Dostoevsky and the Woman Question

Dostoevsky
and the
Woman Question

REREADINGS AT THE END OF A CENTURY

Nina Pelikan Straus

St. Martin's Press
New York

Scholarly and Reference Division,
St. Martin's Press, Inc., 175 Fifth Avenue,
New York, N.Y. 10010

First published in the United States of America in 1994

Printed in the United States of America
Design by ACME ART, INC.

ISBN 0-312-10749-8

Library of Congress Cataloging-in-Publication Data

Straus, Nina Pelikan, 1942-
      Dostoevsky and the woman question : rereadings at the end of a
century / Nina Pelikan Straus.
            p.   cm.
      Includes bibliographical references and index.
      ISBN 0-312-10749-8
      1. Dostoyevsky, Fyodor, 1821-1881—Criticism and interpretation.
2. Women in literature. 3. Feminism in literature I. Title.
PG3328.Z7W657 1994
891.73'3—dc20   93-46929
                                                                      CIP

In memory of
my Russian mother, Vanda Brazel Pelikan,
and for my daughters Laura, Rachel, and Tamara

CONTENTS

ACKNOWLEDGMENTS

I thank Casey Haskins for his encouragement and editing help; Stephanie Sandler and Harriet Murav for their suggestions and criticisms; Albert Guerard, Anna Tavis, Jane Costlow, and my colleagues at SUNY Purchase for their support; Karen Offen and my comrades at the Stanford University NEH on the Woman Question for initiating this book's direction.

NOTE ON TRANSLATIONS AND TRANSLITERATION

Occasional citations in Russian are from F. M. Dostoevskii, *Polnoe sobranie sochinenii v tridtsati tomakh* (Leningrad: Nauka, 1972-). In the body of my text I use the U.S. Board on Geographic Names transliteration system, except when quoting from translators or critics who use other transliteration systems. Quotations from Dostoevsky's works in English are taken from the following translations, abbreviated as indicated:

BK   *The Brothers Karamazov*, trans. Richard Pevear and Larissa Volokhonsky (San Francisco: North Point Press, 1990).

CP   *Crime and Punishment*, trans. David Magarshack (London & New York: Penguin Books, 1951).

D   Boris Brazol's *Diary of a Writer* (Salt Lake City, UT: Gibbs M. Smith Inc., 1985).

EH   *The Eternal Husband*, trans. Constance Garnett, in *Three Short Novels of Dostoevsky* (New York: Doubleday, 1960).

G   *The Gambler*, trans. Victor Terras (Chicago: University of Chicago Press, 1972).

GC   *A Gentle Creature*, trans. David Magarshack, in *Great Short Works of Fyodor Dostoevsky* (New York: Harper Row, 1968).

I   *The Idiot*, trans. Henry and Olga Carlisle (New York: NAL, 1969).

P   *The Possessed*, trans. Andrew MacAndrew (New York: NAL, 1962).

SD   *Diary of Appolonaria Suslova* in *The Gambler*, trans. Victor Terras (Chicago: University of Chicago Press, 1972).

SL   A. Suslova, *The Stranger and Her Lover*, in *The Gambler*, trans. Victor Terras (Chicago: University of Chicago Press, 1972).

I also quote from George Sand's *Mauprat*, trans. Diane Johnson (Boston: Little Brown, 1977) and abbreviated *M*.

Dostoevsky
and the
Woman Question

Introduction:
Dostoevsky and "The Feminine"

This book explores Dostoevsky's major works with a focus on his women characters, his references to rape and men's abuse of women, and his construction of "the feminine." Such an approach to Dostoevsky is "feminist" mainly in the sense that "the woman question" is not subsumed within a larger frame. Intended not to impose feminist ideology upon the writer, but rather to enlarge feminist discourse through Dostoevsky, the following chapters explore new readings with a sense of their positioning at the end of this century.

The project is long overdue if we consider how much more commentary the subject of women in Tolstoy's work has provoked in contrast.[1] It is belated if we consider how critics have mined the motifs of the "margin" and the "threshold," of indeterminacy and the way "conversion hovers at the edge of perversion" in Dostoevsky's work.[2] The blurring of boundaries between erotic and spiritual experience (in Dostoevsky's life as well as in his characters' lives) suggests what is polymorphous in his psychology and polyphonic in his style. If Dostoevsky responded intellectually to a sense of crisis and with an intuition that "the master discourses in the West [were] increasingly perceived as no longer adequate for explaining the world," what he dramatized in fiction was the way men's and women's identities were thrown into question through this crisis.[3] His defense against Western secularization and breakdown takes the form of inscribing "the feminine" as the sacred; but this sacralization is undermined by a deeper intuition of the way certain masculine, sexist impulses exploit and eroticize female spirituality. His contribution to feminist discourse consists of multiple exposures of the way men's liberties conflict with women's liberations.

Elaine Showalter notes that Western consciousness about rape and child abuse has "focused on censoring art and banning pornography rather than on examining the social construction of male sexual violence."[4] Dostoevsky contributes to that examination in ways that neither traditional nor feminist readers have fully explored. As his male convert/pervert pursues his quest for God or salvation, "the feminine" emerges as a problem associated with confusions about the meaning of masculinity and male questing. The plots and structures of the major works make explicit the various attempts by Dostoevsky's heroes to violently repress "the feminine," only to find it returning to destabilize their former assumptions.

Dostoevsky's women carry what is least representable, least vocalized, most marginal, but also most modernist in his fiction. While his "positive" traditionalist women often serve as redeemers of criminal or suffering men, his "new" women perform ambiguously motivated critiques of traditional masculinity. The concept of the "new women," imported from France during Russia's politically turbulent 1860s, was central to debates about Russia's future and Dostoevsky's vision of it. His "negative," hysterical, rebellious, or suicidal women characters make us conscious of the radically transformed social relations the author struggles but fails to repress in his fiction. His obsession with the "new" woman who calls for changed relations between the sexes may symbolize a lifting of personal repression in Freud's sense.[5] The new woman's desires and sufferings, explicitly represented through Polina in *The Gambler* but interrogated in a more complex way through Nastasya Filipovna of *The Idiot* and Katerina Ivanovna of *The Brothers Karamazov*, express the pull toward modernization that Dostoevsky otherwise denies. Dostoevsky's fiction dramatizes what Charles Taylor calls the transforming powers of modern identities even while the novelist opposes them.[6]

Perhaps because Dostoevsky wrote no major novel named for a woman character (*Netochka Nezvanova* is a minor work), readers have not been drawn inevitably to his woman question as in the case of Tolstoy's *Anna Karenina*. Dostoevsky's negative responses to Nikolai Chernyshevsky's socialist heroinism in *What Is to Be Done?* and his explicit support of Slavophiles, Russian imperialism, and the Czars indicate an antifeminist stance. A late-twentieth-century woman reader, finding few direct statements of his commitment to ending women's social oppression, might feel justified in supporting Barbara Heldt's evaluation of the writer as a perpetrator of male chauvinist attitudes and female stereotyping.[7] Yet this judgment does not fit easily with intuitive judgments about the greatness and breadth of Dostoevsky's work or with theoretical justifications for that greatness, particularly in an American reading climate that has welcomed the liberating potencies of Mikhail Bakhtin's theories and deconstruction.

The end of the cold war, with its concomitant assimilations of feminist, gendered, and multicultural discourses, is strongly influencing traditional reading habits, even if gender theory in Slavic studies is still in its early stages. The tendency to line up with either "right"- or "left"-wing readings of Dostoevsky, or to identify him as a liberator or reactionary, has recently yielded to some consensus that Dostoevsky is a "dialogic" writer or, in Gary Saul Morson's terms, a writer who explores boundaries and possibilities that disclose a world of "radical instabilities."[8] Cold war critics of the 1950s who read *The Possessed* as a humorless prophetic attack on Stalinism may seem as narrowly politicized to us today as the "Yipsels" (Young People's Socialist Leaguers) of the 1930s who read *Crime and Punishment* as a guide to *The Communist Manifesto*.[9] Reading horizons necessarily change through time, but visions of change (and the desire for enlarged perspectives and syntheses) become more emphatic, as Frank Kermode reminds us, at the end of centuries.

Recent interpretations of Dostoevsky's works influenced by Bakhtin illustrate this change. Students of literary history may find significant the fact that translations of Bakhtin's texts into English occurred during the same decades that feminist discourse gained wide audiences and that Soviet Communism began to dissolve. Bakhtin, long known to Slavists as a great Dostoevsky critic, was rediscovered in the United States as literary criticism was being drawn to the problem of otherness and "the other" within a post-colonialist, post-cold war, and post-patriarchal culture. Interest in Bakhtin's interpretations of the "dialogic" Dostoevsky against the "monologic" Tolstoy became part of a climate in which the "hegemony" of Euro-American culture was criticized along with "phallocentrism." While Bakhtin's initial introducers and English-language translators of the 1970s and 1980s often discussed the cultural changes that produced Bakhtin's renewed importance, few mentioned "feminism" or "gender" as important dimensions of the change. By 1990, however, Bakhtin's theories about discourse could not be contained by conservative elements within Slavic studies. Literary critics interested in the possible "dialogicity" of writers as different as Matthew Arnold and Joyce Carol Oates were generating a "feminist dialogics."[10] What Bakhtinians shared, whether they were interested in conserving or extending the Russian critic's original insights, was an indebtedness to his model of discourse as tending toward either polyphonic/dialogic (Dostoevskian) or monologic (Tolstoyan) poetics—with the latter frequently described as a form of tyranny over the reader's consciousness.

> Tolstoy's world [writes Bakhtin] is monolithically monologic; the hero's discourse is confined in the fixed framework of the author's discourse about him. . . . Tolstoy's discourse and his monologically naive point of view

permeate everywhere, into all the corners of the world and the soul, *subjugating everything to its unity.*[11]

The discovery that Dostoevsky does not subjugate or impose unity, that he does not inflict his own monologic thoughts upon his characters, inaugurates this book's approach to his fictional women. Bakhtin's remarks about Tolstoy as a subjugator could be mistaken for remarks about Joseph Stalin if we interpret the dialogic-monologic distinction as code language for his criticism of dictatorships. But Bakhtin's praise of Dostoevsky's "distrust of convictions . . . formulas . . . categories and their usual monologic function"[12] also shares a vocabulary with feminist literary criticism concerned with men's monologic impositions upon women's voices. While Bakhtin never refers directly to Soviet or gender politics in his literary analyses, his critique of subjection is as implicitly feminist as it is implicitly antihierarchical and anti-Soviet.

Bakhtin's theories generate ways to analyze links between monologic and patriarchal discourse and between polyphony and women's voices. When he writes that "internally polemical discourse—the word with a sideward glance at someone else's hostile word—literally cringes in the presence or the anticipation of someone else's word,"[13] his description illuminates the psychological condition of those who speak in a context of marginality or fear, as Dostoevsky's lame Maria speaks to the "hero" Stavrogin in *The Possessed* or as the prostitute Sonya initially speaks to Raskolnikov in *Crime and Punishment.* The project of reading Dostoevsky with gender issues foregrounded is part of the larger problem of analyzing "master-slave" relations or what Hans Jauss describes as "the problem of alterity in many areas: . . . between producer and recipient, between the past of the text and the present of the recipient, between different cultures." The interpretations offered in the following chapters follow Jauss's intuition that "human apprehension . . . arises from productive and receptive interaction with art" and that it is "by its very nature an apprehension of the self in an apprehension of the other."[14] Yet the "Dostoevsky" received by our culture so far has mainly been "produced" by men who have not heard "the other's" voice or having heard it, found it "strained."[15]

Very recently, however, the problem of the past and present receptions of Russian texts has been scrutinized by women scholars, with the result that feminist and gender-oriented vocabularies are being assimilated by Slavic studies. In *Sexuality and the Body in Russian Culture*, Jane Costlow, Stephanie Sandler, and Judith Vowles revise the idea that interest in "sexuality is a Western, not a Russian, phenomenon" and find in Dostoevsky the "dark" literary source of more recent Russian and Soviet explorations of sexual desire and dread.[16] Feminist approaches to Pushkin, Tolstoy, Turgenev, Chekhov, and now Dostoevsky, are bringing "the woman question" from the margins of literary criticism to its center. This is not only because the question is bound and determined by our contemporary historical situation. In his September 1877 entry of *The Diary of a Writer*, Dostoevsky himself provides the clue to gender-oriented rereadings of his works:

> Can we continue to deny this woman, who has visibly revealed her valor, full equality of rights with the male in the fields of education, professions, tenure of office, she in whom at present we place all our hopes . . . in connection with the regeneration and elevation of society! (*D*, 846)

The writer's declaration provides no necessary approach to the inscription of "the feminine" in his fiction. Rather, the novels offer sufficient dramatizations of the effects of "the woman question" and Dostoevsky's growing anxiety concerning the treatment of women under the law, an anxiety registered in a story included in the diary's pages: *A Gentle Creature* (otherwise translated as *The Meek One*) of 1876. His comments on women, taken together with his confession of being "haunted" since childhood by the crime of rape, evidences a psychological tremor concerning women and sex that runs through his work as a whole. In his biography of Dostoevsky, Geir Kjetsaa describes the following incident:

> [In 1870] Dostoevsky and his guests were discussing what ought to be considered the greatest crime. . . . "The most fearful crime is to rape a child," the writer said quickly and nervously. "To take life—that is dreadful, but to destroy faith in love's beauty is an even more dreadful crime." And he related the [childhood] episode at [his father's] hospital for the poor [when he learned that a girl who was his friend had been raped and murdered]. . . . "All my life I have been haunted by that memory [Dostoevsky continued], which was the most dreadful crime, the most fearful sin. . . . It was with that crime that I punished Stavrogin."[17]

The literary game of tracing the origin of the ultimate masculinist crime in Dostoevsky's work begins with Strakhov's 1883 letter alleging Dostoevsky's violation of a young girl in a bathhouse. Robert L. Jackson has discussed that letter, Tolstoy's responses to it, and the debate surrounding it "through Bakhtin." Jackson reopens an issue that was of particular concern to psychoanalytically minded critics of the 1950s and 1960s, but it may concern readers in the 1990s for different reasons. For Tolstoy the sexual issue involved judgments as to whether Dostoevsky's character was immoral and debauched, or whether Strakhov was spreading rumors for perverse reasons of his own. For Jackson the issue of sexual violation of females is somewhat resolved by the idea that Dostoevsky, like his own Underground Man, "is in his entirety struggle."[18] Such critical discussions of male immorality and debauchery may not register specific feminist concerns, but they nevertheless move toward the problem of what I call masculinist psychology in Dostoevsky's work.

Whether the psychology of his characters can be best understood in gendered or in sexually neutral terms is a central inquiry in this book. This inquiry acknowledges the writer as one who "in his entirety" expresses dark inner struggles, but it remains skeptical of purely Freudian interpretations of them. Biographical confessions, such as the one about the raped girl, attest to the violence "outside" Dostoevsky's fictions, undermining the idea that "there is no outside to the text"[19] as well as the idea that the novelist's interest in rape was merely a symptom of his private pathology. Because that "outside" of Dostoevsky's work today includes public Euro-American discussions of sexual abuse and sexism, as well as feminist discourse, an interaction between the novelist's work and feminism would appear inevitable.

Dostoevsky's compulsions to depict men's cruelties to women and their variable reactions to these cruelties is more than an element in his work; it is a constitutive part of his vision and his metaphysics. Dostoevsky's contribution to the literature of gender relations may not conform to Western notions of ideological correctness, but it may serve to expose contemporary feminism to some of its own contradictions and limitations: to the way "feminine" and "masculine" constructions of the self depend, for example, on the way "freedom" and "autonomy" are conceived and utilized. Dostoevsky's gift to the reader regarding masculine compulsions and socially constructed male identities stems not from the author's sightings of feminist "light" in our sense, but to his dramatizations of "Russian man's" darkness. It stems rather from an exploration of the masculinity complex in relation to women unmatched by any other nineteenth-century novelist. Dostoevsky's contributions to problems of modernist subjectivity emerge from a particularly Russian context in which contrasts between the exaltation of *symbolic* femininity and the degradation of *actual* women illuminate our ongoing cultural dilemma.

Continuing interest in the Strakhov controversy, together with Dostoevsky's punishments of Stavrogin, Svidrigaylov, Fyodor Karamazov— all of them rapists—suggests why the subject of men's relation to "the feminine" may be important even to readers skeptical of feminism. The novels depict problems of sexual difference, of master-slave relations played out in several different spheres: in the domestic world of intimate male-female relations and family life (for example, the Marmeladov family and Raskolnikov's relation to Sonya and Dunya); in the life of the streets and brothels where men confront vulnerable young females (as the Underground Man confronts Liza and as Fyodor Karamazov seizes and violates Stinking Lizaveta); and in the life of the courts (dramatized most spectacularly in Katerina Ivanovna's reading of the incriminating letter at Dmitri Karamazov's trial for parricide and through Dostoevsky's interest in the Kornilova case, as described in *The Diary*). The domestic, "underground," and legal worlds of these relations expose multiple gender troubles, as legal experts in Dostoevsky's day well knew, and as Dostoevsky recognized as he became increasingly involved with court cases during the 1870s.

As Laura Engelstein reveals in *The Keys to Happiness: Sex and the Search for Modernity in Fin-de-Siècle Russia*, after 1861 the Russian "intelligentsia, influenced by Jeremy Bentham and J. S. Mill, saw 'the woman question' as intrinsic to the problem of social reform."[20] Dostoevsky's personal experiences with emancipated women in the 1860s, exacerbated by his interviews with women criminals and his writing about suicides in the 1870s, brought him close to these questions even as he argued against revolutionary—socialist solutions for them. His awareness of female suffering, along with his admiration for the "new woman" of George Sand's early works, influenced him to create characters and scenes whose significance we have yet to appreciate.

Commentators have remarked upon Sand's heroines as a primary source for Dunya of *Crime and Punishment*, Polina of *The Gambler*, Aglaya and Nastasya Filipovna of *The Idiot*, Lisa Tushina of *The Possessed*, and Katerina Ivanovna of *The Brothers Karamazov*. Dostoevsky was particularly impressed by Sand's *Mauprat* (c. 1837). In her novel Sand tells the tale of Bernard Mauprat in his own words, so that her quasi-feminist agenda is disclosed mainly through the male confessor's self-analysis.[21] Mauprat's obsessive love for his cousin Edmée, the struggle in him between violent sensual impulse and sublimated devotion, and his being accused of attempting to rape and murder her because of frustrated passion—all this is a melodramatic version of the theme of male self-discovery through women which Dostoevsky incorporates into his own work.

Despite its Rousseauist idealism and Gothic ingredients (unmodulated passions, ruined castles, betraying relatives, cunning clergy), *Mauprat* suggested to Dostoevsky the image of a woman as a Christ figure who redeems a "fallen" man while simultaneously confronting him with her feminist advocacy of sexual equality. Resonances between Sand's and Dostoevsky's conceptions of a newly evolving gender culture occur in three kinds of scenes.

In *Mauprat* the hero attempts to rape Edmée, she threatens him with a knife, and he is shamed into releasing her. In *Crime and Punishment*, Svidrigaylov locks Dunya in a room in order to rape her, she shoots at him with a gun (and misses), and he is moved to release her. At the end of this scene, in which Mauprat, like Svidrigaylov, cries out, "you do not love me," Edmée and Mauprat are reconciled. What Mauprat threatens—"I will blow my brains out . . . [if you do not] swear to be mine" (*M,* 61)—Svidrigaylov accomplishes in *Crime and Punishment.*

In the second type of scene, the woman reads a book or books to a man and her voice influences or transforms him. Thus Sonya influences Raskolnikov through her reading of the Lazarus story from the Bible in *Crime and Punishment,* and Edmée serves as Bernard Mauprat's literary educator in *Mauprat.* "I imagined," says Mauprat, "that the ideas of these authors [Montaigne, Monesquieu, and so on] acquired a magical clearness in passing through Edmée's lips, and that my mind opened miraculously at the sound of her voice" (*M,* 143). In the final judgment scene of *Mauprat,* as in the trial scenes of *The Brothers Karamazov,* a woman reads a letter of accusation against a man, testifies to his parricidal impulses, and participates in giving evidence that leads to his conviction and punishment. In *Mauprat,* "the reading of the letter" in which Mauprat expresses his intention of killing Edmée, becomes "the final blow" in his trial (*M,* 282), although he is later released—a situation that parallels Katerina Ivanovna's testimony in court against Dmitri Karamazov.

In the conclusion to this book, I suggest that in Dostoevsky's novels women's potential to transform men emerges from the difference women's sexually vulnerable bodies makes as a conscious part of male sensitization. Sand's theme in *Mauprat* is precisely the sensitization of Mauprat to the question of rape, to what women want, and to the strength of an educated woman's point of view. The "corrected" man Edmée wants must learn that "affection cannot be commanded" (*M,* 113) and that she "would never submit to the tyranny of a man, and no more to the violence of a lover than to the blow of a husband" (*M,* 131).

It is perhaps from Sand that Dostoevsky first discovered how women's voices could produce a "loophole" in his heroes' consciousness, what Bakhtin describes as "the possibility for altering the ultimate, final meaning of one's own words."[22] Sand's voice in *Mauprat* can be read as an attempt to bridge the gap between men's and women's socially constructed language spheres. Her discourse also mediates between traditionally religious expressions of spirituality and romantic-expressive secularizations (and feminizations) of "the spiritual." Edmée is spiritual because she insists on woman's return to a golden age of freedom and equity, but she is feminist because she demands a transformation of Eve's subordinate position to Adam. The female protest scenes Dostoevsky "lifts" from Sand indicate the Russian's attraction to a possible future culture in which sacred and feminist impulses are no longer antithetical and sexual essentialism no longer rationalizes oppression.

With the exception of Tzvetan Todorov,[23] discussions of the philosophical problem of sexual essentialism have been missing from most commentaries on Dostoevsky's "feminine," although psychoanalytic critics have asked certain questions about the novels that also engage feminists. They have asked why, for example, Dostoevsky is drawn in his later work toward feminized male figures such as Prince Myshkin and Alyosha; why representations of rage and murder move from the maternal (in *Crime and Punishment*, 1867) to the paternal level in the final work (*The Brothers Karamazov*, 1881).[24] Such readings have frequently stressed differences between masculine and feminine sexual "natures," or they have incorporated psychoanalytic emphases on a male "complex" concerning the feminine "object." Dostoevsky criticism has generally offered three kinds of interpretations of "the feminine": (1) traditional accounts of human nature written before 1970 that do not problematize gender difference, including Bakhtin's[25]; (2) feminist accounts after 1970 that do; and (3) several commentaries of the 1990s, including Taylor's, Jauss's, and Todorov's, that suggest that rereadings of Dostoevsky's work can themselves transform debates about larger philosophical issues as well as feminist controversies. A reader's-reception history of the novels would reveal the changing status of "the feminine" as it has emerged and shifted, been repressed and disinterred. Although I leave this large task to others, I believe that Dostoevsky's nineteenth-century novels, with their nerve-straining Russian depths, carry more significance for late-twentieth-century women readers than they did for earlier generations.

The novels seem positioned in an unresolved hermeneutic space, somewhere between Western and non-Western, "first" and "third-world" inscriptions; and that may be part of their strength for readers today. Because ideas about fraternity, equality, liberty, and women's rights were imports from capitalist, secularized Western Europe rather than indigenous movements in Dostoevsky's Russia, the Russian woman question serves as a Rorschach test for the wisdom of imposing Western feminist ideologies upon all the world's women. As some recent self-critical feminists argue, more knowledge about cultural and historical differences that affect women must necessarily enlarge the boundaries of gender theory. My attempt to make "the feminine" in Dostoevsky more concrete has been helped by the opening up of feminist theory to autocritique,[26] and by studies such as Engelstein's that link women's lives to larger histories of literature, modernism, and legal reform.[27]

Bringing Dostoevsky's novels into a "living presence of conversation" that emphasizes women through deliberate rereadings is a way to affirm a "unification of two image-fields in a new field of vision."[28] The notion of two image-fields expresses differences between the way men and women (like nations and like theorists) see and read. The concept draws attention to the way Dostoevsky's reception in the West has been shaped by the field of psychoanalysis after the 1920s, by French Existentialism after the 1940s, and by publications of Bakhtin in new translations in the 1980s that led one commentator to praise him as "one of the leading thinkers of the twentieth century" whose theories about "heteroglossia" would confirm a new world vision.[29] In the 1990s, in the wake of deconstruction, feminism, Bakhtin, and the "collapse" of Communism, "post-modern" readings of "the feminine" in Dostoevsky necessitate a hybrid vocabulary. Commentaries in this book on "the engendering of subjectivity"[30] in *Crime and Punishment* and *The Brothers Karamazov*, for example, are intended to complete, when they do not revise, traditional readings that ignored sexual difference.

For traditionalist commentators who did not engage questions of gender in Dostoevsky's work, the novels seemed to represent an essential "human nature." In 1971 Richard Peace suggested "the Karamazovian" as a prototype for the novelist's image of "man" in his commentary on the following passage from *The Brothers Karamazov*:

> [They are] capable of containing all manner of contradictions and of contem-
> plating at one and the same time both abysses: the abyss above us, the abyss of
> high ideals; and the abyss beneath us, the abyss of the lowest and most vile-stink-
> ing degradation. (*BK* xii, ch. 6)

Peace describes Katerina Ivanovna and Grushenka as each containing "within herself both a pole of good and a pole of evil." Each woman's virtue is also her vice, but Peace notes that "in Dostoevsky such obvious polarization never proves to be quite so simple on analysis." Employing no vocabulary that might distinguish the meaning of differences between male and female characters' responses, Peace turns quickly to the subject of "Dmitri's relation-ship to the two women . . . expressed in terms of a very important symbol—money."[31] In his reading, both sexes appear to be psychologically and emotionally one in Dostoevskian "nature," but as Peace himself notes, this description itself seems reductive.

Diane Oenning Thompson, writing in 1991, is sensitive to the way maternity and memory are linked together in *The Brothers Karamazov*, and she offers strong readings of the way Alyosha's mother affects him. But Thompson, like Peace, also avoids feminist terms, even as she emphasizes Alyosha's identification with women. Focusing upon the Christian themes, Thompson writes that "the novel is divided along an axis whose poles are two diametrically opposed religious, philosophical positions embodied in their fictional proponents and brought face to face into intense dialogic relationships."[32] Like Peace, Thompson describes Liza, Grushenka, and Katerina Ivanovna as sharing a psychology and a religious quest with men, even as she notes the structural polarization that, in my reading, also extends to women's socially and historically constructed differences.

Edward Wasiolek initially offers a persuasive analysis of Katerina Ivanovana's character, suggesting that Alyosha's difficulty in understanding her is "our difficulty." But he solves the difficulty by subordinating it to the phenomenon of *nadryv* (self-laceration or strain), which he finds Katerina sharing with several male characters, although not with Grushenka. "*Nadryv* is for Dostoevsky a primal psychological fact," Wasiolek writes in 1964. "It is the impulse in the hearts of men that separates one man from another, the impulse we all have to make the world over into the image of our wills." Men who have the power to expedite this impulse more easily than women are not factored in to produce a discussion of difference. "Katerina *loves* from *nadryv;* Father Ferapont *fasts* from *nadryv; . . .* Ivan raises *nadryv* to a level of universal revolt against God."[33] Like Peace's commentary eleven years earlier and Thompson's twenty-seven years later, Wasiolek interprets Katerina in terms of universal human traits that both Dostoevskian sexes are understood to share.

Robert Belknap's 1967 commentary on the function of *nadryv* in *The Brothers Karamazov* is more suggestive to readers interested in the literary resonances of female "willfulness." Belknap emphasizes a "hierarchy" of human responses that "embody perversity, willfulness, self-consciousness, self-dramatization, absurdity" and "buffoonery." He notes that all the characters in the novel "may be ranked hierarchically along [*nadryv*], with Katerina Ivanovna near one end and Maximov near the other."[34]

Katerina's high-class, feminine self-laceration can be understood, from a feminist perspective that follows upon Belknap's commentary, as a form of resentment against men and against the inhibitions of "the feminine" role—a form distinct from the buffoonery and resentment of Fyodor Karamazov or Maximov. Dostoevsky dramatizes two scenes of "strained" behavior and absurd hand-kissing in the novel—one in which Maximov kisses Grushenka's hand and the other in which Katerina kisses it. Comparisons between these two hand-kissing scenes indicate socially constructed gender differences that have repercussions for the novel as a whole. While

Maximov's kisses hyperbolize conventional male behavior with women, Katerina's kisses express a complicated wish to degrade but also bond with the woman Grushenka against the man Dmitri. When the laceration scene occurs between women, it carries feminist implications that intercept Dostoevsky's attempts to redeem all his characters, male and female, through a finale of Christian forgiveness.

Nina Perlina's 1985 commentary illuminates the significance of specific feminine self-lacerations, although she does not discuss "the woman question" in Dostoevsky as such: "In the narrator's speech, the word 'laceration' appears in quotation marks [that] indicate that some additional information has been inserted into the utterance by the narrator. . . . In other words, the 'laceration' can achieve this additional lexical meaning only in that specific context in which the word is imbedded."[35] The specific context in which Grushenka and Katerina speak is the domestic space, indeed the female space, of the drawing room. Their confrontation is framed by tensions between upper- and lower-class femininity and differences between traditional and "new" feminine identities. The problems of women's specific contextualizations implied in Perlina's discussion and in Belknap's term "hierarchy" differ from universalist or "Karamazovian" approaches to the characters' psychologies. Critics influenced by Bakhtin come closer to feminist analyses when they eschew descriptions of Grushenka as exhibiting essentially feminine and "infernal" sexual traits such as Leonid Grossman, for example, found in her in 1959.[36]

Perhaps Laura Engelstein illuminates Dostoevsky's attitude toward women like Grushenka when she writes that "Russians . . . distrusted bourgeois values of sexual propriety . . . [and were] slow to imitate Western fears of lower-class sexual disorder."[37] Anxiety about such disorder is well illustrated in the following passage from Freud about men's relations to sexually available women, a passage that influenced Dostoevsky commentators during the heyday of psychoanalytic literary criticism in the 1950s and 1960s:

> The principal means of protection against the complaint [of psychical impotence] used by men . . . consists in *lowering* the sexual object in their own estimation, while reserving for the incestuous object and for those who represent it the overestimation normally felt for the sexual object. As soon as the sexual object fulfils the condition of being degraded, sensual feeling can have free play. . . .[38]

If, as Bakhtin argues, Dostoevsky and Freud are incompatible,[39] then what sort of psychology does Dostoevsky's work exhibit and what are its implications for his women figures? Dostoevsky's insistence on punishing his many rapist characters indicates a strong resistance to the necessity of "free play" of male sensuality at women's expense that Freud describes as insuring male potency. What Dostoevsky imagines is a transformed potency that rises from male self-degradation and self-exposure related to female empowerment.

Such a feminist-oriented reading of Dostoevsky risks admonishment for being biased or reductive, but only if we suppose that earlier male-authored commentaries were less reductive because they were "non-gendered." This irony suggests why the category of gender can be considered a "constitutive element of social relationships based on perceived differences between the sexes, and [as] a primary way of signifying relationships of power."[40] What appears "timeless" in Dostoevsky's representations of men and women seems ripe for reinterpretation, particularly when one focuses on the time-bound quality of some literary commentaries.

A critical alternate that seems to avoid the tensions evoked by male-centered or female-centered readings is to construct Dostoevsky's "feminine" in the celebratory mode of what Caryl Emerson calls "the female superiority complex in Russian literature"[41] and what Joanna Hubbs names the woman saviour myth in Dostoevsky.[42] Older commentaries, such as those by Temira Pachmuss, support this approach, offering archetypal descriptions of Dostoevsky's sacrificing women that identify them with "Russia, the Mother, the Wife, the Sister."[43] While such commentaries stand to one side of the Freudian ("lacerated") trace as well as feminist inquiry, they may also appear psychologically naive to late-twentieth-century readers, as they did to Nabokov.

Nabokov's response to "the feminine" in Dostoevsky as the *sentimental* simplifies as it also exposes a complex issue. Interested mainly in literature's aesthetic elements, Nabokov implicitly foregrounds the gendered structures of the novels—what Gary Cox called the master-slave sexual power struggles within them[44]—by criticizing Dostoevsky's "absence of artistic balance."[45] Feminist theorists such as Gayatri Spivak have described how sexist and aesthetic categories frequently cohere in literary works, and how "imbalance" may function as the sign of a disruption in the sexist structure itself.[46] In *Crime and Punishment* it is precisely the disruption of Sonya's prostituted, degraded, but faith-filled female identity in a text apparently masculinist in its discourse that disturbs Nabokov as much as it may delight feminist readers. In the first chapter of this book, I suggest that ideas about the woman question and female imagery increasingly invade the novel, so that differently gendered images of the human confront each other within Raskolnikov's consciousness. What Nabokov calls a structural fault becomes in my rereading the novel's organizing principle.

Nabokov's blindness to the way gender structures *Crime and Punishment* has consequences not only for his criticisms of Dostoevsky, but for his creation of male-female relations in his own *Lolita.* Nabokov's novel performs an aestheticization of rape and child abuse that Dostoevsky would have deplored. This difference illustrates the paradox of Dostoevsky's late-nineteenth-century closeness to late-twentieth-century feminist critiques of "the masculinist" and Nabokov's mid-twentieth-century distance. In contrast to Nabokov, Dostoevsky's works dramatize the gendered ways that ideas live in words.

If Dostoevsky's exposures of masculinist evil seem hyperbolic to Nabokov, these evils fail to resonate in Bakhtin's interpretations of the novels for different reasons. Bakhtin's reading of Dostoevsky is limited by the vision of a hopeful selfhood and a failure to appreciate social pathology.[47] This hopefulness comes in part from Bakhtin's exclusion of a gendered terminology, his seeming neutrality when analyzing certain passages in Dostoevsky's works that thematize men's oppression of women. Bakhtin learned his psychology from Dostoevsky, but he glossed over its more disturbing sexual elements. Dostoevsky's compulsion to describe rapists (Svidrigaylov, Stavrogin), murderers of women (Raskolnikov), and men who drive women to suicide (Matryosha in *The Possessed* and the wife in *A Gentle Creature*), provides evidence of his obsession with an underground hell in which sexist fantasies flourish.

Dostoevsky understood himself to be writing against the feminist and laissez-faire ideals of Western modernism and against the transformation of Russian traditionalism. But his oppositional stance was complicated by his incorporation of George Sandean elements into his own heroines on the one hand, and by his compulsion to fictionalize the darkest male sexual fantasies on the other. Throughout this book, I suggest that the complexity of gender in the novels involves the author's own confusing experiences with "new" women. Dostoevsky's passionate and furious women characters (from Dunya Raskolnikov to Polina, from Nastasya Filipovna to Grushenka and Katerina Ivanovna) evoke the influence of the emancipated Russian women he loved and argued with. Polina Suslova and Anna Korvin-Krupovskaya, each of whom refused him in marriage, confronted him with issues of gender and modernist undecidability. Their fictional surrogates carry the feminist impulse Dostoevsky first repudiates and then assimilates, drawn inevitably to a woman question he was compelled to answer.

What I hope this brief overview illustrates is the variety of discourses "the feminine" evokes. Dostoevsky's women can be interpreted in terms of an essentialist or an archetypal conception of sexual difference, stationed forever between the demonic, the neurotic, and the sublime. Or they can be framed by a psychology that universalizes man's psychology as undifferentiated from woman's, thus muting those differences that emerge so powerfully in Dostoevsky's stories of women betrayed, battered, raped, driven crazy, and murdered by men. The following chapters pursue a third course, which does not attempt to deconstruct the discourse of Dostoevsky's metaphysics so much as to show that "the feminine" is part of it. A book of this kind confronts the reader with the question of whether reading is ever confined within a gendered perspective—or in the words of deconstructionist-feminism, whether "the semiotic" is an "other" of language that is closely connected to femininity.[48]

Some women readers have been daring in their approach to these questions. Harriet Murav's essay suggesting the relation between Liza of *Notes from Underground* and Freud's *Dora*,[49] is the germ for my construction of Katerina Ivanovna's "case" in *The Brothers Karamazov*. Elizabeth Dalton's bold study of Myshkin's "pathology" in *The Idiot* indicates why the quasi-feminist impulses as well as the "holy" intentions of the novel fail. From recent women's interpretations of Russian writers have emerged "other" and "different" voices that have asked new questions and released certain classics from their canonical prisons.

Rereading the female imagery in *Crime and Punishment* in the first chapter, I discover Dostoevsky's exposures of otherness and his longing for the transformation of masculinist will-to-power. Through Raskolnikov's relation to Sonya and through Svidrigaylov's revelations about his impulse to rape Dunya, I consider Dostoevsky's renaming of men's experience in response to feminine difference. His transformation with Sonya at the end of the novel is suggestive of a "feminization of culture" that resonates with George Sandean feminist impulses. Through identifications with women, Raskolnikov becomes a life poised on the threshold of reinvented forms of "the masculine."

My second chapter is a reader's-reception study of *The Gambler* that describes the way interpretations of Dostoevsky's female characters have been produced. When *The Gambler* was packaged in the 1960s along with several of Dostoevsky's letters and (his former mistress's) Apollonaria Suslova's diary and short story, *The Stranger and Her Lover*, it emerged as a thickly contextualized document. The juxtaposition of Suslova's and Dostoevsky's versions of the same story indicates how a man and a woman struggle with the idea of feminine freedom, as well as how commentators writing a century later subordinate that struggle to issues that serve to repress it.

Chapter 3, on *The Idiot*, builds on the problem of "the feminine" as Dostoevsky inscribes it in *Crime and Punishment* and *The Gambler*. His notebooks for *The Idiot* suggest his turmoil regarding masculine identity in the wake of his experiences with Suslova and Korvin-Krupovskaya, both writers, both "new" women who found him too traditional to marry. In *The Idiot* Dostoevsky's confusions about emancipated women and their rage toward men drives him—in what I take to be a literary act of penance and attempted self-transformation—to create another image of the masculine in the perfectly "good" Prince Myshkin. This focus on Dostoevsky's theme of the female characters' flights from masculine expectations of "womanhood" and marriage from "eternal" husbands continues in chapter 4. In chapter 5, on *The Possessed*, I describe the way women expose the nihilist hero Stavrogin. In the once suppressed chapter, "At Tikhon's," in which Stavrogin confesses to the rape of Matryosha, we find the centerpiece of Dostoevsky's "woman question." What is at stake is Dostoevsky's confrontation with his own sexism. Coupled with this revelation, suppressed in *The Idiot*, is his representations of the effect on women of romantic *ubermensch* culture. Dostoevsky's mockery of socialist-feminist enthusiasms, his analysis of negative "liberty" and love of power, is related to debates that remain unresolved among feminists today, as I suggest in my concluding chapter.

In chapter 6, "Female Suicides in *The Diary of a Writer*," I focus on Dostoevsky's analyses of court trials of wife and child beating cases, husbands' murders of wives, and newspaper accounts of female suicides. While much of *The Diary* expresses the writer's nationalistic and utopian impulses, echoed in Myshkin's sensations (experienced before epileptic attacks) of reaching an "acme of harmony and beauty" in the world,[50] the writings also explore and deplore the realities of Russian women's lives. The diarist's meditations on women's experiences lead him to the creation of *A Gentle Creature*, included in *The Diary*'s pages. Robert Belknap describes this story as containing "the most personal, most emotional, most religious and intertextually most moving passage [Dostoevsky] ever wrote."[51] Belknap's consummatory evocation is justified by Dostoevsky's intense preoccupation with the masculinist prerogatives which make female suffering possible, a preoccupation subordinated to others in much scholarly commentary on *The Diary*. *A Gentle Creature*, the story of a cruel husband and his young wife's suicide, is the repository in fiction for Dostoevsky's most intense inscription of gender difference. The story constructs "the feminine" as what has been lost in male-dominated culture and what must be retrieved within male imagination itself.

Dostoevsky's evolution of a feminized male figure in his fiction, in response to perceptions of masculinist pathology, is his most significant contribution to the feminization of culture. Foregrounded in the 1860s with Alexei the gambler's and the Underground Man's identity confusions, the theme evolves through Raskolnikov, through various "eternal" husbands, and through Prince Myshkin—that "absolutely good person" and "idiot" who somehow expedites the death of the woman he loves. The ironies emerging through Myshkin's goodness involve Dostoevsky's suppression of Myshkin's sexuality.[52] Not until Dostoevsky can assimilate sexuality to male goodness in the more persuasively realized character of Alyosha Karamazov can he metaphorize the death of the Father in its most symbolically significant resonance for women.

Dostoevsky's "masculine," like his "feminine," evolves through his rewritings of similar scenarios. Male identity is configured as sexual repression in the service of religious transcendence in Myshkin. It is explored in de Sadean depth through Stavrogin, and then revealed through the sufferings of women at men's hands as recorded in *The Diary*. Only after the inscriptions of masculinity are framed by repudiation and tragedy in *A Gentle Creature* can Dostoevsky imagine the parricide that allegorizes the death of a certain kind of patriarchy.

In chapter 7, on *The Brothers Karamazov*, I suggest how Dostoevsky's dialogism is gendered throughout the novel, and how the subtext of *The Legend of the Grand Inquisitor* is Ivan's relationship to the "new" woman Katerina. The novel appears to have two endings: one cast in the frame of traditional male bonding; the other in modernist ambiguity and gender troubles formed in the wake of the patriarch's symbolically resonant death. What feminists call "the death of patriarchy" is an idea toward which Dostoevsky's fictions evolve and in which not only the Karamazov brothers but their three symbolic "sisters" participate. Dostoevsky's attacks on masculine notions of autonomy, power, and rationality accord with some feminist insights. The evolution I outline here is a way to read Dostoevsky's fiction provoked by the sense of a new historical horizon.

1

Crime and Punishment:
"Why Did I Say 'Women!'?"

While feminist approaches to Dostoevsky's other novels may be promising, the murder-of-women and salvation plot of *Crime and Punishment* offers the most concentrated exposure of the relation between a young man's experience of violence toward women and the construction of his masculine identity. Other Dostoevskian narratives offer the construction (or destruction) of the hero's character in relation to women, yet none explores so relentlessly the identity confusions such relations generate. In *Crime and Punishment* Dostoevsky dramatizes men's experience in response to "the feminine" and points to the possibility of Raskolnikov's becoming a representative "life poised on the threshold"[1] of reinvented forms of the "masculine." In this chapter I indicate how stereotypes about gender have structured previous readings of the heroic in the novel, and how it is precisely these stereotypes that are challenged by Dostoevsky's polyphonic language.

Feminist approaches to the novel may meet with resistance because of Dostoevsky's overt repudiation of a socialism concerned with woman's oppression and his Slavophile nationalism. The recasting of Sonya in his notebooks to embody the philosophy of the soil (*pochvennichestvo*), expressed in her demand that Raskolnikov bow down and kiss the Russian earth, seems evidence of Dostoevsky's conservatism. Yet Bakhtin's description of Dostoevsky's multivoiced discourse invites feminist speculation, particularly in terms of Bakhtin's emphasis on the idea of the *other*. In his notes, Bakhtin offers an image that might serve as the germ of a feminist hermeneutics: "Just as the body is initially formed in the womb of the mother (in her body), so human consciousness awakens surrounded by the consciousness of others."[2]

Several recent studies explore this germ in their shift away from a focus on Dostoevsky's "hero" as a self-sufficient entity, toward an analysis of the male character as an "unaccomplished, incomplete, heterogeneous being"[3] formed by relations to others, especially women. Malcolm V. Jones notes the "transvocalization" of men's and women's voices in the Olya story of *A Raw Youth*, and Elizabeth Dalton describes the incorporation of feminine traits into Myshkin's character in *The Idiot*. Louis Breger's claim, that in *Crime and Punishment* Raskolnikov's "split images of women have been bridged through Sonya's love," further emphasizes the effect of women upon the hero's life. Each of these approaches nevertheless stops short of a specifically feminist orientation. Breger's replacement of the older stereotype of Sonya as a "saint" by the idea that she is the novelist's "fantasy of the perfect therapist"[4] does little to undermine critiques of Dostoevsky's male chauvinism and his "melo-dramatic tradition" regarding women.[5] A Bakhtinian feminism, however, leads in another direction, focusing on Dostoevsky's "new model of the internally dialogized world"[6] by exploring the novel's female imagery in relation to Raskolnikov's self-knowledge.

The question is no longer whether "the emotional core of *Crime and Punishment* is ambivalence towards mother figures and women," as Breger persuasively argues,[7] but whether Dostoevsky creates a one-way bridge from Sonya to Raskolnikov that merely consolidates traditional gender roles. Although feminist issues such as the "woman question" (*CP*, 380) and "the society of the future" (*CP*, 384) are presented satirically throughout the novel, they appear increasingly central to it. Despite critical interest in the "rationality which Dostoevsky attacks" and the puzzle of the "something else in Raskolnikov's make-up which runs contrary to his rationalism,"[8] scant attention has been paid to the problem of the male role's link to rationality and power with which Raskolnikov, and by implication Dostoevsky, struggles. Critics have described the novel's immersion in social problems, particularly in "fallen women" (sparked by M. Rodevich's article of 1862)[9], and the "utilitarian calculus" to which such women were subjected."[10] But none has yet suggested that Dostoevsky's attack on masculine notions of autonomy, power, and rationality accords with some feminist insights; nor have feminists yet explored how women's historically changing roles resonate through Dostoevsky's novels. Such resonances suggest feminism's further dimensions: the struggle with masculinity by the masculine; the testing of the masculinist idea within the male-authored novel. Dostoevsky's obvious mockery of crude feminism of the socialist-utilitarian (Chernyshevskian) type does not resolve the more interest-ing question of Raskolnikov's relation to ideas about "the masculine" or "the feminine," but rather opens that question for reconsideration.

A re-imagining of the novel begins with the reader's capacity for "self-reflection on [his or her] complicity with inherited systems of representation,"[11] as exemplified by assumptions about "the self" that inform, for example, Breger's psychoanalytic approach or Wasiolek's conception of Dostoevsky's "metaphysic." "Raskolnikov killed the money lender for himself, and himself alone," Wasiolek writes. "In the context of Dostoevsky's metaphysic, 'for himself alone' is a profound statement, pointing to the self's capacity to exercise its freedom without limit."[12] Whether Raskolnikov's capacity is a freedom or a pathological fantasy, whether this notion of the self extends both to men and women, remains a puzzle deepened by Bakhtin's metaphor of womblike otherness surrounding consciousness. A Bakhtinian feminism reengages the question of Raskolnikov's motives by suggesting that his "self" is not a self-sufficient entity but is constituted by the variously assimilated voices of others: his mother's and Dunya's voice, the intellectual's voice associated with "Napoleon," and Sonya's voice, to name just a few. A focus on the meaning of the "deep reverie" (*zabyt' ye*, literally, *oblivion*) into which Raskolnikov has sunk when we first meet him is associated less with freedom than with his immersion in female voices and images returning from oblivion or repression (*CP*, 20).

For feminists, "the feminine" may be socially constructed, but for Raskolnikov its polarity to "the masculine" is initially experienced as essentialist. Raskolnikov is obsessed with guilt about his landlady and her daughter, and with responsibility for his mother and sister whose female dependencies "stifle[] and cramp[]" him (*CP*, 57). He is immersed in the dream of the beaten nag and in revolting visions of the female pawnbroker whom he perceives, in contrast to himself, as "vermin." Female images (nag, pawnbroker, landlady, sister, mother) are sources of uncontrollable misery that he longs to transcend through the "fascinating audacity" of a violent, manly act. This act, associated with the fantasy of man's unlimited freedom and the "uttering [of] a new word" (*CP*, 20), receives its charge from the contrasting idea of woman's bondage to an old world: from Dunya's potential bondage to Luzhin in marriage, from his mother's bondage to himself as her "guardian angel" (*CP*, 213), and from Sonya's bondage to prostitution. Raskolnikov's encounters with women continually test whether "everything is in a man's own hands" (*CP*, 20), whether he can conceive of his identity as (metaphysically) bound or unlimited, as (socially) victimized or heroic, as (dialogically) related to women or severed from them in sublime masculinist autonomy. He links women with ideas of cowardice, limitation, and victimization, and masculinity with power, money, courage, and the capacity to create victims. The pawnbroker and Lizaveta are Raskolnikov's victims; his mother and sister are Luzhin's and Svidrigaylov's; and "Mother Russia" is Napoleon's. He murders the pawnbroker as the cab driver of his dream murders the nag, as Napoleon murders "vermin," and as Svidrigaylov may have murdered his wife. Patterned so that Raskolnikov's gendered associations are gradually contradicted, the novel moves toward pandemonium, the "terrible uproar" of the funeral scene in which women scream, Luzhin is unmasked (*CP*, 404), and Dunya resists and defeats Svidrigaylov. Only through the experience of gender roles reversed or conflated can Raskolnikov glimpse the transformed image of manhood Dostoevsky seeks for him.

Dostoevsky's diffusion of sex-stereotyped images is nevertheless at odds with Raskolnikov's initial gender essentialism. The novel begins with Raskolnikov's dream of a (male) cart driver beating a (female) nag and continues with Raskolnikov hacking the female pawnbroker to death, but the image of men beating women is finally inverted. Duplicated images of beating, several of them reversing the gender relations of the others, show how Raskolnikov discovers that what he beats *beats him*. An early image of Katerina pulling her husband "by the hair" (*CP*, 32) is followed by the image of Raskolnikov hitting the "crown" of the female pawnbroker's head with a hatchet (*CP*, 96). Raskolnikov then dreams of "hitting the old woman on the head with all his strength, but at every blow of the hatchet . . . [she] simply rocked with laughter" (*CP*, 194). His fall into a "fathomless chasm" and into a simultaneously "higher" realm where his dialectic "vanishes" (*CP*, 132-3) is also dramatized by Marmeladov's being crushed to death by a horse, implying the retaliation of the beaten mare in Raskolnikov's dream upon her male persecutor (*CP*, 195). The idea of "the feminine" in *Crime and Punishment* is the symbolic hatchet that breaks open men's heads by destroying the distinctions between "low" and "high," "docile" and "powerful," victim and master, the coward and the hero. The hierarchy of Raskolnikov's sexist imagery decomposes as he discovers that he is "a louse . . . nastier than the louse [he] killed" (*CP*, 292) and that his Napoleon fantasy is a "frightful muddle" (*CP*, 470). By exploring the ways in which the masculine-feminine polarities reflected in Raskolnikov's consciousness are undermined, *Crime and Punishment* appears as a text in which Dostoevsky discovers the politics of gender, and in which Raskolnikov's crime and punishment are engendered by them.

Raskolnikov, whose name refers to the schismatic tenets of a sect of Old Believers (*raskol'niki*), soon discovers himself as a "self created within a split—a being that can only conceptualise itself when it is mirrored back to itself from the position of another's desire,"[13] namely women's. His problem with socially constructed femininity is dramatized early in the novel through the characters' ironic discussion of "whether a woman is a human being or not." Razumikhin offers Raskolnikov three roubles for a translation of a German text on this subject that will "sell like hotcakes!" For Raskolnikov the subject hits a nerve. He takes the text and three roubles, walks out of the room, and then returns both text and money. Raskolnikov acts as if he has "the D.T.'s " (*belaya goryachka*: literally, white-hot fever). He explains his "confused" action by murmuring, significantly, " 'I don't want translations' " (*CP*, 130-31). Instead, he wants the real thing, horrific or blissful experience with women. As part of a cluster of female images that gradually transforms Raskolnikov by disrupting his compulsive need to divide "man" into "hero" or "vermin," Sonya exacerbates Raskolnikov's masculinist crisis. She is Raskolnikov's saviour-therapist on a religious or therapeutic level, but his puzzle and poison in feminist terms. Her demand that he confess his crime and "kiss the earth you have defiled" (*CP*, 433) links Raskolnikov's defilement of Mother Russia with Sonya's prostituting herself to men for mere survival and with the degraded femininity of the old pawnbroker. Although the novel initially seems structured as a regression to fantasies of destroying symbolic maternity,[14] it moves quickly from the murder of Alyona toward images of youthful female sexuality embodied by Sonya, Dunya, and Svidrigaylov's raped girls. This is not to say that Raskolnikov's experience radiates less from the act of murdering the pawnbroker, but that this act does not completely account for what else happens in the novel or why it happens.

The relation of Raskolnikov's nonsexual but violent crime against two women and Svidrigaylov's sexual crimes against women can be understood in terms of analogy. The men are "doubles" in terms of a will-to-power expressed through hurting women. Yet something like "the failure of the [double] metaphor to attain and name its proper meaning"[15] is also at work in the novel when it shifts in Part Six from a focus on Raskolnikov to Svidrigaylov and his experiences with Dunya. The woman question enters the text not through any "objectified words in Dostoevsky, since the speech of his characters is constructed in a way that deprives it of all objectification,"[16] but through characterological links between brother and sister (both reformers capable of martyrdom [*CP*, 487-9]), and through the gap that exists between the sexually saturated subplots and the central crime and punishment plot.

Readers who find that Raskolnikov's mother complex does not fully account for his motives for murdering Alyona will ask how the novel's later emphasis on young women and sexual violation relates. It is precisely the relations between the later Dunya-Luzhin-Sonya/Svidrigaylov-Dunya subplots involving attempted or actual sexual violation, and the earlier Raskolnikov-Alyona-Lizaveta murder plot in which sex seems absent, that marks Dostoevsky's novel as bearing a feminist problematic. Dostoevsky dramatizes the transforming powers of the modernist and feminist identities when Dunya enters the text as a heroine who shoots at her potential rapist, Svidrigaylov. The theme of women's protest is carried by the surprising upstaging of Raskolnikov by Svidrigaylov towards the end of the novel, the interrupted focus on Raskolnikov by the Dunya/Svidrigaylov scene, and by Svidrigaylov's dream of the child whore, which bears something like a "side-long glance" at Raskolnikov's dream of the beaten mare.

What is missing from Raskolnikov's discourse and experience is present in the resonating relations between the two men, Dunya, and other women: in their "hidden polemic, polemically colored confession, hidden dialogue,"[17] which defines "man" as he who violates women, which defines masculinity at femininity's expense, and which defines a new kind of woman as a resisting heroine or martyr (*CP*, 487). This hidden polemic about men and women is not disclosed by Raskolnikov's murdering of the pawnbroker. Instead, that crime serves as an opening for Raskolnikov to come in contact with Svidrigaylov, who in turn comes in contact with Dunya which enables both men to admit their to each other their "insect" suffering and hopelessness (*CP*, 305).

Dostoevsky's convergence of the crime and sex-crime categories in the novel's second half forces the woman question and the Napoleonic question (whether Raskolnikov is a "man" or a "vermin") to mirror each other. Svidrigaylov's words about Dunya ("I assure you this look of your sister's haunted me in my dreams" [*CP*, 489]), suggesting obsession with female sexuality, are dialogically related to Raskolnikov's words about the beaten mare in his dreams. The nonsexual words that inform Raskolnikov's dream reveal the contexts of Russian women's lives. In axing the pawnbroker, the symbolic master Raskolnikov will "whip the little grey-brown mare." Taking things into "a man's own hands," he is compelled not to "spare her"; she must be "showered with blows"; she must drown in blood because she is a man's "property" (*CP*, 74-6). Or, in a dreamlike reversal of meanings, he must kill her because she has taken his property (as Alyona takes Raskolnikov's property in pawn), or because he is not, psychologically, his own property. All these words reveal the contexts to which the novel's women are subjugated in varying degrees and the pattern through which Raskolnikov becomes more and more identified with women and their contexts. Katerina carries the load of her family upon her sickly, tortured back, crying out on her deathbed that "they've beaten the mare to death" (*CP*, 448); Sonya can be bought or sold as sexual property; Svidrigaylov beats his wife until she dies; Dunya's virgin blood will flow if she cannot convert the master or persuade him to spare her.

Dunya's relations with men, like Sonya's, disclose the masculinist desire (as dramatized by Luzhin and Svidrigaylov) to purchase woman as a thing, to violate her morally or physically as the instantiation of man's superior power. Raskolnikov's resistance to Sonya, as well as his hatred of the female pawnbroker, demonstrates a terror of the sex-violence complex he associates with men and fears in himself, an association verified by Svidrigaylov's attempted rape of Dunya. The question of what men do to, for, or with women drives Raskolnikov toward others beside Sonya, thus enlarging the dialogue between masculinist identity and crimes against women. His emotional turmoil unravels in relation to Sonya or what Peace calls "the 'Elizaveta' in [Raskolnikov's] make-up";[18] through conversations with Porfiry that trivialize his Napoleonism; but also in terms of the "Dunya" who evolves within him and through the "Svidrigaylov" he confronts.

The pattern that relates Raskolnikov's Napoleon ideology to both his and Svidrigaylov's crimes involves images of violence done to women, even though Raskolnikov's conversations with Porfiry suppress the connection. The novel is saturated with writings about crime (Raskolnikov's article), arguments about crimes redeemed by penitence (with Sonya), conversations about criminal motivation (with Porfiry), and disclosures of the pleasures of sex-crimes (with Svidrigaylov). Yet nowhere does Dostoevsky employ words that describe connections between Raskolnikov's notion that there are "two categories" of human being—the "inferior" and the "talent[ed]" capable of both crime and of saying a "new word" (CP, 279)—and his responses to two categories of the human: the male and the female. These connections are made because Raskolnikov's consciousness is increasingly penetrated by other peoples' words. Women's words in particular tell him a different story than he has told himself. Through Sonya's and Porfiry's words, Raskolnikov begins to understand the connections between his Napoleonic theory and the murder that he, a possibly *talented* young man, has perpetrated against a distinctly *inferior* and nearly *wordless* old woman. As the novel progresses, Raskolnikov's words become more and more a part of "agitated, verbal surface" of a work in which "everything is on the borderline . . . everything is prepared . . . to pass over into its opposite."[19] The crossing over or mutual identification between Raskolnikov and Svidrigaylov becomes increasingly close. Although Raskolnikov commits crimes "on principle" and Svidrigaylov is compelled by sensuality, each man's experience with women mirrors the genderized structure of an action imagined as necessary for male transcendence in the Napoleon fantasy.

The two worst crimes, murder and attempted rape, are positioned at opposite ends of the novel; bookends that symbolize the two "supreme effort[s]" of a perverted masculinist script (CP, 279). While Raskolnikov's article, "On Crime," articulates the supreme fantasy, the novel reveals that fantasy's consequence, which is violence toward "vermin" (who turn out to be female). What the novel articulates as a rethinking of male roles, Raskolnikov's article perverts; yet each reveals that male criminality is never disassociated from fantasies about women and sex. If "it takes a strong soul to endure [Dostoevsky's] works,"[20] this is because the novel and its "intellectual" discussions are haunted by images of battered, violated, and murdered women. Raskolnikov's vision of the "masses" as "cows" (CP, 279) points to "Napoleon" as a bull or phallic signifier. Only a "Napoleon" is capable of violating "Mother Russia." Thus Raskolnikov's question to himself suggests the nature of Dostoevsky's "borderline" feminist inquisition: "Why did I say 'Women!'?" (CP, 268).

Raskolnikov's Napoleonism, like his relation to women, is in Bakhtin's terms a "*live* event," a masculinist "idea-prototype" whose "resonance" must be played out and exposed.[21] Overtly expressed in Raskolnikov's writings and his conversations with Porfiry, the little-Napoleon actions of other male characters in the novel express this idea-prototype in nearly parodic form. Initially experienced through Raskolnikov's murder of the female pawnbroker, whose life "amounts to no more than the life of a louse" (CP, 84-5), the idea is later played out through Luzhin's and Svidrigaylov's relations with Sonya and Dunya. Treated as inferiors, each female figure enters Raskolnikov's "thoroughly dialogized interior monologue . . . a dialogue of ultimate questions and ultimate life decisions."[22] These ultimate decisions are related to problems involving women's bodies, women's social-economic role, and the religious and mythic symbolisms that entrap both sexes. Sonya, Dunya, her mother, Katerina, Lizaveta, and the pawnbroker each represent a familiar feminine situation. All of them indicate how "woman" is a dominant fetish of Raskolnikov's culture, constituted by her lack of phallic, social, and political power.[23]

Sonya's woman problem is that she lacks money and must sell her body to men. Dunya's deprivation and sacrificial impulse for her brother's sake tempts her to sell herself in marriage to Luzhin. If Alyona brokers jewelry, Sonya and Dunya broker youth and sexuality. The pawnbroker's suspiciousness, the way she jumps back "in panic" when a man "advance[s] straight on" (CP, 94), dramatizes the elderly female's experiences of male brutality even before her encounter with Raskolnikov. Lizaveta is not just any docile woman, but one who "always seemed to be pregnant" and who "acquiesces in everything," including sex, as the officers who describe her with "keen relish" indicate to Raskolnikov (CP, 83-4). Along with Katerina, Alyona, and Sonya, she represents the socially degraded female whom Raskolnikov must extinguish within himself in his attempt to establish a sense of male superiority.

Like Svidrigaylov, Raskolnikov must initially mock, penetrate, or hack at a woman to assert a masculine identity otherwise indistinguishable from its status as "vermin."

Dostoevsky represents Raskolnikov as magnetized toward two symbolically gendered extremities, each of which is psychologically imprisoning. Whereas the Napoleon idea embodies masculine fantasies of freedom and modernity, reacting to cruelty by embodying it, the idea of Sonya embodies docility and Christianity, reacting to cruelty by bearing it. In acting out both these roles, Raskolnikov reveals the socially constructed sexual polarities within himself, experiencing fully the Russian "feminine." Not only the novel's women but its central male figures are represented as oppressed by patriarchal hierarchies and by myths about masculine freedom. Svidrigaylov's question, "Am I a monster or am I myself the victim?" (CP, 297), is also Raskolnikov's. The consequence of the "self's capacity to exercise its freedom without limit" is a suffering that Raskolnikov shares with men who make women suffer.

In one such scene of mutual suffering, Sonya attempts to undermine Raskolnikov's masculinist fantasy of some new "law . . . unknown at present" that will bring "into the world by some . . . mysterious process . . . one man out of a thousand" (CP, 280). Reading the Lazarus story to Raskolnikov, Sonya is convinced that such men have already appeared in the form of Jesus and Lazarus. Raskolnikov reacts in the name of the "rational" against Sonya's "feeble-minded" faith (CP, 341)—her holy foolishness or *iurodstvo.* We have already seen the psychological and moral consequences of Raskolnikov's fanatical view of rationality: his hatred of the pawnbroker and his bitter ambivalence toward his mother. The extent to which he understands "rationality" in terms of men's rules or supermen's rules is the extent to which he can initially dismiss women's voices and experiences. Raskolnikov confronts through Sonya a crisis in his conception of a particular kind of masculine reason. If the feminist psychologist Carol Gilligan is even partially correct about the way men and women have been programmed to "convey different ways of structuring relationships . . . associated with different views of morality and self," Sonya and Raskolnikov each distort each other's representations and "mark as dangerous the place which the other defines as safe."[24] Raskolnikov cannot get Sonya to give up her "feminine," communal, and religious approach to experience, and he is pulled toward a gradual self-identification with her that is unexpected, producing in him a terrible anxiety and confusion. He expresses anxiety concerning a transformed form of masculinity suffered by sons who "appropriate those specific components of the masculinity of their father that they fear will be otherwise used against them."[25] Thus Dostoevsky's novel suggests a male psychology that may be closer to Nancy Chodorow's and Carol Gilligan's ideas of gender construction than Freud's. The absence of Raskolnikov's father and the presence of his mother is an important element in his characterization, bringing him psychologically in accord with Chodorow's insight that "for boys, identification processes and masculine role learning are not likely to be embedded in relationships with their fathers or men but rather to involve the denial of affective relationships to their mothers."[26]

Raskolnikov resists Sonya's "relentless condemnation" of his "supreme effort" (CP, 385), and is compelled to reconceive himself in terms of a manhood fearless enough to withstand what men like Napoleon, Luzhin, and Svidrigaylov will use against him. His strategy of resistance against "the feminine" in himself is to emphasize Sonya's degradation as a prostitute. But his strategy is weakened by the fact that he is not repelled by this degradation of her sexuality. Rather, he seems to behold the spectacle of his own folly in hers,[27] intuiting the fit between sex crimes and femininity and crimes of violence and masculinist pathology. What he discovers in Sonya is the courage of the *loophole*: that is, the courage not to define himself solely in masculinist terms. This new version of courage finds its image not only in Sonya but also in Dunya, who outwits the male forces Raskolnikov confronts. Until the last pages of the novel, however, Raskolnikov resists the incorporation of this *other* so close to him. Instead, he imagines that he "alone" must face a "test" that will drive him to "senile impotence" (CP, 531). What is his fantasy? Raskolnikov fears becoming "vermin," a crawling female or cowlike form of life easily squashed by men in power.

At the core of his attraction for and terror of Sonya, at the core of his growing knowledge of Dunya, is the image of himself as a maimed female. He runs from this image of himself but also pursues it. As Wasiolek notes, he is "terrified and crushed by the thought of not being pursued" and "breathes life into the pursuit, providing it with clues."[28] Images of being pursued, of falling to one's knees, and of fainting mark Raskolnikov's journey toward an identification with women, but also toward a difficult new version of masculinity. Marmeladov's description of the way Katerina goes "down on her knees, and kiss[es] Sonya's feet" (CP, 35) inspires Raskolnikov to mimic the gesture in the Lazarus scene, perhaps ironically. Fainting and falling when he first encounters his mother and sister, he is reminded of another pair, the murdered pawnbroker and Lizaveta (CP, 212). His falling replicates the way Alyona "dropped to the floor" at his feet (CP, 96), and it recalls both the meaning of Sonya as a fallen woman and the meaning of Dunya's engagement to Luzhin—"which means you're selling yourself," as he tells her (CP, 249).

Female figures, moreover, reflect the beaten mare in his dream who "collapsed on the ground" and is "whipped across the eyes" (CP, 76-7). Wounded female eyes, associated with the "meek and gentle eyes" of Lizaveta and Sonya (CP, 292), represent a challenge to Raskolnikov's masculinist supremacy associated with his Napoleon theory. As the mirror of Napoleonic masculinity begins to crack, all the women gazing back at Raskolnikov begin to appear in it. As they do, his fainting body speaks against him from within him.

Self-knowledge grows upon him in proportion to his developing sense of Katerina's, Sonya's, and Dunya's female situations in relation to husband, father, fiancé, and brother. Raskolnikov's fear of his "landlady's . . . demands for payment" (CP, 19) and his disclosure in the police station that "from the very first I promised to marry [the landlady's] daughter" (CP, 120) compose elements of a script in which his masculine role is imbedded. Like Marmeladov's, Luzhin's, and Svidrigaylov's scripts, Raskolnikov's script involves complicity in the debasement of women. Luzhin's ability to tempt Dunya in marriage and "debase her spirit and her moral feelings" (CP, 61) is the consequence of Raskolnikov's inability to care for her; a consequence that in the parallel case of Marmeladov drives Sonya to prostitution. Like Svidrigaylov, who locks Dunya into his room with a key, like Marmeladov who "stole by a cunning trick the key from [his] wife's trunk" (CP, 38), Raskolnikov steals into the pawnbroker's room and finds the "notched key" that opens her "biggish box" (CP, 98).

If fainting before women distinguishes Raskolnikov from the men around him, stealing from women or penetrating into women's boxes or bodies is the metaphor through which Dostoevsky connects Raskolnikov to women. Raskolnikov's dream of obtaining heroism by "stepp[ing] over a corpse" (CP, 277-8) and stealing Alyona's money finally cannot be severed from Luzhin's and Svidrigaylov's base heroics using "dirty trick[s]" and "bluff[s]" to seduce women (CP, 415-17). Watching Luzhin and Svidrigaylov in predatory action coupled with cash offerings, Raskolnikov glimpses the sexual-symbolic order in which his image of Napoleonic heroism is grounded. Through the action of other men with women he becomes "dimly aware of the great lie in himself and his convictions" (CP, 553).

No doubt that for Dostoevsky the great lie has an ultimate religious significance. But for Raskolnikov the rupture with lies is apprehended through concrete experience with women who appear as the symbolic vermin of a patriarchal society that he has both incorporated and from which he seeks escape. The escape from the masculinist prison of false heroics and lies begins with Marmeladov's death (CP, 206) and gathers momentum with the knowledge that Svidrigaylov is accused of beating his wife to death and of causing the suicide of a fifteen-year-old girl because he had "cruelly interfered with her" (CP, 314). Luzhin's false accusations against Sonya (CP, 405) quickly follow, with the consequence that Raskolnikov is able to see *himself* in the sexist mirror of Luzhin. If Raskolnikov's "inner speech is constructed like a succession of living and impassioned replies to all the words of others he has heard or has been touched by,"[29] his statement—that he "knew perfectly well [he] was not a Napoleon" (CP, 432)—finally acknowledges what women have taught him. Porfiry's words, "a great act of fulfillment [is] before you" (CP, 472), further stimulate the possibility of an alternate future evolving from Raskolnikov's recognition of the connections between Napoleon's victims, the beaten female horse of his dream, the pawnbroker whom he axed, the tortured Katerina, the prostituted Sonya, and Svidrigaylov's rape victims (who might include Dunya). What Porfiry increasingly exploits as he drives Raskolnikov toward confession is the emotional borderline the young murderer crosses when he is no longer able to distinguish between identifications with masculine or feminine experience.

Running between the physically undeveloped Sonya and the androgynous Porfiry, both of whose bodily attributes signify gender confusions, Raskolnikov is led toward the undermining of his masculine role. Victimized by Porfiry's inquisition, Raskolnikov's sickness appears as a defense against the cruelties of a legal system that treats men without power like women and perpetuates misogyny by allowing men to symbolically retaliate against that system by beating women. Raskolnikov's transformation thus has multiple sources, reinforced by Porfiry's appearance in the novel as a peculiar feminine-masculine compound. "The expression of [Porfiry's] eyes was strangely out of keeping with his whole figure, which reminded one somehow of the figure of an old peasant woman" (CP, 267). Raskolnikov is provoked to partial confession through Porfiry's maternal image and through his strangely castrating discourse: "he'll fly straight into my mouth, and I'll swallow him!" (CP, 355). Attempting to liberate him from the world of dead men's voices, Porfiry insists that Raskolnikov's crime bears "no resemblance whatever to any previous case" (CP, 354). Yet the reader may remember that "exactly the same ideas" about murdering the pawnbroker "just beginning to stir in [Raskolnikov's] own mind" were articulated by ordinary young officers in a Petersburg restaurant a short while before Raskolnikov committed the crime (CP, 84-5). Porfiry's discourse exists alongside other words and images that overlap to form a pattern revealed to the reader: the notion of Raskolnikov's crime as a disease (CP, 90), the resonance between Raskolnikov's Napoleon theory and other misogynist worldviews shared by men of his generation. Because Porfiry has not heard the young officers' words about murdering the old woman, because he has no knowledge of Svidrigaylov's sexual violence toward young women, his solutions for Raskolnikov, like Sonya's, remain partial. Porfiry intuits Raskolnikov's suicidal impulses, but he is not privy to the female-imaged crisis that Raskolnikov's confession to Sonya suggests:

> Was it the old hag I killed? No, I killed myself, and not the old hag. I did away with myself at one blow and for good. (CP, 433)

Related to his growing identification with women, Raskolnikov's suicidal impulses foreshadow the motive behind Svidrigaylov's suicide. Raskolnikov's self-knowledge emerges partially from his ambiguous struggles with Sonya's Christianity and partially through Porfiry's mockery of his Napoleonism. But knowledge also comes to him by way of Dunya's resistance to Svidrigaylov and Raskolnikov's identification with them both. A series of events connected with women leads to the confession of his crime. Svidrigaylov confesses his "disgusting stories" of lust and violence to Raskolnikov (CP, 494); he attempts the rape of Dunya and she shoots at him (CP, 507). In what appears as a non sequitur in the police station, Raskolnikov listens to the assistant superintendent discuss "short-haired young females" who "have a most immoderate desire for enlightenment," and the issue of "what more do [women] want." (CP, 540-1). This textual glancing at feminist questions and Dunya is followed by the announcement that Svidrigaylov has shot himself, and by Sonya's appearance at the police station. Only then does Raskolnikov admit "It was I who killed the old woman" (CP, 541-2). Although Dostoevsky has sought to keep Raskolnikov's crime clean of sexual implications, he is finally unable to forestall the convergence of sex with violence, of Raskolnikov's "disease" with Svidrigaylov's, and of feminist with religious and ethical issues.

The Dunya-Svidrigaylov chapter therefore occupies a peculiar position in the novel because it is explicitly about sexual relations and the masculine problematic. Melodramatic as the Lazarus scene between Raskolnikov and Sonya, it is that scene's reversal, with the man rather than the woman humiliated by the struggle. Dostoevsky's intention to transform man through woman's religious faith is complicated in the second scene by the intrusion of a psychology of a new woman and a transformed man whose life framework is power and sexuality rather than religion and theory. Although Dunya's experience with Svidrigaylov is not mentioned in the police station where her brother makes his confession, the assistant-superintendent's words about "short-haired" (emancipated) women and "educated" men (CP, 540-1) forge dialogic connections between the Svidrigaylov-Dunya scene and the scene of Raskolnikov's confession in the police station with Sonya present.

While Raskolnikov's fantasy is to reform the world of heroes through his Napoleon theory (which Sonya resists), Dunya's "passion for reform" moves in a feminist direction toward advocacy for other women (*CP*, 489) to which Svidrigaylov submits. This glance in a feminist direction through Dunya on Dostoevsky's part is not a fully developed or integrated part of the novel's surface. In fact, the image of Dunya and Svidrigaylov interrupts that surface somewhat the way the central clue to a dream's meaning appears extraneous to the dream's manifest content. It shifts the notion of transformation away from religious conversion to what looks like the feminist conversion of a male chauvinist.

Dunya, much less fully realized as a character than Svidrigaylov, remains part of what Bakhtin calls the novel's "hidden interior," perhaps its most hidden part, justifying the impression that the novel's "narrative practices and psychology [are] violently at odds with [its] ideological intentions."[30] It is the religiously pure and simple Sonya, and not the complex Dunya, who must *appear* to be the source of Raskolnikov's conversion, even if the novel's imagery, its self-interception, and its hidden dialogue suggest the contrary. Slipping from Dostoevsky's anti-feminist/socialist stance, Dostoevsky's "encounter" with Dunya, once set in verbal motion, forms new aspects and new functions of the word for the novel and for the reader. It is only through Dunya's effect on Svidrigaylov that Raskolnikov's confession and self-transformation can be achieved. Only through the connections between religious and feminist ideologies of conversion that "the woman question" can be contextualized. Dunya's visit to Svidrigaylov's rooms explores the question that Dostoevsky has treated satirically through Lebezyatnikov—whether "in the future men and women can have access to each other's rooms" (*CP*, 384)—a question that must henceforth be taken seriously.

Dunya's capacity for a violent act against Svidrigaylov undermines the gendered contraries at the heart of Raskolnikov's fantasy of male freedom and female bondage. Locked in Svidrigaylov's room, threatened with the fact that "rape is very difficult to prove," Dunya shoots at her violator with his own gun, first grazing his hair with the bullet. In the following passage the narrator describes Svidrigaylov's state of mind:

> Now she would kill him—at only two feet away! Suddenly she threw away the gun. A heavy weight seemed to have lifted suddenly from his heart, but possibly it was not only the weight of the fear of death. . . . It was a release from another more forlorn and sombre feeling which he himself could scarcely have defined in all its strength. (*CP*, 506-8)

Dunya's response to Svidrigaylov combines (stereotypically male) self-defense with (stereotypically female) compassion for the other, dramatizing a cross-gendered role that Raskolnikov can "grasp" only "to a certain extent" (CP, 540) and that Svidrigaylov can "scarcely define." Release from Svidrigaylov's masculinist monologue turns upon Dunya's final refusal to use the man's own methods against him, leading to his being "seized by the other's discourse, which has made its home in it."[31] Dunya's image and voice invade Svidrigaylov just as the images of beaten mare, axed pawnbroker, and prostituted Sonya invade Raskolnikov's narcissistic solitude. Her interception in the genderized nightmare destroys stereotypes as it exposes the masculinist disease and "something in common" (CP, 302) from which Svidrigaylov and Raskolnikov suffer.

Woman readers may be particularly sensitive to the implications of Dostoevsky's connection of Raskolnikov with Svidrigaylov. In *Crime and Punishment* the rapist is the murderer's double, and each symbolizes the degenerate form to which the secular Westernized "metaphysic" of free male individuality and genderized oppositions have driven him. Dostoevsky's critique of "man's" freedom suggests the woman-violating form to which socially constructed masculinity is sometimes addicted. The novel makes clear that just as the peasant Mikolka beats the mare because she is his "property" (CP, 77), just as Napoleon is the conqueror of territories, so Svidrigaylov imagines himself the "conqueror of women's hearts" (CP, 488), and Raskolnikov temporarily imagines he can become "one man out of a thousand" by killing a greedy old woman. Svidrigaylov's question to Dunya, "So you don't love me?" (CP, 508) co-exists with Raskolnikov's question, "Why did I say 'Women!'?" and with the assistant superintendent's question, "What more do [women] want?" For both Raskolnikov and Svidrigaylov, disease has its origins in male fantasies that construct women as barriers men must penetrate to achieve masculinity—fantasies symbolized in the novel's last section by Svidrigaylov's dream.

The dream that Bakhtin characterizes as *Menippea* marks the alpha and omega of masculine images of women as it assimilates the temptress to the victim, the Orthodox Madonna to Magdalene, the girl to the woman, and both to the whore who is man's desire and debasement. As Svidrigaylov lifts the covers from the sleeping girl-child, Dostoevsky uncovers the fantastic core of his female image repertoire:

> But how strange! The colour of the little girl's cheeks seemed brighter . . . her
> eyelids were opening slowly, as though a pair of sly, sharp little eyes were

winking at him not at all in a childish way, and as though the little girl was only pretending to be asleep.

Svidrigaylov's dream suggests "the universal genre of ultimate questions"[32] involving masculine relations to power and female sexuality. The dream asks whether women are human, whether women means what they say; whether women desire rape:

> Yes, yes, that was so: her lips parted in a smile; the corners of her mouth twitched . . . . She was laughing! . . . There was something shameless and provocative in that no longer childish face. It was lust, it was the face of a whore, the shameless face of a French whore. . . . But at that moment he woke up. (CP, 520-1)

Replicating fragments of Raskolnikov's experience, the dream echoes the "winking" of the "peasant woman" Porfiry and the laughing of the pawnbroker in his dream, as well as her "sharp, sly" eyes. The child's face mirrors the childish face of Sonya, the fact that Sonya is a "whore," and that whores like Napoleon are "French." Like Sonya, Dunya is tempted to sell herself to men such as Luzhin, but in Svidrigaylov's dream, men also prostitute themselves to degraded identity and dreams that drive them to despair and suicide. Dostoevsky's religious intentions for Raskolnikov do not disguise what his society has projected upon women.

Learning that Svidrigaylov has shot himself, Raskolnikov "felt as if some heavy weight had descended on him and pinned him to the ground" (CP, 541). His feeling inverts Svidrigaylov's sense that "a heavy weight seemed to have lifted suddenly from his heart." The weight of sexual crisis, no longer sublimated into abstract questions of freedom or power, shifts to Raskolnikov. He is weighed down by Dunya's and Sonya's meanings, by the "key" that Svidrigaylov has literally thrown to his sister and, by symbolic implication, to him (CP, 509). If he does not fully incorporate Sonya's Christianity, he nevertheless falls into a new world that Sonya and Dunya occupy. In this world where women affect men intensely, the dialectic between masculinity and femininity, hero and vermin, oppressor and oppressed, begins to close. For Raskolnikov, "Life had taken the place of dialectics, and something quite different had to work itself out in his mind" (CP, 580).

This difference discloses Dostoevsky's new version of a masculinity that will escape violence but resist impotence. Raskolnikov attempts but ultimately fails to live out the most heroic version of male courage available to him (Napoleonism), yet Dostoevsky represents his failure as a triumph. Each defeat of an unwanted sexual advance on the part of other men in the novel can also be read as Dostoevsky's undermining of a false conception of masculinity that must be extinguished in Raskolnikov. Against these masculinist fantasies, Dostoevsky empowers Sonya with a hardly believable compassion and Dunya with a virtue, understanding, and strength that can be read as Dostoevsky's alternative to the virtues of feminine passivity. As matured variants of the raped girl-child figure that haunted Dostoevsky all his life, Dunya and Sonya perform a partial revenge against their male violators. If for Dostoevsky child rape ending in murder was the worst crime, then the resistance to rape by a young woman, leading to the self-conscious transformation of the rapist, would constitute a transformed male consciousness. More importantly it would acknowledge female power in an alternate form to Sonya's. If Svidrigaylov is Raskolnikov's double, Svidrigaylov's conversion from pathological sexuality to a momentary dialogic relation with Dunya is the feminist parallel to Raskolnikov's religious conversion through Sonya.

The impact of "George Sandism" (*zhorzhsandism*) is visible in the Dunya-Svidrigaylov scene given so much weight in this interpretation. Dostoevsky's homage to George Sand after her death emphasized his love for her stories of women who sacrificed for love. But his incorporation of Sandean motifs in his novels also indicate his interest in "new" representations of femininity and in women characters who resist and influence men. Robert Belknap follows Boris Reizov in emphasizing Sand's influence on Dostoevsky's, naming *Mauprat* as "the source for the encounter between Dunya and Svidrigaylov or Katerina Ivanovna and Mitia Karamazov as they stood helpless before an armed man in an isolated room." Like Sand's heroines, both Dunya and Katya are "thrust into a position . . . where [the man] contemplates rape, with an acute consciousness of his brutishness and her noble beauty."[33] From Dunya with a pistol to Pasternak's Lara in *Doctor Zhivago*, who practices shooting and then attempts to shoot her seducer Komarovsky (a Svidrigaylov type), Sand's influence leaks into Russian writers' conceptions of the feminine. Dostoevsky's assimilation of Sandean scenes, of women wringing from men promises to reform, of women putting men on trial, is initiated in *Crime and Punishment* and developed in *The Brothers Karamazov*, through Katerina Ivanovna's judgment against Dmitri, discussed here in chapter 7.

Originating in Raskolnikov's experience with women, Dostoevsky's challenge to himself ends *Crime and Punishment*: "He would have to pay a great price for it . . . he would have to pay for it by a great act of heroism in the future" (*CP*, 559). This heroic act is Dostoevsky's creation of male figures, particularly Prince Myshkin and Alyosha Karamazov, who incorporate socially constructed "feminine" traits and are intensely sensitive to the problem of man's violence against women. In *The Brothers Karamazov*, Alyosha is haunted and motivated by his mother's miserable life. He faints when his father describes how he tortured Alyosha's mother, "the shrieker" (Bk. 3, ch. 8), repeating Raskolnikov's fainting scene with his mother and sister but with a new development in consciousness. Neither Myshkin nor Alyosha can be imagined without their most important predecessor, Raskolnikov. *Crime and Punishment* presents scenes in which no authentic male heroism exists without a man's willing entry into dialogic relations and identifications with women, substantiating certain feminist hopes for the future of both sexes.

2
—

Packaging The Gambler:
The Problem of the Emancipated Woman for
Dostoevsky and His Critics

THE CRITICS' STORIES OF DOSTOEVSKY'S STORY

"Perhaps that's why you count on buying me with money," [Polina] said, "because you don't believe in my noble soul?"

"When did I count on buying you with money?" [Alexei] cried.

"When you let your tongue run away with you, and you've lost your thread."
(G, 43)

For readers sensitive to the cultural climate of the late 1960's and early 1970s Dostoevsky's short novel, *The Gambler* (1866), seemed to perform a critique of market-capitalist values, churning the metaphor of "risk" in all directions: ethical, psychosexual, metaphysical. Resonances between Dostoevsky's "emancipated" 1860s character Polina and a wave of feminist discourse evolving in the early 1970s prompted an American repackaging of the novel, with Victor Terras as translator and Edward Wasiolek as editor. Wasiolek wrote an introduction analyzing the link between *The Gambler's* fictional Polina and Dostoevsky's one-time mistress Apollonaria Suslova (nicknamed Polina), and he included in the package some of Dostoevsky's letters and Suslova's diary and short story, *The Stranger and Her Lover*. Provocatively enough, Suslova's short story ends with her heroine's suicide by drowning. Feminist critics may find interesting resonances between Suslova's story of suicide and other nineteenth-century women writers' imaginings of female lives: Hetty in George Eliot's *Adam Bede*, Shakespeare's sister in Virginia Woolf's *A Room of One's Own*, the feminist heroines of Kate Chopin's *The*

Awakening and Doris Lessing's *To Room Nineteen*. But it is perhaps not surprising that these thematic connections between the unknown Russian woman author and some great women novelists are not mentioned in Wasiolek's introduction. The male critic is interested, rather, in Dostoevsky's theme of the "destructive side" of "the violation of reason," and in "Alexei's passion for Polina," which "seemed to have no bounds, at least no rhetorical bounds...." (*G*, Intro., xxxvii). Boundlessness or "irrepressibility"[1] is offered as the central problem explored in *The Gambler*, a theme associated with sexual liberation, the spending and losing of money, and the unraveling of masculine reason exacerbated by intercourse with emancipated or "free" women.

In his introduction Wasiolek writes that Suslova's "intellectual deficiencies" mark her as a "distinct feminine type, almost indeed the incarnation of the verbal polemics that heated the journals of Russia at this time [1860s] with the 'woman question.'" It is just as well that Dostoevsky's gambler, Alexei, does not go home to Russia from Roulettenberg with Polina and her "vagaries of character," for Polina is just another roll of the "turning wheel, and one suspects for Dostoevsky, the irrationalities of human life." Wasiolek's comments are a synthesis of his responses to Suslova's diary, her short story, and Dostoevsky's portrayal of her in his "wrenching of autobiography into fiction." Yet Wasiolek's persuasive mix of biographical detail and literary analysis also provokes him toward diversionary attacks on the "emancipated" woman type. His introduction sets the terms of *The Gambler*'s reception by telling the reader that emancipated types like Suslova should not be taken seriously: "She could have come out of Chernyshevsky's novel *What Is To Be Done?* with, of course, less resolution and intelligence than his female heroines."

Wasiolek knows what to do with Polina Suslova. Despite her "determination to be a new kind of woman . . . free in her feelings and her acts," he decides that she "wasn't sure how to be it." While he invests the ambivalence of Dostoevsky's male character Alexei with some psychological depth, Suslova's ambivalence (like the character Polina's) appears to him shallow and weepy. Suslova's diary shows that "she didn't want to have children, because she doesn't know how to bring them up, but she cries after saying that." He finds her "understanding" to be "limited" and her attempt to "wrest some significance from the banalities of her life and . . . character" pathetic. This young woman, who "attended the University of Petersburg, participated in demonstrations, traveled openly with a married man," and inspired Dostoevsky's passion, is "always banal" for Wasiolek. She must, he writes, have read *Madame Bovary* but concedes that "even after we make allowances for her need to find a scapegoat for the converging failure and banalities of her life, her anger at Dostoevsky and her interpretation of their relationship may have some truth in it" (*G*, Intro. xviii-xxvi and xxxvii-xxxviii).

Was Suslova's life banal? Marc Slonim, in his *Three Loves of Dostoevsky*, tells us she organized a school for peasant children in Vladmir province and was under police surveillance for being "too free in her opinions," for bobbing her hair, and for not going to church. As Secret Police Case no. 250 for 1868, she was described as "one of the foremost she-nihilists," a threat to the government and a champion of women's rights.[2] Choosing between Wasiolek's negative and Slonim's admiring constructions of Suslova should not influence interpretations of Dostoevsky's *The Gambler*, but the problem of intercepting the fit between biography and fiction becomes especially difficult when sexual relations are involved. Nearly ten years after Wasiolek's introduction, Robert Louis Jackson wrote the essay "Polina and Lady Luck in *The Gambler*" (1981), and his commentary implies that if Dostoevsky was anything like his character Alexei, he lost the chance of a lifetime when he lost Polina.

For Jackson the story is about Alexei's bad luck with the emancipated woman and his refusal to be redeemed by her love. Jackson's approach to Polina suggests some assimilation of feminist discourse. Where Wasiolek finds banality and stupidity in the woman, Jackson finds transcendence and missed opportunity for the man. Do we ascribe Jackson's description of Polina's "love and tenderness" for Alexei to the critic's having stuck to Dostoevsky's text and deciding *not* to refer to Suslova's diary and sketchy short story? The two critics' alternate readings of *The Gambler* suggest contrasting theoretical armatures and temperaments, but also opposing views of the role of "the feminine" in Dostoevsky's work.

For Wasiolek, Dostoevsky explores "the deepest urge in human beings . . . the revolt against definition and the fixities of life; the violation of reason . . . maybe that side he was celebrating in the portrait of Alexei" (*G*, Intro. xxxvii). For Jackson the story explores a "fate-ruled universe [where] there is no tomorrow" or "resurrection" and nothing is celebrated. The gambler's world is "a special kind of hell"[3] in which Alexei refuses salvation by the good Russian woman Polina. Wasiolek's "flux" or Jackson's "fate," the trope of undecidability (symbolized by Lady Luck) is either celebrated or damned, as is Polina and by implication, Suslova.

The meaning of *The Gambler* seems to depend upon the floating feminine signifier, "Polina," associated with all sorts of ideas about woman's freedom and sexuality, emancipated women's capacities for loving men, and the viability of feminist consciousness and activism. Polina is less "in" the story than the story is about her; she is no longer exactly Dostoevsky's character;

she belongs to the idea "woman" and to "the woman question." Dostoevsky's quest for the meaning of the emancipated woman Polina apparently stimulates a similar quest in his male commentators. Is Polina "the eternal mate," a personification of "the liberalizing ideas of a [new] age," as Marc Slonim has described her?[4] Is she a way *out* of a man's pathological gambling with life, as Jackson suggests? Or is she Alexei's (and Dostoevsky's) worst gamble, as Wasiolek attempts to convince us in his introduction? Through a "Polina" constituted by alternative types of sexism, based either on the pedestal theory or an implicit misogyny, each commentator exposes his own uxorious mythology. Who then is Polina for a feminist reader? Is there a Polina in this text?

No doubt Jackson's description of Polina shows that it is better for a woman to be a deliverer than a moron, man's "Lady Luck" rather than his banality, particularly if her only possibility of self-realization is as his wife. Taking these interpretations together, however, Polina seems rather to be the wheel on which Dostoevsky's and his critics' ambivalences turn. Certainly Suslova was the central puzzle of Dostoevsky's life during the years 1863-66, with more than one commentator claiming that Dostoevsky's "experiences with Suslova . . . first laid bare the dark recesses [of the human heart] to his piercing insight."[5] *The Gambler*, like *Notes from Underground*, allegorizes Dostoevsky's sexual confusions and explorations related to his attractions and quarrels with liberalism, modernism, and the West. But Polina, unlike Liza of *Notes from Underground*, is a "lady" whose sexual favors cannot be bought as Liza's can. Conversations between Alexei and Polina—"When did I count on buying you with money?" he asks her—indicate the psychological displacements her nontraditional feminine identity stimulates. Is a "free" woman a whore? What does woman's emancipation set loose in man? These questions are important to understanding why *The Idiot*, *The Possessed*, and *The Brothers Karamazov* still speak to us; but also to understanding the life decisions Dostoevsky made. Should he have lived with or married the emancipated Suslova with all the chances and instabilities that choice signifies? Or did he luck out with a traditional woman who belonged to him like money in the bank (his stenographer, Anna Snitkina, to be exact)?

While the fictive Alexei prefers gambling to being reformed by the fictive Polina, the real forty-three-year-old Dostoevsky asked the real twenty-one-year-old Suslova to marry him; she refused. While the fictive Alexei runs off with the fictive French courtesan-countess Blanche, the real Dostoevsky and Suslova parted, after which Dostoevsky had a short affair with "an adventurer," Martha Brown,[6] followed by his marriage proposal to another emancipated woman and fiction writer, Anna Korin-Krukovskaya,[7] who also refused him. It appears, then, that Dostoevsky confronted a crisis of values with women. Suslova's aftereffect on him was such that he reinvented her repeatedly in his later woman characters. "From Polina," writes Mochulsky, "comes the 'fatal woman' of his novels: Nastasya Filipovna, Aglaya, Katerina Ivanovna, Grushenka."[8] Jacques Catteau finds her most specifically in Katerina Ivanovna. Polina was part of the reason Dostoevsky's life in the 1860s "suddenly broke in two," but this breaking led to his extraordinary perceptions regarding the motivations, fantasies, and consequences of men's treatment of women.

Describing the reality he would enter with Suslova after the death of his wife and his brother, Dostoevsky wrote that "everything was strange and new to me, and not one heart which could replace the two I had lost."[9] Jacques Catteau notes that "from 1863 to 1866 Dostoevsky was confused by his sexual liberation and emotional solitude." The theme of sexual exploration and alienation found in Dostoevsky's *The Gambler* sounds in Suslova's story, *The Stranger and Her Lover,* but her story also suggests a desire to subvert patriarchal authority and a struggle to define her own "space" in a man's world.[10] Dostoevsky's emotional situation during his years of involvement with her was traumatic, unsettled, and un-Russian. In the 1860's, "the woman question" was becoming controversial and fashionable with certain Russian intellectuals who went to France or had French connections,[11] a fact Dostoevsky parodies in *The Gambler* by making Polina's seducer-betrayer a Frenchman. Dostoevsky and Suslova were experimenting with new forms of sexual relations together. They went West together, to Wiesbaden and Paris, to experience Europe's gender revolution—to a world of gambling with love, sex, money, and freedom.

> [Dostoevsky's] first love had faded: [his wife] Mariya Dmitriyevna, ill and erratic, made pointless scenes; he looked after her diligently, but became more and more detached. He fell in love with Apollinariya Prokofiyevna Suslova, whom he had known since 1861 or 1862, and who became his mistress. In 1863, they agreed to meet abroad, in Paris. On his way, at Wiesbaden, Dostoevsky played roulette. He arrived in Paris "too late," as Apollinariya said: she had found consolation in the arms of a Spanish student, Salvador.[12]

Dostoevsky's was "too late" in a number of ways. He was already a man in his forties, suffering from epilepsy, haunted by the death of his wife that seemed a return, psychologically, to the death of his mother. He would have to come to terms with a young woman's preference for a younger man, a younger generation whose ideas would challenge his own. He would be compelled to watch Suslova struggle between himself and Salvador. His attitude toward her would shift between fatherly understanding and the competitor's jealousy; between a sense of his traditional male prerogatives and her rights as a "new" woman whose aggressiveness, pride, and passion attracted and alarmed him. The effect of such a strong and dominating woman on his imagination would be long-term. Again and again in his later fiction he would imagine his hero—whether it was the "perfectly good" Prince Myshkin or the "satanic" Stavrogin—confronted with a woman who would tell the man he *needed a nurse.* Such a woman would also tell the male character—as Aglaya tells Prince Myshkin in *The Idiot,* as Lisa Tushina tells Stavrogin in *The Possessed,* as Katerina Ivanovna tells Dmitri Karamazov in *The Brothers Karamazov*—that he is a liar and a betrayer of himself as well as women.

Suslova's way of life was implicitly a critique of the traditional man Dostoevsky thought he was. He resisted her as he resisted modernism, by incorporating its powers, recreating it as part of the polyphony of his fictions.

DOSTOEVSKY'S STORY

In *The Gambler,* Salvador becomes de Grieux, the "despicable and petty money lender" who comes to Polina "in the guise of an elegant marquis and disillusioned liberal" (G, 195). In real life, Polina and Dostoevsky were reconciled despite Salvador and set out for Baden-Baden, where Dostoevsky's interest in roulette became obsessive. "It is easy to imagine his contradictory emotions," Catteau writes:

> . . . remorse at betraying his sick wife . . . shame for a disturbed and impure love, a sensation of sexual liberation, happiness in loving a woman twenty years younger than himself, who was independent, proud, liberal and ardent, torture at being supplanted by a handsome young man whom, moreover, she did not love, bittersweet reconciliation, redoubled and undeserved humiliations, which the "colossal egoism and self-love" of the imperious Salomé-Apollinariya inflicted upon him, and roulette.[13]

Wasiolek's image of Suslova as confused and unintelligent is countered by Catteau's image of her as the murderous femme fatale Salomé, but both male critics emphasize her nasty female egoism and sexual impurity while treating Dostoevsky's multiple sexual affairs with sympathy. Despite the fact that in a letter to Suslova's sister, Dostoevsky declares that he still loves the egoist,[14] the commentators tend to elaborate on the projections they impose upon her ("Lady Luck," "Salomé," a "banality") rather than on the question of why Dostoevsky fell for Suslova or who *The Gambler*'s Polina might be without these projections.

Confronting possible feminist projections of our own, we need to understand not only why Dostoevsky overtly rejected Suslova's radical ideas about women, expressed by Chernyshevsky's *What Is to Be Done?* (1863) but also why he also pursued Suslova. The problem of "evidence" for literary interpretation now abuts the problem of interpreting historical persons and events. Is there a connection between Dostoevsky's attack on Chernyshevskian socialist feminism and the fact that Wasiolek's, Jackson's, and Catteau's interpretations of Polina emerge within the context of American and French contemporary third-wave feminisms, which they ignore? The gender troubles raised by debates about women in the 1860s influenced Dostoevsky's writing as they did the writings of his literary interpreters in the two decades after 1960. But this parallel remained invisible to the commentators whose writings are most contextualized by it. Did Dostoevsky find himself in a similar situation, overtly rejecting what he would unconsciously absorb?

The woman problem reappears, in twentieth-century commentaries about *The Gambler*, in the denial that signals its silenced presence. Jackson's denial takes the form of disregarding the historical context of *The Gambler* by analyzing it in relation to Pushkin's *Queen of Spades*. He interprets the fictional Polina as the embodiment of a philosophy of love and sacrifice so that she becomes a stereotyped carrier of a salvational ethic the story never finalizes. Wasiolek acknowledges the historical context and Chernyshevsky's influence, but trivializes its influence on Dostoevsky by arguing that the historical Suslova is a trivial person. Luckily, there is also the "Dostoevsky" who does not fit in with this conservative agenda: a man who does not repudiate this free woman for having an affair with a younger man or for not being a virgin. Dostoevsky wants *this* Suslova to marry him. Although he later happily marries his stenographer, Anna Snitkina, the novelist continually "returns" in his fiction to a "flirt[ation] with the revolutionary movement embraced by Petrashevsky and his circle: an illicit liaison which had cost him exile in Siberia."[15] This return indicates a taste for continual self-transformation that informs the gender relations he dramatizes.

Dostoevsky's traffic in things illicit or radical, followed by punishment, is as fundamental to his fictional structuring of male-female relations as to his personal experience of politics. Emancipated women associated with radical politics operate as part of a vacillating magnet in his work whose antitype is conservative loyalty to the Czar and Orthodoxy. This tension between "new" women and the old patriarchy, between the status quo and the longing for an ultimately changed world, shows Dostoevsky to be a "revolutionary and reactionary at the same time."[16] The tension takes a gendered form in his fiction, culminating in the oppositions Ivan fantasizes, in *The Legend of the Grand Inquisitor*, between a type of feminized culture embodied by Christ, and a power-obsessed and pathologically masculinized culture embodied by the Inquisitor—a subject I take up in more detail in chapter 6.

In *The Gambler* the confusions between traditional male and female behaviors, the shifting of conventionally designated masculine and feminine spheres provoke Dostoevsky's explorations of productive forms of "unreason" associated with cultural change. Tzvetan Todorov offers a clue as to how to read Polina's effect on Alexei by suggesting that women who live outside the constrictions of culture's mainstream, either by default or consciously, have the power to break through men's pretensions to superiority. In *Notes from Underground*, Todorov describes the prostitute Liza's female gaze upon the underground man as resembling "neither the master's nor the slave's." For Todorov Liza's "gaze retains its uniqueness" and she "reacts in an unexpected manner . . . that does not belong to the master-slave logic."[17] In *The Gambler*, Dostoevsky describes Polina's gaze as having an even more powerful effect as she points out to Alexei that he is attempting to buy her with money and has lost his "thread." As she listens to Alexei's description of "man" as a "despot by nature" who "loves to be a tormentor," and as he taunts her ("you love it awfully"), she responds by looking at him with a "particularly fixed attention," which makes Alexei realize that his own face is convulsed, his eyes bloodshot, his mouth foaming (*G*, 45). Her gaze, like Liza's in *Notes*, remains unmastered as she flings back his money and his words, denying that she shares his "nature" or his greed.

The resemblances between Liza's and Polina's responses to men in these scenes suggest that women's gestures, particularly the expression of their eyes, work like a language in Dostoevsky. In both texts a woman has a lover whom another man mocks. Just as Alexei scorns de Grieux's letters, which Polina cherishes, so the underground man mocks Liza's letters from her lover, which show she is loved. Both the underground man and Alexei remind the women of their lovers' sexual exploitation of their young bodies. Although Liza is a prostitute whose hopes the tyrannical underground man attempts to crush, and Polina is a "young Russian lady," each embodies the possibility of free love and risky mutual exposures. Each disrupts traditional gender relations, and neither is punished. In two similar scenes between men and women, Dostoevsky illuminates sexual power structures by "simultaneously espousing and subverting them"—a narrative technique Barbara Johnson identifies as fundamental to "perhaps *the* feminist question par excellence . . . : to what structure of authority does the critique of authority belong?"[18]

Dostoevsky raises but does not answer this question. At the same time, *The Gambler* "carries a multitude of quotations within its [language] fabric"[19]—one of which refers to Russia's reception of Western feminism and the problem of authority for Polina. In his explanation to Mr. Astley, another of Polina's suitors, as to why she is attracted to the shallow Frenchman de Grieux , Alexei offers an explanation that appears to be a critique of Russian backwardness:

> "Let me tell you that there is not a creature on earth more trustful and more candid than a kindhearted, clever, and not too sophisticated young Russian lady. A de Grieux . . . wearing a mask . . . can conquer her heart with extraordinary ease. . . . But in order to detect beauty of soul and originality of character *a person will need incomparably more independence and freedom than is found in our women . . . and needless to say, a great deal more experience.* And so, Miss Polina— . . . will need a very, very long time before she can . . . prefer you to that scoundrel de Grieux." (*G*, 195; my emphasis)

Alexei acknowledges that English women have better opportunities for education and self-discovery than do Russian women and that this lack affects Polina's judgments about herself and her choice of men. Although Alexei expresses sympathy for Polina's quest for freedom by acknowledging Russia's cultural limitations, *The Gambler* also shows that men's liberated words can be one thing and their culturally inscribed emotional habits and actions another. Alexei presents himself to Polina as an alternate to de Grieux, but Dostoevsky shows that he is also de Grieux's double. Suslova's critique of the lover's limitations in *The Stranger and Her Lover* is already implicit in Dostoevsky's fictive self-analysis through Alexei. Like de Grieux, Alexei participates in the Frenchman's unauthentic liberalism and capacity for exploiting Polina's idealistic free-love idealism, just as Dostoevsky—according to Suslova's story and diary—presents himself to her as an alternate to Salvador while he shares Salvador's sexual opportunism.

This exposure of how liberal-talking men exploit emancipated women parallels the masculine exploitation of feminine sacralization that otherwise appears in Dostoevsky's work. The insight stimulates Alexei, if not some of Dostoevsky's other characters, to recognize the links between his own and other men's cruelty to women and then to value the experience of punishment for himself. "I absorbed de Grieux's punishment and became guilty without doing too much on my own," Alexei says. His whimsical attempts to punish himself by obeying Polina's humiliating commands suggest that he is divided between allegiances to himself and to her. His inner conflict emerges from his impulse to pay homage to her emancipation at the same time that he feels a deep resentment of it, with the result that he finally flees from her into a kind of emotional oblivion.

Alexei's flight into oblivion has its source in a Raskolnikovian conflict regarding women. Humiliated by Polina's love for de Grieux but unable to condemn it, Alexei finds no resolution for his fragmented masculine persona, and forgetting Polina serves as his only respite. As Polina and Alexei confront each other at an emotional cusp where "love" is destabilized, they discover, as late-twentieth-century men and women are rediscovering, that the challenge of freedom between the sexes can sometimes release enormous hostility on the man's part and mocking defensiveness or withdrawal on the woman's.

Dostoevsky shows that the risks of equality between the sexes unleash punishing emotions that traditional relationships between men and women inhibit. Polina's demands that Alexei "jump down into the abyss" provoke him to enact a stupid joke with a "fat baroness." Alexei speaks of his "irresistible urge to beat you up, to disfigure you, to strangle you. . . . You are driving me mad" (G, 43-6). In his next response to Polina he fantasizes the suicide that Suslova will give to the heroine of her own story. As traditional gender roles shift and Alexei becomes more conscious of their meaning for himself, the "problem of freedom" confronts him as a choice between chaotic license or acknowledgment of the rights of the "other." Paralyzed by these alternatives, Alexei displaces the act of choosing his role as a man to the activity of gambling for money.

For her part Polina tests the degree to which Alexei takes her experiment in self-empowering seriously. She wonders if he could "actually kill" some-body if she told him to, but asks whether he "would come back and kill [her] for having dared to make [him] do it" (G, 46). Experimenting with various identities, she too flirts with the puzzle of liberation versus license, makes crazy and childish demands of Alexei, and then bursts into laughter. Her laughter suggests why Alexei loves her and perhaps why Dostoevsky loved Suslova. Hers is the sort of "demonic" feminist laughter—"the laughter of Medusa"—that represents a demand for pleasure and release. Through laughter and mockery, and by throwing money back in de Grieux's face, Polina disrupts a story about the male gambling obsession and writes herself "into the world and into history—by her own movement." Once there, Polina/Suslova transcends various Dostoevsky critics' ideas of "a universal woman subject who must bring women to their senses and their meaning in history."[20]

Dostoevsky's Polina is not in her right senses in traditionalist terms, and Alexei exclaims that she is "capable of all the horrors of life and passion" (G, 76). In order to play at obeying Polina while simultaneously mocking her need for obedience, Alexei "insults" the baroness by blurting out in French: "I have the honor of being your slave" (G, 49). Alexei's buffoonery releases him from the threat of serious subordination to women. He turns homage into insult and being at Polina's mercy into a mockery of male chivalry when he shows that he will "respect" Polina only by insulting another woman. He will "love" her by creating a "disturbance" (G, 55)—thus affirming his egotistical superiority and controlling her attempt to control him.

Alexei's psychological displacements, mocking Polina by mocking other women, playing the buffoon himself in an effort to control her, mirror Dostoevsky's narrative procedure in *The Gambler*. Reducing the war Alexei wages against Polina's autonomy to a childish but nasty game, Dostoevsky is able to render a satiric slap at *all* the men through the grandiose Grandmother who suddenly steps into the middle of the narrative "out of Russia." The arrival of this Maternal Colossus, scourging her expatriate sons, gives Polina the strength to leave Europe and return home. As the old and new generations of Russian women bond, exiled Russian men begin to suffer and their hungers for sex, power, and money are exposed. Having been pronounced dead by her greedy relatives, the Grandmother surprises everybody by riding into Roulettenberg on a chair "lifted" by several servants. "Leave me alone, you and your point!" she yells at Alexei. "I hope you'll choke on my money!" (G, 122-3). An icon of Mother Russia, Grandmother routes the patriarch general who is Alexei's employer as well as Alexei himself.[21] A servant tells Alexei the story of how a "man . . . stole [grandmother's] money right off the table. She caught him herself, once or twice, and did she give it to him, sir, did she give it to him, calling him all sorts of names, even pulled his hair once" (G, 132).

Through the Grandmother's "giving it" to men, Dostoevsky parodies his own polyphony[22]—moving the woman question backward as well as forward in time through the symbol of the old Russian matriarch. Patriarchs, Grandmothers, fake French countesses, English gentleman, gamblers, and emancipated women converge in Roulettenberg to add their voices to a chaotic babble about love, gender, money, value, and power. But within this chaos Dostoevsky offers a comic and cosmic authority figure who is not male.

The perspective gained by Dostoevsky's comic technique indicates the major difference between what he and Suslova do in fiction with the experiences they shared. While Suslova's feminism is narrowly defined in *The Stranger and Her Lover* as a matter of morality and love, of woman's emotional disappointment in men, Dostoevsky's story completes the picture of disappointment by suggesting the role that money and Western notions of liberty play in Russian male-female relations. The significance of money for Dostoevsky has received much commentary,[23] and in Dostoevsky's works the scene of a woman's flinging back money in a man's face is particularly significant. It symbolizes the writer's disgust with the West's capitalist, laissez-faire cultures, in which human responsibility is reduced to cash nexus. Liza in *Notes from Underground*, Polina in *The Gambler*, Sonya in *Crime and Punishment*, Nastasya in *The Idiot*, Olya in *A Raw Youth*, and Katerina in *The Brothers Karamazov* all enact this gesture that frees them from male dominance connected with economic power. Repetition alone adds to the power of an imagery that ties men's evaluations of women with cash, that symbolizes "the feminine" as a purchasable commodity.

Such "family resemblances" and "chains of episodes"[24] link scenes in *The Gambler* to Dostoevsky's later novels. Foreshadowing more interesting figures like Nastasya Filipovna and Katerina Ivanovna, Polina is represented, for all the text's satire, as a woman fighting with history's symbolization of her. Although the text pays homage to Russian nationality, it also makes a connection between Russia and "the feminine." At the end of the story Alexei is moving toward amnesia, forgetting both his homeland and Polina:

> Polina's image flitted through my mind also. . . . I remember her and knew that I was on my way to her. . . . Yet I could hardly remember what she had told me earlier" (G, 159).

REMEMBERING SUSLOVA

Catteau is convinced that through gambling Dostoevsky "needed to live his dream, to feel true risk, escape from the monotonous ritual of everyday life and enter the game which recreates equality."[25] That Dostoevsky gambled with equality for women should not escape the metaphorist's net. Not only *The Gambler* but Suslova's short story contains the *ur*-scene that Dostoevsky often inscribes in his great novels, a scene in which the male protagonist, confronting a woman, recognizes his guilty tyrannizing of her. Suslova inscribes a variant of this scene in both her private diary and *The Stranger and Her Lover*. Although Suslova's and Dostoevsky's talents and viewpoints differ, each dramatizes sex war and a woman's quest for self-respect. Each narrative dramatizes the psychological sufferings endured by both sexes in an ambiguous world of disrupted ethics and traditions. In Suslova's diary the following conversation between herself and Dostoevsky is recorded:

> When we got to his room, he fell at my feet, and, putting his arms around my knees, clasping them, and sobbing, he exclaimed between sobs: "I have lost you, I knew it!" Then having regained his composure, he began to ask me about the other man. "Perhaps he is handsome, young, and glib. But you will never find a heart such as mine." For a long time I did not have the heart to answer him.
>
> "Have you given yourself to him completely?"
>
> "Don't ask, it is not right," I said.
>
> "Polia, I don't know what is right and what is wrong. . . . Are you happy?"
>
> "No."
>
> "How can that be? You love and you are not happy, how is this possible?"
>
> "He does not love me."

Suslova's selective memory indicates that she needed Dostoevsky's support for her role as a woman who took risks with men without assurances of conventional marriage. That Dostoevsky appeared to be a man who respected such courage in a young woman accounts for her willingness to fully confide in him.

> "Oh, Polia, why must you be so unhappy! It had to happen that you would fall in love with another man. I knew it. Why, you fell in love with me by mistake, because yours is a generous heart, you waited until you were 23, you are the only one who does not demand of a man that he obligate himself in some way, but at what a price; a man and a woman are not one and the same. He takes, she gives."
> (*SD*, 206-7)

Dostoevsky's response to Suslova's risk is a recognition of the price emancipated women pay. Yet he also issues ambiguous warnings: Against whom should Suslova be protected? Against the predatory male companions of sexually free women or against the man who supposedly protects her against these predators? In Suslova's diary we confront the moment Dostoevsky loses his identity and is "divided into two halves." Is Dostoevsky the predator, is Salvador the predator, or are Dostoevsky and Salvador indistinguishable in terms of what Polina can expect from men of her time? If "man and woman are not the same" because she "gives" and he "takes," is

Dostoevsky exempting himself, describing what he takes to be essential differences between men and women, or ironically exposing what he himself condemns?

Processing the hurt that her diary records about Dostoevsky and Salvador, Suslova's *The Stranger and Her Lover* turns on Anna's becoming disillusioned with a certain Losnitsky, whose character is very like the diary's Dostoevsky. Losnitsky returns to Petersburg to see the twenty-two-year-old Anna, whose letters to him indicate that she has become more "serious." Through several encounters, he learns that this woman (whom Suslova describes as Madonna-like, with "an unconquerable strength and passion" in her "gentle and kind features") is in love with a young student. Although Losnitsky comes "too late," he demands to know everything about Anna's affair. When Losnitsky asks whether she has "given" herself sexually to the student, Anna silences him with a sharp frown, but admits that the young man "does not love [her] very much."

Suslova's style is monologic, but she is able to describe Anna as a distinctly difficult character: "no model of moderation either in praise or in censure." She also offers a clear picture of Losnitsky's/Dostoevsky's effect on women. He is a man who does not "dispel depression," but "with a kind of morbid pleasure" becomes "intoxicated by it." As partners in emotional extremity, Anna and Losnitsky are particularly well suited. Suslova gives us the flavor of Losnitsky/Dostoevsky's words as well as her "new" woman's skeptical, sarcastic responses to them:

> "I am no longer a young man" [he says] " and at my age one does not play with one's affections. . . . Your love descended upon me like a gift from God, against all hope and expectation, when I was weary and desperate. This young life at my side promised so much . . . has resurrected my faith and what remained of my former strength."
>
> "You've really put it to good use," thought Anna, but she said nothing. (*SL*, 303-8)

Anna's silence is part of her weariness, the sign of annihilated hope. Her criticisms of Losnitsky's self-centered expectations of her womanly function as a restorer of his virile strength are confined to a "thought," without verbal expression. Missing from Suslova's story is a narrator who can read the ambivalences and gestures of men as well as women, who can simultaneously critique and sympathize with both characters. Suslova seems locked imaginatively into "noble" Anna even if she faithfully records words that Dostoevsky/Losnitsky spoke. But if her fiction served Dostoevsky by confronting him with his own words about women, the quality of her prose is finally less important than the substance of her criticism. Suslova's Anna registers a melodramatic protest against men who cannot remember their idealistic promises to "new" women. The shared experiences of the two writers suggest two different kinds of attitudes toward writing. *The Stranger and Her Lover* functions as a therapeutic catharsis of Suslova's despair about men, while *The Gambler* explores the emancipated woman type as a character and allows Dostoevsky to symbolically punish himself through Alexei. While Suslova's story admonishes Dostoevsky as well as Salvador, *The Gambler* succeeds in retaining its homage to Suslova's protest.

Suslova was one of many women writers who ended their stories with suicide. In *No Man's Land*, Sandra Gilbert and Susan Gubar note that women confront "fears by imagining characters who are unable to achieve the aesthetic release their authors themselves attain by the very creation of these figures."[26] Suslova shares with these authors the theme of a woman's death connected to men's objectifying women as sources of "faith," treating them with condescension, and humiliating them with the double sexual standard.

Anna's suicide is motivated by the realization that her "free" offers of love have been exploited and that she cannot escape the constructions of femininity that define her every act and word. Her "nobility" is humiliated by a young man who promises to love her as an equal and then betrays her, as well as by an older man who says he loves her but is unable to transform his male-chauvinist habits. Losnitsky's question to her is almost of parody of patriarchal speech, foreshadowing Freud's notorious "What do women want?" Losnitsky asks, "Who can figure you out?" to which Anna responds bitterly: "I thought I would find in [my surrender to you] salvation, a goal, a haven, and found nothing but shame and sorrow." Losnitsky offers Anna "shame and sorrow" by "narrat[ing] adventures which occurred during Anna's last absence involving a certain gay lady of the city of B. and various escapades of that frivolous woman, and of a man no less frivolous in his attitude toward her, all told in a casual, cynical tone." When Anna responds angrily to this confession, he says that "this is one of your perfectly feminine traits" and proceeds to lecture her about the necessity of dividing sex from love:

> "Relations between men and woman, such as I have just been telling you about, are most naturally excusable; they are even necessary. Not only do they not interfere with a true and exalted love for another woman, but they actually enhance and support it. Unfortunately, no woman is capable of understanding this . . ." (*SL*, 330)

Anna's disappointment with this condescending man's double standard, scored melodramatically through her suicide, indicates the consequences for both Alexei and Polina (and Suslova and Dostoevsky) of the refusal to remember the past—a theme that ends *The Gambler*. As the supplement to Dostoevsky's story, *The Stranger and Her Lover* indicates what men (Dostoevsky, Salvador, Alexei, Losnitsky) must repeatedly experience and remember if they are not to lose women's love and lapse into the oblivion of egotistical solipsism.

Both *The Stranger and Her Lover* and *The Gambler* expose the consequences of men's resistance to understanding women's quests for emancipation. If suicidal drowning is to gambling as female awakening is to male confusion, Suslova's and Dostoevsky's alternate metaphors together describe a newly gendered landscape. While Suslova's response to their relationship is to write a story that exposes Dostoevsky/Losnitsky, Dostoevsky's is to write a story that exposes the masculinist complex of men of his time. While Suslova's illustration of sex war is single-voiced and narrowly framed, for Dostoevsky the process of getting at the mystery of male-female relations is polyphonic, a defensive incorporation of the recognition Suslova's story and diary records.

The impact of Suslova may have been "unknown and inaudible even to Dostoevsky himself,"[27] with the "Polina" effect lying on a continuum with the George Sand effect. Suslova's complaints to Dostoevsky, that "he killed her faith," are significantly echoed years later in Dostoevsky's words about "destroy[ing] *faith* in love's beauty"[28]—words related to his compulsion to describe sex crimes in fiction and to punish his sensual male "insects" with suicide. Dostoevsky's biographers never fail to record the way Suslova was shocked to find, when she encountered Dostoevsky years after their affair, that he did not recognize her. His amnesia suggests a very deep assimilation, so deep that he could only recognize her when she came from his own creations of Nastasya Filipovna or of Katerina Ivanovna—when she was no longer threatening real but a fiction.

Robert Jackson does not underestimate the impact of Suslova's hungers for emancipation on Dostoevsky when he writes that in *The Gambler* "everything is in flux . . . people, languages, currencies, values."[29] We might now add to this list women's roles, and indeed, the construction of male identity.

3

Flights from The Idiot's Womanhood

The Idiot exhibits an experiment in terms of "the feminine" that marks it off from Dostoevsky's other novels. In *Notes from Underground, The Gambler,* and *Crime and Punishment,* traces of the turbulent 1860s transform relationships between male characters and female characters who embody "new woman" heroinisms. If Sonya and Dunya do not immediately redeem Raskolnikov, and if Liza cannot entirely change the underground man's dedication to spite, their feminine powers are nevertheless acknowledged. If Polina does not bring Alexei toward love and self-knowledge, she at least exercises the wit to escape from his sadistic ambivalence. Up until *The Idiot,* several of Dostoevsky's principle women characters embody a polyphonic and quasi-feminist consciousness that his heroes in part assimilate.

With his apparently favorite hero, "Prince Christ" Myshkin, Dostoevsky breaks this narrative pattern. In the denouement that the whole novel was written for the sake of (as Dostoevsky informed his niece),[1] Myshkin is represented as having assimilated and imitated everything but having understood nothing. Despite Nastasya Filipovna's extraordinary capacity for self-dramatizations of women's sufferings and Aglaya's talk of women's emancipation, Myshkin remains at the end of the novel as he was at the beginning. Caryl Emerson argues that Myshkin is the most "monologic" of Dostoevsky's characters,[2] and one who monologizes others. In this chapter I suggest that this monologism is related to Dostoevsky's displacement of "the woman question" to an "answer" in anachronistic Christianity. Myshkin is offered as a solution for the second sex's problems in Russian society, as an alternative model for masculinity, as an antitype to male violence toward women personified by Rogozhin, and as an antidote to Western patriarchal rationality and secularism. Myshkin is a salve for women's psychological self-degradation, a Christ without a sword who is ready to take on more than one woman as his Magdalene. Dostoevsky's "idiot" fascinates us because he embodies tremendous confusions about gender and sexuality linked to ideas about faith and religion.

As his biographers note, Dostoevsky's period of unrest came to an end shortly after he married Anna Snitkina, and this fact (as well as his desperate need for money) influenced his writing of *The Idiot*. His letters indicate that he found Anna somewhat dull after the heart-rending excitements of Suslova, but that he soon came to love his wife and to anticipate children with her. *The Idiot* registers the "split consciousness" regarding women that Dostoevsky explored in his heroes earlier, but the split is not internalized as it was in Raskolnikov. Rather, it is externalized through the "good" Myshkin and "bad" Rogozhin. Dostoevsky's need to imagine and present to his reading public an "altogether good man" was perhaps prompted by the future he faced as Snitkina's husband and the father of their children. His decision to become a better sort of man himself, felt so deeply as he stood by the bier of his first wife,[3] perhaps motivated his wish to create a hero intent on saving women, rather than one whom women attempt to save. But the novel also expresses large literary-nationalistic ambitions beyond these biographically motivated impulses, and these ambitions account for the novel's chaotically-narrated, structurally a-logical elements.

What is possible or impossible in terms of future relations between men and women is the central problem of *The Idiot*, at least in its most coherent section, Part One. Yet Dostoevsky does not describe the novel in these terms, even though his first notes for the novel record anecdotes about girls and women, nor does Part Two develop the focus initiated in Part One. In *The Idiot*, the tale, the teller, and what is told have unusually labile narrative relations to one another. Discourse that appears initially as polyphony later verges on cacophony, with Myshkin's character remaining oddly monologic throughout. In Part One, for example, the reader may experience a pleasurable sense of collaboration with the author's irony, sharing with him a secret hidden from other characters or even readers: that Myshkin only appears to be an idiot but has come into the world to save women like the beleaguered and proud Nastasya. But this impression does not hold its focus. By Part Two the centrality of Myshkin's relation to Nastasya is dispersed by various subplots. The narration becomes increasingly allusive and paradoxical, intimating that readers are about to witness the modernized crucifixion of a Russian Christ figure but must simultaneously participate voyeuristically in the murder of a beautiful woman. The connections between sex and religion are part of the novel's often discussed "mystery."

Mystery and obscurity are part of the total effect, as is the rivalry/brotherhood between "Prince Christ" and Rogozhin. Perhaps, as Harriet Murav puts it, Dostoevsky cannot imagine an ultimate goodness that does not involve beholding "the spectacle of our own folly."[4] Folly and intelligence, Christian and phallic metaphors are so compounded in *The Idiot*, however, that a feminist reader may suspect she is confronting a series of particularly masculinist confusions. Among them is the author's representation of his hallucinated wish to save women "through Christ," subverted by a perhaps unconsciously dramatized apprehension of the ways Christianity makes that wish impossible to fulfill.

The novel remains the site of contested and perhaps inevitable misreadings that center around the notion of *idiocy*, the holy and sometimes not-so-holy foolishness Myshkin continually exhibits. Contemporary traditionalists like David Bethea who find "danger in reading Dostoevsky through Western eyes" emphasize Dostoevsky's apocalyptic vision and interpret Nastasya's death as a "tragic composite of the two temporalities."[5] Bethea does not imagine how apocalypse could be a danger to Dostoevsky himself. What might the novelist *not* have created if *The Idiot* had met with success? Fortunately for late-twentieth-century readers, the book appears in much criticism as the most puzzling and least popular of Dostoevsky's "great" works. Even Russians at the time of the novel's publication in 1868 greeted Dostoevsky's religious intentions with skepticism. There were nineteenth-century Russians who asked how one could "value" Dostoevsky's version of "this truth" and wondered "who is interested in these pathological sensations, besides epileptics?"[6]

Interpretations of the "mystery" of Prince Myshkin reveal opposing kinds of responses, one of which moves toward Slavophilism and the other towards the presently un-Russian deconstructions of psychoanalytic and feminist theory. Recently some readers have described the "feminization" of Myshkin's character, although they have not pursued "the woman question" as the heart of Myshkin's trouble.[7] Why Dostoevsky reserves a whole chapter for the expression of Yevgeny Pavlovich's idea that Myshkin is obsessed with democracy and the woman question is the piece of the puzzle analyzed later in this chapter.

The puzzle involves the way the novel connects a universalist, supposedly timeless subject, the advent of a "Prince Christ" into decaying Russia, with the timely theme of bringing Myshkin into contact with adventurous young women and changing sexual mores. Modernist negotiations between men and women are framed so that Myshkin's intended innocence and "holy" sickness (epilepsy) subordinate issues of sexuality and women's liberation to transcendent and final liberations "in Christ." Two ideals of liberation seduce the novel's women, and part of their quest is to decide how opposed they are: that is, whether, as Aglaya first supposes, Myshkin could be a good husband for an emancipated woman; or, as Nastasya at first imagines, Myshkin could be her saviour. "Myshkin" develops as a symbol of fantastic investments through which women like Nastasya are seduced into hoping that the dangers their sexuality provokes in men will evaporate. The attempted erasure of sexual desire as part of the "love" Myshkin incarnates for both Nastasya and Aglaya is a symptom of Dostoevsky's experiment with eliminating *eros* and substituting *charitas* as the force that binds men and women together. But Myshkin's nonparticipation in sexual reality also functions as the obscurity around which all problems in the novel circulate. Moving in and out between the sacralized, desexualized heaven that is Myshkin's idea of love—which turns out to be a hell of its own—the women characters of *The Idiot* experience a suspension of the traditional orders of male-female relations.

Nastasya's attraction to Myshkin represents a feminist delusion that she could escape into the nonpatriarchal, nonviolent shelter of presexual innocence. He appears to embody her potential emancipation. Her delusion signals Dostoevsky's attempt to imagine a third sex that is not quite a man, a human being who loves women but not the way men in Russian society generally do. As a dream figure whose attitude to women contrasts significantly with Raskolnikov's, the underground man's, or the gambler's, Myshkin is a man whom, in Dostoevsky's wild fantasy, the emancipated Suslova or Korvin-Krupovskaya *might* have loved (as each did not finally love Dostoevsky), and whom the fictional Nastasya Filipovna *does* accept in marriage, only to die by Rogozhin's knife for that acceptance.

Commentaries on the novel are drawn to the murder scene that ends the novel, and I also approach its woman question by discussing its ending first. I note that Dostoevsky positions Myshkin and Rogozhin near Nastasya's dead body as if the two male characters were meant to interpret the meaning of the scene they are in. This peculiar writing-reading situation, where readers and characters meet together in a final scene that is also a stalemate, indicates how the problem of interpreting the meaning of the dead woman only begins when the novel ends. *The Idiot* conflates what is first and last, backward and forward, what is external and internal, what is idiotic and wise, salvational and destructive, feminine and masculine, even dead and alive. Myshkin is still breathing in the novel's last scene, but he has reverted to a stupefaction that is not exactly "life." It should surprise no reader that at Nastasya's deathbed neither Myshkin nor Rogozhin can interpret what they have done, for without Aglaya's or Nastasya's voices, they have no quasi-feminist discourse and thus no explanation available to them. The last picture in the novel is of the dead Nastasya and the half-dead Myshkin caught in the vice of Russian culture's absolutist polarities, Christianity and sexual liberation, and resurrected by neither.

French feminism's insight that language veers towards incomprehensibility and away from the logic of (arguably male-dominated) "reason" when longings for some New Order are attempted may account for impasses in *The Idiot*. The novel appears utopian and unreasonable; it exhibits a flight from masculinity; it dramatizes the exaltation in depression that Suslova marked in Dostoevsky's personal temperament; it subverts its own raison d'être by compromising the patriarchal-Christian salvational structure in which Dostoevsky believes. Overtly, "Prince Christ" is the savior whom nobody recognizes and who dies to this world because he is too good for it. Covertly, Myshkin is a cultural sponge whose capacity for absorbing pain and evil sacralizes passivity. The novel thus appears to appropriate the "feminine" myth of the *mater dolorosa* so that the last scene is a *pietà* with the genders reversed. This fantasy not only disturbs canonical renderings of Golgotha, but insists upon a surrealist version that is arguably "feminist" in its semiotics because it undermines Jesus Christ's gender role and puts the woman, Nastasya, on the cross.

Provoked by Dostoevsky's comments about the novel's meaning, a feminist reader might be tempted to read this last scene in terms offered by the French feminist Julia Kristeva. Kristeva builds upon Jacques Lacan's theory of the "phallocentric symbolic order" that represses the sense of "the feminine" or "woman" and thus lays claim to "transcendental subjectivity." Kristeva argues

> that there are feminine forms of signification which cannot be contained by the rational thetic structure of the symbolic order and which therefore threaten its sovereignty and have been relegated to the margins of discourse. . . . [Yet for Kristeva] the feminine is a mode of language, open to male and female writers.[8]

Clare Cavanagh's claim that Kristeva's theory articulates an immature, and in Russian-Soviet terms, an ahistorical poetics is persuasive.[9] But if Dostoevsky cannot be consigned to a "feminine mode of language," as he invents the sublime passivity of desexualized Myshkin whose mission is to save women, what description of language suits the discourses of *The Idiot?* The novel's failure to deliver a saviour plus the regressively "feminine" dimensions of Myshkin's character serve as an open target for psychoanalytically minded interpreters. But suggestions that the novel exhibits a pathological structure go only part of the way, for the structure reflects a pathology in Russian society that links femininity, even sacralized femininity, with degradation. Myshkin embodies holiness because he is foolish and he is exalted because he is degraded. But while the figure of the holy fool runs through Russian literature as a whole, Dostoevsky's male and female versions of it have very different functions. Female holy fools, such as Sonya of *Crime and Punishment* and Maria Lebyadkina of *The Possessed*, expose men to what men most deeply deny. Dostoevsky associates Myshkin with "the lower body of Russian culture"[10] that may embody ideas about women, birth, and sexuality, but unlike Dostoevsky's female holy fools, Myshkin can do nothing for the women he encounters. Instead, through "Prince Christ," Dostoevsky marks the place where Christianity and sexual relations destroy each other.

Some psychoanalytic commentators have focused on the relation of Myshkin's "pathology" to the author's, reducing the fiction to autobiography in a way that is both insightful and incomplete. With reference to the fact that Dostoevsky's mother died when he was seventeen, Elizabeth Dalton argues that "Nastasya represents for Myshkin the abused mother, and his identification with her in her masochism is so strong that he can do nothing to prevent her from being destroyed."[11] What also matters as we reread the sado-masochistic, guilt-laden sign language of the novel's last frame, with Myshkin and Rogozhin embracing as they lie near Natasya's dead body, is that images of nineteenth-century Christian suffering have shifted for Dostoevsky from the masculine to the feminine spheres: from Christ and his Father to the Mother and Son, with the son left paralyzed by the shift.

Dostoevsky's intensely religious impulse, represented by Myshkin's wish to transform his mother country and reconcile "all things," finds its expression through a carnal hermeneutics, a staging of bodies intended to speak more, or differently, than words. This staging is configured throughout the text by many moments of speechless gesture and "marginalized" or even incoherent phrases that make Kristeva's remarks about a "feminine mode of language" less implausible. Dostoevsky first foreshadows the final death-stupefaction scene when Nastasya is struck dumb in Part One (the characters say she has become insane) by Myshkin's marriage proposal. The foreshadowing continues each time Myshkin is stricken after his epileptic seizures, and on the several occasions when he is able to do nothing but repeat the words of others like a stuck record. Freud remarks in *Beyond the Pleasure Principle* that repetitions occur when the patient cannot remember what is repressed, and that what he cannot remember is most essential to his cure. Dostoevsky's repetitive discourse throughout *The Idiot* is the condition of the novel's theme, a condition that parallels Myshkin's psychic structure expressed most obviously in the least readable sections of Part Two. Repetition, like ritual, produces the novel's trance-like effect, but it also symbolizes Dostoevsky's attempt to work through anxiety about men's and women's relations in a transitional and quickly changing society.

Readers invariably note the part played in the novel by the print of Holbein's "Dead Christ," with its extremely realistic portrayal of a body from a morgue. Myshkin and Rogozhin are bound by this deadly Christ image as they are bound by their "love" for Nastasya, and perhaps as Dostoevsky was bound imaginatively by composite fantasies of dead wife, dead mother, and the symbolically dead "new" woman (perhaps Suslova) he once loved. "I've seen this [Holbein Christ] painting abroad and I can't forget it," says Myshkin to Rogozhin, noting that it's a painting "that might make some people lose their faith" (*I*, 238). The resemblance between the positioning of the Holbein Christ (with feet pointed toward the viewer's face) and the description of Nastasya's dead body with its "tip of a bare foot" protruding from the sheet reinforces the effect, suggesting exactly how faith is lost. Lying upon the bed murdered, it is Nastasya and not Myshkin who now resembles Christ, a figure de-feminized, de-eroticized, and neutered. "All that could be seen was that a human figure lay stretched out at full length" (*I*, 623). The reduction of her once desirable feminine body to this *kto-to*, literally a "something" deprived of gender, may strike readers cognizant of the history of death and eros in many nineteenth-century novels as an aberration. Instead of the sexual arousal that haunts Thomas Hardy's description of the beautiful hanged body of Tess Durbeyfield; in contrast to the sexual innuendos of Flaubert's Emma Bovary's death (with dark blood like menstrual fluid coming from her mouth); and in particular contrast to Tolstoy's description of Anna Karenina's feminine gestures as she, "with a light movement," plunges under the train to her death[12]—Dostoevsky's female corpse is depicted as altogether sexless. The Nastasya whose "beauty" has acted so demoniacally upon men throughout the novel, providing them with the opportunities for rivalry, madness, and murder, now appears to be de-fetishized. Her transfiguration in death is the opportunity for Myshkin's and Rogozhin's final male bonding, revealing how she has served as "traffic" between them.[13] Her absent femininity suggests a point where the concepts of "good" and "bad" men, the sacred and profane, the personal and the (sexual) political, cancel each other out.

In contrast to this moment of revelation, the living, desirable, fetishized body of Nastasya has appeared as the *prime mobile* of the novel's beginning and middle text. Nastasya has been the main reason for Prince Christ's being *in time*; the main opportunity for his experiment with redeeming the world. Fantasies about "the feminine" thus frame Dostoevsky's notion of the exact time of Christ's symbolic second coming. Descriptions of physically expressed apocalyptic human emotions also parody symptoms of female hysteria connected to certain ideas about how woman's organs influence their emotions. Simone de Beauvoir's theory of genderized binary oppositions—the way femininity is mythologized as *immanence* and masculinity as *transcendence*—throws light on the disturbing compound Dostoevsky invents in *The Idiot*. In this most strained of his novels, to understand Christ is to become immersed in something like feminine hysteria, feminine "weakness," and feminine lack of control. It is to imitate a passive succumbing to a violating, entering God-force, a Spirit that penetrates, possesses, and *epilepsizes*. The passage in *The Idiot* that articulates this fantasy is often quoted:

> Thinking about the [epileptic] moment afterward . . . he often told himself that all these gleams and flashes of superior self-awareness and, hence, of a "higher state of being" were nothing other than sickness. . . . And yet he came finally to an extremely paradoxical conclusion. . . . "What does it matter if it is abnormal intensity, if the result . . . turns out to be the height of harmony and beauty . . . of reconciliation, an ecstatic and prayerlike union in the highest synthesis of life?"

Myshkin concludes that "one might give one's whole life for such a moment!" (*I*, 245-6). The fusion of orgiastic madness with religious ecstasy, of entry into the "demoniacal beauty" of Nastasya as into the frenzy of the "epileptic" moment, is completely symbolized only in the still-life of the denouement. Here Christ's body and Nastasya's become one, echoing the gender fusion Nastasya experiences when she enters psychologically into Myshkin's idiocy also coded as a "higher" level of consciousness. Like epilepsy and like dying, Nastasya quests a terminal experience that would cancel her former degraded identity as Totsky's whore: "I always imagined someone like you," Nastasya tells Myshkin just before she throws Rogozhin's hundred thousand roubles into the fire, "kind, honest, and good, and so stupid he would suddenly appear and say, 'You are not to blame, Nastasya Filippovna, and I adore you!'" (*I*, 192).

What Myshkin is for Nastasya, epilepsy is for Myshkin: a flight into completion and ultimate suspension of the all-too-human and ambivalent self. In both cases these flights involve extraordinary states: the one a brain seizure, racking the whole body; the other a penetration into disembodied *other* consciousness. When Myshkin declares himself willing to marry her, Nastasya appears to lose her mind:

> She continued to sit there and for some time gazed at everyone with a strange, wondering expression, as if she could not understand what had happened and

was trying to make sense of it. Then she suddenly turned to the prince and glared at him with a menacing frown; but for only a moment. . . .

Nastasya's temptation, to identify herself as somebody worthy of "pure" love, is dramatized as a loss of reason that links her consciousness to Myshkin's. If initially, in her role as a "fallen woman," she is capable of irony, a realistic assessment of men's motivations concerning her and even a dangerous playfulness with them, her "pure" self is expressed as a lapse into silence. If Myshkin's epilepsy is a surrogate for Nastasya's erotic passion, her madness is a displaced form of the idiot's eventual insensibility. Her "insane" physical movements carry the text's style, constricting or enlarging its coherence. Only when she inspires love in Myshkin does his emotional life begin. Only her death certifies that the meaning of *The Idiot* has concluded. Her bodily responses are clues to be intensely watched and interpreted, signalled by the most important scene in Part One in which men are assembled to watch her every move and to interpret her choices. As the text's visual fetish, she performs its eruptions, gaps, and closures:

> . . . perhaps she had imagined for an instant that it was all a joke, a deception; but the sight of the prince's face told her at once that it was not. She reflected a moment, then smiled again, as if she herself did not really know what she was smiling at. (*I*, 187)

Nastasya's body does things and she says things that "she herself did not really know." Writing to Aglaya, Nastasya coaxes her to marry Myshkin, but also declares that she is in love with Aglaya, that "every day she looks for an occasion to see [her], even from a distance" (*I*, 454). As Myshkin's Heraclitean flux, Nastasya embodies a ceaseless movement. She is his reminder that he cannot escape from a "fallen" world symbolized by a woman's sex-exploited, "fallen" history that he has come to redeem. This is a rather large prospect for an epileptic who has no theory as to why women are so often subjected and degraded in the first place. In this sense Dostoevsky comes close to writing a tragic comedy, but as I suggested earlier, no consistent tone or choice of literary genre sustains his discourse.

While Myshkin's identity as a redeemer is associated with his ability to remain statically monologic, to merely observe and witness, Nastasya's identity is marked by her compulsion to keep moving. She takes flight toward and away from Myshkin, toward and away from Rogozhin's "knife," toward and away from her "good" and "bad woman" identities, and toward and away from hatred and love of Aglaya. As such, the text imitates a kind of tragic carnival of the feminine body, a movement both toward and away from archetypal images of women that duplicate Dostoevsky's construction of Myshkin as an archetypal saint moving upward and a diseased idiot moving downward in desacralized history. Part of the tragicomedy of Myshkin's failed (sexual) masculinity is that he imitates various stereotypically coded feminine rhythms of hysteria, indecision, marginality, undecidability, and self-degradation, which are Nastasya's forte. Through Nastasya's fainting, running back and forth, flashing of eyes, through the "two spots of color...on [her] cheeks" (I, 163), and her suffering eyes, Myshkin is "pierced" into a resemblance of life. What binds him to women is the physical experience of being pierced or stabbed by excess of feeling. Confronted with Nastasya, he "speaks in a trembling voice" (I, 182); in front of Aglaya even his "lips tremble[ ]" (I, 454). He laughs hysterically and inappropriately when he hears how a man burns his finger in a candle at Aglaya's provocation, then "bursts into tears" (I, 593). After the furious scene between Aglaya and Nastasya, he is found "stroking" Nastasya's head and face "with both hands as if she were a little child . . . laugh[ing] when she laughed and ready to cry when she cried" (I, 589).

The relation of Myshkin's holy foolishness to socially constructed femininity is dramatized by his inability to make up his mind or as his not having a mind to make up. What Michael Holquist calls the novel's "failure to express the holy"[14] is linked to Myshkin's disintegrative bodily and speech rhythms, to a holy foolishness that saves no one, and to the way feminine hysteria and the Prince's epilepsy move along the same discursive continuum in the novel. This brings us to the question of why, at this point in Dostoevsky's artistic career, he was compelled to imagine such a continuum: to create a text whose rhetoric seems to imitate a male's imagining of the movements of a woman's body, perhaps a Suslovian body desired and betrayed. Myshkin's epilepsy appears as a pathological equivalent of, if not exactly orgasm as Elizabeth Dalton suggests, then the climactic emotional frenzies to which "fallen," "passionate" or "new" women are supposedly driven. Like mythologies of femininity that embrace the idea of "woman" as "the body" or "nature," a "tempest" or a "swamp of feeling,"[15] The Idiot deploys its repertoire of gestures to suggest that "Prince Christ" can embody the transfiguring "Beyond" only by figuring himself as female.

Is Dostoevsky hinting that the true Christ is *anima*, a female soul? Are we to understand Myshkin as suffused not with his Father's spirit but with *Sophia*? Dostoevsky insists on epilepsy as the transcendental marker, but that marker is also associated with Nastasya's being driven into epileptic-like frenzies and stupors as she is objectified by Rogozhin as a female commodity. Epilepsy may be the symbol of the Son's connection to his eternal Father, but it is also the sign of Myshkin's hysterical identity with degraded femininity. No attachment to the Father can insure his efficacy in *this* world; yet his feminized soul does not insure his transcendence into the other world either.

Nastasya's and Myshkin's identities are further analogized by violent physical experiences and through the trope of penetration. Dostoevsky brings together strange ideas about woman's biological vulnerability and fantasies about Christ's experience of embodiment so that Christian and feminine subjectivities are allied through the trope of knives and piercing. While Nastasya's madness is linked to her fear of being penetrated by Rogozhin's knife, the movement of the image of the knife structures the text itself. The image of a knife floats within Rogozhin's, Nastasya's, and the idiot's consciousness. The knife floats "outside" too, in the shop window Myshkin sees, and throughout the surrealist atmosphere of the novel that penetrates the reader's consciousness. The Russian verb *pronzat'* (to pierce) is repeated throughout the text in various ways, forming a leitmotif that connects the piercing of Christ by soldiers to the "piercing" eyes following Myshkin in his hallucination, to the way Nastasya's face "had pierced [Myshkin's] heart forever" (*I*, 588), and to Rogozhin's knife piercing Nastasya's body. The "piercing" the characters experience is part of *The Idiot*'s narrative coding of sex and violence as the crucifixion of the Spirit, closely allied to fantasies about the phallus and its destructive potentials.

Christ the male warrior, whose emblem is the sword and not the plow-share, is completely absent from Dostoevsky's conceptualization, as is Christ the church organizer absent from Ivan Karamazov's conception of Jesus in *The Legend of the Grand Inquisitor. The Idiot* foreshadows *The Legend*'s analysis of the problem of Christian (feminine) gentleness as politically impotent, in contrast to tyrannical (male) aggressiveness as ecclesiastical power incarnated in the patriarchal Inquisitor himself. If Rogozhin plays the part of inquisitor-prosecutor in *The Idiot*, Myshkin plays the part of Jesus, with the "new woman" Nastasya caught between them, her tragically ambivalent position foreshadowing "the new man" Ivan's intellectual struggles.

In other ways too *The Idiot* reads like a rehearsal for themes more success-fully realized in Dostoevsky's later work. But the novel remains particularly interesting in terms of the woman question because it displays in its own narrative structure a confusion about one part's relation to another, about orders and hierarchies, and about subordinations and dominations that have gendered connotations. It is significance that Part Four, in which Myshkin becomes the erotic-spiritual fetish literally "fought over" by Nastasya and Aglaya, is a narrative inversion of Part One, in which Nastasya is surrounded by men and is offered the choice between Myshkin and Rogozhin. In the scandalous scene of Part Four, women who were pursued by men become a man's pursuer, and the man who once pursued women becomes the object of female rivalry. In this world of shifting gender roles that leads toward the wedding day and Nastasya's death, Myshkin plays out with Nastasya and Aglaya the role that Nastasya played out earlier with Rogozhin and Myshkin. Instead of men's roubles thrown into the fire, we have letters between the female rivals (which Myshkin hopes will disappear). Instead of Rogozhin exultantly running off with Nastasya, we have a scene in which Aglaya runs out after watching Myshkin run after Nastasya. The gender reversals inscribed in these scenes, the fact that Nastasya chooses the "wrong" man (Rogozhin) in the first scene and Myshkin chooses the "wrong" woman (Nastasya) in the last, suggests that *choice*, sexual and otherwise, is completely de-centered in this novel.

While Part One (ch. 13-16) dramatizes a fantasy in which all the men desire and literally "play for" Nastasya with money and promises, Part Four (ch. 8) expresses a man's desire to be fought over by two beautiful women and to win through to reconciliation with his "world" through love of both of them. What Myshkin discovers, however, is that women cannot be pulled into his synthesis, nor can they accept traditional ideals of Christian reconciliation. Neither Aglaya nor Nastasya serves the patriarchal religious fantasy, even if they are the objects of it and the test cases for Dostoevsky's version of it. Nastasya and Aglaya together, like Grushenka and Katerina Ivanovna in *The Brothers Karamazov*, appear to incarnate forces for dispersal and negation of much that is sanctioned by masculine versions of religious goodness. In *The Idiot* neither woman allows herself to be a vehicle for Myshkin's choice between the two different ideas he believes they represent.

What Mochulsky describes as Myshkin's struggle with an "idea of beauty . . . embodied in the two images of his heroines, Nastasya and Aglaya,"[16] involves a choice between a "new" woman and a "fallen" woman. That both images of women are "beautiful," that both draw Myshkin towards the split that paralyzes him, has been persuasively described by Louis Breger.[17] While Aglaya offers Myshkin the sort of risk that would bring him into a new world of emancipated men and women, Nastasya bonds him to the Christian allegory of forgiveness for sexual sins that throws him back him to the past. But Myshkin cannot and does not choose between these versions of the world, between past and future. Nor is he, ultimately, the only object of their quarrel. The scene between Nastasya and Aglaya suggests a quarrel that is also about the identity of "woman," for which "Myshkin" is an excuse. It is a quarrel between feminism and traditionalism that Katerina Ivanovna and Grushenka will also experience in the chapter called "Lacerations in the Drawing Room" in *The Brothers Karamazov*.

Like Katerina Ivanovna, Aglaya symbolizes ideas about feminine freedom and modernity and naive self-expansion. Olga Matich argues that "Nastasya's incipient and inclusive revolt against the female role . . . characterizes the behavior of her rival Aglaya, whose portrayal is clearly influenced by political considerations." Aglaya reads banned books, wants to become a teacher, and desires a relationship with a man that will defy social conventions. She chooses the "idiot" Myshkin, whom Matich describes as "a man with female attributes" as she describes Aglaya and Nastasya as "nascently masculinized women."[18] While Nastasya's fallen identity is reinforced by the way she succumbs to both Myshkin and Rogozhin, Aglaya acts upon feminist impulses and flies from men's intimidations. Her hope, like Nastasya's initial but undermined fantasy, is that Prince Christ will understand her desire for freedom.

> "I've been thinking about it over a long time [she tells Myshkin], and I've finally chosen you. . . . I don't want them to laugh at me at home. I don't want to be taken for a little fool, I don't want to be teased. I realized all this at once and I refused Yevgeney Pavlovich point-blank because I don't want them always marrying me off! . . . I want to run away from home, and I've chosen you to help me!" (*I*, 448)

Myshkin's ambivalent repudiation of Aglaya, dramatized as a symptom of his infinite "pity" for Nastasya, is the sign that he cannot go forward with the woman question. He reaches an impasse like the Gambler's forgetting of Polina, and like Raskolnikov's fall into "oblivion" after he kills the female pawnbroker. Myshkin's way out is to vow that he wants to love both women. But as Yevgeny Pavlovich rightly observes, this may be an excuse for his loving neither, an intuition that drives both women to enact their disgust with Myshkin's passivity by attacking each other:

> Finally Aglaya looked firmly straight into Nastasya Fillipovna's eyes and at once read clearly all the malice gathering in her rival's look. Woman understood woman. . . . "Ah! So then you have come to 'fight' me? Just imagine, I thought you were—cleverer."
>
> They looked at each other no longer concealing their malice. One was the woman who had been writing such incredible letters to the other. And here all that had vanished into thin air at their first encounter and their first words. . . .

However extravagant the other was with her disturbed mind and her sick soul no predetermined intention of hers could, it seemed, stand against the venomous, purely feminine contempt of her rival. The prince felt certain that Nastasya Fillipovna would not mention the letters herself . . . —and he would have given half his life if Aglaya would not mention them either. (*I*, 582-3)

Positioned precisely between the two women in a way that mirrors the way Nastasya is positioned between her "rivals" Myshkin and Rogozhin, Myshkin's "goodness" appears as a failure of self-recognition and a failure to recognize the larger subject of the women's quarrel. The narrator speaks of "purely feminine contempt" much as Losnitsky in Suslova's *The Stranger and Her Lover* speaks of "perfectly feminine traits." But the narrator cannot control the feminist theme Dostoevsky has set in motion or the reader's reaction to Myshkin's inability to respond to it.

Dostoevsky's strong impulse to create a thoroughly "good" man who will appeal to women's love, as if in penance for his narcissistic rebel figures, operates at last to reveal certain delusions which his other novels have obscured. While Raskolnikov can at least control Sonya to the extent that she is addicted to bringing him to God, Myshkin has no control over either Nastasya or Aglaya as the novel draws to its close. The wish for a termination of the deepest conflicts about women leads to the most intense rendition of confused masculine consciousness that Dostoevsky has yet imagined. While his "kind" and "good" Prince Christ appears initially as a penitential fantasy, by the end "a pattern of sadistic feeling shapes all the principle erotic relationships in *The Idiot*."[19] The act of writing *through* the idea of a "pure" male holiness to discover the sadistic component in patriarchal constructions of "the holy" is a purgation for Dostoevsky that released him toward the critiques of patriarchy and *ubermensch* culture to be inscribed in his last and greatest works: *The Possessed* and *The Brothers Karamazov*. In *The Idiot* Dostoevsky dissolves the sublimity he first constructs, leaving in its wake questions about the "purely feminine" and about masculine motivations for Yevgeny Pavlovich to decipher.

Yevgeny Pavlovich's voice interrupts the narrative precisely the way Porfiry's intercedes in the rationalizing thought processes Raskolnikov indulges in *Crime and Punishment*. Piercing through an increasingly muddy metaphysics, Yevgeny's voice articulates a skeptical modern perspective. As various convincing interpretations for Myshkin's behavior are being offered in the narration, Yevgeny ushers the woman question to the forefront of the conversation. The question of why and how Myshkin became involved with Nastasya is at last addressed.

"You must admit, Prince" [says Yevgeny] "that in your relations with Nastasya
Filippovna there was from the very start something *conventionally democratic* (I put
it this way for the sake of brevity), the fascination, so to speak, of the 'woman
question' (to put it still more briefly)."

In Part Four, chapter 10, Yevgeny Pavlovich is described as "sensibly and
clearly, and we repeat, with extraordinary psychological insight," drawing
for Myshkin "a vivid picture of all the prince's past relations with Nastasya
Filippovna." This man "rose to positive eloquence," the narrator tells us, when
he asserts that "there were lies between [the man and the woman] and
whatever begins with lies must end with lies, for that is a law of nature."
Arguing that "the fundamental cause of all that has happened is . . .
[Myshkin's] innate experience," Yevgeny argues that Myshkin's relations
with women were grounded in nothing but "intellectual convictions."

"For you see I knew all about the curious and scandalous scene that took place
at Nastasya Filippovna's when Rogozhin brought his money. If you like I shall
give you a systematic analysis of yourself, I shall show you yourself in a mirror."

Yevgeny's mirror shows Myshkin a naive but benightedly ambitious
young man who has read too many books, who has "longed for Russia as for
a land which is unknown but full of promise"; but who is finally "seized" in
the "heat of enthusiasm" with the idea of saving some woman. Yevgeny's
rational enlightenment discourse, with its denigration of enthusiasm and
seizures, glances ironically toward Myshkin's own valuation of his epilepsy
as a sign of spiritual depths. Yevgeny's conviction that "everything is perfectly clear" is a bit suspect, however, considering that his own motivation
to analyze Myshkin comes from his disappointment about Aglaya's refusal
of him. He is nevertheless persuasive in describing how, after meeting the
"fantastic, demonical beauty," Nastasya, Myshkin

seized the opportunity to declare publicly the magnanimous notion that [he], a
prince and a man whose life is pure, does not consider a woman dishonored who
has been put to shame not through her own fault but through the fault of a
revolting aristocratic libertine.

Shifting the blame to the revolting Totsky is the smallest part of Yevgeny's
analysis. The point he wishes to emphasize, and with which Myshkin agrees, is
that Myshkin's own feeling may not be "genuine." Yevgeny reveals to Myshkin
that the Prince himself cannot tell the difference between "intellectual" and

"genuine" feelings, between a "fascination (so to speak)" with "the woman question" and a genuine wish or commitment to actually improving the concrete life of a particular woman.

> 'The point is, was this the truth, was your feeling genuine, was it a natural feeling or merely intellectual enthusiasm? In the temple a woman was forgiven, but do you think she was told that she had done well, that she was deserving of all honor and respect?"

Yevgeny moves swiftly through difficult questions about the motives of the woman "chosen," the idea of a man like Myshkin choosing a woman to save, and the problem of men's relations with women in general. He may need to degrade Myshkin to console himself, but Myshkin has no response to Yevgeny's interpretation except to repeat, "Yes, yes, you are right. Oh, I do feel I am to blame!" Unable to resist or answer Yevgeny's skepticism, he can work up no self-transformative *dialogical* energy that would enable him, as it enables Raskolnikov, to break through to more authentic relations with women. Myshkin ratifies, in effect, Yevgeny's diagnosis that his trouble has been some sort of "bad faith" regarding them: what Dalton calls the Prince's passive-aggressive psychology and lack of "genuine" or "natural" feeling.

Myshkin's identity as a failed saviour devoted to the beautiful *image* but not to the efficacy or dialogic potential of Christ, suggests that Dostoevsky might be moving at this late point in his novel toward the redemptive laughter of carnival described by Bakhtin. There is much in *The Idiot* to suggest "the reversal of the hierarchic levels," the toppling of official authority, even some parody of official religion and the figure of Christ himself. But this potentially modernist element is aborted by certain blockings of the "as yet unpredetermined *new word.*" What Bakhtin claims Dostoevsky to be incapable of, a "monosemantic seriousness,"[20] shows up in *The Idiot* as a defense against the revelation that there is nothing funny about Christianity's inability to save women. If any sort of liberation is expressed in the novel, it is achieved at the expense of the author's monologic Christian ideology. The "articulate" Yevgeny Pavlovich voices a dangerously modern clearance in his novel: a moment when the text's official myth of Myshkin's identity collapses and no laughter emerges.

Yevgeny suggests that Myshkin has exploited the role of saviour for his own regressive and delusive purposes. He has "seized the opportunity to declare publicly" his "magnanimous notion" that fallen women should be forgiven and exalted. Myshkin's acts of "love" have been a public spectacle, Yevgeny intimates, and Myshkin has misunderstood his relation to the woman question. Playing an inquisitorial role that is markedly like Porfiry's, Yevgeny elicits a response from Myshkin ("you are right") that echoes Raskolnikov's admission that he is "no Napoleon." What binds the profane hero of *Crime and Punishment* to the sacred hero of *The Idiot* is the "fall" from a superman status.

Bound by conflict, burdened by a traditionalist Christian mythology that strangles men rather than channels them toward new possibilities with women, Myshkin allows Yevgeny to destroy his illusions just as surely as he allows Rogozhin to destroy Nastasya. Shadowing the last chapters that lead to Myshkin's ultimate stupor is a covert idea that connects feminist to religious utopian thinking: *If the true Christ came to Russia, his mission would be to allow women to save themselves from the masculinist erotic culture that confuses love either with the phallic knife or the castrated phallus.*

In *The Idiot*, the narrator's flights, loops, plunges into intertextual interpretation, obscurity, and paradox suggest what Bakhtin calls an "internally dialogic dissociation." Dostoevsky is in love with the freedoms released by the rhetoric of idiocy and the poetics of epilepsy. But this same discourse involves him in regressive Christian delusions of grandeur that the figure of Myshkin cannot realize. Myshkin's relation to "the feminine" serves mainly to defend him against his unresolved feelings about masculine power. Explaining himself to Yevgeny Pavlovich, Myshkin says: "If only Aglaya knew, if she knew everything—I mean absolutely everything. For in this matter, you have to know *everything* about another person, when we have to, when that other person is at fault." This incoherent statement, which the Prince knows is incoherent, ends in further mystification. "There's something here I can't explain to you," he insists, even when Yevgeny insists that "most likely, you never loved either one of them" (I, 599-600). Between the Prince's idea that there is "something here" that cannot be explained and Yevgeny's notion that women are the clue to Myshkin's whole identity, the suppressed "feminine" emerges as the "mystery" of the novel. This mysterious "something" may be related to what Mochulsky and Robert Hingley have described as the germ from which *The Idiot* grew:

An entirely different figure [from Myshkin] had obsessed Dostoevsky from the beginning: a tempestuous woman with a huge sense of grievance, the eventual Nastasya Filippovna. Somehow this image arose out of a real-life court case involving a teen-age Moscow girl, Olga Umetskaya, who had four times set fire to her family home after being savagely misused by her neglectful and sadistic parents.

Hingley concludes that finally "there is far more of Miss Suslova in the finished Nastasya Filippovna" than Umetskaya; and he suggests Anna Korvin-Krupovskaya as the model for Aglaya.[21] But the connection Hingley makes between feminine imagery and the early notes for *The Idiot* is more interesting than finding the exact biographical sources for Dostoevsky's women characters. More suggestive is the link between images of abused femininity and the idea of a feminized male saviour figure. The close identification of Myshkin with women points the late-twentieth-century reader to the transformations in the novel that are now becoming more obvious to us,[22] for "it is impossible to dissociate the questions of art, style and truth from the question of woman":

> One can no longer seek her, no more than one could search for woman's femininity or female sexuality. And she is certainly not to be found in any of the familiar modes of concept or knowledge. Yet it is impossible to resist looking for her.[23]

In *The Idiot* two of Dostoevsky's favorite personas, the idiot-saint and the sexist criminal, cannot help looking for Nastasya. Bakhtin notes that Nastasya is "reduced to a search for herself and for her own undivided voice beneath the two voices that have made their home in her."[24] But two male voices may not be enough to create even one woman's identity. Dostoevsky's male characters continue this quest in *The Eternal Husband*, a short novel that replicates as it revises those scenes of male rivalry and knife/razor play that haunt *The Idiot*. *The Eternal Husband* returns to the psychological realism of *Notes from Underground* and *The Gambler* in which modernist uncertainty, men's impulses to tyrannize over women, and questions about otherness predominate. As a corrective to *The Idiot's* finally exploded fantasy that an asexual Prince Christ could save the world, *The Eternal Husband* offers mocking youthful feminist voices convinced that only *authentic* respect for women's sexuality can transform the future.

4

Eternal Husbands and Their "Traffic" in Women

Dostoevsky's disappointment in the cold reception of *The Idiot* provoked his defensiveness. He argued that such fantastic figures as Myshkin existed, and that to deny them was to ignore the fantastic essence of Russian life. The writer's comments have led to readings of the complete corpus in light of Dostoevsky's "fantastic realism."[1] The "fantastic-realistic" relation between Velchaninov and Trusotzsky in *The Eternal Husband* is a variant on the Myshkin-Rogozhin "doubles" theme of *The Idiot*. While it is possible to interpret the violent relationships with women that occur in *The Idiot* in terms of their "sacred" dimension, *The Eternal Husband* appears as a revision of the novel's romance with Prince Christ's holy foolishness. It also clarifies an insight about the structure of male-female relations obscured by Myshkin's Christian identity. In *The Eternal Husband*, men's "traffic" in women creates a bond of love-hate that blocks the "inescapable seeking after mutuality"[2] otherwise apparent in Dostoevsky's utopian quest.

The novella's hero, Velchaninov, is a somewhat normal middle-aged bachelor: a "strapping fellow . . . even sometimes sensible, almost a person of culture and unmistakable gifts," a "man who had lived fully and in grand style." The reader is introduced to him as he is falling into a "hypochondria" that is recognizably a depression. There is nothing strange about this figure, except that lately he has begun to "suffer from causes . . . of a 'higher'—'if one may use such an expression, if there really are higher or lower causes. . . .' This he added on his own account" (*EH*, 302-3). Quoting Velchaninov as if he were an intimate friend, the narrator is comfortably in accord with Velchaninov's diagnosis of himself as suffering from the return of a certain kind of sensitivity long suppressed, understood as an elevated moral condition.

Even before Velchaninov meets up with Trusotzsky and Liza, he begins to remember certain "incidents in the past," all of which involved humiliating women. He "suddenly, and God knows why," remembers insulting an old man who was "defending his daughter, a spinster, who lived with him and had become the subject of gossip in the town." He "recalled how, simply as a joke, he had slandered the very pretty wife of a schoolmaster, and how the slander had reached the husband's ears." He remembers "a young girl of the working class" whom "he had got [] with child, and had simply abandoned her and his child without even saying good-bye" (EH, 307). These returning memories, especially the last, are mirrored by the actual return to Velchaninov of his natural daughter, Liza, with her surrogate father whom Velchaninov has cuckolded. This return interrupts the latter's focus on his own guilt. Despite the obvious dramatization of the "causes" of Velchaninov's depression (in which "the dream seemed to have merged with reality" [EH, 319]), the narrator moves the diagnostic lens from the adulterer to the cuckolded "eternal husband," from Velchaninov's depression to Trusotzsky's drunkenness and sadistic treatment of Liza. In this way he suggests that Velchaninov's and Trusotzsky's depressions, as well as their attempts to escape them, stem from the same source: unresolved feelings about their relations to women.

The narrative reciprocity between the third and first person point of view is so tight in The Eternal Husband that a blurring of identities (between male narrator and male characters) may suggest that the subject is men in general. The title evokes an equivalent universal typology of "husbands," even when both the narrator and Velchaninov appear to be analyzing and attacking the particular "low person," Trusotzsky, together. This focus on the husband as the object of contempt displaces the reader's attention from Velchaninov's self-condemnation. The voice is so close to first-person narration that it seduces the reader into sympathy for Velchaninov and subverts the recognition that Velchaninov is displacing his own guilt about women to Trusotzsky. Velchaninov's dreams reveal a condensation of himself and Trusotzsky in their imagery, however, as well as a conflict between desire and censorship that illuminates the meaning of Velchaninov's dream figures. Unable to judge himself directly, Velchaninov projects the responsibility for judgment upon the "other people." "Other people who had come in seemed to expect from [Trusotzsky] a final word that would decide Velchaninov's guilt or innocence, and all were waiting impatiently" (EH, 316).

At the beginning of the thirteenth chapter, called On Whose Side Is There More? Velchaninov pronounces a supposedly "final word" about Trusotzsky and himself by asserting that "we are both vicious, underground, loathsome people" (EH, 432). But in the fifteenth chapter he returns to calling only Trusotzsky and not himself a "freak": "Nature is not a tender mother," he says, "but a stepmother to the freak. Nature gives birth to the freak, but instead of pitying him she puts him to death, and with good reason" (*EH*, 446). Velchaninov identifies with Trusotzsky, then repudiates the identification, experiencing a midlife masculinity crisis that results in his vacillating back and forth between blaming Trusotzsky and blaming himself. The question "on whose side is there more [blame]?" only seems to be the story's focus, for it leads, as we see by the story's last paragraph, to a draw. Trusotzsky and Velchaninov are both "freaks" in different ways, but freaks who symbolize two general types of masculine behavior: one passive (a variant on Myshkin), the other predatory (a variant on Rogozhin). The light tone of the story, the relatively noncriminal activities of the two men, and the absence of intentional murder camouflage the pattern of male-female relations that *The Idiot* and *The Eternal Husband* share. By the last chapter it is clear that both "freaks" are to blame for Liza's death, and that her death will haunt them for the rest of their lives: "And Liza, sir?" (*EH*, 460).

Liza, the proud, tortured eight-year-old girl who is Velchaninov's natural child by Trusotzsky's deceased wife, Natalya, is the central figure in a story that records the nightmare of a penitent misogynist. It is to Liza, and to what she knows that the two men don't, that both readers of the story and characters in the story are compelled to return.

What Velchaninov cannot "get to the bottom of," cannot "settle," and is "in terrible haste to find out" about (*EH*, 355) is the structure of a relationship in which he is bound to Trusotzsky *through* Natalya, through the emancipated Zahlebinin women, but especially through Trusotzsky's torturing of Liza. The metaphor of returning and repeating, and of finding out the significance of such returns suggests that the "final word" cannot be uttered by men—perhaps because it is about "the feminine."

Velchaninov is haunted by "hundreds of such reminiscences [involving women]—and each one of them seemed to bring dozens of others in its train" (*EH*, 307). Liza's presence in Petersburg brings Velchaninov back to memories of Natalya, a woman whose domineering, proud, obstinate, and "fascinating" quality is replicated in Liza, described as "a wild creature, sullen and gloomily, resolutely stubborn" (*EH*, 350). Trusotzsky tortures Liza with the idea that she is a repetition of her mother: "You see, she's her mama over again" (*EH*, 347). Bringing home a "wench," he shouts, "She will be your mother, if I choose!" and reminds her, "You're not my daughter, but a bastard!" (*EH*, 369). Liza represents a return of repressed memories to both men, but also what Eva Kosofsky Sedgwick calls "an absolute of exchange value" in "men's gender constitution . . . the ultimate victim of the painful contradictions in the system that regulates men."[3]

Velchaninov and Trusotzsky are "regulated" by "a triangular path of circulation that enforces patriarchal power as being routed through [women]."[4] Velchaninov knows that Trusotzsky "clearly understands the situation [of his cuckoldry] and will take his revenge on me through Liza" (*EH*, 336). But Liza herself is not concerned with revenge or protecting herself. Hers is the "feminist" insight that as "traffic" between the two men her exchange value is duplicated in her relations with Velchaninov even as he tries to save her from Trusotzsky.

> The fact that she was being taken to a strange house [the Pogoreltzevs'] . . . seemed for the time being not to trouble her much. What tormented her was something else. Velchaninov saw that: he guessed that she was ashamed of *him*, that she was ashamed of her father's having so easily let her go with him, of his having, as it were, flung her into his keeping.
>
> "She is ill," he thought, "perhaps very ill; she's been horribly tormented to death. . . . Oh, the drunken, vile beast! I understand him now!" (*EH*, 350)

Liza understands that she is being used, that her father values her very little. Although Velchaninov deplores this, his sensitivity to Liza's suffering is undermined by the way he uses her to divert him from guilty memories and to fill the void in his life: "'Here is an object, here is life!' he thought rapturously" (*EH*, 350). "'My love for Liza,' he mused, 'would purify and redeem my former disreputable and useless life . . . and for her sake everything would be forgiven me and I could forgive myself everything" (*EH*, 386-7). Klavdia Petrovna understands why Liza sickens and dies, reduced to an object shuffled between two men. "She's a proud and sullen child," she tells Velchaninov. "She is ashamed that she is here, and that her father has abandoned her . . . that he let her come here, among complete strangers and with a man . . . who's almost a stranger, too, or on such terms. . . ." (*EH*, 370). The painful contradiction that Liza discovers is that she will either be used by Trusotzsky as a vehicle to revenge himself on Velchaninov, or she will be used by Velchaninov as the "final word" of his own self-vindication. Either way, her subjectivity is reified; her wish for love and for identity is distorted. As traffic, vehicle, love-hate bond, Liza knows herself to be a fetish that the two men work *through*.

Behind this story of a tortured young girl who is witness to her surrogate father's "sodom" (*EH*, 348) is a real scandal, the germ of which was related by Dostoevsky to his friend Sofia Kovalevskaya in 1866. Her memoirs record his telling the story of a middle-aged landowner who recalled how "once, after a night spent in dissipation, drawn along by his drunken companions, he had violated a little ten-year-old girl."[5] The death of the little girl Liza in *The Eternal Husband,* associated with two men whose sexual dissipations and dependencies are the root of their mutual love-hatred, is but one version of the story Dostoevsky told Kovalevskaya. The bolder version is Stavrogin's confession of girl rape in *The Possessed* (c.f. chapter 5). Dostoevsky's compulsion to repeat this story (whose subject is repetition) in variation after variation suggests that resolving the masculinist sexual complex was an important element in his life's work.

The Eternal Husband involves the confessions and obsessions of two men and the evolving meaning of Liza as the key to their identities. Although the narrator's words most frequently come from within Velchaninov's mind, eliciting the reader's sympathy with him (as in the case of the underground man), the story proceeds through seventeen short chapters in which Velchaninov becomes increasingly identified with Trusotzsky until he can confront their relations with women as "loathsome":

> "We are both vicious, underground, loathsome people. . . . And if you like I'll prove it to you that you don't like me at all, but hate me with all your heart, and that you're lying, though you don't know it; you took me there [to the Zahlebinin's] with the absurd object of testing your future bride....you took me there to show me and say to me, 'See what a prize.'" (*EH,* 423)

Male viciousness, Velchaninov says, is directly related to using girls or women as prizes and weapons in the game of masculine competition. Velchaninov seems to have discovered, through his unself-conscious "double," Trusotzsky, a kind of therapy for his disorder. The cure consists of Velchaninov's being so disgusted by the spectacle of his double's insensitivity to women that Velchaninov develops a self-restraint that disables him from enjoying his former games of cuckoldry. Thus Dostoevsky's story shows how "masculinity imagines itself, at most, only by feminizing itself."[6] Velchaninov cannot recognize his masculinist viciousness until he sees it reflected in Liza's sufferings and until he imagines himself *in her place.*

The place of "Liza" as the site of the woman question is replicated symbolically, after her death, in the midsections of the novella by the situations of the Zahlebinin girls, as though the story of this "wild" eight-year-old girl were thrown into the future and she had grown into a socialist-nihilist type. Following chapter 11, satirically entitled *Pavel Pavlovich Means to Marry,* "Nadezhda Fedoseyevna . . . the schoolgirl and Pavel Pavlovich's alleged bride," is described as "a little brunette with a wild untamed look and the boldness of a nihilist; a roguish imp with blazing eyes, a charming but often malicious smile" (*EH*, 400). Attempting to buy this sixteen-year-old with an expensive bracelet, which she and her friends immediately scorn, Trusotzsky finds himself the object of mockery and humiliation. Despite the fact that he reaches an agreement with her father because he has too many daughters and needs to marry them, the girls and their boyfriends succeed in heading off "the eternal husband." Velchaninov is invited to participate in this rebellion against the woman-trafficking patriarchs: "We're all going to make fun of Pavel Pavlovich," one of the girls says to Velchaninov, "and you will too, of course" (*EH*, 404). A certain "Marya Nikitishna" makes Velchaninov promise that he will give the "vile bracelet" back to Trusotzsky "and tell him in the future not to dare butt in with presents." The future generation clearly and pompously declares its creed— in the person of a young man named Predposylov wearing nihilist blue glasses:

> "You must return the bracelet," he blurted out furiously, pouncing on Velcha-ninov. "If only out of respect for the rights of women, that is—if you are capable of rising to the full signification of the question. . . . " (*EH*, 413)

Velchaninov's lessons in feminism continue as Sashenka is commissioned by Nadya to teach the predators about women's sexual and marital rights:

> "It's not enough that [the girls] turn [Trusotzsky] out and put out their tongues at him; he wants tomorrow to denounce us to the old man! Do you not prove by that, you obstinate man, that you want to take the girl by force, that you would buy her of people in their dotage, who in our barbarous state of society retain authority over her?" (*EH*, 428)

Trusotzsky is routed by the younger generation, but Velchaninov is exposed as well: "You haven't surprised us in the least," says the young nihilist. "I knew you were all like that! It's odd, though they spoke to me of you as a man rather new." Stripped of metaphysics, raw in its satire, *The Eternal Husband* pits tradition against emancipation, male chauvinism against feminism. "If she ever falls in love with someone else, " declares the "new" man, Alexander Lobov, "or simply repents having married me and wants to divorce me, I will at once give her a formal declaration of my infidelity—and so will support her petition for divorce" (*EH*, 429).

Would such "new" forms of marriage protect children like Liza? The young man ends his speech by telling the old generation "flatly":

"Such lack of comprehension of the most natural things on your part is due to the perversion of your most ordinary feelings and ideas by a long life spent idly and absurdly." (*EH*, 430)

While the diagnosis may be persuasive, its position in the text trivializes it. Velchaninov knows he is perverted, understands his complicity in Liza's death, and comprehends too well Trusotzsky's desire to hang himself. The reader does not know whether Nadya will find marital freedom in the new world described by her friends, but we do know from Alexander Lobov that after the scene with Trusotzsky "they locked Nadya up . . . There were tears and shouts, but we stood firm!" (*EH*, 449). The influence on Velchaninov of the nihilist/feminist girls and their friends combines with the effect of Liza's death upon him. Mourning for the tortured-to-death girl sensitizes Velchaninov to the horror of an "old" structure of male-female relations personified by the "eternal husband" and the cuckolding lover.

Significantly, Velchaninov falls sick the night after Nadya repudiates Trusotzsky. He feels "poisoned," requests that Trusotzsky stay the night to nurse him, lives out a nightmare struggle with Trusotzsky and a razor blade, and wakes to find his hand cut and bleeding. The scene is described initially as a repetition of the dream Velchaninov experienced before, "but these people seemed to be even more angry at Velchaninov than in the previous dream," and when he wakes screaming, he finds himself struggling with and being cut by Trusotzsky's razor. Dostoevsky captures the non sequitur of hallucination in the following sequence:

What thought guided his first movement and whether he had any thought at the moment it is impossible to say, but someone seemed to prompt him to act fittingly: he leaped out of bed and, with his hands stretched out before him as though to defend himself and ward off an attack, he rushed straight toward the place where Pavel Pavlovich was asleep. . . . Suddenly something painfully cut the palm and fingers of his left hand, and he instantly realized that he had clutched the blade of a knife or a razor and was grasping it tight in his hand....And at that same moment something fell heavily on the floor with a thud. (*EH*, 339-440)

The deliberate blurring of the acted upon and the actor in this extraordinary scene suggests the confusions of Velchaninov's identity. Like the "something" that lies on the bed for Myshkin and Rogozhin to see in *The Idiot*, the "something" that cuts Velchaninov and then falls to the floor in *The Eternal Husband* is a human body abstracted from the individual subject. It is described as an intermediate or transitional object in the psychological sense, canceling out the differences between the *me* and the *not-me*. The struggle of Velchaninov with Trusotzsky occurs in the dark space of dreaming, wish-fulfillment, and psychosis: a condensed imagery that signifies how each man attempts to kill the other in order to finalize a blame they share with other "eternal" husbands and cuckolders.

Velchaninov is blind to the fact that he is not defending himself only, but is very close to murdering Trusotzsky . The "something" that struggles is Velchaninov and Trusotzsky, but it is also Liza, the unnamed entity central to their psychological situations. Dostoevsky does not distinguish here, as Freud would, between dreams and reality. The razor-cutting scene between Velchaninov and Trusotzsky represents a realm of "fantastic realism" that can be occupied physically, not just imaginatively. In this area of half-sleep and semiconsciousness, organically tied to a state of illness and fever, certain dimensions of reality are sharpened, leaving others completely dark. Velchaninov attempts to interpret and demystify what is happening to him in this state by concluding that "Pavel Pavlovich had certainly meant to cut his throat." But he remains "unaware of the fact that one [may] occup[y] a spot *within* the very blindness one seeks to demystify."[7] Velchaninov ratifies his interpretation by getting Trusotzsky "down on the floor" and holding his hands behind his back. But this is not enough for a man whose actions are overdetermined by the fact that he is struggling with *himself* in the symbolic form of Trusotzsky. "For some reason he conceived the desire to tie them behind the man's back." The "reason" Velchaninov ties up Trusotzsky, then puts the razor back in its case, shuts it, and, "when he had done all that," examines his antagonist (*EH,* 440-1) is his need to trap "something" in himself and face it.

The next chapter, *Analysis,* emphasizes Velchaninov's sense of having completed or worked out his problem; but his thoughts also foreshadow the unfinalized quality of his experience with Liza.

> A feeling of immense extraordinary joy took possession of him; something was over, settled; his awful depression had vanished and was dissipated completely. . . . The feeling lasted for five weeks, he scarcely thought of Liza—as though blood from his cut fingers could "settle his account even with that misery." (*EH,* 443)

Distancing himself from Trusotzsky—"in his place I would perhaps hang myself, though" (*EH,* 448)—Velchaninov refuses even to be unsettled by

Alexander Lobov bearing an incriminating letter from Trusotzsky that Natalya once wrote to Velchaninov. When Lobov tells him how they've locked Nadya in, Velchaninov makes no comment. When we meet him "exactly two years" after this "adventure," he is "entirely transformed, or rather reformed" and on his way to Odessa to see a woman, and there is no more mention of Liza, depression, or memories.

Dostoevsky treats Velchaninov's transformation, the result of "healthy" repression and new cash, with urbane irony. The man is troubled no more by "faintheartedness" and memories, and he has a "conviction" that his depression "would never happen again. . . . The cause of all these advantageous and sensible changes for the better was, of course, the fact that he had won his lawsuit." Velchaninov's complacent state of mind, contrasted to his once haunted memory of abused women connected with his "higher " consciousness, is connected to his indifference to all social questions, including the woman question: "No matter how close the social edifice may come to collapse, and whatever may be shouted from the housetops," he says, "whatever shape people and ideas may take, I shall always have just such a dainty, delicious dinner as I am sitting down to now." The delicious "dinner" might even include Trusotzsky's new wife, who arrives on the same train to Odessa. Although Velchaninov does not yet know who she is, "the lady attracted him . . . a conversation began; the lady spoke heatedly and bitterly complained of her husband."

Drawn once again to the system of cuckolding "eternal husbands" that had been subverted by depression and Liza's death, Velchaninov is about to get involved when he "grasped the horror of his position" (*EH*, 453-5). The woman he is courting is married to Trusotzsky, who appears just at the moment the wife introduces Velchaninov "as their guardian angel" and asks him to dinner. Velchaninov's refusal of the invitation is interrupted by the ringing of a train bell, a grotesquely appropriate warning against sexist complacencies:

> In one instant something strange happened to both of them; both seemed transformed. Something, as it were, shook and snapped in Velchaninov, who had been laughing only just before. In an access of fury, he clutched Pavel Pavlovich's shoulder tightly. "If I—*I* hold out this hand to you," showing the palm of the left hand, where a big scar from the cut was still distinct, "you certainly might take it!" he whispered, with pale and trembling lips. Pavel Pavlovich, too, turned pale, and his lips trembled too; a quiver convulsed his face. "And Liza, sir?" he murmured in a rapid whisper . . . tears gushed from his eyes. Velchaninov stood before him stunned. (*EH*, 460)

The reader is faced with a choice in which "the open rejoinders of the one [character] answer the hidden rejoinders of the other." The renewed quarreling between Velchaninov and Trusotzky "occurs not between two integral monologic voices," as Bakhtin reminds us, "but between two divided voices"[8] that forget, until they confront each other, that they are divided. Trusotzky's appearance in the train with his wife and the wife's lover "opens" Velchaninov again to the memory of the "other" (Liza) who once humanized him. Dostoevsky shows that monologism can occur and recur, a form of contraction of consciousness from its "higher" dialogic dimensions into a form that is like psychotic forgetting. In *The Eternal Husband* this lapse is short, and a higher consciousness is renewed through the men's brief re-encounter and the mention of the name "Liza."

As a consequence Velchaninov

> remained at the station and only in the evening set off on his original route in another train. He did not turn off to the right to visit the provincial lady of his acquaintance—he was too much out of humor. And how he regretted it afterward! (*EH*, 460)

In this short work as in others, Dostoevsky's major theme—that "all is permitted" in a world in which skepticism reduces all relations to exploitations—is connected to two recurring themes: the seduction of ethical solipsism, particularly available to men like Velchaninov, and the intervention in that solipsism by girls and young women. The historian Rasianovsky reminds us that "the 1860's and the 1870's with their iconoclastic ideology led also to the emancipation of a considerable number of educated Russian women— quite early compared to other European countries—and to their entry into the arena of radical thought and revolutionary politics."[9] The emancipated girls in *The Eternal Husband* play their part in reminding Velchaninov that "the social edifice may collapse," that new ideas may take shape, and that men like himself may become obsolete. But "emancipation" among Dostoevsky's characters is also achieved by a passionate and voluntary self-condemnation that is called "hypochondria." The lifting of repression of sexist memories leads to Velchaninov's depression but also to a movement toward something like consciousness-raising. As the last line in *The Eternal Husband* shows us ("And how he regretted it afterward!"), more terrifying than that depression is the possibility of socially and economically sanctified recovery from it.

5

Exposing Stavrogin in The Possessed

Like the protagonists in Dostoevsky's *The Possessed*, the Bolsheviks had to spill blood to bind their wavering adherents with a bond of collective guilt.[1]

The Bolsheviks had come to power in 1917 with the emancipation of women on their agenda. As Marxists, they believed that change in the ownership of the means of production signaled a transformation of social and cultural life and with it the end of women's subordination. . . . But the female form played only a supportive role. . . . Woman was the Other, or rather Others, since her personality was split: as working women, she could aspire to political consciousness and public profile; as mother, she was the child of nature, the outsider, forever distanced from social action.[2]

As I noted in the introduction, Dostoevsky's straining against the transformations of modern identity while incorporating them in his fiction made him the genius of self-consciousness or *autocritique*. Reactionary and revolutionary and able to master the discourse of both, Dostoevsky has served as the prophet of various contending ideologies. Yet Dostoevsky's attitudes toward modern social problems in *Besy*, toward his characters' discussions of "the incidence of robbery and violence . . . doubled" (*P*, 326), toward the "unrestrained attitude [that] was the fashion" (*P*, 303), and particularly toward "the woman question," are most frequently read as evidence of his Slavophile conservatism. The novel was understood to attack the terrorist politics and nihilist philosophy of Sergei Nachaev and his followers, among whom were a number of women alleged to have had love affairs with their leader. But Dostoevsky was no ideologically simple Slavophile, and he argued in the Slavophile newspaper *Den* (Day) that their fear "of this passionate negation through laughter, this voluntary self-condemnation, unheard of in any other literature [but Russian] showed how deficient was the Slavophile's sense of reality." Theirs, Dostoevsky wrote, "majestically distances itself from everything that lives and breathes in its vicinity."[3]

The novel's narrator is not thus distanced. *Besy*, translated *The Possessed* or *The Devils*, suggests that the inhabitants of Skvoresniki are "possessed" by a modern revolutionary ideology dedicated to violence and separatism from ordinary community. Yet the novel's narrator is so closely attached to his characters, so fascinated with watching their every move and recording the gossip and mystification that surrounds them, that moral condemnation gives way to a sense of lacerating carnival and Menippean satire: the "passionate negation through laughter" Dostoevsky described as lacking in Slavophilism. *The Possessed* evidences Menippean combinations of the "mystical-religious element" with "crude *slum naturalism*." In this novel, "scandals and eccentricities destroy the epic and tragic wholeness of the world"; they "make a breach in the stable, normal ('seemly') course of human affairs."[4] Dostoevsky's exact attitude toward this "breach" has been the subject of interesting debate, much of it centered around Nikolai Stavrogin and Pyotr Verkhovensky as carriers of the Nachaev mystique. Lunacharsky remarks that "Dostoevsky's split personality, together with the fragmentation of the capitalist society in Russia, awoke in him the obsessional need to hear again and again the trial of the principles of socialism and reality, and to hear this trial in conditions as unfavourable to socialism as possible."[5]

Philip Pomper, in his biography of the famous revolutionary, argues that Dostoevsky "pictured" Verkhovensky as the Nachaev type. But certain facts of Nachaev's life, well-known to Dostoevsky, suggest that the author "split" the real revolutionary's characteristics between his fictional characters, giving the "comic-sinister" aspects to Verkhovensky and the demonic-sexual aspects to Stavrogin. Like Stavrogin, Nachaev was reputed to have been involved with many women, and according to Vera Zasulich, "combined revolutionary activity and romantic conquests."[6] The well-known terrorist Zasulich, whose attempted assassination of General Trepov earned her prison and feminist fame, was among at least five other women who surrounded Nachaev, much as they surround Stavrogin in *The Possessed*. Dostoevsky shows that "new" women's fascination with the combined prowess of sex and violence incarnated by certain leaders was part of the formation of revolutionary socialism—an idea that puts a perverse twist on what late-twentieth-century feminists call *sexual politics*. Although Berdyaev argues that "Dostoevsky inaccurately describes" Nachaev for the purposes of *The Possessed*, he also concedes that the problem of the superman type or *man-deity* is "a very profound one" because the term in Russian was misused in the twentieth century. In Dostoevsky's historical context it meant that "human-ism was to be superseded (*aufhebung*) and not destroyed" and that "it is impossible to remain in this intermediate cultural realm as the humanists of the West would wish." What Nachaev represents for Dostoevsky, Berdyaev argues, is "a rebirth into inhumaneness. Dostoevsky sees this transition in the case of the atheist revolutionary Nachaev who completely breaks away from humanist morality . . . and makes a demand for cruelty."[7]

The demand for cruelty has particular consequences for the girls and women of *The Possessed*. A feminist reading shifts the focus from the frame of political revolution as narrowly defined by men toward the more inclusive problem of men and women in a time of cultural transition. In what sense is Dostoevsky's polemic against socialist/terrorist feminists modernist, and how is Dostoevsky's polemic against modern women disturbed and confused by a "double-voiced discourse" and "hidden polemic"? What does the author mean by surrounding his nihilist hero Stavrogin with several women with whom he is sexually intimate and who successively expose his weakness? I will argue in this chapter that Dostoevsky's "polyphony" affects sympathy for the forces satirized and an exposure, through Stavrogin, of the masculinist tyranny against which feminism emerges.

The Possessed suggests how deeply the question of women engaged Dostoevsky, how in writing against it he would be compelled to explore it, particularly in the once suppressed chapter, "At Tikhon's," in which Stavrogin confesses to his rape of the girl Matryosha. Dostoevsky's association of violence with demonic possession, coded as the "great physical strength" of Stavrogin (*P*, 44) and the phallic "flickering tip of [Verkhovensky's] tongue" (*P*, 172), inscribes biblical allusions that, while losing only some of their original force, can now be re-contextualized within a late-twentieth-century reading horizon of modernist/feminist questions and critiques of masculinist culture. Surprising intersections between Dostoevsky and contemporary feminism emerge from the novel's references to the abuse and rape of girls (*P*, 224-5), "the [terrible] lot of the Russian woman" (*P*, 285), and "women's rights" (*P*, 25). The novelist's difficult relations with feminists (particularly A. Suslova), informed by his reading of Chernyshevsky, leave deep traces in Dostoevsky's discourse—so deep, on occasion, that female voices and ges-tures may occasionally "shout down the author."[8]

In Todorov's retheorizings of Dostoevsky's discourse, the traditional idea that Dostoevsky's women "mirror" the hero is transformed by the idea of a "structure of alterity" and the argument that Dostoevsky's "narrator rejects an essentialist conception of man and an objective vision of ideas." Todorov argues that "we have to transcend the idea of the autonomous text as seen as an authentic expression of a subject, rather than as a reflection of other texts, as play among interlocutors."[9] In *The Possessed*, one of these texts is Chernyshevsky's, and some of these interlocutors are women. Liza Tushina, Maria Lebyadkina, and Matryosha attempt to free themselves of possession by Stavrogin's masculinist power. Rather than reflecting Stavrogin himself, girls and women reflect bits of new consciousness, traces of alien views that Stavrogin must painfully confront.

The challenge of rereading Dostoevsky's references to cruelties experienced by women through men in the novel—beating, rape, and murder—involves resistance to reducing them to symptoms of Dostoevsky's essentialist views or his pornographic and misogynist impulses, as Freud tended to do. As Louis Breger notes, Dostoevsky's depictions of the maternal complex are as central to his fiction as his oedipal and parricide themes. Dostoevsky's maternal metaphors are associated with the idea of the feminine components of faith, with earth and Russia as a mother, and with Jesus as the mother's son incorporating traits of suffering, self-sacrifice, and compassionate love associated with maternity. This sentimental view of femininity nevertheless merges with a powerful vision of female destructiveness, rebelliousness, and disillusion in *The Possessed*. The novel shares with late-twentieth-century feminism various explorations of female victims and critiques of masculine fantasy. Dostoevsky explores the feminine subject, not as feminism does for the specific purposes of liberating women, but for the different purposes of representing the evils of the soul/body schism he associates with a Westernized Cartesian metaphysics; for the purpose of exposing the breakdown of the sacred through the image of sexual violation; and for the purpose of throwing into symbolic relief the picture of Mother Russia raped by her nihilist-terrorist sons.

Dostoevsky's attack on modernist dualism associated with Descartes and masculinist aggressiveness resonates with some recent characterizations of Cartesian philosophy as "the pure masculinization of thought" and a "flight from the feminine."[10] Dostoevsky shares with feminists such as Susan Bordo, but also with philosophers of postmodernism such as Albert Borgmann, a "doubt whether the ego has the indubitable solidity that Descartes claimed for it and . . . whether it could serve as the beginning for the rational reconstruction of reality. . . . The modern project is not simply the advancement of an age-old human striving for more comfort and security but the mobilization of a peculiar masculine aggressiveness that breaks through ancient restraints and reserves."[11]

Stavrogin's involvements with Liza, Matryosha, Maria, and Mary appear in relation to the political activities he inspires as well as to the masculine aura he presents. In *The Possessed* there are no metaphysics without erotics, no political carnivals without bloodshed. Stavrogin's God-defiance takes the form of raping Matryosha and ruining Shatov's wife, as his involvement in the "cause" takes the form of allowing Pyotr Verkhovensky to order Maria Lebyadkina murdered so that Stavrogin can run away with Liza. In whichever direction the reader turns to interpret the novel, a violated female appears, a monstrous image of manhood emerges.

The temptation to idolize Stavrogin is nevertheless a major stumbling block when one focuses on the novel's woman question. This temptation is not confined to characters within the text, but is part of the text's critical reception. Stavrogin's crimes have been described in terms of a masculinist sublime that the structure of the text undermines. *The Possessed* includes scenes of male cruelty and self-empowerment at women's expense that critics identify as Russian Don Juanism, associate with Nietzsche's Superman philosophy,[12] and describe in heroic and metaphysical terms. Mochulsky notes that "four women are grouped around the hero" and that "all of them, like mirrors, reflect various images of the charming demon." Feminist ideas may be more of a problem for Dostoevsky's narrator and less for critics who subsume Dostoevsky's woman question under the stereotype of the "'eternal feminine' in respect of which," Mochulsky argues, "[Stavrogin] commits his greatest crime (Matryosha) and his loftiest action (his marriage to the cripple)."[13] Dostoevsky hints that the secret source of Stavrogin's political charisma is his sexual activity with women—his name indicates the phallic stag horn—and that a cruel sexuality will produce a perverse male following and a cruel politics. A focus on this cruelty indicates Dostoevsky's provocative contributions to gender discourse.

A negative and de-romanticized version of Stavrogin slowly emerges as women close in on him, undermining both his "lofty" and profane activities through their different voices and perspectives. Just as the womanizing Nachaev seems to close in on Dostoevsky's imagination as he constructed Verkhovensky and Stavrogin in his notebooks for the novel, so women perform that revisionist function in the completed novel's structure. Readers remain puzzled about the relation of the Notebooks for *The Possessed* to the novel, as well as the relation of the novel's dual centers. Wasiolek suggests that the reader of the Notebooks will be "skeptical of Dostoevsky's appraisal of Nachaev as naive and ignorant,"[14] but it is precisely Dostoevsky's emphasis on male ignorance of women and love that is exposed as the root of inhumanity in the novel. Stavrogin lives in a world of narcissistic delusion until Dostoevsky dramatizes the way women mock, unmask, and repudiate him.

Yet the novel also contains scenes in which women, particularly socialist women, are sadistically mocked. No doubt that the narrator's satire on

Virginsky's "student sister" who has a "frightful row" with her uncle over "his views on the emancipation of women" (*P*, 375) confirms that Dostoevsky finds women as socialist revolutionaries no less misguided and fanatical than men. Dostoevsky's attack is directed mainly toward women who mouth crude dismissals of family ties and marriage. In the scene where the nihilist girl student calls her uncle a "moron" and argues that his views "explain[] the behavior of all your generation" (*P*, 379) we see a mirror of the "generation gap" violence that haunted Americans in the 1960s. Dostoevsky satirizes girls who savagely attack the older generation, while on the other hand he exposes the consequences of violent male sexism through Stavrogin's relations with the proud Liza, the child Matryosha, the crippled Maria, and the submissive Dasha. Whether or not Dostoevsky explicitly recognized the connection between his own repeated representations of sexually violated and oppressed females and the need for reform and protest against women's condition articulated by feminists, his novel creates a continuum between the schoolgirl's cruelty to her elders, revolutionary ideology's cruelties to ordinary people, and Stavrogin's cruelties to individual women.

Dostoevsky's parodies of women's search for new identities, his consecration of saintly but "mad" female figures like Maria, and his inability to invent a female heroine who is not also a victim of male cruelty have been interpreted as evidence of his male chauvinism. Yet the question of reformulating female identity according to strictly Western feminist models has recently invited a rethinking within feminism that parallels some modern ethicist's embrace of Dostoevsky's critique of modernism.[15] Silvia Tandeciarz, in her reading of Gayatri Spivak, notes some feminists' tendencies to "mechanically apply the same dictums regardless of context and an evident need to reexamine the presuppositions which inform 'the feminist vanguard.'"[16] Dostoevsky directed a similar criticism toward the feminist vanguard of his own time, which appeared as a movement "unparalleled elsewhere in the nineteenth century Western world" in its dedication "to destroying the administrative core of the Empire through assassination."[17] *The Possessed* indicates how the "oversaturat[ion] with ideas about a new movement" (*P*, 22) offers to some women an exciting opportunity not only for criticism of the status quo but also for cruel self-empowerment at other women's expense.

Mrs. Stavrogin and Mrs. Von Lembke "use" Maria Lebyadkina to show how progressive they are. The crippled woman whom Stavrogin marries to "lacerate" himself becomes the temporary mascot of false populist chic, a group supported by inherited monies suggesting Dostoevsky's idea that "the structures of money lay at the heart of socialist thought, although it claimed to dominate them." [18] If Catteau draws our attention to the economic contradictions within socialist revolutionary structures, Joanna Hubbs illuminates the political-religious complexities of Dostoevsky's woman question in her comment about Maria. She is "the icon of Mother Russia abandoned and martyred by those self-willed intellectuals who claim to be her champions and yet, like petty autocrats, despise her." [19] Dostoevsky's portraits of presiding women, exaggerated and sadistic, stimulate a difficult question : "If the psychological power-compulsion of men originated [male dominance], what originated that—and what can supersede it, other than the psychological power-compulsion of women?"[20]

The addiction to cruelty and to the charisma of a cruel male leader is the novel's central theme. If one part of Dostoevsky's attack on socialist nihilism is configured by male violation of females and female rage at their oppressors, another involves his description of the way women are influenced to remodel their personalities on masculine types, resulting, in Liza's case, in "Amazon" challenges "to our society" and a conqueror's psychology (*P*, 104-5). "According to Mrs. Drozdov," the narrator states, "it had all started with Liza's 'headstrong, sarcastic attitude,' which Nikolai [Stavrogin], proud as he was . . . couldn't take and returned in kind" (*P*, 64). Under the pressure of nihilist ideas, the relations between Stavrogin and Liza signal the breakdowns between married couples such as the Virginskys and the Shatovs, leading to further breakdowns of life-confirming restraints on sexuality and violence. Mrs. Stavrogin's contempt for Stepan Verkhovensky's old-fashioned liberalism, like Mrs. Von Lembke's championship of political revolutionaries over her husband's befuddled conservatism, indicates that destroying tradition may duplicate what radicalism seeks to change.

With Liza and Stavrogin's relationship as a paradigm, Dostoevsky reveals the sadomasochistic components in male chauvinism, couples these with the revolutionary impulses of both sexes, and then exposes contradictions as oppressor and victim shift positions. One result is the exposure of masculine naïveté, the result of sexist egotism. Like Nachaev, Stavrogin's limitation may consist for Dostoevsky in his ignorance of love's power, his resistance to the idea that "in women resides our only great hope, one of the pledges of our revival."[21] By dramatizing the connection between bloody revolution and the violation of women's bodies and minds, the writer allegorizes the fit between male terrorist rape and the "Western" modernization of Mother Russia.

Dostoevsky's exploration of masculine violence has engaged readers, particularly after Freud's argument in *Dostoevsky and Parricide* that the author's sympathy for the criminal is boundless. *The Possessed* suggests a turn in sympathy for the second sex, however, dramatized through female characters' gestures of rebellion against men. In scenes involving Stavrogin with Liza and Matryosha, Dostoevsky repeatedly inscribes a gesture of fist-raising that signals a link between feminist and Christian protest. While Dostoevsky mocks the revolutionary participants at the "cell" meeting who "raised their right hands " but then "after raising them at first, at once put them down again" (P, 381), the gesture signifies a difference when women enact it. Liza's anguished relations with Stavrogin culminate with their meeting in Father Semyon's doorway and her raising "her hand to the level of his face" to strike him (P, 318). The gesture foreshadows her exposing and denying him later. The "unconscious fits of hatred that [Liza] couldn't control" (P, 317) also resonate with Matryosha's gesture of raising her "threatening . . . little fist" at Stavrogin after he rapes her (P, 430). For women the revolutionary's fist-clench signifies protest against masculinist cruelty, a gesture Mary Shatova's "Stavrogin's a beast!" (P, 613) verbalizes. After giving birth to Stavrogin's child, Mary's words underscore the consequences of men's addiction to more powerful men: "I bet if I said I wanted to give him that other horrible name [i.e. Stavrogin's], you'd have approved . . . . Ah, you're an ungrateful, contemptible bunch, the lot of you!" (P, 614).

While the bravest women unmask the male-bonded "lot" whose game is exploitation and radical posturing, the silliest women succumb to men's ideas with unbridled enthusiasm followed by indignation. Women play an important part in the novel by establishing connections between what several critics describe as the novel's dual centers of gravity : its one center like a political pamphlet and the other a metaphysical drama;[22] or its division into two plots, one involving Pyotr Verkhovensky and the other Nikolai Stavrogin.[23] Gordon Livermore solves the novel's seemingly fractured structure by emphasizing its "dialectical unity" and the tension between "levels of reality" represented in it by the word "secret."[24] But what is that secret and whose secret is it? The novel's two levels of discourse represent a gendered schism. The revolutionary and religious strands in the novel—suggested by Stavrogin as the leader who will "bring us the New Truth" (P, 404) and Stavrogin as "a complete atheist [who] still stands on the next-to-the-top rung of the ladder of perfect faith" (P, 421)—cannot be severed from Stavrogin's involvement in "sordid" love affairs described as "whims" (P, 118) or from the fact that Stavrogin is unmasked by the several women he harms. Women are the clues to the secret's discovery and to the difference between Stavrogin's levels of being (his appearance and his reality) replicated by the novel's structure.

Stavrogin's secret wife, Maria, unmasks her "prince" as "a bad actor," a "false tzar" and "the pretender" in chapter 3 of Part Two. The story of Matryosha (Stavrogin's confession) unmasks what Stavrogin himself calls his sickness (*P*, 418). Liza exposes Stavrogin in Part Three, chapter 3, as an impotent man in need of a "nurse" (*P*, 545). If "behind it all stood" Pyotr Verkhovensky with his "mysterious network" (*P*, 685), behind this is another network of exploited, but eventually courageous women who grow to hate Stavrogin after once being in love with him.

Considering these exposures, *The Possessed* can be read as a deconstruction of a particular kind of romanticized masculinist sickness with revolution, rape, the will to power, and emotional anesthesia coded as symptoms of a cruel Nachaevian modernism. As in Kafka's world, "it is women who . . . offer the only chance of finding a way past the barrier which separates the alien from the world."[25] From Stavrogin's relations with Matryosha to Shatov's experience with his pregnant (by Stavrogin) wife, men's radical, root-tearing ideologies are challenged by women's grounding in bodily vulnerability and the insights gained as a result. Even Pyotr Verkhovensky's manipulations of Julie Von Lembke backfire upon him as "her eyes opened at last" just moments before the announcement of the fire set by revolutionaries but destroying peasants (*P*, 524). Mikhailovsky notes that Dostoevsky "analyzed the sensations of a wolf devouring a sheep with such thoroughness . . . even love," [26] but does not emphasize how many of these sheep are female. In *The Possessed* devouring is never ungendered, but specifically linked to what Albert Guerard calls the "paedophilic themes in Dostoevsky's works."[27]

Among Dostoevsky critics, Yarmolinsky and Guerard most fully develop the question of why Dostoevsky was haunted by the particular crime of raping a young girl and why he punished Stavrogin with it. While Yarmolinsky underplays but does not entirely dismiss Strakhov's allegation that this secret desire was Dostoevsky's, he notes that "the theme is adumbrated" in "A Christmas Tree and a Wedding," in *The Insulted and the Injured;* that it is explored through Svidrigaylov in *Crime and Punishment;* and that "the same inclination is vaguely ascribed to Versilov in *A Raw Youth*" as well as to Dmitri Karamazov.[28] Guerard argues that Dostoevsky's desire to commit this crime forced the novelist to repeatedly redeem himself symbolically in confessional fiction. Critics who note that Bakhtin's version of Dostoevsky's discourse does not take enough account of "the negative, destructive potential of dialogic discourse in a constant power struggle,"[29] might return again to Yarmolinsky's and Guerard's focus. Power struggles occur between Stavrogin and the women who finally refuse to "mirror" him.

Responsibilities for rape and for female deaths, through suicidal hanging, murder, or after childbirth, are part of Stavrogin's history and significance. His crimes are particularly masculinist. In the shifting gender world where Mrs. Stavrogin can advise Dasha to marry Stepan Verkhovensky for his "helplessness" (P, 67), where Mayor Von Lembke goes "down on his knees to atone" for his words to the perfectly idiotic Mrs. Von Lembke (P, 488), where Lebyadkin can compare himself to an amoeba in a love letter to Liza (P, 126), and where Liputin can thank Stavrogin for humiliating him with his wife (P, 49)—Stavrogin alone plays the role of the essentialist male. Dostoevsky surrounds Stavrogin with those the narrator calls "scum." At the center of what Maria calls "this third-rate crowd" (P, 261), Stavrogin lives out a *macho* advertisement for himself that thrills his radical followers. The worship of power, the idolization of a man "who does not know what fear is," who "could kill in cold blood," who "retained complete control over himself" (P, 194) describes a world of masculinist values familiar to us. Stavrogin embodies the absence of values that feminists such as Annette Baier and Carol Gilligan associate with female ethics: emotional responsiveness as a part of cognition, the values of empathy, and the desire to communicate. As the strong silent type who moving others, remains unmoved himself, Stavrogin receives Shatov's strike merely as an "opportunity to take cognizance of [Stavrogin's] own immense strength" (P, 233).

A Lacanian might find in Shatov's image of Stavrogin's immobility the fantasy of an eternally rigid phallus, but the most important element in Stavrogin's iconography is his refusal to admit pity or terror. "What fascinates [Stavrogin's disciples], of course" says the narrator, "is overcoming their fear" (P, 194). The overcoming of masculine fear constitutes the source of the male-bonding that seduces not only Stavrogin's followers but also some male readers into the masculinist circle.

Although no critic can approve of Stavrogin's actions, echoes between disciples inside and outside of the text remain part of the novel's critical apparatus: "You're the only one who could have raised that banner," says Shatov to Stavrogin (P, 240). "In [Stavrogin's] soul the impulse to crime is paradoxically the impulse to freedom," writes Wasiolek. Responding to critics who describe Stavrogin as the "most complete . . . embodiment of freedom without God, "[30] the feminist reader outside of the circle notes whose freedom is violated in order for that embodiment to be signified. If Stavrogin represents those who "challenge God and society and their own conscience by willful actions 'beyond good and evil,'"[31] why must Stavrogin express his metaphysical defiance through rape or harming of women? Among Stavrogin's followers, only Kirilov asks the important question: "What has Stavrogin's sordid private love affair to do with our movement?" (P, 564). The moment of this answer begins with the narrator's comment that Stavrogin's "viciousness was cold and controlled and . . . reasonable—the most repulsive and dangerous there is" (P, 195) and continues with the images of Liza and Matryosha raising their fists to Stavrogin. The answer climaxes in Stavrogin's confession and with Liza's unmasking of Stavrogin as a diseased man whose freedom is a negation of others that drives him to sexual impotence and suicide.

One sentence uttered by Shatov releases Stavrogin from his silence and drives him to confess at Tikhon's: "Is it true that you entice children and abuse them?" Stavrogin answers Shatov with a lie: "I never harmed children," a statement that Richard Peace takes seriously in his reluctance to find Stavrogin a rapist.[32] Yet the narrator's comment, "He said it after a silence that had lasted too long. He had turned pale and his eyes glowed" (P, 240), points to Stavrogin's preoccupation with his rape of Matryosha. The preoccupation with male sexual violence appears even earlier when Stavrogin is discussing suicide with Kirilov. "Man is unhappy because he doesn't know he's happy," the theory-soaked Kirilov rants. "That stepdaughter will die, the little girl will remain—and everything is good," he continues. "So it's good," says Stavrogin, "that people die of hunger and also that someone may abuse or rape that little girl" (P, 224).

As a figure framed in masculine ambivalence toward women and "modern vacuity and sullenness,"[33] Stavrogin is simultaneously a symbol of the Great Tradition's machismo, the Charles Manson bad-boy inside repressed male consciousness, and the symbolic killer of patriarchy whom some quasi-liberated women hate to love. For men like Pyotr Verkhovensky, Shatov, and Kirilov, Stavrogin is initially a revolutionary icon. As the narrative develops, however, Stavrogin's meaning for the women undergoes change. For Liza, Mrs. Stavrogin, Mary, and Dasha, Stavrogin at first embodies an absence each imagines can be filled with her own presence, either as lover, mother, fellow radical, or nurse. His masklike face, upon which women hungry for power paint their fantasies, his political charisma and muscular sexuality, present a challenge to women because these qualities signify a subversion of Russia's patriarchal order through which "new" women experience their release. Stavrogin represents his mother's "new hopes and even a new daydream of hers" (P, 45). To Liza he embodies a masculine archetype she wishes to confront with her own "uncanny power" and will to "dominate" (P, 105). As a model of rebellion, Stavrogin represents an inventory of potential feminist/subversive attitudes. He is fearless of and irreverent to the establishment fathers. He is unconventional in his sexual behavior, atheistic until confessed, and supposedly dedicated to revolutionary change. Desperate men and frustrated women "thrilled by the thought that he was a killer" (P, 44) love the nihilist as Liza loves the big male spider she imagines Stavrogin will show her (P, 545).

Stavrogin cannot live up to the expectations imposed upon him. This "secret" is never precisely articulated by the narrator, but clearly revealed by women he is involved with. Confronting Dasha, Stavrogin remarks that she seems to be attracted to him as a nurse is attracted to "a particularly charming corpse" (P, 277). At various times in the novel Maria, Dasha, and Liza all imply that he needs a woman's nursing care (P, 261, 545). What appears as the weak tie between the two parts of the novel's structure turns out to occur upon a female borderline where Stavrogin's identity as an erotic and political hero collapses. In scenes involving women, Stavrogin is revealed to be an amateur as a political leader, as a lover, and even as a criminal, picking on the most vulnerable of females and allowing others to do his dirty work with the Lebyadkins. If, as Catteau argues, Dostoevsky's repudiation of revolutionary socialism and Chernyshevskian feminism was part of his critique of Russian utopianism,[34] the utopianism of masculinity, associated with a Cartesian vision of total rationality and control, is just as forcefully critiqued through the novel's strange breed of women.

The unmasking of Stavrogin by women intensifies in the novel's second half, marked by Stavrogin's confession at Tikhon's that Matryosha's gaze frightens him. He also craves the experience of that informing fear: "I wish she would look at me with her big feverish eyes, just as they were then, as if she could see. . . ." Stavrogin leaves this sentence unfinished, crediting Matryosha's view of him with a power and knowledge he ambivalently seeks. He writes that he could "keep Matryosha away if I chose to do so. . . . But that's the snag. I've never wanted to keep her out and I never will. And so it will go on until I go insane" (P, 430). Stavrogin's extraordinary confession suggests the lengths men will go to avoid identifying with female experience and the way they are also drawn back to it as they begin to understand the terrorist consequences of their masculine prerogatives. The description of male eyes watching female eyes accords with an analysis of Dostoevsky's alterity, dramatizing the female subject as a force that, in penetrating male consciousness, is sometimes capable of transforming man's alienation from himself. For Stavrogin (a type of nineteenth-century deconstructionist/nihilist theorist), morality has become a sliding signifier: "I formulated to myself in so many words the idea that I neither knew nor felt what evil is; . . . that it was all a convention." Yet Stavrogin also understands the sexual-political consequences of his self-deconstruction : "I could be free of all convention, but . . . if I ever attained that freedom I'd be lost" (P, 426).

Once Stavrogin's secret loses its mysterious status to become a sordid symptom, it changes the way we read the novel. Not only do Stavrogin's crimes of rape and complicity in the murder of women allegorize the destruction of Mother Russia, but they also illuminate Dostoevsky's response to allegories of the romantic rapist in modern novels since *Clarissa*. Stavrogin's secret points to a culturally constructed masculinist discourse that rationalizes, even cherishes as "charming demon[ology]" in the one sex what it would repudiate without romantic excuses in the other. The Tikhon chapter reveals that Stavrogin's "sordid private love affair[s]" are the central secret readers have been seeking. The crime of rape becomes the paradigm for a violent sexist sickness, delivered finally of romantic associations with aestheticized rapes. Stavrogin's need to "kill" the child in Matryosha and himself, to "see" his/her eyes watching, drives him toward a death that replicates her suicide and identifies his pain with hers. In this chapter the voice and image of the "other" finally penetrates as it dismantles the hero's heroism.

There are readers who nevertheless find Dostoevsky's demystification of Stavrogin disappointing: "Throughout the novel we have a Stavrogin of silence and self-containment," writes Wasiolek, "a portrait that accords powerfully with the silent wasteland that his inner strength makes for him. The analytic Stavrogin of the confessional chapter mars this impassive, unattached air."[35] What Dostoevsky also mars is a romantic masculinist ideal of the unrestricted "will" as the grandest of human attributes. Dostoevsky's decision to connect Stavrogin's confession of rape to his admission that he is "really no socialist," but "has some sort of sickness" (*P*, 418), suggests the fit between *ubermensch* sexism and political nihilism. Repudiating Schiller's romantic conception of "man" as "most sublime when he resists the pressure of nature, when he exhibits 'moral independence of natural laws in a condition of emotional stress,'" Dostoevsky shows that Stavrogin's inability to love "nature" and "women" produces a wasteland that leads to psychological, sociopolitical, and metaphysical terrorism.[36]

Exploring his own nihilism, Stavrogin is intensely involved with women whom he can potentially destroy, with whom he is partially identified, and whose names begin with *Ma* (Matryosha, Maria, Mary), connecting to the Russian *mother* the important icon of the Madonna. He has sexual relations with two of these women, while his sexual performance with Liza appears to be a "complete flop" (*P*, 550). As the source of Matryosha's suicide, Mary's death, and Maria's murder, Stavrogin's involvement with women suggests an unconscious mother complex addicted to paying back or destroying a primal female image. Louis Breger suggests that these women represent split fragments of Stavrogin's own love-denying mother, Vavara, whom he has incorporated as the deadened part of himself. If Matryosha symbolizes the vulnerable child whose expectations of love must be sadistically annihilated as were Stavrogin's in childhood, Stavrogin symbolizes for Matryosha the crippling of love through sexual violence. Dostoevsky himself confirmed Tikhon's statement to Stavrogin that "there is not and cannot be any worse crime than what you did to that little girl" (P, 434).

In his relation to Maria Lebyadkina, on the other hand, Stavrogin is unable to destroy faith in love's beauty, and it is Maria who demolishes Stavrogin's faith in his own impenetrable will and pretensions to metaphysical sublimity. Beaten daily by her brutal brother and crippled physically, Maria does not mirror Stavrogin's masculinist pathology but rather bears its marks on a body detached in the holy fool's autonomy from the world. Stavrogin discovers that Maria is neither holy-foolish nor docile enough to be incapable of recognizing that he is a "fraud . . . impersonating" the revolution's "prince" while becoming its Jack the Ripper. The words of the crippled woman provoke more response in Stavrogin than Shatov's slap in the face: " 'What are you talking about?' " he screams at Maria, "pushing her off so violently that she banged her head and shoulders painfully." With her words in his mind about the "knife" he carries both as phallus and murder weapon (P, 263-4), he runs into the street shouting "a knife, a knife!"— only to meet the low-life criminal Fedka who is his true mirror. Stavrogin's will to repress what Maria knows about him is symbolized in her death by stabbing and the fire that his followers believe he ordered.

In *The Possessed* women do not in fact mirror men but break and shatter the masculine mirror. Through the three women who become disillusioned with Stavrogin and eventually die, Dostoevsky progressively dramatizes the degrees and levels of Stavrogin's ruin. Liza's final destruction of Stavrogin's fetish takes the form, not of Maria's holy fool Christian protest, but that of incipient feminist protest . When Stavrogin admits to her that she has the right to torment him, that "I knew I didn't love you and I've ruined you," she responds by exposing his "noble sincerity" as another form of narcissistic sexism. Her words contain feminist acid:

> "I have not the slightest desire to be a sympathizing nurse to you. I may end up as a hospital nurse if I don't manage to die conveniently this very day, but I'll certainly not nurse you, although, of course, you're as badly off as any poor legless or armless creature." (P, 545)

Liza's description of Stavrogin as limbless puts a sexual twist on Maria's idea that Stavrogin is a fraud whose only power is the knife. Besides a tit-for-tat revenge for his impotence and inability to love her, she engages him in a challenge to his image of her femininity. She imagines that he would take her to "some place where there lived a huge, vicious man-sized spider and that we'd spend the rest of our lives staring at it in fear" (*P,* 545). She wishes to confront the heart of darkness the dominant sex takes so much pride in confronting. Her image of insect horror associates her with several of Dostoevsky male sensualists: with the rapist Svidrigaylov who imagines a hell full of spiders, with Ipollit's spider dream in *The Idiot,* with Dmitri Karamazov who finds "riddles" in "spider" sensuality where "all contradictions live together" (*BK,* 108). But spiders in *The Possessed* are also associated with Matryosha , and with Stavrogin's projection of the insect image upon her which creates the young female as *his* horror. The big male insect Liza wishes to see as the symbol of the tragic riddle of human nature is replicated in miniature in the dream Stavrogin experiences following Matryosha's suicide.

In his confession, Stavrogin speaks of a paradisal dream world that is transformed to nightmare. "In the middle of the bright light" Stavrogin sees a "tiny dot" that assumes the shape of a "tiny red spider" that stabs him. In that light he sees Matryosha standing "reprovingly and threatening me with her little fist . . . that immature creature with her immature brain threatening me . . . but . . . blaming only herself" (*P,* 429-30). In Stavrogin's hallucination he is stabbed by the female spider as he had stabbed her sexually, to be echoed later in Liza's strange words. If for Liza the spider is large and male, for Stavrogin it is small, female, and red, a condensation of his insect sensuality and shame with Matryosha's virgin blood. The fusion of gender horrors, of male and female penetrations and stabbings, reaches its apotheosis in these two scenes. While Matryosha 's response is to kill herself, Liza's is to articulate the wish to castrate Stavrogin, to see the murdered victims (in whose murder she knows herself complicit), and to finally destroy the phallocentric worship Stavrogin's image inspired in her.

Dostoevsky's reduction of Stavrogin is not finally directed only to other men. He also mocks women's addictions to *ubermensch* culture and hero-worshipping, either of utopian socialist ideals or of charismatic individuals. The exposure of women's complicity in the creation of pseudomasculinist heroics is confirmed in Stavrogin's letter to Dasha in which he expresses "no respect" for her willingness to sacrifice herself to him, a man who exhibits "negation without strength and without generosity" (*P,* 690-1).

Not through the submissive Dasha but through the resisting Maria, Matryosha, Mary, and Liza, the answers to Dostoevsky's woman question evolve through the exposure of contradictory themes with which contemporary feminism still struggles: women's seduction by the idea of power, the exhortation to women to empower themselves as men do, and at the same time the feminist critique of power as "patriarchal" along with the description of women as better nurturers or nurses. By representing these unresolved contradictions within the woman's movement, Dostoevsky's discourse in *The Possessed* bridges some gaps between problems shared by nineteenth- and twentieth-century feminists. The novelist warns that the masculine aggressiveness associated with radical politics and violent transformations of tradition may destroy what is best about woman's difference.

By exploring the meanings of Stavrogin's violations of females and their reactions to that violation, Dostoevsky makes his contribution to the politics of rape. By exposing the maimed aesthetics of super-masculinity as incorporated by both men and women, *The Possessed* exposes the paradoxes inspired by the incipient feminization of politics and literature. The "feminization of literature" that occurred during the nineteenth century has been remarked by Terry Eagleton and Rita Felski among others. Felski writes that "an imaginative identification with the feminine permeates much of the writing of the male European avant-garde in the late nineteenth century, a period in which gender norms were being protested and redefined from a variety of standpoints."[37]

In the works that follow *The Possessed*, "the feminine" no longer functions, as it did in *Crime and Punishment*, as the repressed. In *A Gentle Creature* and in *The Brothers Karamazov*, it is yearned for and struggled over as a key to missing links in the human soul.

6

Female Suicides and A Gentle Creature *in* The Diary of a Writer

I am firmly convinced that the majority of the suicides, *in toto*, directly or indirectly, were committed as a result of one and the same spiritual illness—the absence in the souls of these men of the sublime idea of existence. In this sense our indifference, as a contemporary Russian illness, is gnawing at all souls. (*D*, 542)[1]

Dostoevsky's *The Diary of a Writer* is over a thousand pages long. Laced with anti-semitism, nationalist fervor, and the metaphysical philosophies of Solovyev,[2] this strange work, more journalist's column than diary, nevertheless personifies an "ethics of care."[3] Published sequentially for years as it came from Dostoevsky's pen, its structure is octapoedal; it aims to cover huge territories of human concern and includes in its pages one of Dostoevsky's greatest stories about women, *A Gentle Creature* (or *The Meek One*). Bakhtin describes *The Diary* as a "journalist genre . . . full of allusions to the great and small events of the epoch"; it feels "out new directions in the development of everyday life."[4] Dostoevsky was pleased with two thousand subscribers to his *Diary*, with letters from "altogether new types" such as the girl who complained to him that she did not love her fiancé and wanted to continue her studies.

The concerned intelligentsia and girls of the 1870s who asked the writer's advice have little in common with the specialists who read the diary today. Richard Peace finds the work "shorn of dialectic" while Gary Morson argues that it is "semi-fiction" and "polyphonic."[5] Few women readers have had much to say about it. Dostoevsky's polemic, the belief that Russia and Christ will save the world,[6] seems unconvincing at the present moment. But *The Diary* records a less dubious insight: nineteenth-century "Russian man" is so "sick," Dostoevsky shows, that he drives himself and women to crime and suicide.

This theme, represented through various descriptions of the criminal court cases Dostoevsky analyzes, is condensed in the story Mochulsky praises as "unprecedented in literature"[7] and whose ending Belknap describes as "the most personal, most emotional, most religious and intertextually most moving passage [Dostoevsky] ever wrote."[8] In *A Gentle Creature*, the meaning of female suicide cracks open Dostoevsky's patriarchal defenses and leads to statements about women's rights from which the rereadings offered in this book originate.

The textual site of Dostoevsky's story is significant chronologically. It could not be written until Dostoevsky analyzed dozens of real-life court cases taken from newspapers, several of which involved women's suicides. Spanning the years 1873-1881, *The Diary* includes conversations among "Dostoevsky," the readers who write to him, the characters he invents, stories published therein, the multiple hypothetical narrators he imagines, and hundreds of entries from newspapers and journals. As a diatribe against the West's "juridicization of human relations" but also a symptomatic articulation of assimilated Western ideas, one of *The Diary*'s obsessions is the functioning of "reform" laws following serf emancipation within the Russian courts. Some commentators on Dostoevsky's work make no distinction between Dostoevsky's attitudes toward law as expressed in his *Winter Notes on Summer Impressions* (1864) and *The Diary*, written ten years later when the writer came to see the operations of the court up close. "Against the bourgeois ideal of a society based upon the legally guaranteed rights of man and thereby sanctifying the principle of egoism," Andrzej Walicki writes, "Dostoevsky set the idea of the authentic fraternal community . . . in which the individual does not demand his rights but voluntarily submits himself to the collective . . . [while the collective] grants the individual freedom and safety."[9] But the view that Dostoevsky's ideas remained static is unpersuasive if we take seriously Dostoevsky's demand in 1877 that women achieve full equality with men under the law.

Laura Engelstein's descriptions of the Russian legal system account more nearly for Dostoevsky's responses to reform and its consequences for women. "Confusions between police (so called administrative measures) and judicial procedure were a feature of the autocracy's policy of deliberate misrule," she writes. The "reformed" system from which Dostoevsky plucks his suffering characters to analyze in *The Diary* is one in which "disenfranchised" men and women, but especially women, are

> caught between the weight of unconstrained authority exercised from above and the weight of folk tradition that rooted the populace in its communal ways—or,

as a liberal psychiatrist expressed it in 1906, between "the power of darkness below and the darkness of power above."[10]

Nothing is clearer in *The Diary* than that Russian reality presents a contrast to the Holy Mother Russia of Dostoevsky's fantasies. Following the philosophers Solovyev and Fyodorov, Dostoevsky writes that Russia's backwardness preserves the human "relatedness" the West lacks, perhaps as "woman" preserves the "intuition" that "man" has repressed or *Sophia* the wisdom *Logos* denies. Yet the diarist is not sentimental about the suicide, murder, and child and woman abuse this backwardness perpetuates, and he engages the reader in horror stories. Targeting the "liberal" reform lawyers who adjudicate cases by letting criminals go unpunished, Dostoevsky underscores the fact that "reform," Russian-style, may do no more for women and children than the traditionalist legal codes they were meant to transform. Dostoevsky points to an "illness" and an "indifference" in Russia where the poor suffer from brutality and class oppression while the rich suffer from skepticism, pessimism, and uncertainty. Ignoring the possible fit between his critique of patriarchal reform and socialist-feminist ideas, Dostoevsky is driven to confused statements and to paradoxes. The cases he analyzes show that leniency to the offender, in most cases the male head of the household, means continual torture for the household's women and children. Neither the law nor lawyers protect women from domestic abuse and may in fact exacerbate overall crime by driving women to kill their abusers.

If "the sexual abuse of servant girls by their masters is a literary subject in European nineteenth century literature, including Czarist Russia,"[11] Dostoevsky's subtext in *The Diary of a Writer* is that "literature" and "reality" cohere in terms of the gendered master-slave structure that corrupts family life. Laura Engelstein describes the fact that after 1861, "many cases dealing with public problems concerned family affairs."

> The relationships between men and women showed [legal scholars] how the peasant male—who headed the family, ran community affairs, and sat on the peasant courts—wielded his power. It revealed his sense of justice. If the investigators were not gender-blind, it was because the gender issue hit them squarely in the eye. It was also because after the 1860's the intelligentsia[,] influenced by Jeremy Bentham and J. S. Mill, had seen "the woman question" as intrinsic to the problem of social reform.[12]

The gender issues that hit Russia's liberal intelligentsia and its legal scholars "squarely in the eye" hit Dostoevsky in the heart of his fiction-making, as shown in *A Gentle Creature* with its debauched male narrator's direct reference to John Stuart Mill. "During the last decades," Dostoevsky writes, "Russian man has become terribly addicted to the debauch of acquisition, cynicism and materialism. But the woman has remained much more faithful to the pure worship of the idea" (D, 340-1). Whether "pure" or not, female criminals and suicides showed the novelist a world no amount of patriarchal Christian commitment could rationalize. For Dostoevsky the word "patriarchy" could not be free of the connotations of all the "horrors of serfdom and thus the horror of unlimited authority and abuse of force."[13]

While his fiction invariably reveals that women are the last remaining victims of the old order, this awareness nevertheless struggles with several issues that involve Dostoevsky's public persona: his identity as one of the *pochvenniki*[14] with faith in the regenerating capacities of the Russian people; his sense of the powers and limitations of orthodox faith; his skepticism about modernist skepticism itself, and the tension in himself between the "Ivan" he was and the "Alyosha" he wanted to become.[15] What nevertheless intervenes in Dostoevsky's loyalty to the Czar and status quo is his detailed knowledge of persons accused and oppressed, the lessons he learned during his four years of hard labor in Siberia. During those years he "became convinced of the ineffectiveness of the Russian penal system,"[16] and his sense of an effective system of compassion and justice evolved in terms of maternal imagery. His memory of the "muzhik Marei" in Siberia who offered him comforting "maternal tenderness" (*nezhnaia materinskaia ulybka*) helped him attain to "sonship with the people, with Mother Russia, with Mother Earth."[17] His sense of maternal justice was not gender-based. It could be associated with men or women, but never with the harsh fathers, brutal peasant husbands, and indifferent "liberal" lawyers he encountered in Russia's "new" courts.

Affirming his relatedness to Russians as a whole, Dostoevsky inevitably displays much of the masculinist illness he examines, the puzzled sexism he condemns, but also the quest for reform he initially represses. One of the four fictional stories in *The Diary* is about a "ridiculous man" who contemplates suicide; another, *A Gentle Creature*, is about a woman who kills herself. In the journalism that surrounds these fictions, Dostoevsky explores the "unconscious" reasons for family violence, murder, and suicide, basing his analyses on court cases reported in newspapers. Contemplating criminal cases, he becomes convinced that Russia has an unconscious as well as conscious moral life. "In the striving to elucidate to itself through hidden ideas consists the whole energy of [Russia's] life," he writes (D, 14)—an energy that shouts for a cosmic cure and change of human consciousness that legislation alone cannot remedy.

How can a violent and suicidal people, many of them "indifferent to the sublime idea of existence" by Dostoevsky's own admission, contribute to the world through their "unconscious"? What is the relation between *The Diary's* analyses of suicide and its Russian messianism? Gary Saul Morson argues that for Dostoevsky, the world's horrors are the sign that a new Christian order will emerge: "Everything is undermined and loaded with powder, and is just waiting for the first spark."[18] "Suicides in Russia," Dostoevsky writes, "have become so frequent that nobody even speaks of them. The Russian soil seems to have lost the strength to hold people on it" (*D*, 335). An "orphaned mankind" wishes to take its revenge, perhaps on an inhospitable mother-nature-nation. "Because I am unable to destroy nature," Dostoevsky writes in the suicide's voice, "I am destroying only myself" (*D*, 473). It is an oddity of the *Diary* that although Dostoevsky's most vivid comments surround *female* suicide, he usually uses the male pronoun to represent the problem to his readers. The death of women by their own hands is something, Dostoevsky implies, to which men should pay attention, or in which men are complicit. Women's deaths are a hidden sign, something which "gnaws" at men, as indicated in the passage which heads this chapter and by the psychological conditions of Velchaninov, Myshkin, Stavrogin, and the gentle creature's husband.

Dostoevsky does not confront the gender problem head-on until this story. His paradoxical commentary surrounding it includes a critique of judicial "reform" undermined by his own late version of "Russian Socialism." Joseph Frank clarifies Dostoevsky's complex response by quoting Ovsyaniko-Kulikovsky's idea that "'the psychological foundation' of the 'dogma' shared by Dostoevsky and the Russian Left of his time [were] exactly the same" (*D*, Intro., xxv). Critical of "materialistic" Europe, Dostoevsky sounds surprisingly Marxist at times, if not Marxist-feminist. Replicating *Das Capital's* image of "Moneybags" emerging in modern society, Dostoevsky sees that a "new storm was coming up, a new calamity was arising—'the gold bag!' . . . It stands to reason that this former rich merchant worshipped his million as god" (*D*, 484-5). The writer declares that "Russian men" are "materialistic, cynical," but that Russian women are capable of the spiritual "idea." In 1876, Dostoevsky theorizes that serfdom has undermined the stability of patriarchy. There is debauchery among "the last decade of Russian men," disorder and chaos among "the best" of them.

> Serfdom was abolished and everything underwent a profound transformation. . . . the "best men" began, as it were, to vacillate. . . . Moreover, in the understanding of what is best there ensued something altogether confusing and indeterminate. . . . Finally,

are these new grounds known, and who will believe that they are precisely those ones on which so much has to be erected? (D, 483)

Dostoevsky's critique of indeterminacy leads him in the direction of a deterministic nationalist and Christian propaganda, but he cannot erase the power of "new grounds" and new ideas any more than Velchaninov can stop his ears from hearing the student's truth about "new" women and "new" men. Dostoevsky's discourse does not yet participate in images of a physical world ravaged by industrial pollution, but the gendered connotations of a cosmic Russian apocalypse are conjured by his images of maimed and dead female bodies. The text opens in 1873 with the author's analysis of a peasant woman's court case as described in the newspapers:

> A peasant beats up his wife, mutilates her over a period of long years; insults her more than a dog. In despair and in an almost senseless state, having made up her mind to commit suicide, she goes to a village court. There they dismiss her, and, with an apathetic mumble, she is told "You should live on more amicable terms." Is this compassion? (D, 18)

In *The Diary* torture, murder, and suicide exist on a continuum of Russian illnesses. Dostoevsky is compelled to record stories from newspapers and journals about suicide, murder, child abuse, wife beating. His readers are compelled in turn to "answer" these stories and his analyses of them. Dostoevsky cannot omit any detail in his analysis of *why and how* the peasant mother kills herself:

> [The husband] also used to starve her, leaving her without bread for three days. He would put the bread on a shelf[,] would call her and tell her: "Don't dare to touch that bread; it's *my* bread." . . . He demanded that she work; she attended to everything steadfastly, speechlessly, in dismay . . . in a state of delirium. (D, 19-20)

Dostoevsky cannot stop writing about the woman. "I can also visualize her appearance . . . lean as a rake . . . with child. . . . Tying up his wife . . . the blows come down more frequently, more sharply. . . . The animal shrieks of the tortured woman go to his head as liquor." Dostoevsky repeats these horrors, as if to exorcise them from his compassionate (but always implicated) consciousness. But then there is one horror that surpasses all. The peasant hangs his wife by the legs, sits down, eats, then "again starts beating the hanged creature" while their little daughter witnesses the act. The patriarchal courts advised clemency to the peasant father:

Bear in mind that the little girl testified against her father. She told everything, and it is said that she made those present weep. . . . [The father] is to spend only eight months in jail, after which he will return home. . . . Again there will be someone to hang by the legs. (*D,* 20)

Mikhailovsky speaks of the writer's "cruel talent." But where is this cruelty located? Certainly not solely "within" Dostoevsky's imagination or fantasy life, but outside him in the legal system that has been "reformed" by male "liberals":

"*Guilty but deserves clemency.*" . . . "Deserves clemency!" And this verdict was deliberately rendered. They knew what would be awaiting the child. Clemency—to whom, to what?—One feels as if in some whirl; one is seized and turned and twisted around. (*D,* 20)

The links Dostoevsky forges between male debauchery, female suicide, and child abuse include the following "facts" from Russian newspapers: the story of the peasant mother who finally hangs herself in front of her daughter after enduring her husband's drunken torture for years, followed by a story of a mother who boils her child's hand "for some ten seconds" because the child is crying from teething. Such stories are relentless. They appear in Dostoevsky's dreams. He cannot stop thinking about them as keys to the "illness" and the "gnawing" in Russian souls. The images repeat: women and children, most frequently female children:

But the wife hung head over heels, as a chicken! And "this is my bread; don't you dare to touch it!" And the little girl shivering on that oven, listening for a half hour to her mother's shrieks! And, "Mama, why do you choke?"—Isn't all this identical with the little hand under boiling water? (*D,* 21)

In *The Diary* women who mistreat children are themselves mistreated by men. Readers of Dostoevsky know his story about the courier who beat the *yamschik* lad driving the troika who in turn lashed his horses so they dashed "at top speed, as if possessed." Dostoevsky writes in *The Diary* that the disgusting scene remained in his memory all his life: "Never was I able to forget it, or that courier, and many an infamous and cruel thing observed in the Russian people." And the writer adds, "Today . . . couriers no longer beat people, but the people beat themselves, having retained the rods in their own court." The female imagery in Raskolnikov's dream of the beaten mare in *Crime and Punishment* shows up again in Dostoevsky's discourse a decade later.

Sonya and Katerina Marmeladova's stories are replicated in real life stories from the newspapers:

> A drunken husband came to his wife whom he had deserted and whom, along with her children, he had failed to support . . . and demanded vodka from her; he began to beat her so as to extort more vodka from her; then she, that galley-slave working woman (please think of how, thus far, woman's labor has been rated!), who did not know how she could manage to feed her children, seized a knife and thrust it into him. This happened recently and she is going to be tried. . . . Such cases may be counted by the hundreds and thousands. (D, 185-7).

Concerned with how women are treated under the new laws, Dostoevsky notes men's low rating of "women's labor." He describes women pushed by men's cruelties into criminal retaliation, or toward suicide, or toward abandoning their faith in God. The "accursed questions" of metaphysics have been closely bound to problems with women for Raskolnikov and for Stavrogin, as they will be for Dmitri, Ivan, and Alyosha Karamazov. But in Dostoevsky's comments on Russian court cases, where all theories and philosophies confront the test of an all-too-human reality, the accursed questions are even more clearly linked to the woman question. While *Notes from Underground, Crime and Punishment,* and *The Idiot* began with descriptions of a man in a room or on a train, Dostoevsky will begin his last novel, *The Brothers Karamazov,* with a description of Alyosha's memory of his mother, "the shrieker," driven to hysteria and death by his brutal father. The final image in *The Idiot* of a woman destroyed by men seems to haunt Dostoevsky's imagination in *The Diary.* The question of how women's suicides can be understood in psychological, legal, and spiritual terms provokes Dostoevsky to write: "I am receiving a great many letters giving the facts pertaining to suicides, with questions: how and what do I think about these suicides, and how do I explain them?" (D, 542).

The "Great Reforms" of the Russian legal system instituted in 1864 after the emancipation of the serfs were meant to "modernize the judicial system and to guarantee the independence and integrity of the judges." Dostoevsky knows this rhetoric, with its appeals to "the new principle of equality for all subjects irrespective of class" and its promise that "the question of guilt or innocence [is] to be decided by jurors chosen by lot from the local population." The severity of the penal laws under which Dostoevsky himself was punished in Siberia—"beating with rods, whips, or cudgels; running the gauntlet; and branding"—were abolished.[19] And yet beatings, tortures, and murders continue in ordinary Russian households, supported somehow by this "new" and "liberal" kind of justice.

Two images of female suicide in particular engage Dostoevsky: the twenty-five-year-old "zemstvo midwife," Pisareva, who "was able to earn a decent living," and the poverty-stricken woman who jumps to her death holding "a holy image in her hands" (*D*, 470). Dostoevsky is rapturously moved by the second image, which verifies his sense of suicide with a religious difference. He attempts to push the distinction between women who die without faith and those who die in God: "How different are these two creatures; they seem to have come from two different planets!" But the difference begins to dissolve the more he writes about it, until he cannot decide "which of these two souls had suffered more on earth" (*D*, 470). Pisareva, to whom he returns several times in *The Diary*, symbolizes the first type. He theorizes that she could not endure the philosophy of "utilitarianism and egoism. . . . 'If magnanimity doesn't exist, then there's no need even to be useful.'" He describes Pisareva's "snarling, impatient" suicide note that directs the living to "pull off" her "new shirt and stockings" when she is dead. "She did not use the words '*take off*,'" Dostoevsky notes, "but she wrote—'pull off'; . . . All these harsh words are caused by impatience, and impatience by fatigue" (*D*, 336).

Dostoevsky understands that the twenty-five-year-old Pisareva is finally exhausted by "woman's labor." "Why is that dark dull grave so dear to you?" he asks, speaking to Pisareva herself. "How, then, can your mothers help but *howl* over you. . . . You, too, were an infant and you also desired to live" but have lost "the sublime of existence" (*D*, 337). It is not by chance that Dostoevsky's use of the plural ("mothers") emphasizes his identification with them, nor that the passage about Pisareva is followed by the next number called "Unquestionable Democracy: Women." Here he praises Russian women enthusiastically, as if to suppress the questions "Pisareva" raises.

> In [the Russian woman] resides our only great hope, one of the pledges of our survival. The regeneration of the Russian woman during the last twenty years has proved unmistakable. . . . During the last decades the Russian man has become terribly addicted to the debauch of acquisition, cynicism and materialism. But the woman has remained much more faithful to the pure worship of the idea, to the duty of serving the idea. In her thirst for higher education, she has revealed . . . the greatest courage.

The darkened life of women invades this laudatory discourse that elevates Russian women at the expense of Russian men. "I also perceive certain faults in contemporary women," Dostoevsky adds, "her extraordinary dependency upon several essentially masculine ideas: her inclination to accept them credulously and to believe in them without scrutiny." By the end of the paragraph "Pisareva" has slipped into his sentences with their objectivist stance toward the woman question and support for female education. "Let us pray that God will help the Russian woman to experience fewer disillusions, to grow less 'tired,'" than the "poorly rewarded . . . succumbed and vanquished . . . Pisareva." Suicidal women are "unforgettable phenomena" (D, 340-1) who must be exorcised again and again in Dostoevsky's fiction.

A Gentle Creature (1876) is Dostoevsky's answer to the question about Pisareva's drift toward the "dull dark grave." The story puzzles the differences between a man's suicide that a little girl helps to prevent in The Dream of the Ridiculous Man (1877) and a woman's suicide her husband cannot prevent in A Gentle Creature. The two stories, taken together, create a gendered landscape in which men's exploitations of "the feminine" are examined. Eric Naiman's reads The Dream of the Ridiculous Man through Dostoevsky's experiences with Ekaterina Kornilova, a pregnant young seamstress who pushed her step-daughter out the window of their Petersburg apartment and was sentenced to imprisonment and lifelong exile. Naiman interprets Dostoevsky's involve-ment in the Kornilova case (he visited her in prison; he analyzed the motives for her crime) as

> a matter of satisfaction . . . derived from the containment of the irrational and the feminine, as if the incarceration—or quarantine—of birth could, by imposing rational order upon a state of morbid irrationality, defuse pregnancy's contami-nating properties. Indeed, Dostoevskii was happy to inform his readers that Kornilova's character had changed for the better in jail; she had been transformed by prison from a testy woman to "a gentle creature."

Naiman makes a connection between The Dream and A Gentle Creature by putting Dostoevsky's name for the transformed Kornilova in quotation marks. Naiman also links the suffering of Kornilova's stepdaughter and the inarticulate girl in The Dream who saves the ridiculous man from suicide: "In this respect the Kornilova story and the 'Son' [Dream] are mirror images. . . . A central theme in 'Son' is the Ridiculous Man's identification with a dis-tressed child," and the story functions as "therapy for its author." Naiman argues that Dostoevsky believed in "pregnancy's potential for criminal influ-ence."[20] The critic prepares the way for an interpretation of A Gentle Creature in terms of a similar theme of male "containment" of women's "contamina-tion," which initially seems plausible.

But A Gentle Creature offers a different kind of "therapy." A juxtaposition of the two stories reveals that while The Dream succeeds in containing the feminine by de-eroticizing all human relations in an other-world utopia, *A Gentle Creature* is a dystopic counter-discourse suggesting that containing feminine eroticism is itself a form of murder.

In *A Gentle Creature* Dostoevsky indicts another "eternal " husband and foreshadows the opening description in *The Brothers Karamazov* of Fyodor driving his young wife to death. Dostoevsky's misgivings about the constructions of male sexual desire are inscribed in his impulse to punish various husbands and fathers in fiction, an impulse no doubt related to the author's own father's death, whether violent as Joseph Frank has described it, or ameliorated as Geir Kjetsaa has revised it.[21] In *The Diary* we find the peasant husband who hangs his wife by her legs and beats her, Perova's husband who "barbarously butchered her at night . . . and after cut his own throat" (*D*, 160), and references to "decades of Russian men addicted to . . . cynicism and materialism." *A Gentle Creature* emerges from the context of these realities as a fictive contemplation of masculine depression and as a quest for a woman's voice.

Dostoevsky's decision to leave the male narrator and his wife nameless suggests that the author is telling the story of a generic couple, the older man with the much younger woman. In the first chapter of *A Gentle Creature*, "Who Was I and Who Was She," the forty-one-year-old narrator describes their history to himself, but also, as Dostoevsky's preface to the story emphasizes, "sometimes he is addressing an invisible listener, a sort of judge. And, as a matter of fact, this is how it actually happens in real life" (*GC*, 670).[22] The husband knows himself to have gotten away with a crime that has gone unpunished under the laws. In this most "dialogic" of narratives, the speaker is continually twisting toward various invisible responders who may condemn him, "judges" who include readers familiar with J. S. Mill's *On the Subjection of Women* (1869):

> I wasn't going to justify myself, was I? . . . . Mind you, I knew that a woman, and particularly a girl of sixteen, simply must submit to her husband. Women have no originality. That—that is axiomatic. Yes, I regard it as axiomatic even now. Even now! Never mind what's lying there in the sitting-room. Truth is truth, and John Stuart Mill himself can do nothing about it! And a woman who loves—oh, a woman who loves—will worship even vice, the crimes even of the man she loves (*GC*, 685).

Obsessed with being "stern, stern, stern" to his wife in order to control her, the pawnbroker husband reveals personality traits that clinical psychologists today call "borderline," including the obsession with repetition inscribed in his verbal style. Like those men that "Russia" can scarcely root to her soil, the pawnbroker's existential anxiety is such that his quest for security in marriage becomes a kind of "debauchery." His relationship with his young wife is meant to "secure" (his favorite word) "the idea of our inequality" (GC, 700). He shamelessly admits that it "fascinated me—that feeling of inequality. Yes, it's delightful" (GC, 681). Like Luzhin of *Crime and Punishment*, he is drawn to a sixteen-year-old woman who is so destitute she comes to pawn useless things at his shop. To him she personifies traditional femininity in its most vulnerable dimension. He believes, like Luzhin, that poverty and a miserable family background make a woman a better wife. "She had been slaving for her aunts for three years. . . . They even beat her, begrudged her every bite of bread she ate, and they ended up by intending to sell her." He concludes that his offering to buy her in marriage himself appears to her as though he were sent "from a higher world" (GC, 677).

Dostoevsky exposes the precise fit between economics and sexuality in the deal the pawnbroker makes with the gentle creature. Forced to choose between a "fat shopkeeper" or "a pawnbroker who quotes Goethe," she pawns herself to the man for survival's sake but also with a longing for love. "There was also some argument about her trousseau," he remembers.

> She had nothing in the world, literally nothing but then she didn't want anything. I succeeded, however, in persuading her that it was not right and proper for a bride not to have anything at all, and I got her the trousseau. For who else was there to do anything for her? Well, to hell with me! (GC, 681)

This extraordinarily ironic portrait of a man's motivations, his need for a finalized "security"—"I wanted to put her to the test"; "What I wanted was secure happiness"; "I had a right to want to make myself secure at the time" (GC, 672, 625, 686)—dramatizes the connections between procuring women and putting away funds. "Cash-nexus" and "utilitarian" conceptions of marriage connect the gentle creature's story to the real-life histories of young women too exhausted by "woman's labor" to go on living: to both Pisareva and the "holy" suicide who died with an icon in her hands. Dostoevsky synthesizes elements of the two women's real-life stories in *A Gentle Creature*, who is described at the end of the story as taking "a step forward . . . then press[ing] the icon to her bosom and—thr[owing] herself out the window!" (GC, 710). Although Dostoevsky shows that the gentle creature has not lost her faith in God, her personality is finally closer to the raging Pisareva's than to the "holy" suicide.

Rebelling against her husband's tyranny, attempting to kill him with his own gun, the young wife enacts the "new woman's" gestures of protest

Dostoevsky learned from George Sand's *Mauprat* and practiced in fiction through Dunya Raskolnikova and Liza Tushina. The compliance and gentleness that initially serves the husband as a goad for his tyrannies is gradually transformed in the story, leading to what the husband eventually calls his wife's "rebellion and independence" (*GC*, 685). But there are signs of her noncompliance even before the incident with the gun so reminiscent of Dunya's experience with Svidrigaylov. From the beginning her strategies are a "sardonic" smile and an indifference to offers of money, displaying her consciousness of her husband's "utilitarianism and egoism." The more he becomes conscious of her alternate worldview, however, the more he justifies himself and imposes his ideas upon her:

> You see, young people as a rule despise money, so I made a special point of money. I laid particular stress on money. . . . I expected the fullest possible respect from her. I wanted her to stand in homage before me because of my sufferings.

The husband demands that she pay homage to his economic practicality and sympathize with the necessity of his pawnbroking: "I always hated this money-lending business, I hated it all my life" (*GC*, 679). Like the Underground Man and Alexei, the pawnbroker symbolizes "Russian man's illness" associated with a Faustian desire to become a God-man worshipped by women, as Faust himself is at first worshipped by Gretchen. Before proposing to his own Gretchen, the pawnbroker quotes directly from Goethe: "I—I am part of that Power which still doeth good, though scheming ill. . . . You've read *Faust*, haven't you?" Intimidating her with his stammering literary allusions, the pawnbroker is amazed that she could "have been so curious about the words of Mephistopheles when she herself was in such a dreadful position."

> Even at that time I already regarded her as *mine*, and not for one moment did I doubt my own power. It's one of the most voluptuous thoughts in the world, you know. Not to be in doubt, I mean. (*GC*, 675-6)

Yet it is precisely "doubt" that the gentle creature comes to signify. Expressing herself through an "unmastered" gaze that recalls the responses of Liza's from *Notes from Underground* and Polina of *The Gambler*, she refuses her husband's demand for an absolute termination of doubt. His response is to create "a whole system" that sustains their "inequality," even as finds her "gentle face . . . getting more and more insolent," and as he eventually discovers that he is "loathsome to her" (*GC*, 681, 685)

At first she argued. Good Lord, how she argued! Then she began lapsing into
silence. Wouldn't say a word. Only opened her eyes as she listened to me, opened
them wide, those big, big eyes of hers, those observant eyes of hers. I suddenly
saw a smile on her face, a mistrustful, silent, evil smile. Well, it was with that
smile that I brought her into my house. It was true, of course, that she had
nowhere else to go. (GC, 683)

The pawnbroker's demands on his wife represent his masculinist idea that
wives exist to assuage male insecurity and to support male ego. Although he
projects his various desires upon her and is continually watching her, she is
the one whose gaze unnerves and objectifies him. Here Dostoevsky reverses
the "world ordered by sexual imbalance," described by some feminists as one
in which "pleasure in looking has been split between active/male and pas-
sive/female."[23] Dostoevsky shows how the wife's "female gaze" interrupts the
projections of male fantasy, that domesticated version of the *ubermensch*
complex Dostoevsky investigated earlier through Stavrogin's terrorism and
Raskolnikov's Napoleonism. The gentle creature's husband belongs to no
political cause, espouses no revolutionary heroism, and has no ambition to
save Russia from Napoleon using Napoleonic tactics. His meditations about
the voluptuousness of power over the "meek" are entirely concentrated in his
relationship to his wife, with Faust's relation to Gretchen and J.S. Mill's ideas
about women's liberation forming his self-chosen dialectic. In *A Gentle Creature*,
Dostoevsky strips from his self-consciously narrating "hero" the cultural
contexts that lend dignity to heroic aspirations to superiority over "vermin,"
"the masses," or the "ordinary." The novelist presents the woman question in
its rawest form, a form which foreshadows Ivan Karamazov's conversations
with the devil about *Faust* and the important philosophical arguments about
power and powerlessness in *The Legend of the Grand Inquisitor*.

As a small-time inquisitor, the pawnbroker demands a woman's sympathy
and homage, just as the Grand Inquisitor longs for acknowledgment of his
"sacrifice" from the "people." As a meditation upon the origin of "the power-
compulsion in men," which Juliet Mitchell argues is so difficult for feminists
to theorize,[24] *The Gentle Creature* has no parallel in nineteenth-century fiction
for the intensity of its synthesis. Four elements are symbolically synthesized
in the story that remain separate in many of the discourses which compete
as "feminism": (1) a psychological account of gender difference as socially
constructed,[25] (2) something like a "post-structuralist" account of the links
between patriarchal language and foundationalist concepts of "reality,"[26] (3)
an account of the role of religious skepticism and religious belief in men's
relations to women, and (4) a Marxist-like account of the origins of women's

subordination. Among these, Frederick Engels's and Karl Marx's critique of nineteenth century "bourgeois" marriage and women as capitalist "chattel" would seem the most obvious candidate for a description of the marital relationship described in Dostoevsky's story:

> Marriage is determined by the class position of the participants, and to that extent always remains marriage of convenience. In both cases, this marriage of convenience often enough turns into the crassest prostitution—sometimes on both sides, but much more generally on the part of the wife, who differs from the ordinary courtesan only in that she does not hire out her body, like a wageworker, on piecework, but sells it into slavery once and for all.[27]

A Gentle Creature emphasizes the economic base of the pawnbroker's relationship with his poverty-stricken wife, but Dostoevsky also shows that literary culture (from Goethe to J. S. Mill) is a source for the pawnbroker's male chauvinism as well as its potential transformation. Connections between Marxist-Engelian critiques of bourgeois marital relations, Faustian sexist elitism, and the dissemination in Russia of J. S. Mill's and Harriet Taylor's *On the Subjection of Women* produce a thick kind of context for the pawnbroker's woman question. Not only does Dostoevsky's character initially verify his idea of woman's devotion through one of the great classics of world literature—nothing less than the "love story" of Faust and Gretchen, which leads, exactly as in *A Gentle Creature*, to the woman's suicide; but he demands that his wife hand over her autonomy to him, just as the Grand Inquisitor demands that the people "lay the burden of their freedom at our feet" (*BK*, 259).

Dostoevsky inscribes Ivan's Inquisitor as a Faustian hero, and his pawnbroker as a miserable pretender to both those roles. The husband hopes, when he first meets the gentle creature, that her submission to him will secure a foundation and transform the uncertainty of a life in which money has been the central value. Crucial to Dostoevsky's exposure of the husband's psychology is the compounding of economics with erotics and metaphysics. The pawnbroker embodies, for Dostoevsky, the worst aspects of sexual uncertainty, religious skepticism, and profiteering. Each contributes to his anxiety and insecurity, as well as to his pathological quest for a foundation for his life, which in turn leads to the demand that his wife become a substitute for all he lacks. Like certain feminist "poststructuralist" critiques of "foundationalism," Dostoevsky's story exhibits more interest in what the search for security or foundation "authorizes" and "excludes," rather than with asserting what that foundation is.[28]

The pawnbroker's foundationalist fantasy, expressed by his obsessive need for security and control, disables him from acknowledging the otherness of his wife. His initial refusal to hear her voice or sympathize with her suffering buries him in a masculinist monologue. The pawnbroker's imposition of a "stern" and manipulative "silence" parallels the Inquisitor's insistence on "miracle, mystery, and authority" (BK, 255). His insistence that the gentle creature not "meddle" with his "affairs" is a trivial version of the Inquisitor's demand that Christ not "interfere" with his "work." Like the Inquisitor's demand that Christ sympathize with the Inquisitor's sacrifices for the people's sake, the pawnbroker demands that his wife "stand in homage before me because of my sufferings" (GC, 683). Like Christ's, the gentle creature's power comes not from force or argument but from her revealing a new life-interpretation to another and from her expressing a message through gestures and silence. The pawnbroker, like the Inquisitor, has reduced all human interactions to power struggles between the weak and the strong. If *The Legend* is about the Inquisitor's glimpse into a new world order he simultaneously acknowledges and refuses, *A Gentle Creature* is about the pawnbroker's belated breakthrough to another interpretation of life dependent upon his new view of women.

This breakthrough is resisted in a series of increasingly violent interactions. The young wife attempts to do some pawnbroking business herself. Her husband tells her that "the money [is] *mine*." He says that when he asked her to become his wife, he "concealed nothing from her." She reacts to this statement "suddenly" by "shaking all over" and becoming "a wild beast." When he tells her not to "meddle" in his "affairs," she laughs in his face and walks out on him like Ibsen's Nora in *A Doll's House* (but, of course, three years earlier) (GC, 687-8).[29]

What follows is an exposure of the pawnbroker's lies to his wife. She learns from Yefimovich, a former "regimental colleague" of her husband's, that he was turned out of his regiment for being a coward, that he wandered around Petersburg "like a tramp" for three years afterwards, "sleeping under billiard tables" (GC, 690). He lied to her abut being "a financier," lied about "concealing nothing." When he commits the last indignity by spying on her conversation with the tale-telling Yefimovich, the pawnbroker rationalizes the act by telling himself that he is witnessing "the flirtation of a witty, though vicious, creature to enhance her own value." Standing in a room behind closed doors and listening with a gun in his pocket, he discovers instead his wife's extraordinary wit and intelligence. But he also discovers something more terrifying to him: "her unquenchable faith in her ideals":

> For a whole hour I was present at a battle of wits between a woman, a most honorable and high-principled woman, and a man about town with no principles.

... And how, thought I, lost in amazement, how does this innocent, this gentle, this reserved woman, know it all? .... And how scintillating were her words and sly digs! What wit in her quick repartees! What withering truth in her condemnation! And, at the same time, what girlish artlessness! She laughed in his face at his protestations of love, at his gestures, at his proposals ... [and] the bubble of his conscience was suddenly pricked ....The whole truth rose up from her soul.... It was as though I had come across something I had known all my life. (GC, 691)

The pawnbroker brings "the scene to a sudden close by opening the door," grabbing his wife by the hand (as Yefimovich yells sarcastically, "I've certain nothing against the sacred right of holy matrimony"), and dragging her home. Once home, the gentle creature regards her husband with "a solemn and grim challenge in her eyes" and becomes interested in how he loads his gun. The narrator does not tell us her thoughts, but we can guess them from descriptions of her gaze, from the desperation of her attempt to shoot her husband, and from her final inability to commit murder as he lies sleeping on a bed.

She was looking straight at me. Straight into my eyes. And the gun was already near my temple. Our eyes met. But we looked at each other for no more than a second. With a great effort I closed my eyes again, and in that instant I resolved with all my strength I possessed not to make another movement, not to open my eyes, whatever happened.

The pawnbroker initially interprets his act as a victory: "I had crushed her already by my readiness to accept death, and now her hand might falter. Her former determination might be shattered against a new startling impression." He concludes that by his act of heroism, "she was conquered for ever, but not forgiven." But that night begins her sickness that lasts the whole winter (GC, 693-5).

Dostoevsky opens the story at this point to at least two diametrically opposite interpretations. In the first, the pawnbroker finally assimilates his wife's influence, becomes aware of his unjust and oppressive treatment of her, and resigns himself at the moment of crisis to being murdered by her. At the instant of eye contact over the gun, he communicates this to her and her love for him begins. In this nonfeminist version of the story, the reader receives the pawnbroker's words without irony, and with no sense of distinction between the teller and the tale. A few hours before she commits suicide, she "quite suddenly" comes to the pawnbroker and tells him "that she was guilty ... that her guilt had been torturing her all the winter ... that she appreciated my generosity very much," and that she would be a "true and faithful wife" (GC, 709).

But Dostoevsky's story also dialogically forks in another direction. It is clear that the pawnbroker exults in his wife's sickness. Her face in the "exhaustion after her illness" conveys gentleness and humiliation once more, and he is pleased again by "the idea of our inequality" (GC, 700). But as she recovers she begins to sing "as though the song itself were sick," and as the pawnbroker begins to hear "the poor cracked broken note" of her voice, the "scales" fall from his "eyes." He realizes that she sings for herself, that her voice is her own, that she has "forgotten all about" him. When he comes to her and she recognizes that it is "love" he "still wants," she becomes hysterical. The change he undergoes by hearing her "cracked" but authentic voice opens him to a desire for love. But it is too late. When he screams hysterically, "Make me your slave, your lapdog!" she weeps and says, "And I thought you'd leave me alone" (GC, 703-5).

The gentle creature's suicide follows quickly upon this scene and upon her protestations of wifely devotion. But they appear to be conventional words that cover the rage against injustice she has experienced, and they are "cracked" words that mark the death of her once energized rebellion. Once she is actually dead, having pitched herself violently out a window, the pawnbroker contemplates the words of her promises, asking questions that deconstruct his first interpretation of them. Engaged for the first time in his life with what Carol Gilligan calls the significance of woman's "different voice," the pawnbroker is stunned by a new kind of uncertainty. "Why did this woman die?" he asks himself. "Was she afraid of my love? . . . And was the question too much for her and did she prefer to die?" The question keeps "hammering at [his] brain."

The gentle creature asked him for only one thing, that he *let her alone*" and give her freedom. She answered his question, but his will to secure her ultimately interfered with his understanding of it. Wandering through his maze of interpretations, he decides that she "did not want to deceive me with a love that was only half a love, or a quarter of a love. Too honest. . . . I don't know whether in her heart she despised me or not" (GC, 711). Only after her death does he engage the question of her will, her point of view, her right to choose, and he is close to understanding her suicide as a protest.

In his preface Dostoevsky tells us that "a succession of memories which [the pawnbroker] recalls at last leads him inevitably to *the truth*, and truth inevitably elevates his mind and heart" (GC, 669). What is that "truth" for Dostoevsky? It is related to other truths represented by silent gestures, by Christ's kiss that ends his interview with the Inquisitor. Like the kiss that afterwards "burns in [the Inquisitor's] heart" although he "holds to his former idea" (*BK*, 262), the young wife's sacrifice transforms the pawnbroker although it is too late. What the pawnbroker "comes across" is the "truth" the woman herself acknowledges and that J. S. Mill acknowledged in perhaps the most famous male-authored "feminist" document of the nineteenth century. The question of "inequality" is only part of the question, and another question—women's struggle with men for their view of life and their ideals—arises. This question arises at the moment when the gentle creature becomes convinced that her husband "would kill her with the gun," and she levels it at his head.

> At that moment a struggle was going on between us, a life and death struggle, a duel in which—the coward of the day before who had even expelled by his fellow-officers for cowardice—was engaged. I knew it, and she knew it too, if she had guessed the truth and knew that I was not asleep.

The moment with the man, the woman, and the gun has been duplicated, in various versions, in Svidrigaylov's experience with Dunia Raskolnikova, and in Maria Lebyadnikova's exposure of Stavrogin and his "knife." It should now be superfluous to note that this moment in Dostoevsky metaphorizes the struggle between old-fashioned patriarchy and incipient feminist consciousness. In *A Gentle Creature* this moment also leads to the husband's discovery of what women want and the price they are willing to pay for it. "I should have *let you alone*," the pawnbroker says. "You would have talked to me only as a friend, and we should have laughed and been happy together." Twenty-five years her elder, he comes to a realistic assessment of himself and of the young woman's sexuality, an assessment that glances at the words of the "new" men of *The Eternal Husband* who swear to give their wives freedom of divorce and who criticize Velchaninov for his "barbarous" mores. But the pawnbroker's belated generosity is even more extreme:

> And even if you had fallen in love with another man, it wouldn't have mattered a bit. . . . Fall in love if you wish. . . . Oh I don't care what would have happened, only she would open her eyes just once!

The ending of the story contains Dostoevsky's message, which I do not find ambiguous. In this story, and with this ending, we need not *totalize* the notion of Dostoevsky's dialogism. Gary Saul Morson argues that the husband's "horror" lies in large measure in what he does not comprehend: "[T]he 'truth' is, in effect, his inability ever to reach the truth, his inevitable inarticulateness before the horror and his own responsibility for it."[30] But this endlessly deferred "truth" is too easy for Dostoevsky, whose polyphony does not finally exclude an ethics compatible with the most realized intuitions of twentieth-century feminism. The pawnbroker's nearly incoherent last state-ment is that of a man in pain who has destroyed what is most precious to him because he is culturally habituated—by *Faust* and economics and superman psychology—to deny his need for woman's friendship:

> Insensibility. Oh, nature! People are alone in the world. That's what's so dreadful. "Is there a living man on the plain?" cries the Russian legendary hero. I, too, echo the same cry, but no one answers. They say the sun brings life to the universe. The sun will rise and—look at it. Isn't it dead? . . . Dead men are everywhere. . . . "Men love one another!"—who said that? . . . No seriously, when they take her away tomorrow, what's to become of me? (*GC*, 714).

The nameless husband thus adds his experience to Russia's legendary heroes who now, through Dostoevsky, contribute to the discourse of feminism.

In *The Diary*, Dostoevsky devotes some twenty pages to the case of one Kroneberg acquitted for beating his daughter (*D*, 211-237). In the Kroneberg case, Dostoevsky asks one question over and over again: "What is [the lawyer's] purpose in denying so stubbornly the suffering of the little girl?" (*D*, 230). *A Gentle Creature* points to answers. It suggests that the denial of rights and the absence of women's voices in the "reformed" patriarchal legal practice constitute an evil. Dostoevsky's message mixes Christian forgiveness with feminist critique. If Fyodorov could imagine the marriage of East and West, drawing upon "Slavophilism and meteorology with equal facility,"[31] Dostoevsky can draw upon a cosmic "law" of Mother Russia and woman's suffering in his search for a new metaphysically gendered equation.

In his entry for September 1877, Dostoevsky imagines the future. The entry is called "A slight hint at the future intelligent Russian man. The unquestionable destiny of the future Russian woman." The section (*D*, 843-6)[32] begins with the diarist's discussion of what appears to be the Russian man's inferiority complex and his need for self-respect. Dostoevsky does not use this psychological term, but rather the earthy and untranslatable *samoplevaniye* (self-bespitting) to describe Russian self-humiliation and self-mockery. "Nowadays," he writes, "there are strange perplexities and strange anxieties," and Russians literally "fill themselves with fear" when the country achieves victories or successes, as in the Crimean War. In the style repeated throughout the diary, Dostoevsky imagines the voice of a typical Russian man responding with anxiety and "self-bespitting" to the aftermath of national success. "What appears after a victorious war," says this voice, "is self-confidence, self-glorification, and stagnation/depression" (*zastoy*). Dostoevsky argues that the war will "reveal many things" and "change many things"—a statement that moves toward the second part of his subject, women. It is here that the transition between the subject of men's stagnation and self-humiliation and the subject of *new women* begins: "Much will be revealed," he writes, "that used to be regarded by our clever-accuser types as trivial," but that is now a Russian "essence." This "essence" turns out to be the "craving for regeneration," a craving that will be expedited "practically" and with "modesty" by "new men" unafraid of self-respect: men who describe themselves as "bene-fitted by modern woman."

> But the principle and most salvational regeneration of Russian society will fall to the part of Russian women. . . . After the present war, during which the Russian woman has revealed herself so loftily, so brightly, so sacredly, no one can doubt the high destiny that awaits her among us.

Dostoevsky argues that "the age-old prejudices will finally fall, and that 'barbaric' Russia will show what place she will offer [*otvedet*] to the 'little mother,' the 'little sister' of the Russian soldier, that self-sacrificer and martyr for the Russian man." Dostoevsky's language becomes emphatic and lyrical. In my translation the impulsiveness of his diction is lost, but not his emphasis on the need for women to enter public institutions of "office" and the "professions":

> Can we continue to deny this woman, who has so obviously displayed her valor, the brimful equality of rights with the man in education, in the professions, in tenure of office—she in whom we now place all our hopes, after her exploit, in terms of the regeneration and elevation of our society! This would be shameful and unreasonable, especially because [this denial] would altogether depend on us [men], since the Russian woman of her own accord has over-stepped those stages [*sama pereshagnula te stupeni*] which until now had set the limits to her rights.

Dostoevsky's words resonate with a late-nineteenth-century sensibility that finds prejudicial laws against women to be a "shame" and an act of unreason. With words like "rights" and "professions," Dostoevsky joins thinkers like J. S. Mill whose personal experiences with emancipated women have transformed them. The novelist's attitude towards Jews and Russian Messianism may continue to shock his admirers, but his attitude towards women can now be understood to have stepped out of the racialist-nationalist and male chauvinist circle.

7

The Brothers Karamazov:
Rereading "the Feminine" and "the Corpse of the Father"

Discussing *A Gentle Creature* in the previous chapter, I drew a parallel between the philosophical underpinnings of the story and *The Legend of the Grand Inquisitor*. Tensions between a universalist, monologic, and totalized view of human relations and one grounded in freedom and uncertainty are at the core of the husband's and Ivan Karamazov's sufferings. While for Ivan the choice lies between recognizing difference or "uniting everyone at last into a common, concordant, and incontestable anthill" (*BK*, 259), the choice for the husband lies between attempting to "conquer" the gentle creature or leaving her alone in freedom.

The pawnbroker experiences these tensions personally through his relationship with a young woman. He does not elaborate philosophically upon why he finds the "inequality" between himself and his wife so "delightful," but his vision of the will-to-power is gendered. He does not say, like the underground man or the gambler, that "[s]avage, unlimited power, if only over a fly, is also a kind of pleasure," or that "[m]an is a despot by nature, and loves to be a tormentor." He does not rationalize the delight he takes in controlling his young wife by saying, as the Inquisitor says, that he is doing it for her (the people's) own good. The pawnbroker rationalizes his behavior by saying that J. S. Mill is wrong and that "a woman . . . simply must submit to her husband" because "women have no originality." His wife's originality is not discovered until after her death when the pawnbroker recognizes that his misogynist oppressions are the source of her suicide.

I have argued, building upon Dostoevsky's own interpretation of his story, that the husband achieves a belated revelation of the "truth" that his need to "secure" the woman's subordination destroys her. The husband's image of "love" is his "rebellious" wife's coming to him voluntarily and laying her life at his feet, an impulse that Ivan's Inquisitor argues is the essential arrangement for human happiness: "Man was made a rebel; can rebels be happy?" asks the Inquisitor of Christ.

> "You rejected the only way of arranging human happiness, but fortunately, on your departure, you handed the work over to us . . . you gave us the right to bind and loose. . . . Why then, have you come to interfere with us?" (BK, 251)

Parallels between the way the "gentle creature" and Christ are bound and loosed, and between the pawnbroker and the Inquisitor, resonate with important nineteenth-century debates about liberty, democracy, and happiness. Like other novelists who wrote after 1869 when Mill's *On the Subjection of Women* was published, Dostoevsky dramatized the effects of liberal and socialist ideas on male-female relations. Ideas about freedom and transforming culture are rarely represented in these novels as detached from ideas about women's sexuality, as shown in several canonical works written in England, France, and Russia in the decades after Dostoevsky wrote *A Gentle Creature* and *The Brothers Karamazov.* We might expect George Meredith's *The Egoist* (1879), for example, or Tolstoy's *Anna Karenina* (1875-7) and *The Kreutzer Sonata* (1889), or Thomas Hardy's *Tess of the d'Urbervilles* or *Jude the Obscure* (1893-6), if not Emile Zola's *Nana* (1880), to explore the woman question more profoundly and precisely than Dostoevsky does. Yet a rereading of his work yields a surprising depth of exposure in comparison.

With the character of Grushenka in *The Brothers Karamazov*, Dostoevsky breaks with a long-standing nineteenth-century literary tradition in which, as Karen Horney puts it in *Feminine Psychology*, "the adoration of 'pure' motherliness, completely divested of sexuality, [coexists with] the cruel destruction of the sexually seductive woman."[1] One need only think of the sexually energized Anna Karenina and Emma Bovary and their "inevitable" suicidal ends, of the last chapter of Hardy's *Tess* in which his voluptuous heroine is hanged, and of the disgusting "postules," "bubbling purulence," and "black ruinous hole" of Nana's face as Zola describes her on her death bed—not as a prostituted *demi-mondaine* exploited by men, but as a poisonously autonomous creature who has "assimilated" the "gutters"[2]—to appreciate Dostoevsky's positive view of strong feminine sexuality.

To understand how sexual conventions, religion, and the woman question illuminate each other in Dostoevsky's novels, we need a psychologically oriented language, particularly in a late modernist climate when problems of faith and God are often relegated to specialized theological discourses. Jung's rather than Freud's[3] theories provide a better frame for a discussion of feminine "spirituality" in Dostoevsky in relation to sexuality. Ann Belford Ulanov, a Jungian psychiatrist, describes "the feminine style of consciousness in the revelation of Christ" in a way that coheres with my rereading of *The Legend of the Grand Inquisitor*. Ulanov's phrase, "the redemption of the sexual polarity in the Incarnation,"[4] is close enough to some feminist notions of cultural androgyny, and to the Solovyevian religious ideas that intrigued Dostoevsky, to indicate how male-female relations in *The Brothers Karamazov* differ from those in other great nineteenth-century novels.

Mary Ellmann's description of how "the spiritual" in women is organized in Tolstoy's *War and Peace* indicates the contrast in Dostoevsky I am attempting to draw. For Tolstoy, as for Freud, "the mind was an instrument of aggression, and education the learning of systems of attack—which given to women would, he feared, destroy the man's ideal of their *delicacy*." In *War and Peace*, and in a more complex way in *Anna Karenina*, "the particular pleasure of the woman's mind is called its 'spirituality,' i.e., its separation from the purposeful and productive world of masculine thought." The reader can compare Katerina's or Grushenka's complicatedly sexualized expressiveness to this "virtue of dedicated imbecility . . . celebrated in [Tolstoy's] Natasha as the young mother, who studies nothing but the contents of soiled diapers."[5] Something like an ancient goddess-worship motif can be traced in the Karamazov father's and son's obsessions with Grushenka, and Katerina Ivanovna's "mad" wish to become Dmitri's God (*BK*, 189) has no parallel among the heroines or madwomen who populate other male-authored nineteenth-century novels. Dostoevsky's work contrasts with those in the inscriptions of his wish to release the symbolically "feminine" dimensions of "the spirit"—as evoked through sexy women characters as well as feminized male figures such as Myshkin, Ivan's Christ, and Alyosha—from bondage to a "Roman" culture associated with patriarchal tyranny and the repression of sensuality and freedom.

The writer's critique of "Rome," however, does not exclude compassion for the sufferings of those who reject the Russian Christ. In *The Diary*, Dostoevsky puzzles over the question of whether a woman who commits suicide without "faith in God" suffers more than one who does. In *The Gentle Creature* he shows that through the sorrow of losing his wife and confronting his guilt, the pawnbroker husband achieves the same release from a constricting faithlessness in human nature that the Inquisitor experiences momentarily as he feels Christ's kiss burning "in his heart."

After this kiss the Inquisitor lets "the prisoner" Christ go even as he "holds to his former idea" (*BK*, 262). Ivan Karamazov's Inquisitor retains the belief that human beings find the burden of freedom intolerable, and for this reason they will condemn, burn or crucify every liberating Christ in their midst as "the most evil of heretics" (BK, 250). With astounding irony, Dostoevsky represents the pawnbroker as crucifying "the feminine" in a way that makes the Inquisitor's treatment of Christ look tolerant in contrast. What the pathetic pawnbroker inadvertently accomplishes—the condemnation of a female rebel/heretic—the Inquisitor has the sense to refrain from doing to Christ a second time.

The gentle creature's rebellion is heresy in the sense that she disrupts the male-centered order of the husband's nineteenth-century culture, just as Christ disturbs the patriarchal-inquisitional order of fifteenth-century Seville. Women's relations to men in Dostoevsky can be read as replicating Christ's relation to men who have inherited but misinterpreted Christ's mission. This theme is represented through Sonya in *Crime and Punishment*, in a most perplexing form in *The Idiot*, and through Maria Lebyadkina in *The Possessed*. But the sentimental attachment to the infinitely meek man or woman whom Dostoevsky favors in his early work is missing after 1876. The gentle creature is not sacralized. She does not read the Bible to her pawnbroking husband. In *The Brothers Karamazov*, Grushenka's motherly feelings for Dmitri are linked to her seductive, erotic ones. Lise, Alyosha's "little demon," plays sado-masochistic games with the tender hero and lives in the novel to be loved and praised. What Grushenka and Lise share with the more complicated Katerina Ivanovna is a voice that articulates needs that cannot "continue to be denied." The question "How can we continue to deny Christ?" is connected in Dostoevsky to the question "How can we continue to deny this woman?"

Cruel images of those who deny faith in Christ haunt Ivan's imagination, but the image of "a gentle creature" who makes faith possible is also the source of his *Legend*. Men's relations to women are not directly represented in the Inquisitor's conversation with Christ, but only if we forget the context surrounding Ivan's "muddled poem," which is his doubt as to whether Katerina loves him or his brother Dmitri. Connections between men's doubting women's love and doubting their faith in God are made throughout Dostoevsky's work, but in *The Brothers Karamazov* Ivan is represented as having excellent reasons for suppressing these connections. As the carrier of atheistic doubt in the novel's discourse, Ivan has every reason to displace his unresolved relation with Katerina to an abstract level of contemplation in which the gendered connotations of the Inquisitor's and Christ's debate remain hidden. Ivan is caught philosophically between the Inquisitor's cynical argument for power and Christ's silent rejoinder of love. But he is also caught psychologically between his "Karamazovian" temptation to treat Katerina in the same way that his father and Dmitri treat women and the possibility of relating to her in freedom as suggested by his version of Christ.

Unable psychologically to inquisition himself directly about Katerina, Ivan writes a philosophical fable in which all his erotic and charitable, murderous and forgiving, power-hungry and freedom-loving impulses, but above all skeptical and faithful impulses are explored. The kiss Ivan inscribes into his poem in the finale provokes Alyosha to plagiarize it, but Ivan's poem also represents a wish to be kissed and forgiven by his feminine inquisitor, Katerina Ivanovna. It is at this point in *The Brothers Karamazov* that the religious question and the woman question meet most profoundly in Dostoevsky's work. But this is not to say that Dostoevsky himself realized the connection.

If, according to Bakhtin's reading of Dostoevsky, "life" exists in its potential, in its unceasing movement, in voices projected out towards others and into the future—and not in the fixities to which monologue aspires— Katerina's presence in *The Brothers Karamazov* is a kind of "feminist dialogics" linked to Ivan's dialogue within himself and with Alyosha as to whether God exists. Katerina attempts, like Ivan, to create a future for herself for which she has no language or model. She must piece together from other people's words and ideas, often contradictory on all sides, a self, a significance, and a faith in life. Katerina's "hysteria" can be understood as a language in search of a meaning beyond the identity her society offers. As "new" men and women who refuse to "spit upon themselves," Katerina and Ivan share a sometimes "demonic" pride that disables them from the love-in-humiliation and submission that Dmitri and Grushenka ultimately experience. As intelligentsia, Katerina and Ivan press against official versions of masculinity and femininity. Ivan's skepticism and his critique of all authority, including God's, is paralleled by Katerina's incipient feminism. Her "hysteria" mirrors his "brain fever." His obsession with collecting stories of abused children is echoed by her obsession to "save" first Dmitri and then, during the trial, Ivan himself. The new woman, like the new man, is a character in process—alienated, de-centered, and often on the verge of madness—the least resolved and most modern element in Dostoevsky's last novel.

Katerina's life is represented as a series of discontinuities and sudden changes. Early in Part One she is asking Dmitri for money to save her father; a few pages later she is suddenly an heiress and her father is no longer mentioned. She is contaminated on all sides by expectations and modernist problems that make Grushenka's life look traditionalist in comparison. Grushenka ("little pear") is a delicious Russian type, a dangerous but finally reformed femme fatale whose desires eventually conform to her society's ideals of Christian redemption. While Dmitri believes that Katerina "loves her own virtue, not me" (*BK*, 117); Grushenka finally loves Dmitri better than virtue, which satisfies him. In Grushenka Dostoevsky celebrates feminine sexuality and the loving power of a "disreputable" woman who foreshadows Joyce's Molly Bloom. In Katerina, on the other hand, Dostoevsky celebrates feminine aspiration and intellect but shows the woman besieged, a theme he shares with women novelists from Jane Austen through George Sand to Virginia Woolf.

Katerina is a complicated "new" type of woman, Suslovian in her confusions and her independence, humorless in her passion for autonomy: difficult for men to understand. She arrives in the town of "Beast Pen" (Skotoprigonyevsk) from St. Petersburg, perhaps a shock in itself. Her relationship to the characters is new, and unlike Grushenka she is at first protected from certain realities by her status as an "educated young lady." Inside the Beast Pen she encounters her fiancé, the eldest Karamazov son, a primal victim of mother neglect and father abuse, a man capable of brutal passions but finally willing to go to Siberia "for the wee one" (*BK*, 569, 507). Confessing to "games[s] of insect sensuality" with women (*BK*, 109), Dmitri's relation to Katerina is a test and a competition. She is the first woman, as he admits to Alyosha, whom he finds more than equal to himself:

> "I felt that 'Katenka' was not like some innocent institute girl, but a person of character, proud and truly virtuous, and above all intelligent and educated, while I was neither the one nor the other. You think I wanted to propose? Not at all, I simply wanted revenge because I was such a fine fellow and she didn't feel it." (*BK*, 111)

Dmitri's "incident" with Katerina dramatizes the class and money struggles that Dostoevsky engages as part of the woman question elsewhere. The scene reaches through Dostoevsky's work to the underground man's and Alexei's throwing money at Liza and Polina, money which the women hurl back in contempt; to the scene where Rogozhin attempts to buy Nastasya and succeeds in carrying her off in Part One of *The Idiot*; to the relationship of the pawnbroker and the gentle creature whom he marries because she is poverty-stricken. But Katerina and Grushenka differ from these women in a major respect, which indicates an evolution in Dostoevsky's awareness of women's changing status. Each has money and therefore more choice; neither Grushenka nor Katerina can be "bought" like Nastasya Filipovna or the poverty-stricken gentle creature. Although Grushenka's lower-class sexual powers compete with Katerina's "noble" class powers, each woman actively participates in culturally symbolic transactions involving money that allow her to remain independent of men's evaluations of her to some extent. Katerina suffers from the psychological detachment her social privilege, education, and wealth involves, but she is also the head of her household and in a position to "give" financially . Grushenka suffers from her reputation as a sexually "loose" woman whose money has been earned through her "old man," Samsanov, but she finally cannot be tempted by Fyodor Karamazov's offer of ten thousand roubles tied in red ribbon.

Grushenka's game with money, like Katerina's, takes the form of retaliation against men who believe that women are objects to be bought and secured. The feminist theme shared by the two very different women has its source in resentments grounded in being humiliated by men. The Polish officer who seduced Grushenka provokes in her the same wish for restitution and revenge that Katerina experiences with Dmitri. In retaliation for Dmitri's humiliating her, Katerina attempts to bind him to her by lending him money. Katerina and Grushenka attempt to use money to achieve power and independence, either through their understanding of the way money seduces (Grushenka), or of the way money creates guilt (Katerina).

As a "disreputable" woman, Grushenka is habituated to the connections between money and sex. Katerina's first experience with these connections is traumatic, intensified by her later realization that Dmitri has humiliated her further by telling Grushenka that she "came" to him as if she understood that such debts must be paid for sexually. Katerina's wish to experience relations with men on a "higher" level, emancipated from sordid sexist transactions, is from a feminist point of view understandable and admirable. Differences between Katerina's and Grushenka's attitudes to sex and money, to loving, giving, and getting, structure the novel's early "laceration" scenes, scenes that tempt the reader to choose between an intellectual and a sensual woman, between a "new" woman who is self-destructive and self-delusive, complex and aspiring, or a delightfully "fallen" woman who is sensual and simple, cunning but finally satisfied with the status quo. The tensions between Grushenka and Katerina may appear as a sub-theme to the grand theme of parricide, but these tensions affect every event in the novel. Without the motivation of his love for Grushenka and his debt to Katerina, Dmitri would never have shown up at his father's house on the night of the murder. Without the motivation of his love for Katerina and jealousy of Dmitri, Ivan would not have taken Smerdyakov into his confidence and laid the seeds of moral and religious doubt that provoke the "lackey" to murder their father, Fyodor Karamazov.

Until the night at his father's when Dmitri beats Grigory and runs to the inn for his orgy with Grushenka to discover that she loves him, Dmitri's character is nearly a parody of a man's obsession with male dominance. Confessing to Alyosha about Katerina earlier in the novel, Dmitri chooses a metaphor to describe his game with her that replicates Stavrogin's with Matryosha in "At Tikhon's." Like Stavrogin, whose rape of Matryosha engenders his dream of her returning to him as a stinging red spider, Dmitri understands himself as "bitten by a spider," poisoned by a "insect" resentment that reaches a crisis in his relationship to a woman who will not subordinate herself to him.

> "[Katerina] was there in the majesty of her magnanimity and her sacrifice for her father, and I was a bedbug. And on me, a bedbug and a scoundrel, she depended entirely . . . this thought, this spider's thought, so seized my heart that it almost poured out from the sheer sweetness of it. . . . I was breathless. Listen: naturally I would come the next day to ask for her hand, so that it would all end, so to speak, in the noblest manner, and no one, therefore, would or could know of it. . . . And then suddenly . . . someone whispered in my ear: 'But tomorrow, when you come to offer your hand, a girl like this will not even see you. . . . She'll have the coachman throw you out: Go cry it all over the town, I'm not afraid of you!' I glanced at the girl . . . . Anger boiled up in me. I wanted to pull a mean, piggish, merchant's trick. . . . I looked at this [woman] . . . with terrible hatred—the kind of hatred that is only a hair's breadth from love, the maddest love!" (*BK*, 113-4)

This extraordinary confession expresses the love/hate inspired in a traditional man by a "new" woman who is "not afraid" of him, even though, a moment before, she seemed "entirely dependent" on him. Katerina begins to carry the woman question of the novel when she and Dmitri are coerced into a mutually revealing dependence on one another, when each becomes pathologically engaged in proving something to one another. It is with the privileges of the male sex that Dmitri can humiliate Katerina, but it is with the privileges of her upper class, educated, and wealthy status that she can humiliate him. Dmitri is aware of her resentment: "You could see it in the look on her face," he says (*BK*, 114). While he resents the "noble" class power she claims over him, she resents the sexist system he symbolizes.

The connections between money, sex, and Katerina's need to make men feel her willpower have an earlier origin in her relationship to her father. He is man who is short five hundred roubles of government money and will face court-martial if Katerina does not come to Dmitri "secretly" to ask for it. Katerina is torn between allowing herself or her father to be humiliated (there is no mother in the picture), and she makes the virtuous daughter's choice. But because the man is her father, her position as a woman is finally worse than Grushenka's. Grushenka's deal with her surrogate father (once lover) Samsanov is without nuance and a matter of survival. Katerina is programmed early in her life to associate virtue with sacrifice, but she also links sacrifice for men's sakes with a deep humiliation and wish for compensation. The parallels between Katerina and Grushenka, as beautiful female commodities whom men attempt to buy as though they were prostitutes, are more developed versions of the Dunya-Sonya parallel made in *Crime and Punishment*. Yet unlike Sonya and Dunya, Katerina and Grushenka remain antagonists when other relationships in the novel appear to be resolved. Two different kinds of resentment, grounded in two contrasting experiences of femininity, carry the feminist themes of the novel through its last pages and beyond.

Alyosha's understanding of Katerina's "strong faith in herself" is partial, for he favors Grushenka's simplicity. As the narrator's beloved hero, Alyosha remains "chilled" and out of tune with Katerina (*BK*, 101); but this does not mean that the late-twentieth-century reader need be. When Alyosha describes how Ivan, sent by Dmitri to see Katerina, immediately "fell in love with her," and "is in love with her still" (*BK*, 112), we may wonder why Alyosha offers no analysis of why Ivan should love her, only one of why Katerina loves Ivan. Alyosha recognizes that before becoming intimate with Ivan, Katerina must work out her pain through Dmitri. He believes that Katerina was "tormenting herself with her affected love for Dmitri, out of some kind of supposed gratitude," but concludes that a "character like Katerina must rule, and she could only rule over a man like Dmitri but by no means over a man like Ivan" (*BK*, 186-7). Alyosha emphasizes Katerina's willpower, but does not set enough value on her wish to transform a sexist relation into friendship, expressed in her following protest:

> "I set myself only one goal in all of this: that [Dmitri] should know who to turn to, and who is his most faithful friend. No, he does not want to believe that I am his most faithful friend, he has never wanted to know me, he looks on me *only as a woman*." (*BK*, 147; emphasis added)

Katerina's addiction to Dmitri suggests a quest for acknowledgment of her humiliation, a cathartic working through of her relation to a "brutal" masculine type necessary for her later relation to the more complicated "new" man, Ivan. Insisting on pursuing her "love" for Dmitri, Katerina exposes herself to what Simone de Beauvoir calls "the brutish life of subjection to given conditions," the compulsion to "assume the status of the Other."

Katerina's displacement of resentment to "love," described in much commentary about her as masochism, is a symptom of her search for what "only woman" means. In a famous passage often quoted by feminists, Simone de Beauvoir gives voice to the feminine situation for which Katerina has no feminist words:

> Now, what peculiarly signalizes the situation of woman is that she—a free and autonomous being like all human creatures—nevertheless finds herself living in a world where men compel her to assume the status of the Other. They propose to stabilize her as an object and to doom her to immanence since her transcendence is to be overshadowed and forever transcended by another ego (*conscience*) which is essential and sovereign. . . . How can a human being in woman's situation attain fulfillment?[6]

Katerina struggles against the overshadowing of her powerful ego, and in doing so she attains neither the loving responses nor personal fulfillments that are Grushenka's. But Katerina also eludes the punishing "stabilization" or "immanence" of conventionalized femininity, and does not end up like Emma Bovary, Anna Karenina, Tess Durbeyfield, or Dostoevsky's "gentle creature" whose resolution to the "woman question" is an early death. Katerina's desire to be known fully as a person is attached to the wrong man, but Dostoevsky does not let us forget that as she makes demands of Dmitri, she is also attached to Ivan:

> "Why, why does he not know me, how dare he not know me after all that has happened? I want to save him forever. Let him forget that I am his fiancee! And now he's afraid before me because of his honour! He wasn't afraid to open himself to you, Alexei Fyodorovich. Why haven't I yet deserved the same?" (*BK*, 147)

Katerina's proud words request an answering voice from a man who will ratify her resentments and perceptions, but her search also draws her to Grushenka. As she speaks these words to Alyosha, she is overexcited because Grushenka is "in the next room." Katerina fantasizes that she can bond with and dominate the lower-class woman. Introducing Alyosha to Grushenka, Katerina "delightedly kissed her several times on her smiling lips. She seemed to be in love with her," especially her "swollen . . . lower lip" (*BK*, 149). Her response to Grushenka's sensuality is itself sensual, as if she trusts her sexual responsiveness with a woman more than with a man.

Katerina's "case" sets in motion much of what is undecidable in the novel besides the sexual psychology of women: whether, for example, Katerina's "hysterical" desire to be Dmitri's "God, to whom he will pray" (BK, 189), is madness or an incipient feminine theology; whether her imperiousness is a symptom of pathological egotism or a defense against the male tyrannies she has already experienced with Dmitri. Alyosha finds her powerful and strange:

> Her image he recalled as that of a beautiful, proud, and imperious girl. But it was not her beauty that tormented him, it was something else. It was precisely the inexplicable nature of his fear that now added to the fear itself.

Her psychological complexity, corresponding to Ivan's, evokes a sense of the uncanny in the men around her. "[T]rying to save . . . Dmitri, who was already guilty before her" (BK, 101-2), her strangeness suggests a compulsion to test her own and others' suffering and power through a "nobility" measured through men's ignobility.

Katerina's desire to bond with Grushenka is understandable if we grant the justice of her resentment. The chapters entitled "The Two Together" and "Strain [or lacerations] in the Drawing Room" represent fundamental differences between Grushenka, who is rooted in traditional folktale ethics of the "little onion," and the "new" woman Katya drifting in an identity without roots. Grushenka and Katya test their own and each other's powers, and the educated "noble" woman is decidedly at a disadvantage. Victor Terras emphasizes the scene's homoerotic elements, but what matters is that Grushenka wins in the game of female laceration because she is the mistress of the traditionally feminine role—a role from which history has expelled Katerina as it continues to expel women today.

The scene explores themes which Holquist, Wasiolek, and Belknap have found central to the novel's meaning:[7] the way psychological stress functions to reveal the characters and their ideas of life to one another. Less frequently described is the way that *nadryv* or "laceration" takes on a different dimension when women are participants. Katerina and Grushenka experience confrontations and strains in terms of specifically feminine sensitivities to words and gestures associated with sexual advances and humiliations by men. From the first chapter's description of Fyodor's cruelty to Alyosha's mother and his memory of her, to the last chapter, in which Alyosha encourages the boys to remember "only one good memory" to "serve[] some day for our salvation" (BK, 774), Dostoevsky's novel exposes the sources, methods, and consequences of male brutality for women.

Alyosha's memory of his mother, a memory with which at least two biographies of Dostoevsky begin,[8] is inscribed in *The Brothers Karamazov* as a primal scene that enables Alyosha's sensitivity to both Katerina and

Grushenka. In that scene a male child is held up to the icon of the Mother of God (with whom he confuses his own mother) in a gesture of salvation against a raging or mocking father. Such pictures, taken from life and exaggerated in fiction, mark "major turning points" in culture, suggesting new strains and stresses on women's lives "affecting childbirth, sexuality, family structure."[9] Crucial to Dostoevsky's image repertoire, the picture of the lacerated mother asking blessings for her child from a female deity is related not only to the image of Madonna and the Christ child, but to a particular historical moment in Russian history: the advent of serf emancipation with its accompanying dissolutions of patriarchal authority, and the beginning of the "woman question" as it emerged in the 1860s. As the male recipient of female intercession against the father's power, sculpted by his mother, Alyosha lives on the borderline between himself and others with more sensitivity than other men, and his identification with women relates to his early memories. Despite Zosima's teachings about compassion and forgiveness, something in Katya inspires the "chill [that] r[u]n[s] down [Alyosha's] spine the closer he came to her house" (*BK*, 101-2) because he does not recognize in her the requisite maternity he values in women.

Alyosha believes that a man could love Katya passionately but not for long. Her psychological complexity, like that of Freud's Dora, is described by Alyosha as well as by some traditional critics (Holquist, Wasiolek, Belknap) as illness rather than insight. But Katerina's affect on Alyosha suggests something more. Remembering the "strains" in the drawing room, he dreams all night as if the scene contained a clue to his mother-dominated hauntings as well as "to this rivalry [that] was all too important a question in the fate of his brothers and all too much depended on it." As Ivan's female "double," Katerina seems to suffer as he did from a maternal deprivation, a lack of primal care that makes her especially vulnerable to losing her identity or assimilating that of others. Grushenka wins in the game of female laceration in the drawing room because she is able to mold herself into being the mistress of traditionally feminine sexuality.

Katerina wishes to bond with Grushenka in sisterhood grounded in resentment at betraying men. At the same time she wishes to sever the bond with Dmitri that drives them together in the first place. Although Katerina hopes to discover in Grushenka the humiliated consciousness that lacerates her, Grushenka's responses are not at all what Katerina expects. Grushenka is at once the "angel" and the "slut" (*BK*, 147, 152), the *Other* and the *Same*. The knowledge that Grushenka delivers to Katerina, which drives Katerina to the final outburst in court, is that class and money cannot protect "woman" from being "only woman" in the world they share:

"So I'll go right now and tell Mitya that you kissed my hand [says Grushenka], and I didn't kiss yours at all. How he'll laugh!"

"You slut! Get out!"

"Ah, shame on you, young lady, shame on you! It's really quite indecent for you to use such words, dear young lady!"

"Get out, bought woman!" screamed Katerina Ivanovna. Every muscle trembled in her completely distorted face.

"Bought, am I? You yourself as a young girl used to go to your gentlemen at dusk to get money, offering your beauty for sale, and I know it." (*BK*, 152)

During their encounter Grushenka evidences the skill of a consummate actress playing "woman" to the hilt. She embodies what Katerina's culture values but what Katerina resists in herself. Grushenka is the text's walking "Venus de Milo," as the narrator suggests. Alyosha finds in her "an impossible contradiction" as she plays the obsequious "childlike" peasant girl to Katerina's "lady" and as she exploits a traditional feminine psychology by insisting on her inalienable (feminine) right to change her mind about promising to give up Dmitri: "Oh, no," she says, "I never gave you my word. It's you who were saying all that." Forging the construction of woman as "fickle," as having "such a tender, foolish heart," Grushenka cons her way through Katerina's attempts at manipulation and female bonding (*BK*, 147-152).

Appropriating the role of seducer, Katerina's appeal to Grushenka's feminine vanity by kissing her hand backfires. If a "denial of a sense of connectedness and isolation of affect may be more characteristic of masculine development" than feminine,[10] Katerina has experimented with a "masculine" persona, which Grushenka, exploiting "feminine" intimacy, uses against her. What horrifies Katerina is that woman's sexuality, whether withheld or sold to the highest bidder, signifies the same exchange. Grushenka says that the "lady" is merely the "slut" in disguise.

Lacerating herself with the idea that she is like Grushenka, and everybody knows it—"He told this creature what happened then, on that fatal . . . accursed day!" (*BK*, 153)—Katerina's hierarchy of values, her notions of "good" and "bad" women collapse. When she discovers that women like Grushenka can mock and reverse the double class and gender structures that frame women's lives, her consciousness of what feminists call "gendered subjectivity" is born. Alongside Ivan's articulation of skepticism, the voice of woman's consciousness in patriarchal society asserts itself through Katerina's hysteria. Grushenka, like many of Katerina's critics, sees nothing in Katerina but female jealousy and competition. From this moment, Grushenka becomes Katerina's demonic alter ego, an inner self with which she struggles through and beyond Dmitri 's trial.

By the time the narrator of *The Brothers Karamazov* brings the reader into court with the lawyers, the accused, Alyosha, Grushenka, and Katerina Ivanovna, she will be known more familiarly as "Katya." She listens while the lawyer for Dmitri's defense argues that Fyodor Karamazov was not a "real father." Fetyukovich implies that some fathers are so cruel they deserve to die and that their murderers deserve our sympathy. The narrator seems particularly surprised that the "ladies" in the audience (who *have* fathers) are moved by this argument. But he also emphasizes that "our peasants" (who *are* fathers and make up the jury) ultimately "stand up for themselves," remain unmoved, and render a verdict of guilty against Dmitri as parricide (*BK,* 753).

The responses of the court are divided in terms of gender, with the male narrator recording the events. Part of the emotional strain on readers of the novel involves making a decision in favor of interpretations based on attitudes toward a male-voiced narration, further engaging attitudes toward patriarchal legal and social structures. Katya's interruption in the court's all-male discourse is presented as a kind of scandal. Late-twentieth-century readers are compelled by the events at Dmitri's trial to confront their allegiances to patriarchy, their ambivalence about it, their anxiety about what sort of world they would occupy without it, but also their pleasure in symbolically destroying it, a pleasure voiced by Lise, who reminds Alyosha that "everybody loves it that [Dmitri] killed his father" (*BK,* 583).

The confrontation with a nineteenth-century patriarchal structure in which fathers can legally torture their children and wives is emphasized in the opening chapter through Alyosha's memory. Katya's confession to the court of Dmitri's betrayal of her carries that memory into the present. She forges the link between the sexist crimes of the father and the son, a link that some traditionalist critics, influenced by Freudian interpretations of female "hysteria," reduce to masochism or "a purposeful and pleasurable self-hurt " related to the "impulse we all have to make the world over into the image of our wills."[11] But Katya's impulse to transform the world is one she shares with Dostoevsky himself, and it should not be reduced to her revenge upon Dmitri. Symptomatic of a larger wish to destroy conventions of male domination that victimize Ivan as well as herself, Katya's wish for self-empowerment appears less a feminine sin than a feminist challenge.

Her situation and words mirror interpretive problems that parallel those of Freud's *Dora,*[12] a text in which Freud verifies, as do Freudian readings of

The Brothers Karamazov, the psychoanalytic "truth" that frigidity is the "cornerstone of hysteria and its most profound symptom."[13] Katya's case, like Dora's, has frequently been handled through a "patriarchal" critique of femininity that obscures the woman's own story. On the other hand, the feminist theory that hysteria is a "political weapon" seems alternately reductive, and even perhaps romantic in Katya's case.[14] Parallels between Dora and Katya nevertheless expedite discoveries about the function of women's voices in *The Brothers Karamazov*. Like Dora, who "believes (and Freud agrees) that she is being used as a pawn in a game between her father and Herr K., the husband of her father's mistress,"[15] Katya knows she has been a pawn in the game between Grushenka and Dmitri involving Dmitri's father. Like Dora's, Katya's hysteria appears as a form of revolt against male power, which Dostoevsky's narrator describes as Dmitri's "betrayal." As in the case of interpreting Dora, there is much in Dostoevsky's text regarding Katya to convince us that "men" believe that "femininity, bondage, and debasement [are] synonymous." On the other hand, there is much in Freud's *Dora*, as there is much in Dostoevsky's *The Brothers Karamazov*, that reveals how Dostoevsky's and "Freud's concept of the feminine was incomplete and contradictory." While Dostoevsky's narrator acknowledges his uncertainty about Katya, Freud denies it by suggesting that he had "restored what is missing" in Dora's "fragmentary" account.[16]

In both cases, the unsolved meaning of female hysteria generates anxiety in the narrators. In both, the text's gender troubles invite rereadings. These troubles may account for an impression that *The Brothers Karamazov* has not one but two endings, that in the last two chapters polyphony explodes to tell differently gendered stories. Five of the novel's chapters are particularly concerned with differences between how men and women see the world: "The Two Together" (Book 3, ch. 10) which resonates with "Strain [or Lacerations] in the Drawing Room" (Book 4, ch. 5), both of which concern Grushenka's and Katya's relationships with men; "A Sudden Catastrophe" (Book 12, ch. 50), in which Katya reveals Dmitri 's letter; and the last two chapters of the Epilogue. The different endings for the novel in "The Lie Becomes Truth" and "Ilyucheshka's Funeral" dramatize alternate ways of envisioning human relations. While Alyosha's life solution inscribed by the boy's last "hurrah" encourages a traditional ending in which parricidal impulses are resolved and women are absent, the *other* last chapter keeps alive the questions about patriarchy and its consequences for both men and women.

As the most difficult of the symbolic Karamazovian "sisters," Katya is Dostoevsky's last incarnation of the woman problem. Like Dunya, Polina,

Nastasya, Liza Tushina, and "the gentle creature," Katya has been violently dominated (humiliated, harassed, bullied, exposed to rape) by a man who is later "tried" or exposed by the woman's words, gestures, and in the case of the pawnbroker's wife, by her act of suicide. While such scenes have been a sensational staple in the gallery of male-female confrontations in Dostoevsky's works, what marks off Katya's trial of Dmitri from the others is its fully *public* character. Her reading of Dmitri's letter to the court, like Ivan's reading of his *Legend of the Grand Inquisitor* to Alyosha, positions her on both sides of the "masculine" (autonomous/dominant) and "feminine" (dependent/submissive) dualism as it is constructed in Russian society.

She plays out the role of Dmitri's inquisitor as well as, paradoxically, the Christ who might save Ivan. Her testimony seems to the narrator as if she is "throw[ing] herself off a mountain," an image that echoes the moment in *The Legend of the Grand Inquisitor* when Satan tempts Christ to "prove what faith you have in your Father" by "cast[ing him]self down" from "a pinnacle of the Temple" (*BK*, 255). The resonances between the two "falls," the one resisted and the other accomplished, plus the resonances between earthy and heavenly authorities, forge links between feminist and religious disenchantments with traditional patriarchy. Or as Fetyukovich reminds the court, everything has stemmed from mainly *"one fact: the corpse of his old father"* (*BK*, 741)—a phrase that resonates with *the death of God*.

During Dmitri's trial Katya becomes the interpreter of other women's situations, particularly those connected with skepticism about the father's authority in the widest sense. The death of the father makes everybody in the novel articulate, and Katya's voice emerges more powerfully as the fantasy of herself as a martyr collapses. She confesses her resentment about being betrayed by Dmitri, and in the process reveals her deeper link to Ivan.

> "How, how could [Dmitri] *not* understand that I was telling him right to his face: 'You need money to betray me with your creature, here is the money, I'm giving it to you myself, take it, if you're dishonorable enough to take it . . . !' I wanted to catch him out, and what then? He took it, he took it and went off and spent it with that creature there, in one night. . . ." (*BK*, 688)

Condemning Dmitri and "shuddering with malice," Katya's discovery of her resentment against male dominance is tragically belated in one sense but therapeutic in another. Her public confession propels her into recognizing the delusion of her self-identification as a "noble" traditionalist woman who sacrifices for men who do not appreciate her. With the collapse of this delusion, Katya is ready to turn towards the uncertainty of her relationship with Ivan. Everything about this potential relationship is difficult and un-formed, a psychological chrysalis. Ivan lies sick with brain fever; Katya is hysterical. Her situation sets off a train of self-contradictory interpretations on the narrator's part that suggests her interesting future.

As evidence is "extract[ed]" from "the raving hysterical woman," her words move closer and closer to revealing her closeness to Ivan: "He could not bear it that his own brother was a parricide!" Katya shouts. "Already a week ago I saw that he had become ill from it . . . and all because of the monster, all to save the monster!" Through her insistence on Dmitri's monstrosity, Katya's suffering through her father and through her culture comes to a symbolic head. Her insistence that Dmitri is the murderer is psychologically over-determined by her need to vent hatred for a male-dominated system that continually humiliates her. The narrator describes her as "gloating" in her wish to "ruin" Dmitri, as "hurrying convulsively," and as giving vent to "hysterics, sobbing and screaming" (*BK*, 692). But the turns and twists of the narrator's interpretations and descriptions of her behavior raise more ques-tions than they resolve.

> Oh to be sure, one can speak thus and confess thus only once in one's life—in the moment before death, for instance, mounting the scaffold. But it was precisely Katya's character and Katya's moment.

The narrator's words seem especially "overpopulated"[17] in reference to her. Katya speaks as if in "the moment before death," which recalls Dostoevsky's experience before the firing squad for his involvement in the Petrachevsky circle. In both cases the speaker risks death for criticizing a powerful authoritarian structure, and Dostoevsky's language connects Katya's resistance to Russia's sexual politics to his own memory of political resistance. *The Brothers Karamazov*, evolving in polyphonic complexity as Dostoevsky writes the trial sequence, suggests that the patriarchal (Czarist, Russian Orthodox) world of allegiances is being dismantled by some one else's words—that the "teller" and his "tale" may be suffering the same disjunction as does the female "hysteric." Dostoevsky's narrator does not linger over this possibility, but jumps ahead to another interpretation of Katya's action in court.

> It was the same impetuous Katya who had once rushed to a young libertine in order to save her father; the very same Katya who proud and chaste, had just sacrificed herself and her maiden's honor before the whole public by telling of "Mitya's noble conduct," in order to soften at least somewhat the fate in store for

him. So now, in just the same way, she again sacrificed herself, this time for another man, and perhaps only now, only that minute, did she feel and realize fully how dear this other man [Ivan] was to her!

This interpretation, however, is interrupted by another: "was she lying about Mitya in describing her former relations with him?" And again by another: "or perhaps this strained love would have grown into real love, perhaps Katya wished for nothing else, but Mitya insulted her to the depths of her soul with his betrayal, and her soul did not forgive. . . . She betrayed Mitya, but she betrayed herself as well!" (BK, 691-2). As the focus of a multitude of interpretations—including Grushenka's that Katya is Dmitri's "serpent"—Katya's meaning eludes the narrator's grasp.

Caught between arguments by the defense and the prosecution, and by the women's agenda that Katya's words suggest, the courtroom is immersed in reevaluations of values and in quasi-feminist threats. Through Katya the choice between condemning and exonerating Dmitri is intensified. Her testing of Dmitri's capacity to betray her instantiates her suspicion that men cannot love "independent," "proud" and "educated" women with "princi-ples"—that women like herself will remain unloved. By the end of her confession, Katerina knows herself to be cast off the "mountain" of the traditional male-female relational structure. "The tension broke, and shame overwhelmed her" (BK, 691). At the same time she moves toward a new identity.

Katya is not redeemed within the conventional Christological pattern that frames Dostoevsky's imagination, but neither is she stabilized as the negative pole to Grushenka's positive goodness. Diane Oenning Thompson argues that "in a nineteenth century novel, the redemptive pattern has to be a memory structure (a memory of a memory)."[18] What we know of Katya's "memory structure" involves an absent mother, a wish to sacrifice herself and "save" men (her father, Dmitri, then Ivan), and various acted-out and exper-imental identities that fall away during her testimony at Dmitri's trial. As a "new woman" Katya cannot identify herself as a femme fatale, as Grushenka does, by exploiting her own sexuality, making money through Samsanov, and playing men off against each other. Nor can she totalize herself as the good mother, as the finally penitent Grushenka tries to do. Katya's social position and education at "the finest institutions for young ladies" imprisons her psychologically in a "pedestal theory" reinforced by her virginity. Her protest against Dmitri is a private release from sexual as well as social repression, a riot against male chauvinism that parallels the ladies' near "riot" in response to the verdict of "guilty" enforced by the all-male jury (BK, 753).

Through Katya, Dmitri learns in court that he is being tried as a victimizer of women as well as a murderer of fathers. At the same time Ivan, experiencing his devil hallucinations at home, is on trial for his ambivalence about patriarchal institutions and God, associated with his ambivalence about loving Katya and community. Dmitri's outcry to Katya in court, asking her to forgive him, marks the moment he discovers the differences between traditional and futuristic forms of the "feminine." In response to her reading of his letter to her, he cries, "If I hadn't been drunk I'd never have written it . . . !" (BK, 689). This response echoes the excuses of drunken men tried, as described in Dostoevsky's *Diary*, for treating their women like cattle or chickens. Katya's testimony makes clear that Dmitri cannot understand why he is being tried for parricide unless he understands his woman problem. Ivan cannot solve his religious question without simultaneously solving his God problem, his father problem, and his relation to Katya. Katya cannot solve her "Dmitri" or "Ivan" or "father" problem without facing her society's male sexism.

In *The Brothers Karamazov*, each brother's attitude to fathers, to God, and to modernist skepticism is turned and twisted by his relation to a woman. Releasing the repressions that block men's insights into the social and sexual orders, women interpret men's dreams. Lise interprets the dream of demons and pitchforks she shares with Alyosha; Grushenka interprets Dmitri's dream of the "wee one" to his brothers. Dmitri's dream inspires him to ask "why is the wee one crying?" and "why are these burnt-out mothers standing there?" (BK, 507). Grushenka's transformed image as the good mother influences him to "go to Siberia" for "that wee one" even though he is no murderer (BK, 569). Henceforth he will identify his manhood with compassionate maternity, and he will make claims about the nature of women's love, believing that every man needs to be under some woman's thumb.

Katya also stimulates Ivan's capacities for new kinds of dreaming. His *Legend of the Grand Inquisitor* ends with a longed-for kiss. The hallucinated devil speaks a language of double-entendre that suggests how Ivan's disenchantment with "God" and "man" is fused with his disenchantment with woman's love. The devil's "method" is to "sow just a tiny seed of faith" in Ivan by "leading [him] alternately between belief and disbelief " (BK, 645), a method that mirrors Katya's erotic tormenting of Ivan with doubt about Dmitri. Ivan's madness, linked to his complicity in Smerdyakov's murder of their father, is also expressed by his inability to "talk" to Katya, as Alyosha talks to Lise and as Dmitri talks to Grushenka. Discussions between Ivan and Katya are hidden behind "doors" in the text, suggesting that their language cannot fit the frame of traditional love affairs. Ivan's and Katya's selfhoods may be struggling through "Freudian" (Western) scientific models that Dostoevsky (before Freud) dramatizes and critiques. While for Freudians "the postreligious 'scientific spirit' is a mental and cultural advance, through the agency of renunciation . . . and beyond Christian illusion,"[19] for Dostoevsky neither the scientific nor the religious view structures Katerina's and Ivan's love.

Each brother is exposed and broadened by women, and each woman's identity is realized by her resistance to men. Alyosha, teased by Lise because he wears "skirts," is embarrassed into moments of transformed insight by her expectations of what he will become as her future husband. Lise's sickness, like sand irritating an oyster, produces pearls of psychological insight that Alyosha's health denies. He needs "the little demon" as the voice that humanizes and undermines his utopian and idolatrous tendencies. "Wickedness is sweet," Lise says. "Everyone denounces it, but everyone lives in it, only they all do it on the sly and I do it openly" (BK, 173). If Lise undermines Alyosha's overly determined goodness through naughty girlish irony, Grushenka detonates the violently virile Dmitri through her erotically maternal force,[20] and Katya's hysteria dives deep enough to contact Ivan's madness. Women's capacities to transform men are associated with the powers of earthy sexual attraction (Grushenka), with the sharpening of the imaginative powers sometimes associated with disease (Lise), and with a strained and evolving intelligence (Katya). Each woman's powers arise from their specifically feminine social positions. Lise's hysteria, like Katya's, is a result of unlived life, of powers unused and repressed. Each woman has a motive for wanting Fyodor Karamazov dead, for the "father" symbolizes the order that frames and represses her.[21]

Like the brothers, Katya, Grushenka, and Lise are each complicit in the murder of Fyodor Karamazov; but they "love it," as Lise says, in different ways. Lise loves Fyodor dead because the event of his death opens her doors to the world. Gossiping and interpreting motives, she can indulge in forbidden self-expressions and conversations; in challenging and "wicked" worldviews that make her feel less cloistered and more alive. "Wicked" imaginings are the surrogate lives that Lise's physically and emotionally confined world denies to her. Grushenka loves Fyodor dead, on the other hand, because his death detonates her narcissism, the femme fatale's fantasy of having men die for her. His actual death stirs her impulses of responsibility. For the first time in her life she understands the consequences of her actions in terms larger than self-interest. Katya loves the idea of the father's corpse for the most philosophically complex reasons. Karamazov's death enables Katya to adjudicate, to condemn, but also to discover who and what she truly hates and loves—a freedom she denied to herself before the moment of the trial.

Reading Dostoevsky against Tolstoy, George Steiner reminds us that Dostoevsky gathered materials for the fictive trial of Dmitri Karamazov from the real trial of the feminist-terrorist Vera Zasulich. The association suggested to Dostoevsky "spiritual links between a private act of parricide and the attempts of a terrorist on the life of the Czar—the father—or one of his chosen representatives."[22] Zasulich's attempt on the notorious police prefect Trepov signaled a feminist political assault that paralleled the psychological struggles women experience with men as dramatized in *The Brothers Karamazov*. In renouncing obedience to the fathers and recognizing a world beyond the one bounded by such obedience, the women of Dostoevsky's last novel suggest connections between dialogic poetics and the feminization of culture.

That the real Vera Zasulich was acquitted by a "jury that shared her outrage over the beating of a political prisoner," that she had to be "spirited out of Russia by her comrades when the czar ordered her held pending further instructions,"[23] influenced Dostoevsky when he invented Dmitri's fate. At the end of *The Brothers Karamazov*, Dmitri's comrades, like Zasulich's, are making plans to spirit him away so that he will not face the horrors of Siberian exile. Alyosha, the most recognizably Christ-like character in the novel, is involved in these plans, as well as the difficult and rebellious Katerina, and of course, Grushenka. Yet the two women are still quarreling at the very moment of planning, not about Dmitri but about their identities as women.

This leads to the problem of the novel's resolutions in the final chapters. It ends in two ways—one cast in the frame of hagiography, male bonding, and ethical Christian closure; the other in modernist ambiguity and gender troubles linked with philosophical skepticism. The first ending is represented through Father Zosima's teachings about love and the "mysterious sense of our living bond with the other world." The "mysterious sense" is engendered by reparenting oneself with a good father (what the boys find in Alyosha). But neither Katya nor Ivan are reparented in any way. Katya, unlike Grushenka, displays few maternal traits. Like Ivan, she is not "good" in Zosima's sense, nor will she become Ivan's surrogate mother. Katya and Ivan thus remain alone upon "bad" modernist borders, orphaned to the past as modern readers may find themselves orphaned. While Grushenka's erotic-religious solution involves her sacrificing femme fatale cunning to a type of traditional maternal loving, Dmitri's erotic-religious solution sacrifices male dominance to female dominion. His patriarchal Christianity assimilates the "feminine" as it also conveniently detonates it. In contrast, Ivan's and Katya's incomplete relationship is framed within their "abusing" a God who makes women and children suffer. This is a bad "God" whose "corpse," incarnated in Fyodor Karamazov, Dostoevsky never quite succeeds in burying.

In "Ilyucheshka's Funeral," however, the bad father *appears* to be dead. The all-boy audience cheers the arrival of the good father Alyosha, and women are decidedly invisible. If this ending strains modern sensibility as it attempts to erase the complexities the novel has disclosed, it is because the next-to-last chapter speaks to us more clearly than it did for Dostoevsky in 1881. In "The Lie Became Truth" Grushenka and Katya speak to each other in "venomous voice[s]" that refuse to be silenced by men's words. Alyosha and Dmitri struggle when Dmitri says to Grushenka, "You don't want to forgive!" Although Alyosha intervenes, shouting at his brother, "Mitya, do not dare to reproach her!" he only exacerbates what he has come to resolve. Alyosha is not forceful in his insistence upon mutual forgiveness. The women remain unruly. As he catches up with the fleeing Katya, her words resonate with a venom that presages a new version of love, aimed at constructing a value for the rebelling women:

> "No, I cannot punish myself before that one [Grushenka]!" [says Katya]. "I said 'forgive me' to her because I wanted to punish myself to the end. She did not forgive. . . . I love her for that!" (*BK*, 767)

The last image of Katya is that her "eyes flashed with savage wickedness," the wickedness of a rebellion and skepticism she shares with Ivan. Katya loves Grushenka because she remains independent of the demand for "forgiveness" enforced by the most gentle carriers of patriarchy, Alyosha and Dmitri. If feminist critiques of Freud's *Dora* suggest that "the indeterminacy of sex roles, like the indeterminacy of narrative form, represents a state of not being in control,"[24] Katya's indeterminate configuration in the text's Christological structure produces the central loophole in the narrative. She and Ivan are the "individuals" in the novel whose independence presents the greatest challenge to Alyosha's (and Dostoevsky's) final solution. They remain persons who set themselves up as "individuals[s], proprietor[s] of [their] own nature[s], which [they] pit against the nature of others."[25]

The transformation of Katya's perceived "wicked" nonsubmission depends on the possibility of male-female relations transcending a patriarchal dispensation. The tale called *The Brothers Karamazov* is not contained by its teller/narrator, not even by its author, and it is not only about brothers. Dostoevsky's last novel envisions transformed men and women living together as they confront the still-warm father's corpse.

Conclusion

DOSTOEVSKY AND GENDER CRITIQUE

"Strong" critics of the past two decades have undermined several ideas that have sustained readers of Dostoevsky for generations. Roland Barthes and Foucault argued for the death of the author, Hayden White for the death of history or at least the fictionality of all historical schemes.[1] Feminist critics have argued that "men are not born with a faculty for the universal," although "the universal has been, and is . . . appropriated by men"[2]—with Dostoevsky offered up as no exception among appropriators. This feminist skepticism is what I have attempted to refine in the preceding chapters first by suggesting that Dostoevsky's greatness is related to his exposure of what he calls "Russian man's illness" and what I call masculinist disease; second, by indicating points of contact between some kinds of modern feminism and Dostoevsky's exhaustively dialogical autocritique; and third, by suggesting the significance of Dostoevsky's God-discourse as it relates to gender issues.

What is appropriated in Dostoevsky's as well as other male-authored writings, one feminist argument suggests, is a "world" constructed by men without including women's desires or voices within it. But Dostoevsky's work shows that "the feminization of literature" and debates about "the woman question" can be described as man-centered only if we reduce "feminism" to a monologic discourse written only by women or if we identify it with a contemporary concept of liberty disassociated from nineteenth-century Russian concerns. Laura Engelstein has argued that forms of gender critique were operating in Dostoevsky's Russia. She shows the ways in which gender issues were obvious to the Russian intelligentsia who observed the court system's sexually asymmetrical definitions of crime and its meting out of punishment. I have argued that Dostoevsky's work manifests an immersion in these same gender issues, and that a rereading in terms of them has become appropriate at the end of this century.

But approaching Dostoevsky with a focus on the problem of sexual difference needs some further theoretical justification. There is no *one* gender theory or *one* feminist conversation; rather, there are different kinds of feminisms. Throughout this book I have quoted from various kinds, some incompatible with others. If Dostoevsky makes contributions to feminist and gender discourses now, which kinds are verified by his insights? The answer bears upon quarrels among feminist theorists themselves, which Toril Moi's response to Luce Irigaray's notion of "the feminine" exemplifies: "Any attempt to formulate a general theory of femininity will be metaphysical," Moi argues. "This is precisely Irigaray's dilemma: . . . she falls for the temptation to produce her own positive view of femininity. But, as we have seen, to define 'woman' is necessarily to essentialize her."[3] The problem of "essentializing" or universalizing "woman" remains at the core of the debate among contemporary feminists, as it remains for those who attempt to interpret "the feminine" in Dostoevsky. Feminist literary criticism of male-authored novels has tended to move between two opposite scenarios: one claims that men and women share the same desires and potentials, but that men (and male authors) repress this knowledge and stereotype women; the other claims that men and women are radically inscrutable to one another,[4] so that women, if they want to know about themselves, should write their own books.

While the latter suggests sexual essentialism, the former explains perceived differences between men and women literary characters by describing the author's time-period or his personal prejudices. One kind of feminist analysis tends toward a carnal hermeneutics, emphasizing women's different physical or sensual apprehension of the world and the idea that "discourse is sexed."[5] The other emphasizes the socially constructed subject, with one radical version leading to the notion that gender can be indeterminate or can "float" between men and women as a signifier.[6] But the idea that "the feminine" is *only* socially produced leads to a paradox that has been used to support some Slavists' avoidance of feminist terminology altogether. Elizabeth Grosz describes it as follows:

> If we are not justified in taking women as a category, then what political grounding does feminism have? Feminism is placed in an unenviable position: either it clings to feminist principles, which entails its avoidance of essentialist or universalist categories, in which case its rationale as a political struggle centered around women is problematized; or else it accepts the limitations

patriarchy imposes on its conceptual schemas . . . and abandons the attempt to provide autonomous, self-defined terms in which to describe women and femininity.[7]

Caught in a conflict between standards of intellectual rigor and the effort to liberate women in and outside texts, some feminists argue that feminism needs to acknowledge its immersion in "patriarchal" frameworks and begin its critique from there. In this book I have understood the word "patriarchal" to refer not to a specific language of "men" but rather to a harsh social and legal system that some members of the Russian intelligentsia of both sexes sought to transform. The idea of a feminist no-man's-land from which to critique Dostoevsky's novels does not seem helpful, since there is no essentially "woman's language" I can't, in principle, share with men. The debates on parricide in the trial scenes of *The Brothers Karamazov* "speak" to women like Katerina Ivanovna of her resentment of the male-dominated world that humiliates her. The subject of father-killing is not confined to father-son relations or a male audience but is part of a larger social frame that includes women's struggles with symbolic fathers and traditional roles. Joseph Frank has recently (1993) described Dostoevsky's "grand dialogue with his time in all its aspects, from sensational crimes . . . to the great philosophical debates over the destiny of Russia and the existence of God"—and his effort "to establish contact with the Other on every level."[8] When traditionalist commentators comfortably employ words originally associated with de Beauvoir's feminist critique of male dominance (woman as the "Other"), Dostoevsky is *already* being reread from an interpretive perspective in which feminism has been assimilated. What Bakhtin describes as Dostoevsky's polyphony is not incompatible with the idea of "floating" signifiers, sexual or otherwise, that are part of a world conceived as unfinalized. Bakhtinians, as well as feminists who deconstruct sexual essentialism, might agree that both men and women in Dostoevsky's novels are "populated" by various voices, modes of thought and feeling, and interpretations of the world, all of which remain in open process until each novel ends.

But the Bakhtinian account of discourse as gender neutral does not accord with interpretations of how that world *feels and appears* to Dostoevsky's women who do not have access to the intellectual culture and social powers that men do. The novels offer us no female intellectuals of Ivan Karamazov's stature, and debates about "the woman question" are waged mainly between men. Yet women, like men, struggle with faith and skepticism and with what Isaiah Berlin calls "negative" and "positive" freedom; with the difference that men are more able than women to act upon negative freedom as license, freedom as a release from social responsibility or from "God's law." Dostoevsky's heroines have less access to the educated languages of philosophical paradox, to ideas that arise from contact with centers of power (academies, churches, government); and this difference is not severable from male-dominated social structures or from women's sexual vulnerability. Dostoevsky represents nineteenth-century Russian women's access to important debates between Slavophiles and Westerners, progressives and traditionalists, conservatives and revolutionaries, Christians and atheists, as marginal. But women themselves, as figures of influence and force, are not marginalized.

What some commentators have described as woman's "superior" position in Russian literature and in the Eastern Church indicates the oxymoron (*superior inferiority*) that "the feminine" evokes in Dostoevsky. In traditional commentaries of the novels, women's powers to influence men are understood to emerge paradoxically from their legal and sexual disempowerment, from a Russian context in which women's sufferings are closely associated with Christian martyrdom and crucifixion. What must now be added to this commentary is a recognition of the way Dostoevsky's "modern" women attempt to overcome not only their own cruel and self-destructive desires, but patriarchy's legal, social and psychologically supported cruelties against them. A traditional reading of the novels concludes that women's task is to embrace love rather than (feminist) resentment or revolution. This accords with Dostoevsky's professed commitment to the Eastern Orthodox "aim in life" which is "not to get into another world, but to work toward the deification of the world in which we find ourselves." To work toward salvation for "creation as a whole," with "our only hope for salvation lying in self-forgetfulness and *active* love in the world,"[9] involves a problem for women, however; for it is exactly their limitations as *actors* in the world that make their possibility of salvation different.

The problem of women and action is resolved traditionally in *Crime and Punishment*, if not for Dunya, then for Sonya. But its more difficult aspect emerges in *The Brothers Karamazov* when Katerina Ivanovna declares that she will "save" Dmitri by sacrificing herself to him. While Ivan reacts to this declaration with mocking irony, suggesting that this suffering will give a purpose to her life and justify her old age, Alyosha at first takes Katerina seriously. As she continues to dramatize and vocalize her sacrifice, however, he begins to recognize another meaning for it. *It is as if you are in a theater, playing a part*, Alyosha tells her. The part Katerina plays is an imitation of Sonya, itself an imitation of the Madonna or Magdalene. In *The Brothers Karamazov* modern women who play the role ring false.

The female martyr role is most authentic when played by an uneducated or simple woman like Sonya, who embraces the passionate passivity of holy foolishness without ambivalence. But Sonya's quality of "infinite compassion," her lack of irony and self-questioning, gives way in Dostoevsky's later novels to an association of female holy foolishness with idiocy. Stinking Lizaveta, the holy fool of the "Beast Pen," is Dostoevsky's final version of victimized womanhood. The evolution of the "feminine" from *Crime and Punishment* through *The Idiot, The Possessed, The Gentle Creature,* to *The Brothers Karamazov* signals the devolution of the writer's sentimentality. Not women's "self-forgetting" but their protest is associated with salvation. Maria Lebyadkina's denunciation of Stavrogin, not her self-forgotten dreaming, drives him toward confession and "God." It is Katerina's exposure of Dmitri's male chauvinism and Grushenka's sexual one-upmanship that leads him to self-transformation. The pressure of modern ideologies of women's emancipation on Dostoevsky, though resisted, is assimilated. After the watershed of *The Idiot,* no unambivalently faith-filled women who are sane appear in the novels. Alyosha's mother, the "shrieker," shrieks not only because she longs for God but because she has been tortured by her husband.

The promise of "the sacred" and the perpetuation of "the profane" create a terrible mental tension for women even if, in the Eastern Church, "the sacred is not something promised for an 'other' world, but is something surrounding us here and now, permeating all of life, even though our pride keeps us from seeing it."[10] Dostoevsky's "emancipated" women are at risk for breakdown or psychosis of a kind that distinguishes them from their religious counterparts. Such women's "higher" social education produces awareness of paradox, separation, difference, injustice, and otherness. Alyosha's mother's pride is broken, but Katerina's pride enables her to foresee the modern world of paradox and skepticism associated with Dmitri's betrayal of her and Ivan's emotional detachment from her—a world finally incompatible with Alyosha's vision of the marriage at Cana.

What Dostoevsky's traditional women resolve through self-humiliation, his modern women pull asunder through hysteria and pride. Yet each is linked to the other through patriarchal structures stronger than class difference. What links upper class women like Katerina and lower class women like Sonya is their potential to transform men when acts of sexual violation are involved, when the difference women's sexually vulnerable bodies makes for men becomes a conscious part of male sensitization. In this sense women intersect intellectual debates about God and political debates about revolution, for "the woman question" is *their* question. Whether women can transform male consciousness or religious symbolism; whether emancipation for

Russian women can take some form other than Western (liberal capitalist) feminism; whether socialist revolutionary politics can work for or against women: all this constitutes "the woman question" connected to the "accursed" questions of the writer's time. And each of Dostoevsky's female characters, simple or complex, can be understood in relation to it.

MEN'S LIBERTY AND WOMEN'S LIBERATION

In analyzing "the feminine" as assimilated into the conception of Christ through Dostoevsky's creation of "new" men like Raskolnikov, Prince Myshkin, and Alyosha, I have attempted to persuade rereaders that the great Russian writer's work contributes to the feminization of both religious and secular culture and to feminism's search for new moralities.[11] What may deter Western feminists from accepting this contribution is Dostoevsky's refusal to allow a solution to male-female difference that remains unconnected with the problem of faith or belief. His woman question is not carried autonomously by any one feminist heroine, as it is in *Jane Eyre*, but "is contained in its transfer from one mouth to another, from one context to another,"[12] through the interaction of women with men. What Dostoevsky refuses to ignore, despite his claim that Russian men can no longer deny women equality, is the paradox at the heart of the rhetoric of self-empowerment and the metaphysics implicit in exercises of power and freedom. Irving Howe puts this in the most general terms in describing the "source of Dostoevsky's greatness":

> . . . [S]urely part of the answer is that no character is allowed undisputed domination of the novel, all are checked and broken when they become too eager in the assertion of their truths. . . . He *exhausts* his characters. . . . No one escapes humiliation and shame, none is left free from attack . . . no one is spared, but there is the supreme consolation: no one is excluded.[13]

Dostoevsky is interested in the liberation of personalities, but he continually reminds us of freedom's underground: the faithless floating of autonomous and alienated intellects, addicted to forms of separatism, competition, and self-empowering at Others' expenses. Through the "doubling" of the woman-murdering Raskolnikov and the rapist Svidrigaylov, as well as through Stavrogin in *The Possessed*, Dostoevsky indicates the ideological continuity between liberating sex and liberating violence. His dialogically interactive positioning of the woman question shows that men's "liberties" may be incompatible with women's "liberation." Radical separatism from community is nihilism for Dostoevsky, for it negates the Other's inclusion in a shared world. Reformed civil laws may do much to create equal justice, but for Dostoevsky law needs the surplus of emotional commitment to an ideal image (*obraz*) of perfected humanity (Christ and his mother or a feminized Christ) if human defacement (*bezobraziye*) is to be transformed. Sonya and Dunya's exposures of Raskolnikov, like Matryosha's, Maria's, and Liza Tushina's exposures of Stavrogin, show how certain ideas about "liberty" can deform personality, especially male personality, to reproduce the tyranny that "liberalism" is intended to transform.

Isaiah Berlin's well-known distinction between "positive" and "negative" liberty is useful for identifying Dostoevsky's criticism of Western conceptions of freedom, particularly as they were received in Russia. Dostoevsky quarrels with a tradition based on the Enlightenment belief that freedom is identical to Reason or that "positive" freedom and "negative" freedom (freedom *to* and freedom *from*) are compatible. And this delusion (in Dostoevsky's view) of compatibility enables the "reformed" lawyers of Russia's courts to operate in such a way that they "pardon" men who string up their wives like chickens or torture their children. Berlin expresses the general idea of "negative" liberty as follows: "I am normally said to be free to the degree to which no man or body of men interferes with my activity," and "the wider the area of non-interference the wider my freedom."[14] In Dostoevsky's novels it is clear that certain classes of people (peasant husbands, upper class men, and to a lesser extent, upper class women) experience a "wide" area of freedom while the freedom of other classes is extremely limited. Dostoevsky dramatizes anxiety about negative freedom that Berlin analyzes as follows:

> What troubles the consciences of Western liberals, is not, I think, the belief that the freedom that men seek differs according to their social or economic conditions, but that the minority who possess it have gained it by exploiting, or, at least, averting their gaze from, the vast majority who do not.

In emphasizing how Liza (of *Notes*), Dunya, Polina, and Katerina look into men's eyes and refuse to let men avert their gaze from women's situations, Dostoevsky marks the difference between a liberty that exploits and a liberty that empowers women. Polina, the "gentle creature," and Katerina Ivanovna incarnate the longing for a "positive freedom" associated with the "wish" (as Berlin puts it) "to be a subject, not an object." Such women struggle against being "decided for" and long to be "self-directed and not acted upon by external nature or by other men as if [she] were a thing, or an animal, or a slave incapable of playing a human role." The "negative" goal of "warding off interference" and the "positive" freedom of "being one's own master" may seem, as Berlin suggests, "at no great logical distance from each other—no more than negative and positive ways of saying the same thing." Yet Berlin's argument couples with feminist arguments about the way "liberty" has been constructed historically to reflect masculine prerogatives: "Positive and negative notions of freedom historically developed in divergent directions," Berlin writes, "until, in the end, they came into direct conflict with each other."[15] Dostoevsky represents this conflict as gendered through the pawnbroker's demand that his "gentle" wife not "interfere" with his freedom or his desires and her suicidal protest against being totally "decided for" as if she were a "thing." The conflict is given voice through Katerina's protest against Dmitri's treatment of her as a sexual object, and most profoundly, through Ivan's story of a gentle Christ whose ideal of positive freedom clashes with the Inquisitor's negations. Dostoevsky shows not only that liberty can exhibit "two profoundly divergent and irreconcilable attitudes towards the ends of life"[16] but also how the commitment to either has consequences for women.

Unobstructed "negative" freedom, as dreamed about by Raskolnikov and Stavrogin, as practiced by the Inquisitor and as worried about by Ivan, is for Dostoevsky *the* problem of secularized, money-centered culture and *the* problem for women. His attack on Enlightenment conceptions of Reason coheres with certain feminist and deconstructionist critiques of traditional foundational epistemology[17]; but not because Dostoevsky believes all values are contingent. Rather, it is because he understands human interaction to be unstable and therefore in need of necessary fictions of stability. His "new" women have more trouble embracing (the necessary fiction of) "God" because images of stability tend to be masculine. Dostoevsky argued that *even if it were proved that Jesus Christ never existed, he would believe in Christ.* The desire for an ultimate value or a stable icon is fulfilled in the experience of Dostoevsky's male heroes, but his modern heroines' desires for a transcendent icon of their own remains unfulfilled. Women's unfulfilled desires for ideal models, for freedom that is neither negative nor a negation, disrupt Dostoevsky's Christological narrative structures, suggesting what is incomplete in the author's religious vision.

The desire for transcendent, noncontingent values—for God—does not translate into a coherent or harmonious world of male-female relations in Dostoevsky's novels. Concepts do not fit or hang together harmoniously in the novelist's discourse; there are no necessary links that are ultimately coherent with Reason, as Dostoevsky's comment about Christ reveals. And there are no necessary links that bring either men or women to God either. It is from this chiasma, this gap between desire and Reason, that the idea "God is dead" emerges.

The "death of God" debate among characters in the major novels is not limited to theology and philosophy, but relates to the gender crises that link Dostoevsky's times to our own. Nietzsche testified to the enormously generative force of the idea—"If God does not exist, everything is permitted"— he found in Dostoevsky. If feminists today contemplate the death or end of Patriarchy, they do so to some extent within a tradition that goes back to anti-authoritarian religious discourses of the eighteenth century and to Dostoevsky's and Nietzsche's responses to a perceived crisis. Feminist preoccupations with transforming patriarchy can be interpreted as part of a larger climate of criticism in modern thought that analyzes the way authority is symbolized or activated. Dostoevsky's heroes do not simply symbolize authority as "God" if they are believers, and as "Man-God" (superman) if they are atheists. His destructive and self-destructive heroes are involved in the deification of man himself, but never woman; while his positive heroes move toward a reconception of God through the antipatriarchal assimilation of traits associated with "the feminine."

Dostoevsky's focus on a utilitarian, rather than a more nuanced idea of how freedom is configured in the West, serves to rationalize his idea of Russia's special religious mission: to preserve the world's soul symbolized by the communal faith of the Russian people. "The feminine" in Dostoevsky is thus partially associated with souls represented as having not been neuroticized by (Western) skepticism and death-of-God individualism. Myshkin as well as Sonya, Alyosha as well as Maria Lebyadkina symbolize that sort of soul. But "the feminine" also signifies another kind of soulfulness, involving woman's power to expose the evils of a male dominance and negative freedom that "kills God."

The woman question in Dostoevsky exhibits tensions between traditional, Madonna-like women and "new" women; but with both types of women subject to rape and both capable of exposing masculinist "disease." While both traditional and emancipated expressions of the feminine are related to Solovyev's influence on Dostoevsky and his emphasis on *Sophia*, the World Soul or "eternal womanhood,"[18] the tension between emancipatory and religious tendencies in his women figures is not resolved. "The feminine" appears polyphonic in Dostoevsky. It is connected to a maternalist Christianity (the Church as the holy mother) on the one hand, and to (Western) reform and women's rights on the other; but also to the ambiguities and undecidabilities, the symptoms of "split" consciousness that result from interacting with this tension itself. The writer cannot interact with the polyphony of women's voices, with modern and anachronistic images of women, and keep his conservative vision intact. Whereas Sonya disrupts the dangerously Western Napoleonic model of "dialectics" and negative freedom so seductive to Raskolnikov, Nastasya's fate disrupts the Christian salvational myth embodied in Myshkin that is so seductive to Dostoevsky himself.

What can we make of the representation of women's disrupting of both traditionalist *and* modernist schemes in Dostoevsky? of both Slavophile and Western attitudes? The most general answer is that women point to a future that has not been traversed, a possibility their legal and psychological difference signifies. Women and "the feminine" also carry ideas and emotions that, in *Crime and Punishment* and *The Idiot,* suggest a flight from masculinity and its burden. If men must be transformed through women who foreshadow *the way,* this is not only because the way lies through spiritual and physical suffering, but because women's experience expands men's identifications of what is possible for all humans.

The tensions between modernist and traditionalist forms of "the feminine" constitute part of a dialogical network that has been obscured in Dostoevsky criticism through approaches that essentialize masculinity and femininity; through gender-neutral Bakhtinian descriptions of Dostoevsky's discourse; and by feminists who reduce Dostoevsky's vision to stereotypes about women. But the dialogic of the feminine operates even in Dostoevsky's most didactic writings. Russia's missionary future, belabored in *The Diary,* is juxtaposed, as I suggested in chapter 6, with visions of female suicides and commentaries on injustices against women perpetrated in Russian courts. While Dostoevsky's ideal Russia projects an anachronism forward through an Orthodox Church associated with the writer's dreams of utopia, his *actual* Russia emerges as a gendered nightmare in which the Russian man's "disease" and its consequences for women are disclosed.

Dostoevsky's paradoxical intuitions are carried by Ivan's and Katerina's experiences with freedom and faith. Their modernist recognitions produce psychological breakdowns that also function to signal breakthroughs to new quests for reality. Ivan's quest brings him to an understanding that patriarchal "liberty" can mean the power to lock a female child in an outhouse, to rape an idiot female innocent, to set dogs on a peasant boy, to define the masses as incapable of wanting freedom for themselves as the Inquisitor does. Katerina's quest brings her into struggles with all the central characters (Grushenka, Dmitri, Ivan, and even Alyosha) and into a self-lacerated awareness of her "problem without a name" connected to being treated as "only a woman." The minds of Dostoevsky's most interesting heroes are full of female images: of a mother shrieking as her husband humiliates her faith, of beaten children, of raped Matryosha raising her little fist, of the beaten mare and the hacked female pawnbroker, of Dunya shooting her way out of a forced seduction; and of Nastasya Filipovna and Katerina Ivanovna confronting the fact that men cannot "save" them.

The two conceptions of freedom that Dostoevsky explores in their consequences for women carry implications for our own day. Should men's free access to pornography that degrades women be curtailed? Should certain kinds of liberty associated with male pleasure or empowerment but with female humiliation be limited or censored? In *The Diary of a Writer*, Dostoevsky was already showing that the uneducated peasant's "freedom" in the reformed courts made him more of a monster towards his wife and children. To understand the masculinist hell which is the consequence of a certain form of liberation as Dostoevsky conceived it, we might digress for a moment to consider how one debate about liberty is inscribed in our contemporary American context.

At the moment of writing I am stirred by certain parallels between debates in Dostoevsky and Ronald Dworkin's review of Catharine A. MacKinnon's *Only Words*.[19] Discussing the question of whether pornography should be censored, MacKinnon argues that pornography contributes to the economic and social subordination of women. Dworkin responds by suggesting that we do not know pornography's effects on men for sure, and that curtailing First Amendment liberty is worse than allowing pornography (which he says "almost all men" are "disgusted by"). This is a distinctly gendered debate of the kind that is implicit in Dostoevsky's discussions of the Russian courts in *The Diary* and in his exploration of the husband's tyranny in *A Gentle Creature*. In the American debate, Dworkin argues that "only one answer is consistent with the ideals of political equality" and that answer is that "no one may be prevented from influencing the shared moral environment, through his own private choices . . . just because these tastes or opinions disgust those who have the power to shut him up or lock him up."[20]

Perhaps MacKinnon's feminist argument could be better served against Dworkin's if she tackled the problem of negative versus positive freedom so important to Dostoevsky. For in his novels, some men justify their continued engagement in activities that degrade women by appealing to abstract principles of liberty as noninterference. They may use "liberty" to psychologically intimidate and silence women; and feminists can argue that the masculinist bias in the idea of what constitutes freedom makes it so difficult to transform ideas of just laws and rights. The philosopher Charles Taylor argues in *The Ethics of Authenticity*, moreover, that our culture's dominant discourse of freedom and its authority as untrammeled expressiveness—basically, negative freedom—founders on philosophical incoherence. Such "freedom" can function to undermine the very forms of community it purports to support unless it is grounded, at some deeper level, on a notion of positive substantive ends[21]—on what for Dostoevsky was *obraz*: that image of futurity important for *sobornost*.

Dostoevsky's notion of how liberty operates differently for women and men has its source in his awareness of female sexual vulnerability and men's exploitation of it—an awareness feminists might share. In late-twentieth-century readings of *The Idiot*, such as my own or Elizabeth Dalton's, this exploitation does not preclude the "innocent" type Myshkin manifests, for Myshkin's relation to Nastasya is not exempt from the influence of male-modeled violence or the way will-to-power is inscribed in the symbolic structure. I concluded in my last chapter that a gendered symbolism underlies Ivan's *Legend of the Grand Inquisitor*. This suggests that for Dostoevsky a transformed feminized version of man's imitation of Christ would be needed alongside any transformed civic organization that guaranteed women (or the nonmasters who include women) rights to liberty, justice, and the pursuit of happiness. If "woman is determined as the symptom of man,"[22] not just part but the whole of the patriarchal structure, including religion, needs transformation.

For readers struck by the way Dostoevsky's narrative practice appears at odds with his ideological and religious intentions, "the feminine" functions to extend and enlarge that modernism that the term "polyphony" implies. Because the power of the writer's polyphonic discourse appears greater to many late-twentieth- century readers than his inscription of the Christian agenda, his attempt to control the meaning of women's sufferings by allying them with that agenda appears as a productive failure. It produces female holy fools, such as Sonya Marmeladova and Maria Lebyadkina, who are powerful only to the degree that they are simple and uneducated, rendering incoherent Dostoevsky's statement that Russian women's "valor" requires education and equality. Sonya's poverty, sexual degradation, and lack of education lock her out of the realm of ideas that stir, enlarge, and distemper Raskolnikov's search for integration. But Dostoevsky values precisely those limitations in Sonya because one tendency in his thought depends on the belief that *those who do not celebrate God celebrate only their own egos*. This message is the extent of Dostoevsky's monologism and it exists in tension with the dialogic in his work. It is the message of Zosima to Alyosha, of Sonya to Raskolnikov, of Tikhon to Stavrogin; but this message is also deadlocked with another without which the first would lack power. For Dostoevsky also values the tension itself, the breadth of the "new" women whose egos are like the author's own, like Raskolnikov's and Ivan's. And it is these women's attempts to extend themselves, even in self-destruction, that continues to fascinate.

The deadlock between emancipated and traditional identities illustrates a transformative moment in the history of sexuality[23] expressed most complexly by Nastasya's situation in *The Idiot*. Through Nastasya Dostoevsky explores tensions between the social positions of men and women, between assertion and passivity, between the feminine enslavement to a sexual "fall" and the masculine freedom to exploit the fallen. But the novel shows that these tensions are too modern for "Prince Christ" to resolve. The dilemma Dostoevsky engages through Nastasya bears the same sort of significance for feminism as do the fates of Emma Bovary, Anna Karenina, and Tess Durbeyfield; for all these female characters carry the weight of their author's skepticism.[24] Each disrupts the author's longed-for narrative closure. Like Flaubert's Emma, Tolstoy's Anna, and Hardy's Tess, Dostoevsky's Nastasya is involved in a suicide/murder that symbolizes skepticism about sexual conventions and religious traditions.

While a general nineteenth-century philosophical crisis of skepticism vitalizes the fictions of all four writers, it takes a specifically metaphysical turn in Dostoevsky's novel because of connections he makes between masculinist sickness and religious questing. *The Idiot*, like *Anna Karenina*, *Madame Bovary*, and *Tess of the d'Urbervilles*, dramatizes the betrayal in love of a beautiful young woman and her death. But only in Dostoevsky's novel is this betrayal associated with a hero imagined as a Christ. Myshkin's stupefaction, as he sits beside her dead body at the end of *The Idiot*, suggests that "Christ" needs to be remodelled, that Nastasya's fate may be the clue to how, and that a resolution of religious skepticism is dependent upon men's confrontations with "the feminine." This connection is made explicit in the last paragraph of *The Gentle Creature* when the pawnbroker's crying out for God coincides with his acknowledgment of his wife's need for freedom.

In his letters and nonfictional writings, Dostoevsky clings to the model of Christ as the ideal man and to the icon of the Madonna as Christ's feminine counterpart. While his novels contain allusions to these images, his male and female characters are not construed in terms of them but in terms of what deconstructionists call *différance*. The jargon notwithstanding, *différance* suggests Dostoevsky's apprehension of the "nothing" against which metaphysics and iconographies wage their battle to create final or transcendent meanings. In Dostoevsky the idea that "God does not exist," the force of modern skepticism, stands as the motivation for passionate commitment. This is a commitment to an "as if" society—to a sacralized human communitarianism that is continually deferred. Without this endlessly deferred "final word," the dialectic between modernism and traditionalism, skepticism and belief, would simply mean strife, but in Dostoevsky's discourse it means something else: the exploration of self- and world-affirmation through multiple voices. The philosopher Charles Taylor puts it this way:

> Whether we go on seeing ourselves as dependent on God for this transformation, like Dostoevsky . . . or not, like Nietzsche, . . . [both] have a thoroughly modern conception of what transformation involves. This conception has its roots in the post-Romantic notion of the creative imagination, which helps complete what it reveals.[25]

The subject matter of Dostoevsky's novels is not incommensurable with the subject matter of feminist critique, for both explore the incomplete revelations of patriarchal dispensation and each struggles to give voice to what is becoming. If Dostoevsky's explorations of the masculinist will-to-power complex add to our knowledge of how society has come to be structured as it is, his dramatizations of women's creative rage and their exposures of men's delusions suggest his own version of "what is to be done."

Dostoevsky loved both traditional and emancipated women and felt the confusions for male psychology involved in the alternate kinds of love each woman gave and demanded. His fiction contains traces of his own lost mother (dead when he was seventeen), and he searched all his life to understand her death and to resurrect her image. In 1992, Gary Saul Morson, citing the influence of Bakhtin on non-Slavists, hoped that "the resurrection of the Russian literary tradition itself has begun."[26] But another sort of hope—that the tradition's resurrection will now admit the insights of feminist readers—is perhaps as justified considering Dostoevsky's contribution to the woman question. Women's presence and influence in the great Russian's work reminds us that "the unity of a text is not in its origins but in its destinations."[27] Rereading that work exposes what women and men might further imagine about their collective futures together.

Notes

Introduction

1. See, for example, Judith Armstrong's *The Unsaid Anna Karenina* (New York: St. Martin's Press, 1988); Mary Evans's *Reflecting on Anna Karenina* (London: Routledge, 1989); Amy Mandelker's *Framing Anna Karenina: Tolstoy, the Woman Question, and the Victorian Novel* (Columbus: Ohio State University Press, 1994); and *Tolstoy Studies Journal* (vol. 3, 1990), edited by Amy Mandelker and devoted to feminist and women's issues.

2. This is Robin Feuer Miller's phrase, offered in her talk on "Dostoevsky and the Homeopathic Dose," given April 25, 1993, at Dostoevsky Laboratory II, Yale University.

3. See Alice Jardine's discussion of literature and the "Crisis in Legitimation" in *Gynesis* (Ithaca: Cornell University Press, 1985), p. 99ff.

4. Elaine Showalter, *Sexual Anarchy: Gender and Culture at the Fin-de-Siècle* (New York: Viking, 1990), p. 4. Eva Kosofsky Sedgewick and Laura Engelstein also contribute to the examination of the social as well as the legal construction of male sexual violence. See Engelstein's *The Keys to Happiness: Sex and the Search for Modernity in Fin-de-Siècle Russia* (Ithaca: Cornell University Press, 1992) and Sedgwick's *Between Men: English Literature and Male Homosocial Desire* (New York: Columbia University Press, 1985).

5. See Sigmund Freud, *The Standard Edition of the Complete Psychological Works of Sigmund Freud*, vol. XIII, trans. James Strachey (London: Hogarth Press and the Institute of Psychoanalysis, 1953).

6. Among those who examined this fertile contradiction is the philosopher Charles Taylor, who devotes several pages to *The Possessed* in

his *Sources of the Self: The Making of Modern Identity* (Cambridge, MA: Harvard University Press, 1989), p. 447ff.

7. Barbara Heldt, *Terrible Perfection: Women in Russian Literature* (Bloomington: Indiana University Press, 1987).

8. Gary Saul Morson, *The Boundaries of Genre: Dostoevsky's Diary of a Writer and the Tradition of Literary Utopia* (Austin: University of Texas Press, 1981), pp. 4-7.

9. Eugene Lyons, in *Assignment in Utopia* (New York: Harcourt Brace, 1937), describes attending "Socialist Sunday School" with "a volume of Dostoievsky under my arm" (p. 7).

10. Dale Bauer, ed., *Feminism, Bakhtin, and the Dialogic* (Albany: State University of New York, 1991).

11. Mikhail Bakhtin, *Problems of Dostoevsky's Poetics*, trans. Caryl Emerson (Minneapolis: University of Minnesota Press, 1984), p. 56. Emphasis added.

12. See Bakhtin's remarks on carnival and Menippea in *Problems*, p. 124ff.

13. Bakhtin, *Problems*, pp. 196-7.

14. Hans Jauss, *Question and Answer: Forms of Dialogic Understanding*, trans. Michael Hays (Minneapolis: University of Minnesota Press, 1989), pp. 208-9.

15. Gary Saul Morson argues that "while English or comparative literature professors can easily be unaware of the differences between the Slavic theoretical tradition and their own, Slavists usually cannot. The spectrum of Slavist's responses is predictable. Some become wary of theory altogether. Others strain as much as possible to be like their non-Slavist counterarts, but the signs of strain tend to be visible." ("Introduction: Russian Cluster," *PMLA* 107 [March 1992]): 228.

16. Costlow, Sandler, Vowles, eds., *Sexuality and the Body in Russian Culture* (Stanford, CA: Stanford University Press, 1993), pp. 8 and 30.

17. Geir Kjetsaa, *Fyodor Dostoevsky: A Writer's Life*, trans. Siri Hustvedt and David McDuff (New York: Viking, 1987), p. 327ff.

18. Robert Jackson's talk, given at the Dostoevsky Laboratory II at Yale University, April 25, 1993, entitled: "A View from the Underground: On Nikolai Nikolaevich Strakhov's Letter About His Good friend Fyodor Mikhailovich Dostoevsky and on Lev Nikolaevich Tolstoy's Interesting Response to It."

19. The idea that the text is a self-contained artifact was a truism of New Criticism, reinforced in the 1980s by Jacques Derrida's ideas about "the 'deconstruction' of the history of metaphysics" and the idea "of writing as a game within language." See Derrida's *Of Grammatology*,

trans. Gayatri Spivak (Baltimore, MD: Johns Hopkins University Press, 1976), p. 83 and 315.

20. Engelstein, *Keys to Happiness*, pp. 115-6.

21. George Sand, *Mauprat*, trans. Diane Johnson (New York: Da Capo Press, Inc., 1977).

22. Bakhtin, *Problems*, pp. 233-4.

23. Tvetan Todorov, *Genres in Discourse*, trans. Catherine Porter (New York: Cambridge University Press, 1990), p. 89.

24. Louis Breger discusses this question in psychoanalytic but not feminist terms in *Dostoevsky: The Author as Psychoanalyst* (New York: New York University Press, 1989), p. 125.

25. See Caryl Emerson's and Gary Morson's critique in *Mikhail Bakhtin: Creation of a Poetics* (Stanford, CA: Stanford University Press, 1992); and Joe Andrew's argument that "Bakhtin was gender blind" in his review of Michael Holquist's *Dialogism, Bakhtin, and His World* in *The Slavonic and East European Review* 70, no. 2 (April 1992): 326-7.

26. Julia Kristeva describes a feminist semiotics that is "an open form of research, a constant critique that turns back on itself and offers its own autocritique." See Kristeva's introduction in *Desire in Language*, ed. L. Roudiez (New York: Columbia University Press, 1980).

27. For discussion of revolutionary and "new" Russian women, see Barbara Engel's "Women as Revolutionaries: The Case of the Russian Populists," in *Becoming Visible: Women in European History*, ed. Bridenthal and Koonz (Boston: Houghton Mifflin, 1977); and Richard Stites's *The Women's Liberation Movement in Russia: Feminism, Nihilism, and Bolshevism* (Princeton, NJ: Princeton University Press, 1978, 1991).

28. Jauss, *Question and Answer*, pp. 216-7.

29. See Michael Holquist's introduction to *The Dialogic Imagination by M. M. Bakhtin*, trans. Michael Holquist and Caryl Emerson (Austin: University of Texas Press, 1981), pp. xvi-xvii.

30. Vincent M. Colapietro describes this term as "the process by which a human organism, as a result of being initiated into various systems of representation, becomes a subject, a split being (conscious/unconscious) with a sexual or gendered identity. The expression involves a pun, since it plays upon two sense of *engendering* (the process of bringing something into being and the process of acquiring a gender)." See Colapietro's *Glossary of Semiotics* (New York: Paragon House, 1993), p. 98.

31. Richard Peace, *Dostoevsky: An Examination of His Major Novels* (Cambridge: Cambridge University Press, 1971), pp. 230-2.

32. Diane Thompson, *"The Brothers Karamazov" and the Poetics of Memory* (New York: Cambridge University Press, 1991), p. 55.

33. Edward Wasiolek, *Dostoevsky: The Major Fiction* (Cambridge, MA: MIT Press, 1964), p. 160. The italicized words are from the original.

34. Robert Belknap, *The Structure of "The Brothers Karamazov"* (The Hague: Mouton & Co., 1967), p. 47.

35. Nina Perlina, *Varieties of Poetic Utterance: Quotation in The Brothers Karamazov* (Lanham, NY, and London: University Press of America, 1985), p. 186.

36. Leonid Grossman, *Dostoevsky: His Life and Works*, trans. Mary Mackle (Indianapolis, IN: Bobbs Merrill, 1975), p. 576.

37. Bakhtin, *Problems*, p. 252.

38. Engelstein, *The Keys to Happiness*, p. 4.

39. Freud, Standard Edition, vol. XIII.

40. See Tzvetan Todorov's discussion in *Michael Bakhtin: The Dialogical Principle*, trans. Wlad Godzich (Minneapolis: University of Minnesota Press, 1984), pp. 30-34.

41. See Joan W. Scott's "Gender: A Useful Category of Historical Analysis," *American Historical Review* (March 1987): 1067-8.

42. Caryl Emerson, "Bakhtin and Feminism: Why is It So Problematic?" paper delivered at Modern Language Association Conference, New York, December 1992.

43. See the conclusion of Joanna Hubbs's *Mother Russia* (Bloomington: Indiana University Press, 1988).

44. Temira Pachmuss, *F.M. Dostoevsky: Dualism and Synthesis of the Human Soul* (Carbondale: Southern Illinois University Press, 1963), p. 115.

45. See conclusion, Gary Cox, *Tyrant and Victim in Dostoevsky* (Columbus, OH: Slavica, 1983).

46. Vladimir Nabokov, *Lectures on Russian Literature* (New York: Harcourt Brace, 1981), p. 110.

47. See Gayatri Spivak's "Finding Feminist Readings: Dante-Yeats" in *American Criticism in the Post Structuralist Age*, ed. Ira Konigsberg (Ann Arbor: University of Michigan Press, 1982), p. 47.

48. See objections to Bakhtin's interpretation of Dostoevskian psychology in Emerson and Morson's *Mikhail Bakhtin: Creation of a Poetics*.

49. There are now thousands of available discussions about women's writings. See, for a good example, Stephanie Sander's "Embodied Words: Gender in Cvetaeva's Reading of Pushkin," *Slavic and East European Journal* (Summer 1980): 139-57. A range of theories about writing and gender can be found in the politically moderate anthol-

ogy *Feminist Literary Theory*, ed. Mary Eagleton (New York: Basil Blackwell, 1986), and in the more recent and radical *Feminists Theorize the Political*, ed. Judith Butler and Joan W. Scott (New York: Routledge, 1992).

50. Harriet Murav, "Dora and the Underground Man," in *Russian Literature and Psychoanalysis*, ed. Daniel Rancour-Laferriere (Amsterdam/Philadelphia: John Benjamins Pub. Co., 1989), pp. 418-30.

51. See Gary Saul Morson's *The Boundaries of Genre*.

52. Robert Belknap, *The Genesis of the Brothers Karamazov* (Evanston, IL: Northwestern University Press, 1990), p. 35.

53. Elizabeth Dalton, *Unconscious Structure in The Idiot; A Study in Literature and Psychoanalysis* (Princeton, NJ: Princeton University Press, 1979).

Chapter One

1. Mikhail Bakhtin, *Problems of Dostoevsky's Poetics*, trans. Caryl Emerson (Minneapolis, University of Minnesota Press, 1984), p. 63.

2. Tzvetan Todorov, *Mikhail Bakhtin: The Dialogical Principle*, trans. Wlad Godzich (Minneapolis: University of Minnesota Pres, 1984), p. 96.

3. Ibid., p. 103.

4. Louis Breger, *Dostoevsky: The Author as Psychoanalyst* (New York: New York University Press, 1989), p. 53.

5. Barbara Heldt, *Terrible Perfection: Women in Russian Literature* (Bloomington: Indiana University Press, 1987), p. 37.

6. Bakhtin, *Problems*, p. 291.

7. Breger, *Dostoevsky*, p. 16.

8. Richard Peace, *Dostoevsky: An Examination of His Major Novels* (Cambridge: Cambridge University Press, 1971), p. 34.

9. Donald Fanger, *Dostoevsky and Romantic Realism* (Cambridge, MA: Harvard University Press, 1967), pp. 185-6.

10. Joseph Frank, "The World of Raskolnikov," *Encounter* 26, no. 6 (June 1966): 32.

11. Alice Jardine, *Gynesis* (Ithaca, NY: Cornell University Press, 1985), p. 64.

12. Edward Wasiolek, *Dostoevsky: The Major Fiction* (Cambridge, MA: MIT Press, 1964), p. 77.

13. Jacques Lacan, *Feminine Sexuality: Jacques Lacan and the École Freudienne*, ed. Juliet Mitchell and Jacqueline Rose, trans. Jacqueline Rose (New York: W. W. Norton and Pantheon Books, 1985), p. 5.

14. Adele Barker, *The Mother Syndrome in Russian Folk Imagination* (Columbus, OH: Slavica, 1985), p. 123.

15. Shoshana Felman, *Writing and Madness*, trans. Martha Noel Evans (Ithaca, NY: Cornell University Press, 1978), p. 128.

16. Bakhtin, *Problems*, p. 203.

17. Ibid., p. 203.

18. Peace, *Dostoevsky*, p. 54.

19. Bakhtin, *Problems*, p. 167.

20. Jacques Catteau, *Dostoevsky and the Process of Literary Creation*, trans. Audrey Littlewood (New York: Cambridge University Press, 1989), p. 455.

21. Bakhtin, *Problems*, pp. 88-92. The italics are Bakhtin's.

22. Ibid., p. 74.

23. I use the work *lack* in the sense of Lacan's interpretation of Freud's notion of the female as "castrated," stressing a linguistic rather than physical meaning. Raskolnikov's Napoleonism can be understood as a symptom of phallocentric narcissism in the sense that "the human social order . . . refracted through the individual human subject is patrocentric," reflecting not biological but "cultural-symbolic language conditions" (Juliet Mitchell, Intro. I to Lacan, *Feminine Sexuality*, p. 23).

24. Carol Gilligan, *In a Different Voice* (Cambridge, MA: Harvard University Press, 1992), p. 62.

25. Nancy Chodorow, *The Reproduction of Mothering: Psychoanalysis and the Sociology of Gender* (Berkeley: University of California Press, 1978), p. 176.

26. Ibid., p. 177.

27. I am paraphrasing the last sentences of Harriet Murav's *Holy Foolishness* (Stanford, CA: Stanford University Press, 1992), which reads: "To belong to the new community, to be a good reader of Dostoevsky, requires that we be willing to behold the spectacle of our own folly" (p. 174).

28. Wasiolek, *Dostoevsky: The Major Fiction*, p. 7.

29. Bakhtin, *Problems*, p. 238.

30. Michael André Bernstein, "'These Children that Come at You with Knives': Ressentiment, Mass Culture, and the Saturnalia," *Critical Inquiry* 17 (1991): 365.

31. Bakhtin, *Problems*, p. 219.

32. Ibid., p. 146.

33. Robert Belknap, *The Genesis of "The Brothers Karamazov"* (Evanston, IL: Northwestern University Press, 1990), pp. 40 and 60.

Chapter Two

1. Nina Perlina notes that "scholars have shown that . . . the concept of irrepressibility/*bezuberzb* appears in . . . *The Gambler* as an echo and reflection of Pushkinian motifs from *The Covetous Knight* and *The Feast during the Plague," Varieties of Poetic Utterance: Quotation in the Brothers Karamazov* (Lanham, NY and London: University Press of America, 1985), p. 166.

2. Marc Slonim, *Three Loves of Dostoevsky* (New York: Rinehard & Co., Inc., 1955), pp. 179-80.

3. Robert Louis Jackson, "Polina and Lady Luck in *The Gambler*," in *Modern Critical Views: Fyodor Dostoevky*, ed. Harold Bloom (New York: Chelsea House, 1988), p. 209.

4. "The Eternal Mate" is Slonim's title for the chapter on Suslova in *Three Loves of Dostoevsky*. See pp. 111-13.

5. Hallett Carr, *Dostoevsky* (London: George Allen & Unwin Ltd., 1931, 1949), p. 112.

6. Little is known of Brown except that Dostoevsky met her through a writer named Gorsky, who contributed tales of slum life to the periodicals *Vremya* and *Epokba*. Brown was a native Russian of the lower middle class who had married an American sailor in England. In her letters to Dostoevsky, she described herself as a "pauper and vagrant." When she was sick and hospitalized, Dostoevsky visited her and gave her money. She wrote to him: "It is all the same to me whether our relationship lasts a long time or not, but I swear to you that far beyond any material advantage, I prize the fact that you have not scorned the fallen part of my nature, that you raised me above the letter on which I stand in my own estimation" (quoted in Avrahm Yarmolinsky, *Dostoevsky: Works and Days* [New York: Funk & Wagnalls, 1971], p. 201ff).

7. Anna Korvin-Krupovskaya, a beautiful young blond in 1865, had a considerable impact on Dostoevsky's life and perhaps more on his writing than critics allowed before Robert Belknap's 1990 long overdue comparison between her story "Mixail" and Dosteovsky's Alyosha of *The Brothers Karamazov*. When the parallels were pointed out to Dostoevsky in 1881, he said, "You know, it's really true!" Critics writing in the 1970s and 1980s (Yarmolinsky, Jackson, Wasiolek) concentrate on Anna as Dostoevsky's love interest, but Belknap argues that "she fascinated him in large part because of her writing, and because he shared her interest in certain . . . technical

problems [such] as the creation of an unremarkable hero" (see Belknap, *The Genesis of "The Brothers Karamazov,"* [Evanston, IL: Northwestern University Press, 1990], pp. 92-5). Dostoevsky himself wrote that Anna was "one of the finest women I have ever met. She is exceedingly wise, has a literary education and true and good heart. She is a girl with high moral qualities, but her beliefs are diametrically opposed to mine, and she is much too honest to abandon them. A marriage to her would therefore have not been happy." For her part Anna wrote that Dostoevsky "needs a wife who can give her entire life to him, who will think only of him. I can't do that. I want my own life. Besides, he is very nervous and demanding, and he seems to grab hold of me and suck me into him. I am never myself when he is around" (quoted in Geir Kjetsaa, *Fyodor Dostoevsky: A Writer's Life,* trans. Siri Hustvedt and David McDuff [New York: Viking, 1987], p. 175).

Although Anna could not love him, her sister Sofia, fifteen years old at that time, did. Later Sofia became the first woman professor of mathematics at the Hogskola in Stockholm. Anna, however, was not permitted to study. Her father found her involvement with writing and with being published by Dostoevsky dangerous: "Now you sell your stories," her father said, "perhaps you will be selling yourself next!" The two sisters' situations indicate the ambiguities of upper-class women's lives in Russia, as Barbara Engel suggests in *Mothers and Daughters* ([Cambridge: Cambridge University Press, 1972], pp. 66-7). A career in medicine or mathematics was possible for a young woman, but a literary career seemed somehow immoral. Anna's father, however, could not prevent Anna from eventually leaving these constraints and marrying the French socialist Jaclart. Both she and her husband were active in the Paris Commune and eventually returned to Russia. After Dostoevsky married, he remained friends with both sisters and their families (c.f. Kjetsaa, *Fyodor Dostoevsky,* pp. 174-5, and Yarmolinsky, *Dostoevsky: Works and Days,* pp. 201-5). Richard Peace adds to this history an analysis of Anna as the "prototype for Aglaya . . . a young girl with nihilist leanings," in *The Idiot.* "Aglaya tells Mishkin that she has read all the banned books, and wants to devote herself to something useful, not spend her life going to society balls; the moral charge which she throws at her rival, Nastaya Filipovna, is that she does not work" (*Dostoevsky: An Examination of His Major Novels* [Cambridge: Cambridge University Press, 1971], p. 81).

8. Constantin Mochulsky, *Dostoevsky: His Life and Work*, trans. Michael A. Minihan (Princeton, NJ: Princeton University Press, 1967), p. 318.

9. Quoted in Jacques Catteau, *Dostoevsky and the Process of Literary Creation*, trans. Audrey Littlewood (New York: Cambridge University Press, 1989), p. 142.

10. Sandra Gilbert and Susan Gubar in *No Man's Land* (New Haven: Yale University Press, 1988) ask the question that Suslova's story provokes: "If literary men in the late-nineteenth-century and early-twentieth-centuries portrayed women's invasion of the public sphere as an act of aggression that inaugurated a battle of the sexes, did late nineteenth-and-twentieth century literary women transform their words into weapons in order to wrest authority from men?" (p. 65).

11. For a discussion of the debate about women provoked by Chernyshevsky and Mihailov during the 1860s, see Richard Stites, *The Women's Liberation Movement in Russia: Feminism, Nihilism, and Bolshevism* (Princeton, NJ: Princeton University Press, 1978, 1991), pp. 38-44.

12. Catteau, *Dostoevsky*, pp. 143-4.

13. Ibid., p. 145.

14. F. M. Dostoevsky, *Pis'ma v 4-kh tomakh*, ed. A. S. Dolinin (Moscow-Leningrad, 1928-59), p. 121.

15. Peace, *Dostoevsky*, p. 301. Perhaps one needs to be reminded again of the suffering Dostoevsky experienced for his involvement with the radical-socialist Petrashevsky circle in 1849. Yarmolinsky's description of the mock execution Dostoevsky and the other Petrashevskians endured gives some idea: "The severity of the sentences could be accounted for only by the hysteria which seized the Russian government as it watched the thrones of Europe rock in the revolutions of 1848. . . . The Emperor had a weakness for theatrical effects, in addition to immense self-righteousness. He gave orders that the death sentence should be announced to the prisoners in a public place in the presence of the populace and the troops, and that only after the men had gone through all the preparations for their execution were they to be informed at the last moment that the Czar in his ineffable charity had made them a present of their lives" (*Dostoevsky*, p. 88). Dostoevsky's sentence was then commuted to five years of penal servitude in Siberia.

16. See V. Pereverzev, "Dostoevskij i revoljucijaj," in *Tvorchestvo Dostoevsogo* (Moscow: Gosizdat, 1922), p. 6.

17. Tzvetan Todorov, *Genres in Discourse,* trans. Catherine Porter (New York: Cambridge University PRess, 1990), pp. 90-1.

18. Barbara Johnson, *A World of Difference* (Baltimore, MD: Johns Hopkins University Press, 1987), p. 70. The emphasis is hers.

19. Perlina, *Varieties of Poetic Utterance,* p. 7.

20. Hélène Cixous, "The Laugh of the Medusa," reprinted in *Feminist Literary Theory,* ed. Mary Eagleton (New York: Basil Blackwell, 1986), pp. 225-7.

21. Perlina argues that "Dostoevsky was the first writer of the modern world who understood the applicability of polyphonic search as a 'specific mode of thinking'" (*Varieties of Poetic Utterance,* p. 9). The Grandmother personifies a specifically Russian mode of polyphony. She is "Mother Russia," who both satirizes others and is lovingly satirized.

22. The idea that Dostoevsky's discourse parodies its own polyphony is Perlina's following Bakhtin. Perlina argues that Dostoevsky's art is a "collocation of quotations." The characters quote each others' words, sometimes with intensions to distort or parody (Ibid., pp. 4-17).

23. See, for example, the endless chronicle of Dostoevsky's financial troubles in biographies by Yarmolinsky, Joseph Frank, and Geir Kjetsaa, as well as Jacques Catteau's significant contribution to Dostoevsky's views of the links between socialism and money.

24. Using this Wittgensteinian terminology, Malcolm Jones has traced a Rousseauian motif in Dostoevsky's novels that involves a man's theft of money from a girl or woman, his blaming her for the loss, and his guilt. His discussion of the family resemblances of scenes in *Crime and Punishment* and *The Devils* (*The Possessed*) is particularly revealing. See Jones's "Dostoevsky, Rousseau and Others," *Dostoevsky Studies* 4 (1983), esp. pp. 89-90.

25. Catteau, *Dostoevsky,* p. 145.

26. Gilbert and Gubar, *No Man's Land,* p. 162.

27. Perlina, *Varieties of Poetic Utterance,* p. 162.

28. See my introduction on Dostoevsky's obsession with rape as the worst crime because it murders love.

29. Jackson, "Polina and Lady Luck," p. 189.

Chapter Three

1. "Almost the whole novel," Dostoevsky informed his niece in a letter, "was thought and written for the sake of the denouement."

See F. M. Dostoevsky, *Pis'ma*, Vol. II, ed. A. S. Dolnin (Moscow-Leningrad: 1928-59), p. 138.

2. Caryl Emerson, "Problems with Baxtin's Poetics," *Slavic and East European Journal* 32, no. 4 (Winter 1988): 503-25.

3. See Dostoevsky's letters and his various biographers' descriptions of this event.

4. Harriet Murav, *Holy Foolishness: Dostoevsky's Novels and the Poetics of Cultural Critique* (Stanford, CA: Stanford University Press, 1992), p. 174.

5. David M. Bethea, *The Shape of Apocalypse in Modern Russian Fiction* (Princeton, NJ: Princeton University Press, 1989), p. 101.

6. See Murav's description of Dostoevsky's dissatisfactions with the novel and her analysis of the "two tendencies"—including Burenin's as cited above (*Holy Foolishness*, pp. 73-4).

7. See, for example, Mochulsky's or Pachmuss's commentaries supporting the religious interpretation in contrast to Peace's and Holquist's more skeptical commentaries.

8. Chris Wheedon, *Feminist Practice and Poststructuralist Theory* (Oxford: Basil Blackwell, 1987), p. 69.

9. Clare Cavanagh argues in "Pseudo-revolution in Poetic Language: Julia Kristeva and the Russian Avant-garde," *Slavic Review* (Summer l993), that in Julia Kristeva's work the "'Symbolic Order,' the 'Father' or the 'Law' . . . all seem to mean simply society as such with no regard as to whether the particular 'society' is democratic or tyrannical" (p. 29).

10. Murav, *Holy Foolishness*, p. 6.

11. Elizabeth Dalton, *Unconscious Structure in "The Idiot": A Study in Literature and Psychoanalysis* (Princeton, NJ: Princeton University Press, 1979), p. 173.

12. The description of Anna's last moment conforms to a stereotyped vision of femininity, including the accoutrement of the "red handbag" that is flung aside before she jumps. See Leo Tolstoy, *Anna Karenina*, trans. Joel Carmichael (New York: Bantam, 1960, 1988), p. 816.

13. Again, I refer the reader to Eva Kosofky Sedgwick's discussion, in *Between Men: English Literature and Male Homosocial Desire* (New York: Columbia University Press, 1985), of women as intermediate objects or "traffic" between men who cannot otherwise establish their (homosexual or homosocial) bonds.

14. Michael Holquist, *Dostoevsky and the Novel* (Evanston, IL: Northwestern University Press, 1986), p. 196ff.

15. See the chapter "Myths," in Simone de Beauvoir, *The Second Sex*, trans. H. M. Parshley (New York: Knopf, 1952).

16. Constantin Mochulsky, *Dostoevsky: His Life and Work*, trans. Michael A. Minihan (Princton, NJ: Princeton University Press, 1967), p. 380.

17. See Louis Breger's chapter on *The Idiot* in *Dostoevsky: The Author as Psychoanalyst* (New York: New York University Press, 1989).

18. Olga Matich, "The Idiot: A Feminist Reading," in *Dostoevsky and the Human Condition After a Century*, eds. Ugrinsky, Lambasa, Ozolino (New York: Greenwood Press, 1986), pp. 55-6.

19. Dalton, *Unconscious Structure*, p. 97.

20. Mikhail Bakhtin, *Problems of Dostoevsky's Poetics*, trans. Caryl Emerson (Minneapolis: University of Minnesota Press, 1984), pp. 165-6. Also see Bakhtin's discussion of the carnivalesque in *Rabelais*, trans. Helen Iswolsky (Bloomington: Indiana University Press, 1984), p. 303.

21. Ronald Hingley, *Dostoevsky: His Life and Work* (New York: Charles Scribner's Sons, 1978), p. 414ff.

22. In the early 1990s, two male-authored feminist novels received much attention: Norman Rush's *Mating* (New York: Random House, 1991) and Peter Haug's *Smilla's Sense of Snow* (New York: Farrar, Straus and Giroux, 1993). Both novels explore feminist questions, are narrated by women's voices, and are authored by men.

23. Jacques Derrida, "Becoming Woman," *Semiotexte* 3 (1978): 130.

24. Bakhtin, *Problems*, p. 235.

Chapter Four

1. See Malcolm V. Jones's *Dostoevsky After Bakhtin: Readings in Dostoevsky's Fantastic Realism* (New York, Cambridge University Press, 1990).

2. Writing of Dostoevsky's psychology in Bakhtinian terms, Gerald Pirog argues in "Bakhtin and Freud on the Ego," in *Russian Literature and Psychoanalysis*, ed. Daniel Rancoeur-Laferriere (Amsterdam/Phil-adelphia: John Benjamins Pub. Co., 1989) that "what is lacking in Freud is a principle which accounts for the need of the other in terms of an inescapable seeking after mutuality" (p. 401). As *The Eternal Husband* shows, certain seekings of "mutuality" may be perverse—a phenomenon for which Freud and feminism *does* account.

3. Eva Kosofsky Sedgwick, *Between Men: English Literature and Male Homoso-cial Desire* (New York: Columbia University Press, 1985), p. 134.

4. Ibid., p. 179.

5. Quoted in Constantin Mochulsky, *Dostoevsky: His Life and Work*, trans. Michael A. Minihan (Princeton: Princeton University Press, 1967), p. 387.

6. Philippe Lacoue-Labarthe, quoted in Frank Lentricchia's "Patriarchy Against Itself: the Young Manhood of Wallace Stevens," *Critical Inquiry* 13 (Summer 1987): 742.

7. Shoshana Felman, "Turning the Screw of Interpretation," in *Literature and Psychoanalysis: The Question of Reading: Otherwise* (New Haven: Yale University Press, 1977), p. 199.

8. Mikhail Bakhtin, *Problems of Dostoevsky's Poetics*, trans. Caryl Emerson (Minneapolis: University of Minnesota Press, 1984), p. 256.

9. Nicholas V. Riasanovsky, *A History of Russia*, fourth edition (New York: Oxford University Press, 1984), p. 382.

Chapter Five

1. Richard Pipes, *The Russian Revolution* (New York: Vintage, 1990), p. 788.

2. Elizabeth Waters, "Female Form in Soviet Political Iconography," in *Russia's Women*, ed. Barbara Engel (Berkeley: University of California Press, 1990), pp. 231 and 242.

3. See Aileen Kelly, "Irony and Utopia in Herzen and Dostoevsky," *The Russian Review* 50 (October 1991): 409.

4. Mikhail Bakhtin, *Problems of Dostoevsky's Poetics*, trans. Caryl Emerson (Minneapolis: University of Minnesota Press, 1984), pp. 115 and 117.

5. Anatoly Lunacharsky, "Dostoevsky," in *Marxism and Art: Essays Classical and Contemporary*, ed. Maynard Solomon (Detroit, MI: Wayne State University Press, 1979), p. 219.

6. Phillip Pomper, *Sergei Nechaev* (New Brunswick, NJ: Rutgers University Press, 1979), pp. 107-8.

7. Nicholai Berdyaev, *The Russian Idea*, trans. R. M. French (Hudson, NY: Lindisfarne Press, 1992), pp. 108-9.

8. Jacques Catteau, *Dostoevsky and the Process of Literary Creation*, trans. Audrey Littlewood (New York: Cambridge University Press, 1989), p. 3

9. Tzvetan Todorov, *Genres in Discourse*, trans. Catherine Porter (New York: Cambridge University Press, 1990), p. 89.

10. Susan Bordo, "The Cartesian Masculinization of Thought," *Signs* 11, no. 3 (Spring 1986): 441.

11. Albert Borgmann, *Crossing the Postmodern Divide* (Chicago: University of Chicago Press), pp. 50-1.

12. See Marc Slonim's afterword to the MacAndrew translation of *The Possessed* (New York: NAL, 1962).

13. Constantin Mochulsky, Dostoevsky: His Life and Work, trans. Michael A. Minihan (Princeton, NJ: Princeton University Press, 1967), pp. 434-5.

14. Edward Wasiolek, ed. *Dostoevsky's Notebooks for the Possessed,* trans. Victor Terras (Chicago: University of Chicago Press, 1968), p. 19

15. See, for example, Charles Taylor and Albert Borgmann.

16. Silvia Tandeciarz, "French Feminism in an International Frame: A Problem for Theory," *Genders* 10 (Spring 1991): 88.

17. Richard Stites, *The Women's Liberation Movement in Russia: Feminism, Nihilism, and Bolshevism* (Princeton, NJ: Princeton University Press, 1978, 1991), p. 125.

18. Catteau, *Dostoevesky,* p. 157.

19. Joanna Hubbs, *Mother Russia* (Bloomington: Indiana University Press, 1988), p. 229.

20. Juliet Mitchell, *Women's Estate* (New York: Vintage, 1971), pp. 178-9.

21. Dostoevsky's phrase in *The Diary of a Writer* (Salt Lake City, UT: Gibbs M. Smith, Inc., 1985), p. 846. See also my introduction to this volume.

22. Edward Wasiolek, *Dostoevsky: The Major Fiction* (Cambridge: MIT Press, 1964), p. 111.

23. Albert Guerard, *Triumph of the Novel* (New York: Oxford University Press, 1976), p. 262.

24. Gordon Livermore, "The Shaping Dialectic of Dostoevsky's Devils," in *Dostoevsky: New Perspectives,* ed. Robert Jackson (Englewood Cliffs, NJ: Prentice Hall, 1984), p. 185.

25. Gunther Anders, *Franz Kafka,* trans. A. Steer and A. K. Thorlby (London: Bowes & Bowes, 1960), p. 32.

26. Nikolai Mikhailovsky, *Dostoevsky: A Cruel Talent,* trans. Spence Cadmus (Ann Arbor, MI: Ardus, 1978), pp. 11-12.

27. Guerard, *Triumph of the Novel,* p. 93.

28. Avrahm Yarmolinsky, *Dostoevsky: Works and Days* (New York: Funk & Wagnalls, 1971), p. 312.

29. Malcolm Jones, *Dostoevsky After Bakhtin: Readings in Dostoevsky's Fantastic Realism* (New York: Cambridge University Press, 1990), p. 196.

30. Wasiolek, *Dostoevsky,* pp. 131 and 136.

31. Slonim, afterword to *The Possessed,* p. 700.

32. Richard Peace, *Dostoevsky: An Examination of His Major Novels* (Cambridge: Cambridge University Press, 1971), pp. 211-13.

33. Borgmann, *Crossing the Postmodern Divide*, p. 6.

34. Catteau, *Dostoevsky*, p. 380.

35. Wasiolek, *Dostoevsky*, p. 32.

36. Discussing Schiller's remark, Isaiah Berlin makes clear what sort of dangers Dostoevsky dramatizes through Stavrogin: "the disintegrating influences of romanticism, both in the comparatively innocuous form of the chaotic rebellion of the free artist of the nineteenth century and in the sinister and destructive form of totalitarianism." See "The Apotheosis of the Romantic Will," in Berlin's *The Crooked Timber of Humanity* (New York: Random House, 1991), pp. 84-5.

37. Rita Felski, "The Counterdiscourses of the Feminine in Three Texts by Wilde, Huysmans, and Sacher-Masoch," *PMLA* 106, no. 5 (October 1991): 1094.

Chapter Six

1. The reader may be interested to know that *The Writer's Diary*, from which I quote in this chapter from the Brasol translation, is being retranslated by Kenneth Lantz in a Northwestern University Press publication and with an introduction by Gary Saul Morson. The second volume of the new translation is due to be published in June 1994, too late for my use here.

2. Among the ideas of Vladimir Solovyev (1853-1900) that influenced Dostoevsky were the notion of Christian unity, the reconciliation of Rome and Russian Orthodoxy, the intellectual and moral crisis of the West, and the union of *Sophia* (the World Soul and feminine principle) with the *Logos*, God with man, and the implicit union of men with women.

3. Carol Gilligan's analysis of the differences between men's and women's voices suggests the Bakhtinian distinction between monologic and dialogic poetics. An important element in *The Diary* is Dostoevsky's conception of interlocution with others that dismantles the favored Western notion of the writer as a solitary or autonomous voice. As Joseph Frank makes clear in his 1979 introduction to *The Diary*, "nothing could be more false than to see [Dostoevsky] . . . as a genius creating solely out of his own inner life, and as obsessed exclusively with and by his own personal fantasies. For Dostoevsky's novels are steeped in the social-cultural

reality of his time, and cannot really be understood unless we grasp his relation to . . . [the Diary's] sketches of various social types, and comments on the latest cultural events . . . [his] walking idly through the streets and chatting with his readers about everything" (pp. x-xi).

4. Mikhail Bakhtin, *Problems of Dostoevsky's Poetics*, trans. Caryl Emerson (Minneapolis: University of Minnesota Press, 1984), p. 118.

5. Richard Peace argues that "when Dostoevsky is attempting to pres-ent firm concepts and irrefutable conclusions, as in much of the *Writer's Diary*, the result is merely bizarre dead formulae," *Dostoevsky: An Examination of His Major Novels* (Cambridge: Cambridge University Press, 1971), p. 311.

6. This sort of nationalist conviction, which the philosopher Tom Rockmore calls "metaphysical racism," is less alien to the late-twen-tieth-century reader after the cataclysm in Bosnia. Harriet Murav argues that in advocating Russia's world-redemptive role, Dostoevsky knew that his audience could find him a "madman . . . *iurodivyi*" (holy fool), and that he answered, "Let it be *iurodstvo* [holy foolishness] as long as the great thought does not die" (quoted in *Holy Foolishness: Dostoevsky's Novels and the Poetics of Cultural Critique* [Stanford, CA: Stanford University Press, 1992], pp. 167-8).

7. Constantin Mochulsky, *Dostoevsky: His Life and Work*, trans. Michael A. Minihan (Princeton, NJ: Princeton University Press, 1967), p. 548.

8. Robert Belknap, *The Genesis of "The Brothers Karamazov"* (Evanston, IL: Northwestern University Press), p. 35.

9. Andrzej Walicki, *Legal Philosophies of Russian Liberalism* (Notre Dame, IN: University of Notre Dame Press, 1992), pp. 74-5.

10. Laura Engelstein, *The Keys to Happiness: Sex and the Search for Modernity in Fin-de-Siècle Russia* (Ithaca, NY: Cornell University Press, 1992), pp. 22-24.

11. The feminist historian Gerda Lerner puts this abuse in the large historical frame that Dostoevsky claims for his vision of history, a vision that moves towards the transcendence of master-slave rela-tions. See Lerner's *The Creation of Patriarchy* (New York: Oxford University Press, 1986), p. 88.

12. Engelstein, *Keys to Happiness*, p. 115-6.

13. Ibid., p. 120.

14. Victor Terras describes the *pochvenniki* (from *pochva*, "soil," hence "men of the soil") as those "whose Slavophilism was more democratic and down-to-earth than that of mainstream Slavophiles. Apollon Grigoyev (1822-64) was the initiator of the movement and Fyodor

Dostoevsky its most effective proponent. The *Pochvenniki* discounted the romantic mysticism of the Slavophiles as mere theory and sought to develop their own nationalist ideology on the basis of what they thought were the 'facts' of Russian life. . . . They suggested that [the world] would be regenerated by Russian civilization, a creative synthesis of the great national cultures of the West. Dostoevsky's celebrated 'Discourse on Pushkin' (1880) is a concise statement of their perspective," *A History of Russian Literature* (New Haven: Yale University Press, 1991), p. 287.

15. In the introduction to Temira Pachmuss's *F.M. Dostoevsky: Dualism and Synthesis of the Human Soul* (Carbondale: Southern Illinois University Press, 1963), Henry T. Moore wrote that "Dmitri was what Dostoevsky had been . . . Ivan was what he had become, and . . . Alyosha was what he would have liked to be" (p. viii).

16. Belknap, *Genesis*, p. 59.

17. Harriet Murav, "Dostoevsky in Siberia: Remembering the Past," *Slavic Review* (Winter 1991): 431.

18. Gary Saul Morson, *Dostoevsky's "Diary of a Writer": Threshold Art*, Ph.D. diss., Yale University, 1975 (Ann Arbor, MI: University Microfilms International, 1986), p. 88. See also Morson's later commentary on the diary in *The Boundaries of Genre: Dostoevsky's Diary of a Writer and the Tradition of Literary Utopia* (Austin: University of Texas Press, 1981).

19. For a general discussion of the reforms of 1864, see Jesse D. Clarkson's *A History of Russia* (New York: Random House, 1961, 1969), p.304ff.

20. Eric Naiman, "Of Crime, Utopia, and Repressive Complements: the Further Adventures of a Ridiculous Man," *Slavic Review* 50 (Fall 1991): 512-20.

21. Dostoevsky's father was assumed to have been murdered by his serfs in 1839 when Dostoevsky was eighteen. Documents discovered by Geir Kjetsaa and described in his biography of Dostoevsky (*Fyodor Dostoevsky: A Writer's Life* [New York: Viking, 1987]) revised the murder theory. Kjetsaa argues that the father died of illness and that the murder story was a cover-up. "Both versions of his father's death must have been known to Dostoevsky, and there is nothing to indicate that he had more faith in the murder rumors than in the official report that his father had died of his illness" (p. 34). There is nothing, that is, except the story of Fyodor Karamazov's death in Dostoevsky's novel. The murder of a drunken and cruel landowning father still remains part

of the Dostoevsky tradition as Joseph Frank conceives it in *The Stir of Liberation: 1860-1865* (Princeton, NJ: Princeton University Press, 1986).

22. Although *The Gentle Creature* is found within the pages of Boris Brasol's translation of *The Diary* (and entitled *The Meek One*), I have chosen to use Magarshack's better translation of the story and Dostoevsky's comment about it from *Great Short Works of Fyodor Dostoevsky*, as indicated in my Note on Translations and Transliteration.

23. Laura Mulvey, *Visual and Other Pleasures* (Bloomington and Indianapolis: Indiana University Press, 1989), p. 19.

24. C.f. chapter 4, note 20.

25. For example, Nancy Chodorow's and Carol Gilligan's contributions to theories about differences between boys' and girl's upbringings and men's and women's voices, and French feminist theorizings about how female libido is constituted. See, for example, Luce Irigaray's *This Sex Which Is Not One*, trans. Catherine Porter (Ithaca, NY: Cornell University Press, 1985); and Hélène Cixous's appropriation of Lacanian psychoanalysis in "The Laughter of the Medusa," in *Feminist Literary Theory*, ed. Mary Eagleton (New York: Basil Blackwell, 1986).

26. Post-structuralist accounts include political theorizings (see, for example, Judith Butler's and Joan C. Scott's anthology, *Feminists Theorize the Political* [New York: Routledge, 1992]), and some of the political ruminations of Julia Kristeva about language in *Revolution in Poetic Language*, trans. Margaret Waller (New York: Columbia University Press, 1984).

27. Frederick Engels, *The Origin of the Family, Private Property, and the State*, trans. Evelyn Reed (New York: Pathfinder Press, 1972), p. 79.

28. In "Contingent Foundations: Feminism and the Question of 'Postmodernism,'" Judith Butler addresses the problem of philosophical foundationalism that engages Ivan in *The Brothers Karamazov* and that the pawnbroker husband's hunt for "security" is a symptom of in *A Gentle Creature*. Butler writes: "To establish a set of norms that are beyond power or force is itself a powerful and forceful conceptual practice that sublimates, disguises and extends its own power play through recourse to tropes of normative universality. And the point is not to do away with foundations, or even to champion a position that goes under the name of anti-foundationalism. Both of those positions belong together as different versions of foundationalism and the skeptical problematic it engenders. Rather, the task is to

interrogate what the theoretical move that establishes foundations *authorizes*, and what precisely it excludes or forecloses"(*Feminists Theorize the Political*, ed. Judith Butler and Joan W. Scott [New York: Routledge, 1992], p. 7).

29. Ibsen's *A Doll House* was written in 1879, Dostoevsky's *The Gentle Creature* in 1876.
30. Morson, *Boundaries of Genre*, p. 14.
31. Ibid., p. 46.
32. In the Russian language edition, pp. 31-33.

Chapter Seven

1. Karen Horney, *Feminine Psychology* (New York: W. W. Norton, 1967), p. 113.
2. Emile Zola, *Nana*, introduction by Ernest Boyd (New York: Random House Modern Library Edition, n.d.), p. 544.
3. In Ann Belford Ulanov's *The Feminine in Jungian Psychology and in Christian Theology* (Evanston, IL: Northwestern University Press, 1971), she reminds us that, especially in the Protestant West, "the psychology of the feminine is the psychology of its suppression. The feminine is characterized by sexual passivity (see Havelock Ellis), by sexuality per se to the exclusion of rational capacity (see Otto Weininger), by penis envy (see Freud), by social inferiority (see Adler), by cultural conditioning (see Karen Horney), by societal organization (see Margaret Mead). . . . [But] humanity has paid a high price for its . . . exclusive reliance on the male viewpoint" (p. 317).
4. Ibid., pp. 304-5.
5. Mary Ellman, *Thinking About Women* (New York: Harcourt Brace Jovanovich, 1968), pp. 25-6.
6. Simone de Beauvoir, *The Second Sex*, trans. H. M. Parshley (New York: Knopf, 1952), pp. xxxiii-xxxiv.
7. Robert Belknap suggests that "buffoonery and the *nadryv* may be said to be . . . the axis which has done most to make Dostoevsky the old testament of the existentialists." See *The Structure of "The Brothers Karamazov*," (The Hague: Mouton & Co., 1967), pp. 41-7.
8. Avrahm Yarmolinsky's *Dostoevsky: Works and Days* (New York: Funk & Wagnalls, 1971); and Geir Kjetsaa's *Fyodor Dostoevsky: A Writer's Life*, trans. Siri Hustvedt and David McDuff (New York: Viking, 1987).
9. Joan Kelly-Gadol, "The Social Relations of the Sexes: A New Methodology for Women's History," *Signs* 1 (1976): 812.

10. Nancy Chodorow, *The Reproduction of Mothering: Psychoanalysis and the Sociology of Gender* (Berkeley: University of California Press, 1978), 169.

11. Edward Wasiolek, *Dostoevsky: The Major Fiction* (Cambridge, MA: MIT Press, 1964), p. 160.

12. I am indebted here to Harriet Murav's "Dora and the Underground Man," in *Russian Literature and Psychoanalysis*, ed. Daniel Rancour-Laferriere (Amsterdam/Philadelphia: John Benjamins Pub. Co., 1989), pp. 418-30.

13. Maria Ramas, "Freud's Dora, Dora's Hysteria," in *In Dora's Case: Freud-Hysteria-Feminism*, ed. Charles Bernheimer and Claire Kahane (New York: Columbia University Press, 1985, 1990), p. 150.

14. See Toril Moi's critique in "Representations of Patriarchy," in *In Dora's Case: Freud-Hysteria-Feminism*, ed. Charles Berhneimer and Claire Kahane (New York: Columbia University Press, 1985, 1990), of Hélène Cixoux's notion of Dora "as a radiant example of feminine revolt." Moi argues, along with Catherine Clement, that "hysteria is . . . a cry for help when defeat becomes real, when the woman sees that she is efficiently gagged and chained to her feminine role" (p. 192).

15. Ibid., p. 182.

16. Ibid., pp. 183-6.

17. Bakhtin uses the word "overpopulated" to suggest why "language is not a neutral medium that passes freely and easily into the private property of the speaker's intentions." In arguing that Katerina, like Freud's Dora, escapes from the narrator's controls, I'm reminded of Bakhtin's warning: "[Language] is populated—overpopulated—with the intentions of others. Expropriating it, forcing it to submit to one's own intensions and accents, is a difficult and complicated process" (*The Dialogic Imagination:: Four Essays*, trans. Michael Holquist and Caryl Emerson [Austin: University of Texas Press, 1991], p. 294).

18. Diane Oenning Thompson, *"The Brothers Karamazov" and the Poetics of Memory* (New York: Cambridge University Press, 1991), p. 68.

19. Judith Von Herik, *Freud on Femininity and Faith* (Berkeley: University of California Press, 1982), pp. 196-7.

20. In this connection, see Louis Breger's discussion of Dmitri and Grushenka (*Dostoevsky: The Author as Psychoanalyst* [New York: New York University Press, 1989]).

21. In Mary Eagleton's introduction to *Feminist Literary Criticism* (New York and London: Longman, 1991), she explains "the symbolic order" in Lacanian terms: "In Lacanian theory the moment of the Oedipal crisis and the repression of desire for the mother is also the

moment of acquisition of language and the entry into the symbolic order" understood as "patriarchal" (p. 15).

22. George Steiner, *Tolstoy or Dostoevsky: An Essay in the Old Criticism* (New York: Knopf, 1959), pp. 145-6 and 159.

23. Barbara Engel, "Women as Revolutionaries: The Case of the Russian Populists," in *Becoming Visible: Women in European History*, ed. Bridenthal and Koonz (Boston: Houghton Mifflin, 1977), p. 365.

24. Madelon Sprehngnether, "Enforcing Oedipus: Freud and Dora" in *In Dora's Case: Freud-Hysteria-Feminism*, ed. Charles Berhneimer and Claire Kahane (New York: Columbia University Press, 1985, 1990), p. 271.

25. Vladimir Lossky, *The Mystical Theology of the Eastern Church* (Crestwood, NY: St. Vladimir's Seminary Press, 1976), p. 122.

Conclusion

1. Hayden White, *Metahistory* (Baltimore, MD: The Johns Hopkins University Press, 1973), p. x.

2. Elaine Showalter quoting Monique Wittig in the introduction to *Speaking of Gender*, ed. Elaine Showalter (New York: Routledge, Chapman and Hall, 1986), p. 1.

3. Elizabeth Grosz, "Conclusion: A Note on Essentialism and Difference," in *Feminist Knowledge: Critique and Construct*, ed. Sneja Gunew (New York: Routledge, 1990), p. 341.

4. The analytical philosopher Donald Davidson offers the strongest critique of the idea that we have incommensurable views of the world. Although few feminists have yet responded to Davidson's ideas as yet, Davidson can be understood to pose a challenge to certain kinds of feminist theorists who define "sexual difference" in radical terms: who argue, for example, that there is such a thing as a specifically woman's "world" or a woman's "language" incommensurate with "men's" language. See Steven E. Cole's analysis of Gayatri Spivak's feminist claims in "The Scrutable Subject," in *Literary Theory After Davidson*, ed. Reed Way Dasenbrock (University Park, PA: The Pennsylvania State University Press, 1993), pp. 59-91.

5. Luce Irigaray, *This Sex Which Is Not One*, trans. Catherine Porter (Ithaca, NY: Cornell University Press, 1985), p. 136.

6. See Judith Butler's "Contingent Foundations: Feminism and the Question of 'Postmodernism,'" in *Feminists Theorize the Political*, ed. Judith Butler and Joan W. Scott (New York: Routledge, 1992).

7. Grosz, "Conclusion," p. 342.

8. Joseph Frank, review of Catteau's *Dostoevsky and the Process of Literary Creation*, in *Common Knowledge* (Fall 1993): 129.

9. Charles B. Guignon, *Dostoevsky: The Grand Inquisitor* (Indianapolis, IN: Hackett Pub., 1993), p. xii. The italics are mine.

10. Ibid.

11. See, for example, Virginia Held's *Feminist Morality: Transforming Culture, Society, and Politics*, with a foreword by Catherine R. Stimpson (Chicago: University of Chicago Press, 1994).

12. Mikhail Bakhtin, *Problems of Dostoevsky's Poetics*, trans. Caryl Emerson (Minneapolis: University of Minnesota Press, 1984), p. 202.

13. Irving Howe, *Politics and the Novel* (Freeport, NY: Books for Libraries Press, 1957, 1970), p. 75.

14. Isaiah Berlin, *Four Essays on Liberty* (New York: Oxford University Press, 1969), p. 123.

15. Ibid. pp. 131-2.

16. Ibid. p. 166.

17. See, for example, Barbara Herrnstein Smith's work in this field. At the moment of writing, I refer the reader to her recent "Unloading the Self-Refutation Charge," *Common Knowledge* (Fall 1993): 95.

18. Andrzej Walicki is not the first reader to suggest that Alyosha Karamazov is modeled on Solovyev and that Solovyev's ideas of synthesis between the "patriarchal" and the "matriarchal," Western philosophy and Eastern Christianity, are "obvious in the theocratic utopia of Ivan Karamazov" (*Legal Philosophies of Russian Liberalism* [Notre Dame, IN: University of Notre Dame Press, 1992] p. 170).

19. Ronald Dworkin's review of Catharine A. MacKinnon's *Only Words* in *The New York Review of Books*, October 21, 1993, pp. 36-42.

20. Ibid., p. 41.

21. Thanks to Casey Haskins for pointing out this connection between Dostoevsky's thought and Taylor's contemporary philosophy.

22. Slavoj Zizek describes Jacques Lacan's "teaching" in terms of a "universalization of the symptom . . . so that finally even woman is determined as the symptom of man" (*The Sublime Object of Ideology* [London: Verso, 1989], p. 72).

23. See Michel Foucault, *The History of Sexuality, Volume I*, trans. Robert Hurley (New York: Vintage/Random House, 1980). Although Foucault's work does not refer to feminism, his idea that there are various discourses of and about sexuality, and that these are crucial to the workings of institutional power, indicates a direction Dostoevsky

critics might take. Foucault's indirect influence is felt in Laura Engelstein's *The Keys to Happiness: Sex and the Search for Modernity in Fin-de-Siècle Russia* (Ithaca, NY: Cornell University Press, 1992).

24. See my discussion in "Emma, Anna, Tess: Skepticism, Displacement, Betrayal," *Philosophy and Literature* (Fall 1994).

25. Charles Taylor, *Sources of the Self: The Making of Modern Identity* (Cambridge, MA: Harvard University Press, 1989), p. 449.

26. Gary Saul Morson, "Introduction: Russian Cluster," *PMLA* 107 (March 1992): 230.

27. See Roland Barthes, *The Semiotic Challenge*, trans. Richard Howard (New York: Farrar, Straus & Giroux), p. 105ff.

Works Cited

Anders, Gunther. *Franz Kafka*, trans. A. Steer and A. K. Thorlby. London: Bowes & Bowes, 1960.

Andrew, Joe. *Narrative and Desire in Russian Literature: 1822-49*. New York: St. Martin's Press, 1993.

Baier, Annette. "The Moral Perils of Intimacy," in *Pragmatism's Freud: The Moral Disruption of Psychoanalysis*, ed. L. Smith and R. Kerripin. Baltimore: Johns Hopkins University Press, 1986.

Bakhtin, Mikhail. *The Dialogic Imagination: Four Essays*, trans. Caryl Emerson and Michael Holquist. Austin: University of Texas Press, 1991.

―――. *Problems of Dostoevsky's Poetics*, trans. Caryl Emerson. Minneapolis: University of Minnesota Press, 1984.

―――. *Rabelais*, trans. Helen Iswolsky. Bloomington: Indiana University Press, 1984.

Barker, Adele. *The Mother Syndrome in Russian Folk Imagination*. Columbus, OH: Slavica, 1985.

Barthes, Roland. *The Semiotic Challenge*, trans. Richard Howard. New York: Farrar, Straus & Giroux, 1988.

Bauer, Dale, ed. *Feminism, Bakhtin, and the Dialogic*. Albany: State University of New York, 1991.

Belknap, Robert. *The Genesis of "The Brothers Karamazov."* Evanston, IL: Northwestern University Press, 1990.

―――. *The Structure of "The Brothers Karamazov."* The Hague: Mouton & Co., 1967.

Berdyaev, Nikolai. *The Russian Idea*, trans. R. M. French. Hudson, NY: Lindisfarne Press, 1992.

Berlin, Isaiah. *The Crooked Timber of Humanity*. New York: Random House, 1991.

———. *Four Essays on Liberty*. Oxford: Oxford University Press, 1969.

Bernstein, Michael Andre. "'These Children that Come at You with Knives': Ressentiment, Mass Culture, and the Saturnalia." *Critical Inquiry* 17 (Winter) 1991: 358-72.

Bethea, David M. *The Shape of Apocalypse in Modern Russian Fiction*. Princeton: Princeton University Press, 1989.

Bordo, Susan. "The Cartesian Masculinization of Thought." *Signs* 11, no. 3 (Spring 1986): 439-56.

Borgmann, Albert. *Crossing the Postmodern Divide*. Chicago: University of Chicago, 1992.

Breger, Louis. *Dostoevsky: The Author as Psychoanalyst*. New York: New York University Press, 1989.

Butler, Judith. "Contingent Foundations: Feminism and the Question of 'Postmodernism,'" in *Feminists Theorize the Political*, ed. Judith Butler and Joan W. Scott. New York: Routledge, 1992.

Carr, Hallett. *Dostoevsky*. London: George Allen & Unwin Ltd., 1931, 1949.

Catteau, Jacques. *Dostoevsky and the Process of Literary Creation*, trans. by Audrey Littlewood. New York: Cambridge University Press, 1989.

Cavanagh, Clare. "Pseudo-revolution in Poetic Language: Julia Kristeva and the Russian Avant-garde." *Slavic Review* 52, no. 2 (Summer 1993): 283-97.

Chernyshevsky, Nikolai. *What Is To Be Done?* trans. by Michael R. Katz. Ithaca, NY: Cornell University Press, 1989.

Chodorow, Nancy. *The Reproduction of Mothering: Psychoanalysis and the Sociology of Gender*. Berkeley: University of California Press, 1978.

Cixous, Hélène. "The Laughter of the Medusa," reprinted in *Feminist Literary Theory*, ed. Mary Eagleton. New York: Basil Blackwell, 1986.

Clark, Katerina, and Michael Holquist. *Mikhail Bakhtin*. Cambridge: Belknap Press, 1984.

Cole, Stephen E. "The Scrutable Subject: Davidson, Literary Theory, and the Claims of Knowledge," in *Literary Theory After Davidson*, ed. Reed Way Dasenbrock. University Park, PA: The Pennsylvania State University Press, 1993.

Costlow, Sandler, Vowles, eds., *Sexuality and the Body in Russian Culture*. Stanford, CA: Stanford University Press, 1993.

Cox, Gary. *Tyrant and Victim in Dostoevsky*. Columbus, OH: Slavica, 1983.

Culler, Jonathan. *On Deconstruction Theory and Criticism after Structuralism*. Ithaca, NY: Cornell University Press, 1982.

Dalton, Elizabeth. *Unconscious Structure in "The Idiot": A Study in Literature and Psychoanalysis*. Princeton, NJ: Princeton University Press, 1979.

de Beauvoir, Simone. *The Second Sex*, trans. by H. M. Parshley. New York: Knopf, 1952.

de Man, Paul. *Blindness and Insight*. Minneapolis: University of Minnesota Press, 1971, 1983.

Derrida, Jacques. "Becoming Woman" *Semiotexte* 3 (1978): 128-37.

Dostoevsky, F. M. *Pis'ma v 4-kh tomakh*, ed. A. S. Dolinin. Moscow/Leningrad, 1928-59.

Eagleton, Mary. *Feminist Literary Criticism*. New York and London: Longman, 1991.

Ellman, Mary. *Thinking About Women*. New York: Harcourt Brace Jovanovich, 1968.

Emerson, Caryl, and Gary Saul Morson. *Mikhail Bakhtin: Creation of a Poetics*. Stanford, CA: Stanford University Press, 1992.

————. "Problems with Bakhtin's Poetics." *Slavic and East European Journal* 32, no. 4 (Winter 1988): 503-25.

Engel, Barbara. *Mothers and Daughters*. Cambridge: Cambridge University Press, 1972.

————. "Women as Revolutionaries: The Case of the Russian Populists," in *Becoming Visible: Women in European History*, ed. Bridenthal and Koonz. Boston: Houghton Mifflin, 1977.

————. (ed.). *Russia's Women*. Berkeley: University of California Press, 1990.

Engelstein, Laura. *The Keys to Happiness: Sex and the Search for Modernity in Fin-de-Siècle Russia*. Ithaca, NY: Cornell University Press, 1992.

Fanger, Donald. *Dostoevsky and Romantic Realism.* Cambridge, MA: Harvard University Press, 1967.

Felman, Shoshana. *Writing and Madness,* trans. Martha Noel Evans. Ithaca, NY: Cornell University Press, 1978.

Felski, Rita. "The Counterdiscourses of the Feminine in Three Texts by Wilde, Huysmans, and Sacher-Masoch." *PMLA* 106, no. 5 (October 1991): 1094-1105.

Frank, Joseph. *Dostoevsky: The Stir of Liberation: 1860-1865.* Princeton, NJ: Princeton University Press, 1986.

———. "The World of Raskolnikov." *Encounter* 26, no. 6 (June 1966): 30-5.

Freud, Sigmund. *The Standard Edition of the Complete Psychological Works of Sigmund Freud,* trans. James Strachey. 24 volumes. London: Hogarth Press and the Institute of Psychoanalysis, 1953.

Frye, Northrop. *Anatomy of Criticism.* Princeton, NJ: Princeton University Press, 1957.

Gilbert, Sandra, and Susan Gubar. *No Man's Land.* New Haven: Yale University Press, 1988.

Gilligan, Carol. *In a Different Voice.* Cambridge, MA: Harvard University Press, 1992.

Girard, Rene. *Violence and the Sacred,* trans. Patrick Gregory. Baltimore, MD: Johns Hopkins University Press, 1972.

Guerard, Albert. *Triumph of the Novel.* New York: Oxford University Press, 1976.

Guignon, Charles B., ed. *Dostoevsky: The Grand Inquisitor.* Indianapolis, IN: Hackett, 1993.

Grossman, Leonid. *Dostoevsky: His Life and Works,* trans. Mary Mackle. Indianapolis, IN: Bobbs Merrill, 1975.

Grosz, Elizabeth. "Conclusion: A Note on Essentialism and Difference," in *Feminist Knowledge: Critique and Construct,* ed. Sneja Gunew. New York: Routledge, 1990.

Heldt, Barbara. *Terrible Perfection: Women in Russian Literature.* Bloomington: Indiana University Press, 1987.

Hingley, Ronald. *Dostoevsky: His Life and Work.* New York: Charles Scribner's Sons, 1978.

Holquist, Michael, ed. *The Dialogic Imagination by M. M. Bakhtin*, trans. Michael Holquist and Caryl Emerson. Austin: University of Texas Press, 1981.

————. *Dostoevsky and the Novel*. Evanston, IL: Northwestern University Press, 1986.

Horney, Karen. *Feminine Psychology*. New York: W.W. Norton, 1967.

Howe, Irving. *Politics and the Novel*. Freeport, NY: Books for Libraries Press, 1957, 1970.

Hubbs, Joanna. *Mother Russia*. Bloomington: Indiana University Press, 1988.

Jackson, Robert Louis. "Polina and Lady Luck in *The Gambler*," in *Modern Critical Views: Fyodor Dostoevsky*, ed. Harold Bloom. New York: Chelsea House, 1988.

Jardine, Alice. *Gynesis*. Ithaca, NY: Cornell University Press, 1985.

Jauss, Hans. *Question and Answer: Forms of Dialogic Understanding*, trans. Michael Hays. Minneapolis: University of Minnesota Press, 1989.

Johnson, Barbara. *A World of Difference*. Baltimore, MD: Johns Hopkins University Press, 1987.

Jones, Malcolm V. *Dostoevsky After Bakhtin: Readings in Dostoevsky's Fantastic Realism*. New York: Cambridge University Press, 1990.

————. "Dostoevsky, Rousseau and Others." *Dostoevsky Studies* 4 (1983): 81-94.

Kelly, Aileen. "Irony and Utopia in Herzen and Dostoevsky." *The Russian Review* 50 (October 1991): 397-416.

Kelly-Gadol, Joan. "The Social Relations of the Sexes: A New Methodology for Women's History," *Signs* 1 (1976).

Kjetsaa, Geir. *Fyodor Dostoevsky: A Writer's Life*, trans. Siri Hustvedt and David McDuff. New York: Viking, 1987.

Kristeva, Julia. *Desire in Language*, ed. L. Roudiez. New York: Columbia University Press, 1980.

Lacan, Jacques. *Feminine Sexuality: Jacques Lacan and the École Freudienne*, ed. Juliet Mitchell and Jacqueline Rose, trans. Jacqueline Rose. New York: W. W. Norton and Pantheon Books, 1985.

Lerner, Gerda. *The Creation of Patriarchy*. New York: Oxford University Press, 1986.

Livermore, Gordon. "The Shaping Dialectic of Dostoevsky's Devils" in *Dostoevsky: New Perspectives*, ed. Robert Jackson. Englewood Cliffs, NJ: Prentice Hall, 1984.

Lossky, Vladimir. *The Mystical Theology of the Eastern Church*. Crestwood, NY: St. Vladimir's Seminary Press, 1976.

Lunacharsky, Anatoly. "Dostoevsky," in *Marxism and Art: Essays Classical and Contemporary*, ed. Maynard Solomon. Detroit: Wayne State University Press, 1979.

Matich, Olga. "*The Idiot*: A Feminist Reading," in *Dostoevsky and the Human Condition After a Century*, ed. Alexej Ugrinsky, Lambasa, and Ozolino. New York: Greenwood Press, 1986.

Mikhailovsky, Nikolai. *Dostoevsky: A Cruel Talent*, trans. Spencer Cadmus. Ann Arbor, MI: Ardus, 1978.

Mitchell, Juliet. *Woman's Estate*. New York: Vintage, 1971.

Mochulsky, Constantin. *Dostoevsky: His Life and Work*, trans. Michael A. Minihan. Princeton, NJ: Princeton University Press, 1967.

Moi, Toril. "Representations of Patriarchy," in *In Dora's Case: Freud-Hysteria-Feminism*, ed. Charles Bernheimer and Claire Kahane. New York: Columbia University Press, 1985, 1990.

Morson, Gary Saul. *The Boundaries of Genre: Dostoevsky's Diary of a Writer and the Tradition of Literary Utopia*. Austin: University of Texas Press, 1981.

―――. *Dostoevsky's "Diary of a Writer": Threshold Art*. Ph.D. diss., Yale University, 1975. Ann Arbor, MI: Michigan University Microfilms International, 1986.

―――. "Introduction: Russian Cluster." *PMLA* 107 (March 1992): 226-9.

Mulvey, Laura. *Visual and Other Pleasures*. Bloomington and Indianapolis: Indiana University Press, 1989.

Murav, Harriet. "Dora and the Underground Man," in *Russian Literature and Psychoanalysis*, ed. Daniel Rancour-Laferriere. Amsterdam/Philadelphia: John Benjamins Pub. Co., 1989.

―――. "Dostoevsky in Siberia: Remembering the Past." *Slavic Review* (Winter 1991): 430-40.

―――. *Holy Foolishness: Dostoevsky's Novels and the Poetics of Cultural Critique*. Stanford, CA: Stanford University Press, 1992.

Nabokov, Vladimir. *Lectures on Russian Literature*. New York: Harcourt Brace, 1981.

Naiman, Eric. "Of Crime, Utopia, and Repressive Complements: the Further Adventures of a Ridiculous Man." *Slavic Review* 50 (Fall 1991): 512-20.

Pachmuss, Temira. *F. M. Dostoevsky: Dualism and Synthesis of the Human Soul*. Carbondale: Southern Illinois University Press, 1963.

Peace, Richard. *Dostoevsky: An Examination of his Major Novels*. Cambridge: Cambridge University Press, 1971.

Perlina, Nina. *Varieties of Poetic Utterance: Quotation in The Brothers Karamazov*. Lanham, NY, and London: University Press of America, 1985.

Pipes, Richard. *The Russian Revolution*. New York: Vintage, 1990.

Pirog, Gerald. "Bakhtin and Freud on the Ego," in *Russian Literature and Psychoanalysis*, ed. Daniel Rancoeur-Laferriere. Amsterdam/Philadelphia: John Benjamins Pub. Co., 1989.

Pomper, Philip. *Sergei Nechaev*. New Brunswick, NJ: Rutgers University Press, 1979.

Ramas, Maria. "Freud's Dora, Dora's Hysteria," in *In Dora's Case: Freud-Hysteria-Feminism*, ed. Charles Bernheimer and Claire Kahane. New York: Columbia University Press, 1985, 1990.

Riasanovsky, Nicholas V. *A History of Russia*. Fourth edition. New York: Oxford University Press, 1984.

Sand, George. *Mauprat*, trans. Diane Johnson. Boston: Little Brown Pub., 1977.

Sedgwick, Eva Kosofsky. *Between Men: English Literature and Male Homosocial Desire*. New York: Columbia University Press, 1985.

Showalter, Elaine. *Sexual Anarchy: Gender and Culture at the Fin-de-Siècle*. New York: Viking, 1990.

Slonim, Marc. *Three Loves of Dostoevsky*. New York: Rinehard & Co, Inc., 1955.

Sprehngnether, Madelon. "Enforcing Oedipus: Freud and Dora," in *In Dora's Case: Freud-Hysteria-Feminism*, ed. Charles Bernheimer and Claire Kahane. New York: Columbia University Press, 1985, 1990.

Steiner, George. *Tolstoy or Dostoevsky: An Essay in the Old Criticism*. New York: Knopf, 1959.

Stites, Richard. *The Women's Liberation Movement in Russia: Feminism, Nihilism, and Bolshevism*. Princeton, NJ: Princeton University Press, 1978, 1991.

Tandeciarz, Silvia. "French Feminism in an International Frame: A Problem for Theory." *Genders* 10 (Spring 1991): 75-90.

Taylor, Charles. *Sources of the Self: The Making of Modern Identity*. Cambridge, MA: Harvard University Press, 1989.

Thompson, Diane Oenning. *"The Brothers Karamazov" and the Poetics of Memory*. New York: Cambridge University Press, 1991.

Todorov, Tzvetan. *Genres in Discourse*, trans. Catherine Porter. New York: Cambridge University Press, 1990.

———. *Mikhail Bakhtin: The Dialogical Principle*, trans. Wlad Godzich. Minneapolis: University of Minnesota Press, 1984.

Ulanov, Ann Belford. *The Feminine in Jungian Psychology and in Christian Theology*. Evanston, IL: Northwestern University Press, 1971.

Von Herik, Judith. *Freud on Femininity and Faith*. Berkeley: University of California Press, 1982.

Walicki, Andrzej. *Legal Philosophies of Russian Liberalism*. Notre Dame, IN: University of Notre Dame Press, 1992.

Wasiolek, Edward. *Dostoevsky: The Major Fiction*. Cambridge, MA: MIT Press, 1964.

——— (ed.). *Dostoevsky's Notebooks for The Possessed*, trans. Victor Terras. Chicago: University of Chicago Press, 1968.

Waters, Elizabeth. "Female Form in Soviet Political Iconography," in *Russia's Women*, ed. Barbara Engel. Berkeley: University of California Press, 1990.

Wheedon, Chris. *Feminist Practice and Poststructuralist Theory*. Oxford: Basil Blackwell, 1987.

White, Hayden. *Metahistory*. Baltimore, MD: The Johns Hopkins University Press, 1973.

Yarmolinsky, Avrahm. *Dostoevsky: Works and Days*. New York: Funk & Wagnalls, 1971.

Zizek, Slavoj. *The Sublime Object of Ideology*. London: Verso, 1989.

INDEX